Midnight Trauma

A Native American Mystery

PHYLLIS A. FAST

Midnight Trauma: A Native American Mystery
2nd in a series

Copyright © 2017 by Phyllis A. Fast. All rights reserved.
Revised First Edition.

Fast, Phyllis A.

ISBN: 978-0-9974977-3-1 (trade paperback)
ISBN: 978-0-9974977-4-8 (ebook)

Library edition ISBN: 978-1537172149

Keywords:
1. Fiction—mystery. 2. Native American—fiction. 3. Alaska Native—fiction. 4. Artists—fiction.

Denaakk'e words are in the Koyukon Athabascan Dictionary (2000) by Jules Jetté and Eliza Jones. The editor-in-chief was Dr. James Kari, linguist. It was published by the University of Alaska Fairbanks. Significant linguist sources are Dr. Elisa Peter Jones of Koyukuk. Alaska and her daughter, Susan Paskvan of Huslia, Alaska.

Cover painting "Meditation or Medication" by Phyllis A. Fast, acrylic, 2002.

Book design and prepress services by Kate Weisel (weiselcreative.com)

DEDICATION

To my uncle, Francis Harper

ACKNOWLEDGEMENTS

I am indebted to the people of Fairbanks, Alaska, where I lived a good many years of my life. I am especially grateful to the many Alaska Native people who befriended me, including Poldine Carlo and her family, as well as my many cousins, aunts and uncles.

I thank Kate Weisel who helped me in every aspect of producing this novel. I also thank my friend and colleague, Ann Jache, who insisted that I write about intergenerational trauma. In addition, I thank my friend and colleague, Jane Harper for arguing with me over many points. She is a creative writer as well as a lifelong friend. I am grateful to Jan Harper Haines, author of *Cold River Spirits*, for providing constant reminders of the essence of good writing. I also thank Darryl Lundahl and Barbara Haury of Luebeck, Germany for their constant encouragement.

Midnight Trauma centers on the horrific theme of historic trauma (also called intergenerational trauma), which forms the core of Anthropology, Indigenous Studies and many other academic areas. It has been a force in all of my paintings and now fiction. Each of us reacts to trauma in the privacy of their minds, souls, and homes. I am indebted to many Alaska Native artists, painters, carvers, writers and actors who have dedicated themselves to teaching others about it, including Susie Qimmiqsak Bevins Ericsen, Diane Benson, and many others, for teaching. In 2001 Susie Silook invited me to join them in the art and performance exhibit, "Ceremony of Healing" which focused on Alaska Native women who have been ravaged by murder, rape, stereotyping, and criminalization. I am proud to be part of those who try to create a web of safety.

LIST OF CHARACTERS in MIDNIGHT TRAUMA

Deloo Dena Goode   The protagonist is an Alaska Native woman, age 21, whose mother (Taale) is Tleeyegg'e hʉt'aane (also known as Koyukon Athabascan), Athabascans who live on the lower Yukon River in Alaska. Since people of the Tleeyegg'e nation follow the mother's line by cultural custom, therefore so is Deloo. Deloo's father is a deceased white American whom she never knew. Deloo (pronounced duh-LOO) is short for Delookeełt'aa, and means she's cute in Denaakk'e (the language of the Tleeyegg'e nation).

Baasee'   Spirit guide for Deloo. The storyteller is both telling as well as playing very active trickster-like role. In Denaakk'e her name means 'Thank You'. The name is pronounced bah-SEE). It rhymes with bossy. She is proud of her fourteen thousand plus years of life and afterlife.

Taale Dena   A Tleeyegg'e hʉt'aane (also known as Koyukon) Athabascan. Her nickname name rhymes with "rally."

Lizzy (Virginia) Grant   Deloo's friend and Floyd Charles' cousin.

Earlene Shoepack   Taale's friend, owner of Earlene's Beads.

Vindee Shoepack   Earlene's daughter.

Pauline Dena   Taale's aunt, Deloo's great aunt.

Floyd Grant   Deceased. Lizzie's cousin.

Jack Cruikshank   Detective, Fairbanks Police Department.

Francis (Frank) Harper   Detective, Fairbanks Police Department

Prize Woman   Also called Ming Liu Wu, is half Chinese and half Inuit of Canada. She is fluent in Inuttitut of northern Québec (her first language), Inuktitut (spoken in other parts of Canada), English, French, and Mandarin.

Chuan Wu   Ming's husband. He is Chinese, speaks Mandarin and English, and several computer languages.

Brent Clerick   Archaeologist. He is a white man from Alaska.

MoLi Liu, or the Little Ghost   Deceased, she is Ming Liu's twin sister.

Woody (Woodrow) Morrow   The late Arthur Goode's best friend, soon to be married to Zigwan.

Zigwan Woody's fiancée and mother of Nibuna.

Nibuna Age six, daughter of Woody and Zigwan.

Arthur Goode Deceased. Deloo's husband. He died five months after they married.

DENAAKK'E ATHABASCAN WORDS
(language of Deloo and Taale).

baasee' thank you, borrowed from French fur traders of the 19th century. Pronounced *bah-SEE*

Denaakk'e The Athabascan language (one of 11 in Alaska) spoken by the Koyukon people.

hutłanee a warning of bad luck. Pronounced *hoot-LAN-ee*. The ł is called the Indian-L or Bar-L. You can pronounce by pressing your tongue upward against the roof of your mouth and hissing like a cat.

Koyukon a fabricated name for the Tleeyegg'e hut'aane Athabascans who occupied the area around the Yukon River at the mouth of the Koyukuk River. There are eleven separate nations (once called tribes) of Athabascans in Alaska.

Naagheltaale the Big Dipper constellation. Pronounced *Nah-rell-TALL-eh*. **gh** is made by a the twist of sound at the back of the tongue.

Tleeyegg'e hut'aane the word used in Denaakk'e for their own nation.

More Denaakk'e words are in the *Koyukon Athabascan Dictionary* (2000) by Jules Jetté and Eliza Jones with the mastery of Dr. James Kari, linguist. It was published by the University of Alaska Fairbanks.

Gwich'in Athabascan words are available in the *Gwich'in Junior Dictionary* by Katherine Peter. It was published by the University of Alaska Fairbanks.

CHAPTER 1

Day 1 Monday evening

In mid-July the shadows were barely noticeable, giving Taale a clear view of the scrubby trees sheltering a house on the other side of the street. She saw someone staring at her. The attire was gender unspecific, but something about the person caught at Taale's mind. She didn't recognize the face because of an ugly scar showing through buzz-cut black hair and making its serrated way downward toward the chin. She wouldn't have forgotten such an ugly welt. She gasped when their eyes met and held for a flicker of time. She turned toward her daughter.

"That's a cop!" Deloo's voice was loud enough through Taale's open windows to alert the scar-faced person as well as everyone else in the vicinity. Deloo, however, was staring at the policeman on the opposite side of the street and didn't notice the person Taale saw.

"Deloo-Loo, did you…" The sudden sound of sirens alarmed her. Taale stopped, surprised to see lights in the bead shop on a Sunday. She also forgot she was using her private nickname for her only daughter.

Deloo pointed to a spot nearby, "We'd better check it out. That parking spot is close enough. Let's go in." She hopped out of the car as soon as Taale pulled into the space. Taale's eyes searched for the scarred person, but instead saw two people, arms wrapped tightly around each other, hustling away.

"Mom? Are you coming?" Deloo asked.

With a final glance toward the far side of the street, Deloo's mother got out of the car. Then, just as her feet touched the sidewalk, a deep shiver flooded Taale's spine and all thought of the pair fled her consciousness.

But wait, let me give you some background. Only then will you understand how easily a simple murder became part of a precisely timed pattern of history. First, let me introduce myself. I am Baasee', Deloo's invisible spirit guide. I am not all-knowing, but in this tale, I assure you the passage of time means everything.

It started when a traffic light forced Deloo and Taale to wait at a street corner in Fairbanks, Alaska. I, Baasee' the Intrepid, was taking stock of some jittery news. I compared notes with Zephyr. We agreed. Trouble was about to change the lives of both of our mortals, Deloo and Taale. Deloo was my fabulous mortal. Her mother, Taale, belonged to Zephyr. My name sounds like bossSEE and means 'Thank You' in Denaakk'e, Deloo's Athabascan language. Her name rhymes with KuhCHOO and means 'She's Cute,' which she is. Taale has the most unusual of names. Hers is short for Naagheltaale (pronounced Nah-rell-TALL-eh), and refers to the Big Dipper in a few Athabascan languages, including Denaakk'e.

It had been a difficult year for my small mortal, Deloo Goode. She's twenty-one and already a widow. Like her mother, she's an Alaska Native born and raised in Fairbanks, "Alaska's Golden Heart" as the tourist brochures claim.

Taking a quick look around I, Baasee' the Stalwart, hitched up my dazzling spirit-guide belt and communed. ~ *At least here in Alaska they won't be so suspicious of my little baby. She's not their target this time round.* ~ I was referring to problems we'd had in Canada not long ago. It'd taken a special trip by Taale to explain things to the authorities. Well, that and some mighty fine spirit guide tricks by yours truly.

Earlier in the day, Deloo and her mother had gone to the university and strolled through the Wood Center on their way toward the bookstore. Zephyr and I floated above them, enjoying the easy way we had with each other. The mortal pair were at the University of Alaska Fairbanks where Deloo had seen signs for careers in medicine.

Eager to grow up and take over running her own life, Deloo urged her mother, "Come on, Mom. Maybe there's a need for artists in medicine."

All was well and ordinary until a child raced down an aisle. He knocked Deloo off balance. She fell against a case. It crashed with a shatter. People turned toward her. Someone pulled Deloo out of the splintered glass while Taale checked her daughter. There was nothing serious enough to call for a stretcher, although a man wheeled his display gurney out of a corner while others murmured calming words to Deloo. Dozens of people bearing blankets, band aids and ointment scurried around them, all eager to show off how to deal with an emergency. Taale counted her daughter's pulse beats, using her smart phone's digital timer.

I commune silently to Deloo. ~ *You've survived. It's time to get up.* ~ The jade ring on her left hand blazed.

Deloo did not notice her ring, and I wondered if the freak band of light had anything to do with the accident. After shooing away the last of the helpful hands, the mother and daughter sat on a nearby bench until Deloo caught her breath. As both of them knew, the universe doesn't recover well from periods of genuine horror. All right, all right. I know what you're thinking. A little fall is not in itself horrific, but you just wait. Deloo, habitually oblivious to passing time, was fascinated by the course of Historic Trauma. It was her history, after all.

"Look. A timeline of the traumas for each Alaska Native generation beginning in 1850." Deloo mused, "I guess Sintannah was born about then, right?"

"Sintannah?" Taale peeked at her cell phone and answered absently. "Yes. She was my great-great-grandmother. She was born a little later. Something wiped out her family way up north on the Koyukuk River. Other people sent Sintannah and her sisters down that river to get husbands. There were new people to choose from: Russians, Americans, and Canadians."

"Says there were lots of contagious diseases came into Alaska at that time like measles and small pox. Children like Sintannah were orphaned and there were no elders left to raise them in the small villages. That's why they had to find husbands as soon as possible."

"A lot of intermarriage happened then. Those outsiders were glad to get a woman, but usually didn't treat them like they did women in the lands that they came from. So Aunt Pauline says," Taale muttered. "A lot of those men went back home without their Alaska Native wives when they got rich, or else died young themselves without anyone knowing."

"Ha! Nothing's changed in that regard since then. This poster says their children, people of Grandmother Ruth's generation, as well as her parents, went through starvation if no one in the family could hunt. If they survived, it was often thanks to the church orphanages." Deloo pointed at another poster. "The great worldwide flu took a lot of lives in the early twentieth century."

"Yes. Some of the Native men tried to help by traveling great distances. When they found a widow with kids, they'd go hunting for them. Such meat would last for a month or two. The widows and kids lasted a little longer because of those caring people," Taale said.

"One of my friends is still teased because her great-grandmother sold herself to a miner for a can of grease. The grease lasted for a winter and the nickname 'Cannagrease' lasted for generations," Deloo pointed at the poster while looking at her mother. "Do you remember Milly? That was her great-grandmother."

Taale rebuked her daughter. "Don't call people names. *Hutlanee.*" *Hutlanee* means bad omen in Denaakk'e, their ancestral language. "If you say anything bad about someone else, the same thing could happen to you."

"I'm sorry, Mom," Deloo apologized. "Back in the day, Grandmother Ruth and Great Aunt Pauline went through a lot to survive on their own as well to help their big families. This poster calls them the Mid-Twentieth Century Survivors. It says here the gold miners brought alcohol to Alaska. Later American soldiers brought drugs into the state."

"The U.S. army and air force created a lot of military installations in Alaska after World War II," Taale affirmed. "Some people called Great Aunt Pauline's generation the Welfare Women because the War on Poverty supported unmarried mothers with food and other subsidies. It still does. Native women took the head of household roles and Native men had less and less to do. Where previous generations got sick by disease, Aunt Pauline's generation turned into drunks and drug addicts. We've still got those problems and Aunt Pauline hates it. She decided to call our neighborhood Little Tanana (pronounced TAN-uh-nah), which means a place for healing. For Aunt Pauline, that has always meant no booze allowed. If she catches anyone drinking or offering alcohol in Little Tanana, she'll kick them out. She is strict."

"Mom, you said our neighborhood, Little Tanana, was the first place to get sober. Her generation also brought us ANCSA and later the Sobriety Movement," Deloo smiled.

I listened with pride. I didn't have much to do with Deloo's Great Aunt Pauline. It was hard enough to keep Deloo alive as the daughter of a single woman who would have, without her Aunt Pauline (my Deloo's Great Aunt Pauline), been trapped in the welfare cycle. Take the trouble we had a while back, for example, when Deloo's mother inadvertently turned thieves onto Deloo. It took an ounce or two of magical prevention. Now back in Athabascan country in Alaska, we've got to find out why Deloo's mom has a fabulous quantity of gemstones. Earlene, the woman who gave the gems to Deloo's mom, harbors the secret. We thought the problem was simple: Ask Earlene how she got them. Now we're asking, where's Earlene?

Earlene's disappearance stinks of something from another time and place when patterns emerged and have stayed for generations. Vicious, controlling people had deemed Alaska Natives as worthless in a quest for personal gain. The posters in the university gallery call it Historic Trauma. I call it intergenerational trouble. I have too much experience with the notion, having witnessed the damage for several thousand years. I, Baasee' the Ancient and Forlorn, see it as the fallout after new people barge into foreign countries without concern for the rights of the original owners. Deloo and her mother continued reading posters.

~ *Pauline's right, Deloo,* ~ I communed in spirit-guide fashion, which is silent, ~ *your forebears survived a lot of misfortune. Be proud of them for working so hard after what happened to their families.* ~

I loved giving Deloo advice, but now it was time for payback in fashion choices, such as which is more alluring, fake sapphire fangs or false ruby molars. Deloo was of no help, since she couldn't see me yet.

"Hey! Look at this!" My mortal pointed at a scrap of paper on one of the posters. "That's Great Aunt Pauline's list. It's her idea of what causes Historic Trauma."

"What? Where?" Taale rooted in her bag for reading glasses and peered at the poster.

"You had her list on the fridge at home. Did you put it here on this poster?"

Taale shook her head. "No. Someone in Little Tanana must have done it."

"Oh no! Please tell me it's not true!" Deloo wailed and pointed to an adjacent poster about the new generation. "I didn't know Josephine was dead."

Strong arms encircled Deloo's shoulders. Thinking it was Taale, Deloo leaned into them. "She hung herself when you were in New Mexico, Deloo," a voice murmured.

Deloo whirled to see who was behind her. "Hung herself? She was my age. Why?"

CHAPTER 2

Day 1 Monday, early afternoon

The speaker was Lizzie Grant, one of Deloo's close friends in high school. "Lots of things, I guess. Josephine was dating an older guy who was a heavy drinker. She dropped out of school because she got into drugs and booze. Rumor was he forced her to have sex with not just him but all of his friends, too. She didn't tell anyone what was going on, and besides a lot of kids killed themselves last year. Josephine might have thought it was expected, to kill herself I mean. That's why I got involved with this Historic Trauma poster session. So people would know what's really happening when a kid commits suicide or maybe worse. There've been shooting sprees here, too. It's not just in Europe or other places in the United States. The Alaska Native statistics are horrendous. They're much worse in coastal villages like Kotzebue."

"Lizzie!" Deloo's clotted throat choked on the name. "I should have known, but I've been away from here for a while."

"It's good to see you, Deloo. Welcome home." The slim young woman with thick glasses and a mass of frizzy brown hair rocked Deloo. It had been three years since the two had spent time together. The long hair confused Deloo. Even I, the Astounding Baasee', didn't recognize her. As I remembered it, the girl had always worn her hair very short. Nonetheless, they had been inseparable since they were toddlers. Lizzie, like Deloo, was Fairbanks-born. Unlike Deloo, she was a white American with many ties to Alaska's Native community.

Meanwhile, Taale was snuffling herself. With her face toward yet another poster, she whispered, "Four of these people are related to us. They are my cousins. They all died twenty to thirty years ago. You were too young to know them, Deloo. I knew these five too, but they aren't related to us. They died a year or two ago." Taale peered at the bottom edge of the poster. "I wonder who made this poster. I'd like a copy." She spotted the name then and said aloud, "Virginia Grant. The name is familiar. Do you know her, Deloo?"

"Yes, Mom. Of course I do." Before she could explain someone leaned into her.

"I made it," Lizzie put a hand on Deloo's shoulder. "I can get you a copy."

Taale peered at the thin young woman, reluctant to take her eyes from the photos of her cousins. She dug around in her purse for something to wipe steam and tears from her glasses. When they were clean she looked again at the young woman beside Deloo. "Ah Hah! Now I can see you. In fact, how could I forget? We slaved over your computer in the middle of the night for six hours in April. As I recall, my supervisor wrote a letter to the professor on your behalf. How'd that go, Virginia?"

Deloo looked surprised. "Virginia? Mom? Since when did you ever call Lizzie by her birth name?"

"What?" Taale looked at her daughter, eyes blank. "Do you know Virginia, too?"

Lizzie smiled. "Of course, Taale." She put glasses on and pulled her shaggy hair away from her face. "Look at me again."

Taale took off her glasses and examined Lizzie's face. "Oh my word! Lizzie! I didn't recognize you with all the hair. Besides, when I'm working all I see is the computer screen. My eyes are good enough without glasses, and way worse with these computer glasses—except when I have to read a screen. I forgot all about the way you changed your name."

When Lizzie was five years old, she announced to everyone in her family and Deloo's that her name was Lizzie (short for Queen Elizabeth I of England) and not Virginia, the state whose name stems from the great monarch. From then on she wouldn't answer to any other name.

"You wrote Virginia on the form. You were so upset, I didn't waste time on figuring out what you looked like. Students' problems always come first in UAF's computer labs. You and I got so busy with your Mac I didn't have a spare second to think about you as a regular person. You were my computer patient. How about you? Did you recognize me, Lizzie?"

The wannabe Alaskan reincarnation of the sixteenth century Virgin Queen of England, Lizzie, shook her head with vigor. "It was the worst nightmare of my life! You could have been a gorilla. I didn't care about anything except my computer problem. You are a genius, Taale." Lizzie looked at her with awe. "Your fingers danced on the keyboard and you kept saying 'Everything will be fine, Virginia. Just take another deep breath and sit beside me.' I sat, I breathed, and all of a sudden my data appeared on the screen." Lizzie leaned her head on Deloo's shoulder. "My biology research paper was due at midnight. I had thirty minutes left by the time your mother got my data back on the screen."

Deloo gripped her friend's hand and vowed, "My mother knows everything!"

Suddenly, I got zapped by two spirit-guide messages. First, Taale would suffer for her knowledge of "everything," second was a vivid reminder of the old King Kong movie starring Fay Wray. In my mind I examined the charismatic blue eyes of the movie star, wondering if I would be working with her ghost, since she was dead. No answers came forth, so I returned to Taale's computer skills.

"Yes, Taale is remarkable. It was all there, but I still had one more data set to enter, and then I had to run the computations. Then check them over. Your mom stayed with me the whole time. She didn't move except once. That's when she claimed she needed to go to the bathroom. Instead, she came back with her supervisor and explained what had gone wrong, and how long we had spent trying to salvage the tables. He got my student ID and wrote a letter with both of your signatures on it. My prof accepted the report."

Taale pretended to puff out her chest. "You worked all year on it in the professor's lab. Of course he accepted it. He saw you do the work. The computer problems were not your fault." Taale paused, looked at Deloo, and added, "She wrote about Arthur in that paper."

"My Arthur?" Deloo's face flushed. She started to drop away from Lizzie's grip.

Deloo's first reaction to hearing anyone mention her beloved, although dead husband, was jealousy—as it had been ever since he died a few months ago. She tended to get jealous of anyone who had known or talked to him. In my long experience as a spirit guide, the jealousy phase of grief often dissipated in a week or so. Not so, Deloo. She was still stuck in it months later. I used magical power to soothe her. To help her over the rough patch, I urged her to think about what Arthur did. *~ Ask her why and how. Arthur was a research professor, after all, not a teaching prof. I think you'll love what she has to say. ~*

Lizzie smiled at Deloo's question, and answered, "Your Arthur had a lab space near my course professor's office up on the West Ridge. Sometimes when my professor was in class or off somewhere, Arthur would help me, even though it wasn't his job." She shook her head. "He was a real whiz, Deloo. He could see connections to the ordinary world I couldn't imagine. I wish I could have spent more time learning from him." Lizzie hooked her arm tighter around her friend's shoulders. "I'm so sorry he's gone."

"Yeah. Me too," Deloo shook off her ache. "So now I'm back here. I'm going to work on a B.F.A. in Art starting in the fall. They just accepted my application."

Taale asked, "So, Lizzie, besides making this astonishing poster, how did you do on that course?" She pointed at the sign above the medical career table.

Lizzie answered, "Yes. My professor gave me an A for my research paper. He's been helping me qualify for a pre-med program. However, since I started the Biological Sciences major a little late, I'll have to go another two years before I get into a pre-med program."

"That's awesome, Lizzie," Deloo said. "We might graduate together."

Taale gazed again at the array of Historic Trauma posters. "These are awesome, too. It's important to see how many of our Alaska Native generations have been devastated by traumatic death and for so many terrible reasons. Posters like these put it into personal perspective. My family is here and I'm with them again just by looking at their faces." She sighed and nodded at Lizzie. "I would like a copy of your poster. Just a photo would do for me."

Taale jumped when she heard her cell phone ding and then tapped its screen and turned to the others with a strained smile. "What a day! We'd better go soon, okay, Deloo-Loo?"

* * *

Day 1 Monday earlier that afternoon in downtown Fairbanks
Clumsy adolescent feet ascended the bead shop's stairwell. Something hit the paneling and caught in one of the vertical grooves. An older man hid behind the door at the top of the stairs and listened to the clumsy one swear softly. Unexpectedly, the wood panels cracked and the stairwell walls splintered. The hidden man forced himself to take a deep breath. They weren't his walls. He heard the steps continue; he saw a shadow. His lips stretched across dry teeth when a steel pipe gripped by the younger man's tan hand entered the room. The big man behind the door snagged the pipe with his own calloused white fist. He jerked the person, a lanky teenager, inside the room.

In my spirit-guide way, I felt a cringe come. My interest, of course, rests solely in my cherished mortal, Deloo, but I still have a little cave-girl nosiness that never got washed out of me. Whatever the cause, I know what happened on this day foretold catastrophic events for my Deloo. I sighed for Deloo. Wasn't it enough to be a widow at twenty-one? A cranky roar from the ether told me to prepare for more.

Day 1 Monday afternoon at the University

While Lizzie took a picture of her two posters, a table next to Lizzie's caught my attention. Passersby stroked the soft, long fur of a stuffed and mounted wolverine. A science club student explained the wolverine came from the Athabascan village of Northway, about two hundred miles east of the university. "Wolverines are known for the thick, warm fur treasured by Alaska Native skin sewers."

The student droned on, explained it was a male wolverine who once weighed about forty pounds. His appetite was geared for eating rabbits and ptarmigan. I wished the wolverine spirit well and returned to Deloo. My new goal for her future excluded anything to do with taxidermy.

As I flowed along above her, I felt an ethereal touch along my backside. I examined my surroundings with care. It was the sort of casual signal a recently-dead person might make. Ancient spirits like me, with over fourteen thousand years under my aura, are more formal. A tiny sparkle of black and gold caught my eye. MoLi, a little ghost I'd met a while back, flickered at me. I spirit-smiled and cast a tendril around her in greeting.

~ *MoLi, what are you doing here?* ~ She was the deceased twin of a living woman whom Deloo dubbed "Prize Woman". I was sure we'd seen the last of Prize Woman, but MoLi wouldn't have left her twin for anything.

MoLi simpered pleasantly and explained, ~ *Chuan and Ming are working on some sort of project for the Chinese government.* ~ having stretched her spirit language skills as much as possible, she stopped. I, the patient Baasee', held off on asking for more.

Using my magical ways, I tugged at Deloo's hair. ~ *Deloo, look around for Ming, the woman you call Prize Woman. Her twin's spirit, MoLi, is here. You know, the little ghost. Ming must be in Alaska as well. Maybe over there.* ~ I indicated the far corner with spirit guide precision.

"Huh? Where?" Deloo spun around on one foot, scanning the crowd, all while grousing, ~ *We're in Alaska, Baasee'. Lots of women look Asian, just as Ming does. It's common in this part of the world. I don't see her.* ~

In one short month Deloo and I had become comfortable with each other. Deloo still doesn't see me except in dreams, but she's trying. Meanwhile, I've assembled a sizeable collection of fake eyelashes and toenails by which to amaze her when the time comes. Otherwise, I keep very busy training her to deal with life's problems, such as how to live a mortal life without her husband.

Deloo and Taale left the building a few minutes later. They heard a clatter of footsteps and a pair of ravens, *dotson* in Deloo's language, landed on the grass and concrete as a loud, if tiny blockade. They danced, eyes alert, refusing to get out of the way. I looked around for something physical like Deloo or immaterial like me, and heard it easily. Lizzy was screeching, "Can I get a ride?" As she drew closer, the ravens threw their beaks airwards and flew away. I flew with them for a short way, but they spotted a mortal human replete with hot French fries, and settled at his feet. I felt snubbed so I returned to Deloo. I could hear the three mortal women once again in animated discussion about Historic Trauma.

Deloo and Taale experienced two different generations of intense Historic Trauma among Alaska Natives. The very nature of that history gave them an intimate view of poverty and a woman's version of Native American wealth. They never got a chance to see much actual money until I, Deloo's doting spirit guide, spotted an opportunity a little over a year ago and went for it. I think of myself as Baasee' the Significant. I was glad to butt into their discussion with my views on the poster exhibit. Deloo disgorged shorter versions of my thought, serving to sound more informed about the subject than either her mother or Lizzie.

Although it took an extra half hour to take Lizzie to her aunt's house in Ester, conversation flowed easily. When they reached Lizzie's destination there was a tangible feeling of regret they tried to remove with extended words of parting.

Once back in the car with Taale, I pinned myself to Deloo's flowing hair and pretended the wind buffeted me from side to side. Zephyr did the same with Taale's hair. We, the spirits, were half in and half outside of the car. Taale hit a bump, so Zephyr faked a wound. I raised the ante by fighting non-existent head winds in a life-and-death effort to save her. It was one of our favorite games. I didn't know it would be our last time for a few months to taunt death. However, I knew everything was about to change. Entering the bead shop, we found two policemen in uniforms, a man of about forty and a teenager who hovered around his father. All of them asked or wondered who Taale was. Taale introduced herself as a friend of the owner.

"I called Mr. Cunningham earlier today."

A middle-aged man thanked her for coming and extended a hand.

"I'm afraid we'll have to meet later on this week. There's been a terrible incident here."

Beside her mother, Deloo recognized one of the policemen. "Hi Tim," she favored him with a big smile, "what happened here?"

The young officer turned a cool stare on my mortal's changeable green eyes and then relaxed. "Hi Deloo. You'll have to go back to your car. There's been an accident."

~ *Not an accident, Deloo. Your friend's supervisor has called the homicide line. They are expecting crime scene investigators and at least one detective to get here any minute.* ~ I swept around the shop to do my own version of investigation.

"Hello, Timothy," Taale stretched out her hand toward him. "I haven't seen you in a while." He was one of Deloo's high school friends, one of a pack of young people who used to eat as much as they could find in Taale's refrigerator.

"Hi Ms. Dena." Officer Brumley shook Taale's hand.

"Ms. Dena? Taale?"

A man's voice behind my Deloo sent a warning vibration throughout me. In the air above them I studied the newcomer. I didn't recognize him, but got a high-speed message from his guide indicating Zephyr and I had better screw our Athabascan spirit tunics on a bit tighter. A death would soon take up our mortals' time.

"Yes?" Taale turned toward the voice. "Do I know you?"

Forty-five to fifty, the stranger wore dirty jeans and a torn tee shirt. Blood soaked. Taale stared.

"Hi Deloo." From behind his father, Leroy Cunningham, a teenager peered at Deloo.

"Tony," Deloo moved to stand beside Taale and smiled. "You've grown like a weed. How long has it been since I babysat you?"

"I'm fifteen now." Tony's mouth moved toward a grin, Stopped. Warped. His tee shirt was wet. He looked down.

Deloo gasped, "What's going on here, Tony? Why are you both … so bloody?"

It was then one of the policemen ushered the women out of the shop and asked them to wait. Shocked, they nodded.

It occurred to me, the usually more vigilant Baasee', to study Taale from a police perspective. While I was as empty of knowledge as the two mortals with me, I knew the authorities were all thinking horrified thoughts about murder. Sadly, of all those present, she might seem to be the most promising suspect they had in all of Fairbanks.

Taale was an unwed mother who continued to struggle to keep her child, now an adult, away from busy bodies. Deloo's biological father had been a handsome student from a university in Kansas. He had come to Alaska to explore the wilderness before heading back to his real life. Family life, meaning the burden of an unexpected baby, wasn't going to be part of his 'real' life. He left Deloo's mother the morning after she found out she was pregnant.

A few months after Deloo's birth, Taale tracked him down and demanded information about his health records. She also asked for child support. Typical of non-men, as Deloo's Great Aunt Pauline termed them, he gave excuses about the money, referring to his status as a poor college student, but he did send the information she requested about his family health. It was clean of all the known debilitating fatal illnesses except one: incompetence. He died in a boating accident when Deloo was seven. Deloo never met her father.

As Taale had done all of her life, she scrambled to pay for basic needs and was too poor to afford a lawyer like Mr. Cunningham to sue the father's estate on Deloo's behalf. Although occasionally sorry he had died and left her and Deloo without hope of an alternative income, she did what she could to make a life for herself and her little girl. Taale and Deloo never got to know what he was like, but it was obvious he fit all of Great Aunt Pauline's criteria for what she termed non-men. Non-men thought it was their right to get girls drunk, drugged, raped, and then leave them pregnant, or broke or dead without seeing any of it as a man's responsibility, legal or otherwise.

The year Deloo turned nine was the year Taale got a part time job at a restaurant near her own home, leaving her with no time for long, leisurely chats, so she and Deloo didn't visit Earlene's Beads as often as they used to do. Taale hit the job ceiling for women. Even though Taale had nearly enough college credits to get an Associate of Arts degree, she didn't land a good job. People continued slamming her into the stereotype of women too dumb to finish high school. Besides her ethnic background, she also hit the white American race barrier in the job market. Besides a non-degreed skill in computer programming, she had terrific knowledge of Alaska Native arts, hunting, tanning, and cooking. None of those skills fit American jobs and served instead as an excuse to let employers give her applications a no-go rating. She fit the unskilled labor pool descriptions.

Having a job at the restaurant, however, meant she could call and even feed Earlene at the restaurant after the lunch rush ended. From then on, the two adult women met where Taale worked or at the university, rather than Earlene's Beads.

When I arrived on the job as a spirit guide at Deloo's birth, I took Pauline seriously when it came to Athabascan ethics. I was determined that what had happened to the mother would not happen to my Deloo. By a miracle I found my Deloo a rich young man who was destined to die young—a perfect fit for Deloo's financial straits. And besides, she loves her deceased Arthur still, perhaps because most of my hopes for him (okay, money issues) have gone as planned.

Deloo's father-in-law, Zachary Goode, helped with a surprising discovery of valuable gemstones subtly tucked into Taale's beading. The discovery left Deloo and Taale more puzzled than elated. I was beyond elated. Had I launched both mother and daughter into satisfactory wealth? What more could an industrious spirit guide want?

Other things have happened in the past few weeks as well. A Native American friend, Woody, told Deloo and Taale he landed a job in south-central Alaska. His fiancée, Zigwan, and daughter Nibuna would join him there. Woody's job wouldn't be starting for a couple of months, so he would have time to help us all figure out what happened to Earlene, who seemed to know how everything worked together regarding fabulous gems. However, Earlene was missing and almost presumed dead. It was time for Baasee' the Righter of all Wrongs, to come to the rescue.

CHAPTER 3

Day 1 Monday afternoon

Somewhere beyond my spirit guide awareness and yet nearby, a frumpy woman emptied a dustpan into a garbage can on her porch. The house attached to the porch looked as old as Fairbanks, meaning well over a century. Fairbanks, known for its below-freezing temperatures, is not kind to most dwellings or humans. The house was probably younger than the woman. Half of the exterior paint had flaked away long ago, and what was left of it had faded to the same color grey as the exposed and snow-stained wood below. The woman looked like most dog-eared Fairbanks residents: sturdy, grouchy, and toughened by weather and people. Dustpan watched a brown-haired woman walking along the street. What struck Dustpan as most odd about the brown-haired lady was that she was walking. She was batting away mosquitoes like a new-comer, but using her feet like a Fairbanks old timer. However, she was walking in good leather shoes, not sneakers. She looked like a woman who had grown used to accepting rides everywhere. Her kind didn't walk more than a block. Her kind didn't walk up to a perfect stranger, even another woman.

"Excuse me?" the brown-haired woman chirped.

Dustpan wiped filthy hands on her jeans legs, and met the other woman's eyes, or at least as much as she could since the other woman wore dark glasses. "What do you want?"

"Do you know if this place is for rent? Or sale?"

"What? You're crazy. It's my house, and I don't expect to move any time soon." The woman picked up her dust pan and turned her back. The house was empty of furniture as was obvious through any window.

"My father used to live here," the brown-haired woman declared, touching her neck as though a cold draft had risen around her.

"My house was built in 1974." Dustpan lifted a brow and looked at the newcomer with humor. She noted a few light grey hairs near the woman's temple and figured her to be getting close to fifty. "If your father lived here, it was probably when you were a child. Was he here then? Where were you?"

Brown Hair decided to take that as an invitation and stepped onto the porch. Close up Dustpan saw she must have been a great beauty when she was younger. The brown-haired woman's nose, a perfect diamond shape, breached forward from the face far more than did most. The tilt of her chin taunted both love and hatred. The skin around her eyes had loosened, sagged, and covered the loveliness they once must have held, giving her a haunted look. Brown Hair lied again, "You are right. I was a child. He left me and my mother when I was an infant. I am trying to understand what his life was like. I grew up in Bellingham Washington." Deceit was not her forte, but her quavering voice made her seem innocuous.

Dustpan frowned. "All right. I charge two thousand per month plus utilities."

"How many rooms does it have?" Brown Hair asked, peering around Dustpan into the house.

"Five, if you count the porch. It's a big porch." She spread an ample arm across the dilapidated entryway.

"Six hundred."

"One thousand. And I'll pay for electricity until the end of August."

They both laughed. They both knew there was little need for artificial lighting or heat during June, July or August of any given Fairbanks summer. Brown Hair, alias Fay, considered. "We need two bedrooms. Does it have that many?" Fay asked. She was Fay Wray Clerick, named for the twentieth century movie star. "And we need a fridge."

"One bedroom and there's no fridge. Nine hundred."

"Seven."

They settled at eight hundred a month, free electricity until September first with first and last months' rent as deposit. Fay knew that was all they'd ever pay her. After the landlady left, a black-haired woman in an ancient Ford hatchback pulled into the unpaved driveway. A tiny pink gorilla jiggled under the rearview mirror. The gorilla was her granddaughter's contribution to Fay's King Kong fantasy of being a movie star. Fay pretended to pat her own back. She used her acting skills where they counted.

A man stood on a porch a block to the west, enjoying the labor of the new arrivals. He'd visited the owner, the one the women thought of as Dustpan, numerous times. It was a tiny place with a token single bedroom barely large enough for one. There was definitely no room for a second person. He figured the middle-aged woman with brown hair must be the new tenant and the black-haired woman might be a friend. They didn't have much: a couple of suitcases apiece and three or four bags from Fred Meyer. The major work came when the grimy delivery van pulled up in front of the house.

Out of his hearing, Carmen, the black-haired woman, saw the delivery truck and said to the other woman, "Fix your wig! They're here."

The other woman twisted the wig into place without looking in a mirror. The brown wig was a little askew, but no one complained. Two men unloaded a used refrigerator, a television set, a couch and a bed. The brown-haired woman stood to one side to supervise the men. The watcher kept an eye on the place. Neither of the women seemed to leave. Shrugging, the neighbor gave up his vigil and turned on his TV.

Unaware of the neighbor, the two women made sleeping arrangements. Fay automatically assumed the bedroom was hers, although they were splitting the rent. She took off her brown and gray wig for a final time that day and put it in the bedroom. Carmen took the couch. Although plagued by mosquitos, Carmen figured out a solution to the small insects. She attached a fly swatter to her belt and carried another in an oversized bag while she set up the couch in the living room for herself. Fay and Carmen had just arrived by air and bought a rickety car from a used car lot within their first hour in Fairbanks. They were glad the place was so close to Earlene's Beads. Their friend, Earlene, wouldn't have found a better location for them. Hadn't, actually. They found it themselves.

Carmen plumped the pillow she had carried for years. Its bright embroidery reminded her of the smells and colors of her South American past. She needed it as she settled for the night in a place so far from home. Sadly, the fates had seen to shift her ever farther north. She heaved a tired sigh. Sunlight still flooded the house, as it would for several more weeks in Fairbanks, where midnight sun really meant sleeplessness for those used to darkness at night. Many holes in the ragged curtains above the couch gave her good views of the street outside as well. Tomorrow would be a good day to search for heavy, dark fabric. Despite the light, her transition from being awake to asleep happened before she reached her pillow.

A couple of hours later she awoke to a musky scent. Was it the curtains? She groped for the light switch. It was on the opposite wall. Looking around, she realized electric light was unnecessary. Her watch pointed to 12. For a moment she thought it was noon. A second glimpse at the gloomy room suggested it was actually midnight, and she grinned. Midnight sun only if you imagined it to be a cloudy day.

Nearly two decades earlier in 1997, Carmen Hauser had arrived in

Bellingham, Washington with her father. Her goal was to meet their relative, Fay Clerick. The family relationship could be seen in their big,
blue eyes. Fay and Mr. Hauser had the same eyes. Mr. Hauser offered to
pay for Carmen's room and board. Because his monetary gift was huge,
Fay agreed to host Carmen for a month. Mr. Hauser quadrupled his gift,
and Fay no longer set a time limit to Carmen's stay. Before Mr. Hauser
left his daughter, he revealed why Carmen wanted to meet Fay. Fay's son
was a man whom Carmen had met in 1990 when she was nineteen. No
other man had pleased her as much. When she heard her father's next
business trip would be to one of the towns in which her one-time heart-
throb might be, she begged to go along. He finally consented and made
arrangements to meet with Fay. Carmen was elated. At last she would
see the man whom she thought loved her as much as she loved him.

At first Fay was amused and cautiously allowed Carmen to call her
Suegra, or Spanish for mother-in-law. As time wore on, she realized she
was stuck with a woman who had nowhere else to go and no other vision
of reality than her son.

Fay cautioned, "My son and I haven't talked in decades and besides
he's now wandering the world as an archaeologist. If you think calling
me a mother-in-law means I'll take care of you, I can't and I won't."

Carmen replied with a sad shake of the head, "No, Suegra, I agree.
He doesn't treat any woman right. You have helped your parents to live
safely at home until they died. Now that you grow old, someone needs to
take care of you. Maybe I'll learn what evil there is about your son that
one month of romance didn't help me figure out."

Carmen arrived in Washington the same summer Vindee Shoepack,
a teenager with sandy brown hair, arrived in Bellingham alone. She was
Earlene's daughter and Fay's granddaughter. Earlene took her to visit her grandmother Fay during the summers beginning in 2006 when
Vindee turned twelve.

From the beginning Earlene realized how impoverished Fay was,
and thought she could help by paying Fay to keep Vindee once a year
for a month. Fay agreed to get five hundred dollars for Vindee's room
and board.

Although or perhaps because Carmen was to learn Vindee was her
pined-for boyfriend's illegitimate daughter by another woman, she became fascinated with the child. It didn't take long for Fay and Carmen to
realize Vindee must have been conceived by Carmen's boyfriend shortly
after leaving her in 1994. Facing the truth of BeeZee's shallow interest

in her, Carmen put aside two decades of hope and became Vindee's Bellingham guardian and tutor. Tutoring Vindee was easy, since the girl was a genuine scholar who studied all the time. Vindee took a fancy to trying Spanish, and in the course of her first afternoon with Carmen, Vindee learned to speak a few words, thus winning Carmen's heart.

It didn't take long for Fay Clerick to realize that with the extra money, she could afford to keep her house in the Sehome district of Bellingham. She decided it would be sensible to invite Carmen to live with her as long as she wanted to stay. Carmen agreed to call Vindee her "step-daughter," and took care of her with Fay during the summers. Carmen taught Vindee how to speak her own style of Spanish. In good time Fay assured Carmen she considered her a daughter-in-law rather than guest. Although at first elated, Carmen soon learned the words brought her no closer to the man from whom she now sought some sort of retaliatory victory.

Over time Carmen's relationship with Fay settled into an easy companionship. Many years passed and Carmen's overwhelming infatuation with BeeZee disappeared completely. In fact, her feelings for him became open hatred as she realized how much pain the man had caused his own mother.

Of late, the two older women had spent an uncomfortable fall in Bellingham, awaiting word from Alaska. On Thanksgiving Day, the phone her father had given her months earlier dinged politely. She grabbed it and looked at the screen. "Plan B. I." There was no other message. Carmen stared at the screen and then rushed inside. Just as the four of them planned, the simple message told them too much. One of the other two, Earlene or her daughter Vindee, was down, the other was carrying on alone. Carmen prayed they were both still alive, but the odds were too harsh and in favor of Fay's son. The second thing was a little better. Fay's son had not figured out what happened to the last beaded jacket. He was still on the hunt for it.

She flapped it at Fay. "Plan B. Earlene wouldn't send it unless she or Vindee was sure your son hasn't figured out what happened to his last jacket. He is desperate for all of the money he has cached away. We're to go to Fairbanks."

Fay studied the phone's screen and frowned. "Why doesn't she say more?"

"She can't, Suegra. That's what we agreed to do last summer. There's to be no contact with them until we get a second text message, or else we find out another way he's dead. Meanwhile we have to follow Earlene's directions. You must get rid of all unneeded things. We have to go on the first of July." Carmen sucked in a noisy breath, trying to keep her emotions in order. "You know what the agreement was. All we can know is she lives. Your life is still in danger, since he knows where you live. You've got to get out of here. Me, Too. It will be easy for me. I've never had the money to buy things. Two bags, and I'm done."

"But all we know my granddaughter is alive. How will we ever get that last message? We're moving to Fairbanks. We don't even know if she, I mean, if Earlene made it. Why can't we call them?"

"Earlene knows what you know about him. He is evil and smart. Your son is going to blame you because you're kinfolk. He would assume we know something others don't. That's his style. Remember what Vindee said about seeing him at the store all those years ago. Thanks to her new glasses, she could see him and his blue eyes, but he didn't see hers. We know it's him. Earlene warned us if he showed up, we'd have go to with the other plan. Plan B means follow her plan in detail and "I" means we'll all be incognito or in disguise."

"It means she—our little Vindee—is alive." Fay shook. First her head, then her entire body shook with bigger and bigger waves of fear and guilt. "What did I do to him, Carmen? Why did he turn out this way, this horrific way?"

Carmen knelt beside the older woman's chair and whispered, "How he got to be the way he is cannot be your fault. I'm lucky he was only with me for one summer. It was a great time, but even then I knew not to say or do certain things. He's twisted inside. You know he is." She held Fay's hand in both of hers. "We have got to begin moving out of our home today." Carmen gazed at Fay. "Your stuff is going to take a lot of time, Suegra, since you have a lot of rooms, maybe things you don't remember. Do you want to work on it this afternoon?"

Fay stared at the other woman, aware of her total dependence on the younger Carmen. She'd been unbelieving until she saw her son walking in the store a few years back. He hadn't been in contact with her for years. Why now? She tormented herself for answers, and finally accepted the truth. Above all, he wasn't trying to make contact with her or his late grandparents. He was watching. Perhaps by now, he'd found out the grandparents had passed. She knew it was her son, even though he seemed to wear disguises from time to time. Most people wouldn't notice unless they'd seen him taking his first steps as a baby. One leg was shorter than the other. It was cute then. Frightening now as they had compared Earlene and Fay's complementary stories. He was not like other people.

"Yes." Fay opened her eyes. "Yes. Let's move my things as soon as possible. I don't have much, but as you say, there are lots of nooks and crannies my parents and I used for decades. There's more cleaning to do than packing."

They were glad Earlene had cushioned Plan B with so much time. Fay didn't own much worth keeping, but they kept discovering more things to sell or give away as the months passed. One day Carmen found an old photo of Fay's father, mother and Fay's son. She reached for her almost mother-in-law's hand and whispered, "Do you miss them, Suegra? Do you miss your parents? Or the man who is your son?"

Her throat thickened. Fay muttered, "Yes, both. I miss my mother more than my father, but do I miss my son? No. I miss the little boy he was before his father died. When he realized his father was never going to come back, something happened to the soul he used to have. The child I loved never came back either. I lost both my husband and my son at once."

Another flow of tears launched itself along Fay's lined face. Carmen handed her a tissue. "Mi suegra, your son, he thinks we women are all ignorant. Maybe we were. We have done nothing, yet he has done brutal things to others. He doesn't know I am here or that he has a daughter. Moreover, none of us have ever guessed he is so rich. Let it go, Suegra mia. Earlene is the one who works on computers. Leave her to know those details. Thanks to Earlene, you and I have a chance to live the way we imagine he does."

"Earlene risked her life for us," Fay said. "Her soul is good. My son has never had a good or kind soul."

CHAPTER 4

Day 1 Monday afternoon

Brent entered the house cautiously. It had been a year since his last stay. His flashlight glimmered against the wire filament he had put in place last year. None of it had been touched except by assorted insects. His bare mattress peeked at him from the bedroom. Since he was tired from the long trip, he decided to dispense with the insects as quickly as possible by using the vacuum cleaner. Soon he covered the mattress with the mothball smelling sheets and lay on top of it. Brent slept without dreaming.

A mile or two away a mother wolverine nursed her two kits and reached mentally toward the new arrival in her world, meaning the human who had moved into the house she considered part of her territory. Like most mothers, she defended her infants without regard to personal safety. She had explored the perimeter of the house when young and decided then the single rope of barbed wire pegged to the lower edge of the wall was warning enough to stay away. Besides, in their mental way, the bear had assured her the man had murdered many of them, bear and wolverine, throughout the years. The man did not distinguish between species, often taking the lives of wolves and wolverines simply to practice his aim. The human never collected the meat or hide afterward. In Deloo's Tleeyegg'e hut'aane ancestry (also known as Koyukon Athabascan), the wolverine is one of the three animals that hold a place of honor in Athabascan legends. The wolverine is a mustelid known for its savage destruction of any threat. In the old days it was hutłanee to speak another person's name aloud, so people substituted metaphors about the person instead. Most of the time such metaphors were tame. For example, if the person was well known for demonic fury, she or he might be called wolverine. The other two legendary Athabascan animals are the bear and the wolf, both of which are predictably vicious, if not so damaging as the wolverine.

Unaware of the animals nearby, Brent awoke and rolled over to look at his suitcase. The bag had been in his backseat for a few thousand miles and probably smelled both noxious and tantalizing to small creatures. Lifting himself easily to a sitting position, he draped his long legs over the side of the bed and got up. He caught a glimpse of himself in the door mirror. His belly was flat once again after months of getting fat while searching for the lost jacket. Moreover, sitting day after day in his car while he drove from one end of Canada to another left him with nothing except thirty pounds around his gut and the loss of an old friend. His friend's widow had left a single note at the end of his obituary in the Boston Globe: "Contact Harold Johnson for further information." He decoded the words to mean get out. Brent began driving north as soon as possible.

* * *

Day 1 Monday
The patch would have worked if Leroy Cunningham's client had been there. She would have heard the electric saw and seen the first drops of water. But Earlene Shoepack remained missing and thus did not call the plumber or clean up her own mess. If Leroy had known what would happen to his teenaged son's best friend... .

Instead, Leroy had received a thick letter from Earlene on the morning before Thanksgiving several months earlier. It contained changes to her will which she had drafted and signed in front of witnesses, as well as a big check to cover routine bills and unexpected costs, such as plumbing. She also wrote a note asking him to check her shop once in a while and to change the alarm code after reading her instructions. The entire amount of her check was far more than she'd paid him in any given year.

Earlene's shop was a block away from his office in one direction and two blocks in another from his own home. As it happened her note alarmed him so much, he stopped by two days before Thanksgiving to talk on his way home. She was there and mentioned her plumbing problems. Despite the fact he was a lawyer, she asked him to make a small patch on her outside wall as a makeshift repair. All she had was interior sealant, so he promised to come back soon with the right kind of patching material. They changed the alarm code together. That was the last time he saw her.

Now, eight months later young Floyd Charles was dead and the attorney Leroy Cunningham was sure it was his fault. He had ignored the oddity of Earlene's disappearance because they had talked the day before she disappeared in November. She had mentioned she would be traveling. Maybe she was still enjoying herself. All she asked him to do was pay her utility bills and drive down her street to make sure the bead shop looked empty and untouched. Except for one minor incident involving young children and firecrackers, everything remained silent in Earlene's Beads.

Sensing his luck had turned sour, he drove by the store on the morning after the break-in and saw a steady flow of water along the sidewalk and into the street. An hour later he came back with his son and ended up spending the entire day there. The flooring looked ruined. Some of the sheetrock in the stairwell and store was damaged and sagging. Tony offered to get his buddy, Floyd, to help him pull sheetrock and move furniture.

Tony and Floyd, both sixteen and best friends since they were four, had worked out a two-stage system at the store. During stage one, Tony and Leroy tore out rotten sheetrock and piled it up near the back door. Then Floyd carried it in quick trips to and from the dumpster. Around six that evening they finished stage one and the boys wanted to quit for the night. Leroy convinced them to move some of the store contents up to the second bedroom which they both knew as Vindee's room.

"Okay," Floyd agreed, "We'll be done in a few minutes." The three of them moved Earlene's bed and two dressers farther into her bedroom and some furniture into Vindee's room. By the time they finished, they had trouble closing the door to the smaller room, so they decided to leave it open.

"We're done!" In spite of their claims of being tired, they seemed to glide over the staircase as they took the steps three at a time. Tony grinned at his father from the back door. "Let's go get some pizza."

"Wait," Floyd pulled an odd length of steel pipe out of a pile near the back stoop. "I remember seeing the other half of this upstairs in the little bedroom. I'll put this one up there too."

"Okay," Leroy draped a sweaty arm around his son's shoulders, "We'll be in the car out front. Just pull the back door shut before you leave the shop and leave by the front door. I'll wait there for you. Once we close the front door, we'll trigger the alarm system."

Floyd retrieved the pipe and carried it upstairs. He accidentally rammed it into the stairwell. The door to the spare room was closed. He recalled trying to shut it earlier, but something had jammed it. Neither he nor Tony had been able to figure out the problem and left it ajar. Shaking his head, he pushed it farther open and stepped forward to put the pipe on the floor next to its twin. That's when a hand grabbed the steel out of the boy's hands and struck his young head. Floyd crumpled. The assailant lifted Floyd's inert body as if it weighed nothing, carried him to the top of the stairs, and flung the body down the steps.

"Floyd!" Leroy shouted when he saw the boy's head through the front door window. It dangled, face upward, hair falling from his innocent forehead. No one observed the dark figure who slithered into the shadows of the upstairs area and inserted his body into a narrow space. Later, when there was a tempest of activity inside the building and the crowd was focused on the departing body, the figure slipped through a narrow hatch, made his way downstairs. There he walked away through the open back door. No one saw him.

Leroy, at the onset of the nightmare, unlocked the front door and turned off the alarm. Tony rushed to his friend's side at the back door. "Floyd. What's the matter? Get up."

From the front doorway Leroy could tell Floyd didn't hear anything. Shaky fingers found 9-1-1 and he explained what happened. Leroy Cunningham then pulled his son away from Floyd. "Let me see him, Son."

* * *

Day 1 Monday evening

Now, a year after their decision to move from the state of Washington, Carmen raged about coming to Fairbanks, Alaska. She hung her head. "I was angry—angry at your son, angry at Earlene." She turned immense, sad eyes on Fay. "Suegra mia, we should have left things as they were."

"No, my Carmen. You know things are better because we have Vindee near us again. Let's do as Earlene wanted it to be done. You know she's right about all of it." She got up, patted Carmen's shoulder. Fay tried to straighten her back as she hobbled to her bedroom. She made it, turned and smiled again, and disappeared into her room.

Carmen patted her temporary bed on the couch and sighed when she saw it was ten PM. She heard a sound and sat up. Carmen looked through a gaping hole in the curtain first to the left and then to the right. Earlene's Beads had been an ordinary yellow in the day. In Fairbanks' evening sunlight, the walls took on a deeper shade, giving the building a coppery look. Carmen sighed again, wondering if she was letting her mind go wild when something moved against the bead shop's addition. The house was tiny. Each floor featured five hundred square feet. Fay's Bellingham house was much larger.

She stared, trying to pick out the shape she'd seen move. A man. He was standing beside the add-on at the edge of the wall. On the outside the addition looked to be about the size of a small room, maybe eight-feet by eight-feet square. Carmen shook her head.

Unaware of her, the man laid a bag on the ground and pulled out some sort of tool. She figured it was battery-powered, as she didn't see him plug it in to a socket. Soon the tool was whining. Although her carpentry experience was limited, she knew the pipes connected to the shop's main water line somewhere near where he was drilling. The man would get wet. She shrugged. The guy would figure it out soon enough. And did. She heard the shrieking whine change pitch. Heard metal break. Despite excellent night vision, she couldn't make out any of the man's features. Or what he was doing beyond using a loud tool.

"Suegra, come look!" she hissed, catching a glimpse of Fay moving in the dark hallway beside her bedroom. By the time Fay reached Carmen, water started gushing out of a hole in the bead shop's wall. The man swore once, collected his tools, and ran to a vehicle parked a short distance away from him. Carmen squinted at the tousled whitish hair, and shook her head. "This kind of light is too grey and I can't see well," she murmured. "It looks like he was trying to cut a hole in the bead shop's wall." The car sped away.

Carmen tapped 9-1-1 on her phone. "Better get ready, Suegra. The police will want to talk to us."

"They may interrogate us," Fay responded.

"Maybe they will, but I'm tough," Carmen quipped. "Police do not scare me for telling the truth of what I see." Carmen was proud of her independent ways.

The police came and went without asking many questions. Since there was no sign of the man who cut a hole in the wall, they wrote a report about a civil disturbance. The police filed a report, complete with a good photo of a shoe print. The call they made to the owner was automatically forwarded to a lawyer. On the following morning attorney, Leroy Cunningham, called people who patched both the hole in the pipe and the wall. As soon as the plumber removed the damaged piece of paneling, a carpenter replaced it with something also white and with a similar pattern to cover the small addition housing a crumbling fireplace. Leroy tested the work by pushing on it with his full body weight. It held.

"Isn't this the same panel you replaced last winter?" Leroy asked.

"I didn't replace it in January. All I did was shove it back into place and brace it. This time I took the old sheet of paneling out and replaced it with this and braced it with a couple of two-by-fours. If you look at the upper edge of the panel I took out, you can see what he did."

Leroy examined the piece of wood. "I don't…. Oh. There's some kind of lock up here."

"Yup. It's a spring-loaded lock. If you tap it twice, the little panel pops open unless you leave it ajar like he did last winter. We had a freeze in mid-December. Froze it open. You would have had a flood then, but you turned down the heat and drained the water on the first of December. Saved yourself a bunch of money."

"Thanks." Leroy paid the carpenter, remembering the December issue when Earlene had gone missing. No one had heard from her since.

CHAPTER 5

Day 1 Monday evening

They came. Spirits like me or ghosts like the others. I was the oldest spirit present—at the moment. The young ghost who clutched Floyd's eternal remains turned a forlorn ocular at me. *~ Do you know how to do it? ~* He communed. I send a quick plea for help to Grandfather Kwaikit.

~ Of course. ~ My reply covered a huge lie. I'd done the final transformation a mere ten or twelve times over the course of thousands of years. Others did it more often. *~ Do you want me to guide you? ~* I asked the young ghost.

He squirmed. *~ Yes. No. I've never done it. He's the first. ~*

I fabricated a sigh to those who knew me, prayed Grandfather Kwaikit would get my request and then I began the part I knew by heart. *~ First, ~* I communed, *~ you and I must pray for accuracy. Then tell me about him. What's special about Floyd? ~* I nudged the young ghost through a meager five minutes of memories about Floyd.

From out of nowhere, Grandfather Kwaikit appeared and asked, *~ How did he earn these three insignia? ~*

~ Ah, yes. He always helped his friend, Tony. Even when it meant giving up something more pleasant, like this evening. A very pretty girl asked him to stop by for a visit to help her with homework, but Tony asked first. I didn't have to do much to remind Floyd to help those in need. And the second one is for helping Tony get his father's car out of a ditch late at night. This one is for helping Tony tonight, even though he had damaged his left knee last week. ~

Grandfather Kwaikit showed us both how to register those feats officially. I set up the rest, and Floyd's first step was finished. Grandfather Kwaikit checked my records, asked a few more questions, and then mumbled some magic words I never quite got. It took all of twenty minutes to sum up the boy's life. If Floyd had been older, accomplished more, like marriage, children, and a job, it would have taken a lot longer. As it was, I figured asking for more details about the night he helped Tony with Mr. Cunningham's car would happen later. And then I saw a wondrous golden column which meant Floyd had accomplished greatness. It seemed like Floyd was in good shape despite an untimely death. I hoped Deloo would be lucky enough to earn such an award. She was, thank goodness, far from death. I hoped.

I looked around to find my charge and spotted her in the midst of a crowd. Two police cars stopped traffic on each end of the block. The body was about to be carried out of the front door. Grandfather Kwaikit and I assembled in front of Floyd's sprite and led the Great Walk of Death in our old ways out of the bead shop. We, the spirits, were far above Floyd, but not so high we couldn't hear the soft strains of an old potlatch memorial song. Two elders sang while the rest mumbled along with them.

An older spirit floated toward us and communed. ~ *I heard you in there. That golden column is for all the help he was to his father.* ~

~ *Ah!* ~ Grandfather Kwaikit thanked the spirit and added something to Floyd's transformation. Two people rushed at Floyd's body. The older man was ashen. The woman flung herself onto Floyd's body and wailed at the empty sky. I gathered she was Floyd's mother and swaddled her in comfort.

When the singing faded, I located Deloo and plopped down beside her just as Mr. Cunningham approached Taale and began, "I would like to meet with you...."

"Excuse me," a stranger interrupted them. The second man looked Native, but not someone Deloo knew. "I would like to speak to Mr. Cunningham first." The two men stepped to the side to mutter in low voices, both looking at Taale. Floyd's body was placed in an emergency vehicle and the crowd dispersed. The pair of men returned to Taale and Deloo.

"Ms. Dena, I would like to speak to you. My name is Detective Francis Harper."

Taale eyed the stranger. His tone of voice irritated her. There was no option. He demanded time to talk. He was a tall dark man who appeared to be about her age or older, maybe as much as forty-five. "Do I know you? Where are you from?"

He looked perplexed at the second question. "You're the fourth person to ask where I'm from. I was raised in Iowa. I'm new at the Fairbanks Police Department. I just started a week ago. I am investigating the murder of Mr. Floyd Charles."

"Murder?" Taale's eyes widened.

"Yes. Mr. Charles appears to have died by unnatural causes. Do you have time to answer a few questions?"

Taale opened her mouth and couldn't speak for a moment. Then she rasped, "Do you mean here?" She looked around. Several people looked back. People she knew.

"It'll be easier to talk to you later at the department. Right now I'm looking for those who might have seen anything unusual. I also need to find out why you in particular are here."

"Oh. Well, I stopped by to see when Earlene is due back. She noticed him writing notes and when he asked for her name, she said slowly, "T-A-A-L-E, it's short for Naaghetaale. My last name is Dena, D-E-N-A. I do beading for Earlene once in a while. I wanted to find out if she needed any more of my work." Detective Harper gave her first name a try and gave up with a polite smile. He nodded and continued, "Your address and telephone number?" Again, she dictated while he wrote in his notebook.

"Thank you very much. I'll call you for a longer chat." Detective Harper scribbled some information and closed his notebook. He turned to Deloo and asked, "Who are you?"

Deloo brightened. "I'm Deloo Goode. I'm Taale's daughter." Deloo tipped her head toward her mother. "She brought me back from Cambridge Massachusetts, and I'll be living here for a while."

"Do you mean you will be living with Ms. Dena?"

"Uh, yes. I will. For a while." Detective Harper's look prompted her for information. "Well I might live next door if Great Aunt Pauline approves. She doesn't know. I haven't asked her—yet."

Detective Harper made a noise sounding like a suppressed chuckle and he closed his notebook. "Thank you." He nodded to Taale and turned to someone else.

Taale turned back toward Mr. Cunningham who asked, "Do you have time tomorrow to speak to me?"

"Uh," Taale managed.

"In view of what happened tonight, there is a legal matter I would like to discuss with you, but I should wait for permission from the police." Mr. Cunningham touched his neck as if to loosen a tie. He wasn't wearing one so he dropped his hands.

Taale nodded. "Legal?" He shrugged. Taale queried, "Do you have a card? I'll call you tomorrow."

Mr. Cunningham fumbled with pockets and found nothing. "Sorry. I don't have one with me. I'll give you my telephone number. The matter is important."

After he left, Taale and Deloo looked around, saw no one else they should talk to and headed back to Taale's car. "I can't believe what happened to Tony," Deloo murmured.

"Me either," Taale replied. "Listen, Honey, there's something I've got to tell you."

Taale's agitation was so thick it was making it very difficult to be in the car with the two of them. Nonetheless I swooped down to Deloo, ~ *Get ready, my resilient wolverine. She's got more bad news.* ~

Deloo sat up bolt straight and eyed her mother. "What, Mom?"

"I talked to my boss this morning." She stopped.

"What happened?"

Taale made two wrong turns in a row and almost hit a pedestrian.

Alarmed, I communed to Deloo, ~ *stop her! She's going to kill us!* ~

~ *I see that.* ~ Deloo replied the commune way. Speaking aloud, she said, "*Hutlanee*, Mom, you'd better slow down. Pull over there." Deloo pointed at a convenient empty parking spot.

Taale saw it a bit too late. She squealed to a halt, jerked the car back and forth until she achieved technical parking status, and turned off the engine. "He fired me," she said without warning.

"What? Fired you?"

"Sort of. He put me on one-quarter time for one month. On August fifteenth he'll consider making it half-time."

"He can't do that. Can he?"

"Yes," Taale stared at her window, and added after a moment. "He is just following the rules. You know the one: The last to hire is the first to fire. There've been some cutbacks in other departments, too."

An older Deloo might have figured out something to say right away, but my girl was caught off guard and remained silent. This was a job for Super Spirit Baasee'. I leapt into the fray and communed ~ *It's not a problem, Deloo. You have all the money she needs for the time being. Remind her she's got something more important to do. She has to find out why Earlene put those gemstones into those beads. Tell her so.* ~

Deloo glanced upward to an imaginary spot in which she assumed I reside. ~ *Right. I'll do so.* ~ Aloud she said, "Mom, remember, I have a lot of money from Arthur's life insurance. Let's live on me for a while. You need to find Earlene. That will take a lot of time and energy. Your boss let you do it by cutting your hours."

Taale stared at her daughter with her mouth sagging open. Zephyr, her adroit spirit guide, touched Taale with a tendril of comfort. Taale responded with a weak smile. "Thank you, my dear. I needed that. You're right. I must find Earlene and talk to her about those gemstones. They're worth a lot more money than a part-time job." Taale stared back toward the bead shop and started her car. She pulled onto the empty street with jerky twists of the steering wheel and lots of sudden brakes.

"Are you all right? Maybe I should drive."

Taale apologized and pulled into yet another parking spot. "Thanks to you I am better. First thing tomorrow I will call Mr. Cunningham." Just as she spoke her phone's general-public ring tone sounded. She touched the icon to accept the call.

"Hello." She repeated yes several times, glanced at her watch, and then ended the call. Her shoulders sagged and she put the car into drive. "That was Detective Harper. He wants to speak to me now. I'll take you home first. This shouldn't take long."

Deloo looked at the car's clock. It was late. Almost eight. She shrugged. *~ Mom will be home by nine, right? ~*

I searched for an answer my way and replied, *~ this is Detective Harper's first murder case since he was hired in Alaska. He's got to be thorough to prove he was the right person for the job. You won't see her for a while. ~*

Taale was at the police station until well past midnight. Deloo had been pacing for hours, wondering if she should go down to the station to rescue her. When her mother appeared at the door, Deloo was full of anger and burst out "What happened? What did he do? I thought you got arrested."

Taale sagged against the door. "He kept asking me the same questions over and over and over. I think he hates me. Then Jack Cruikshank came in. Remember him? Finally, Detective Harper explained it was because I was in the Will."

"What Will" Deloo asked.

"Earlene's Will. She named me in her Will along with her daughter, Vindee." Taale responded.

"Is she dead? Did they find her body?" Deloo looked at her mother with alarm.

"No. They haven't found a body, but she's been gone for six months, and someone tried to break into Earlene's Beads a few nights ago and again tonight. Then Floyd got murdered." Taale groped her way to the couch and slumped on it. "I suppose I would do the same if I were Detective Harper."

~ At least Taale's here. They're just eliminating as many people as they can and something about being in Earlene's Will makes your mother a juicy suspect. Ask her if they told her to stay in town. ~ I communed.

Deloo squeezed in beside Taale on the couch and gave her a big hug. "Look on the bright side, Mom. They let you go. Did they have any other suspects there?"

Taale embraced her daughter hard and gave a little laugh. "Just me. They're trying to locate Vindee now, but I haven't seen her for years. Have you?"

Deloo shook her head. "Not since she went to Bellingham to live with her grandmother."

Taale continued, "Right." Taale's lips formed a tenuous smile. "At least I was able to set him straight on why people keep asking where's he's from. I told him he looks Native, but not quite from the interior. Turns out his mother was from Cordova. She signed the papers to let him be adopted a day or so before she died. His birth father is like yours. He skipped out on her as soon as he found out she was pregnant."

"Wow! Is that why he moved here?"

Taale shook her tired head. "I didn't ask. Anyway, Detective Harper did not talk to anybody else tonight. He said something about me not leaving town and it was late. He took his car keys off the desk. I think he went home when I did."

CHAPTER 6

Day 2 Tuesday morning

Chuan pulled a worn three-by-four-inch notebook out of the computer bag he'd owned since his Harvard days. Those were the days of magic when he met and married the only woman he would ever love. She'd always looked twenty, even now when they were both over forty. On his suggestion, they were in Fairbanks, where he thought they would find the answers they needed. If that also satisfied the ghost of Ming's twin sister MoLi, they would all be content. MoLi had come to Ming in many ways for the past couple of weeks. Chuan wished his parents were with him rather than at their home in China. They had taught him how to deal with the spirit world. They would know even more methods of communicating.

Chuan opened his laptop and allowed his agile fingers to do their work. More out of decades of habit than success, he barbed his search with a variety of misdirection and identity traps to perform a cursory examination of his former employer's accounts. As they had been for weeks, none of them were active. Then he followed those of the head of a big Chinese mafia, through cloudy trails of public banking. He didn't bother the rest of the suspects because they were known to use retaliatory codes.

It was time to move on. It was time to find out more about MoLi. She'd gone to China with Ming as a final summer of freedom before she married. Since she, unlike Ming, wasn't in China as a student, MoLi took to exploring her Chinese background. She visited the famous sites both in and out of the Chinese borders, sometimes without telling her twin sister what she was doing. Her disappearance was explained away as MoLi's enthusiasm for the beauty and grace of everything Chinese. Chuan had many doubts about her disappearance as being the result of a pleasure trip.

Twenty years had passed since then. Now the ghost of MoLi was back. Ming didn't comprehend but her husband, Chuan, did. Why now? Why force Ming to go to Fairbanks, Alaska? Why not fly to Beijing instead, Chuan wondered. They needed help. He turned to Ming and asked, "Shall we take a little ride out to where our friend lives?"

A half hour later they found the address and tried to find a safe place to park and watch. The neighbors were sparse, but close enough someone was bound to see them if they tried to pull into an empty drive-way. The July foliage of the surrounding aspen, willows and cottonwood obstructed most other locations. Then Chuan found an old, rutty road that allowed him to pull within a few hundred feet of the small house. Ming produced a small pair of binoculars. She used them while Chuan got out to see how close he could get to their friend Brent's house. Dozens of mosquitoes, drawn to his exposed skin, began biting him until he ducked back into the car. He had to back into a thicket of willows in order to turn around, leaving a few tire gashes in some tender, albeit prolific Alaskan brush of willows and spruce.

* * *

Day Two, Tuesday morning

I watched Taale leave the house before Deloo awoke. After learning she'd talked to the police detective, Leroy Cunningham had asked to meet with Taale well before eight in the morning. Taale was just returning to the house when Deloo poured her first cup of coffee.

Deloo looked at her mother in surprise. "I didn't hear you leave. Were you back at the police station?"

"No," Taale smiled and accepted the cup of coffee her daughter handed her. "I got another job."

"What? I thought we talked about this. What about searching for Earlene?"

"That's just it," Taale laughed, "This morning I met with Mr. Cunningham. I asked him how to find Earlene. He doesn't know where she is. He asked me why I wanted to know. I told him about the jacket I got on my doorstep last November. I told him I wasn't sure if I should keep it or not and I wanted to ask Earlene for confirmation. Instead of answering, he asked me why the cops let me go last night. It's like he wanted to be sure I'm not a murderer."

"What? That's nosy of him. Why should it matter to him?" Deloo snarled.

I, the invisible Baasee', created a current to tug at Deloo's very straight, smooth hair, making it stand out from her head.

Taale stretched a hand out to smooth her daughter's hair. "Your hair always flies up. I never figured out how," she remarked and began pacing.

I asked Zephyr what else happened.

Below us, Deloo caught her mother's hand with hers while she grumbled silently at me, *~ Stop doing that! ~*

~ All right, but your mother likes me to do it. ~ Then I sighed, spirit-guide style. *~ Keep her on track with Earlene. Has the lawyer heard from her? ~*

"Has he heard from her?" Deloo asked her mother.

Taale paused and then resumed pacing. "Not at all," Taale shrugged. "He told me it's about time for him to pull together her records as well as repair the bead shop walls. He showed me a copy of the letter she wrote to him last winter. In it she says if she didn't talk to him by December first to assume she was dead. She had updated her Will a week before Thanksgiving. In it she named me as one of her two heirs. If Earlene's daughter dies before me, then I inherit everything, meaning all of the bead shop. I doubt if she ever had anything else. Great Aunt Pauline helped her as much as possible, but I usually brought Earlene lunch and sat at the counter with her now and then."

"Her daughter inherits that old bead shop? Vindee? I haven't seen her since we were in high school. She used to hang around the shop. Where did she go?" Deloo asked.

"Vindee graduated from Western Washington University last June. It was a week or two after you and Arthur got married. She came back to Fairbanks once or twice while she was a student. I don't know where she went after graduation."

Deloo put a warm hand over her mother's. "You've been busy these past few years yourself, Mom. Now both of us have graduated from college. You can relax."

"You have a two-year degree. You still have to get your B.F.A. Waiting as long as I did to finish nearly finished me."

"I will, Mom. I promise. So what are you going to do now?"

"With Earlene missing, I suppose I also won't get to find out more about those gemstones." Taale had been pacing in her small house. She swung around to face Deloo. "He wants my help to clear up her estate. Earlene told him I was her best friend and I was also knowledgeable about computers. The two of us took courses together. He wants me to find her computer to locate all her assets. One of the weird things Earlene did was to give Mr. Cunningham a quarter million dollars as an advance. She's never done that before. She's never had so much money before. I don't know where she got it. It must have cost all of her savings to put Vindee through an expensive university like WWU."

"Scary." Deloo turned pale when a thought occurred to her. She stood and paced beside her mother. "Did you say Thanksgiving? She disappeared when Arthur died."

The two women stared at each other for a long moment. Taale said, "That's right. I got the jacket the night before he was …" She couldn't finish the sentence.

Deloo did it, her voice harsh and somewhat hoarse. "Killed. When he was killed."

They both sat down hard on the couch. After a while Deloo whispered. "What did you tell Mr. Cunningham?"

Taale laid her head back on the couch before answering. "I told him I had to tell you and then think about it. He agreed with me, but he wants to know before the end of this day." Taale sat up and turned toward Deloo. "So I went to talk to my boss at the University. I asked him what my schedule would be at one-quarter time." She rested her head on the couch again.

Deloo prompted, "And?"

Taale turned bleary eyes to Deloo. "He said I would be working ten hours a week. Saturday nights from seven until six on Sunday mornings with an hour break."

"Yo! That's the worst graveyard shift I've ever heard of." Deloo frowned. "What do you want to do?"

"Working at the shop might help me figure out why she gave me back the jacket. If she's dead, and Cunningham is right, it might help us find her murderer. Even if I don't find her, I'd be paid for what I know how to do on computers. I want to take Cunningham's job." Taale stood again and walked around her small room. "I also want to keep my job at the University just so I have something to go back to at the end of all this."

Deloo raised her eyebrows. "Except for knowing how exhausted you'll be with the Saturday all-nighter, I don't object. When do you start—either job?"

"I have to tell both of them my answer today. Would you like to help me at the shop? Besides going over her accounts to pay bills, Mr. Cunningham needs somebody to call the skin sewers and beaders about their merchandise, supervise the carpenters, and do the rest of the cleaning. I can't do all of it."

"Sure, I could help when I'm not painting. I've got that commission to do. How many hours a week?"

"I'll call Mr. Cunningham about when we should start. Maybe he'll let us start tomorrow, and your hours could be as little or as much as you'd like to do." Taale sat down beside Deloo again and picked up her smart phone to press a few icons. In a moment she was speaking with Leroy Cunningham. After preliminaries she announced her decision. "We want to know when we should start." She pushed the icon to use the speaker and told him of Deloo's plans.

"How about tomorrow morning at seven-thirty? The carpenters will be there at eight to install new sheetrock."

Deloo nodded. Taale said, "Yes. We'll be there."

He spent a few minutes talking hours and wages and then ended the call. Taale put her phone in her pocket. "I'll tell my boss at the university later today. This has been an ordeal for me," she produced a thin smile for Deloo, "with Floyd's death on top of it." She yawned and tousled Deloo's hair. "I'm going to take a nap. Talk to you when I wake up."

Something occurred to me, the greatest spirit guide in the house, if not the universe. Something Taale herself told us a couple of weeks ago. Taale seemed very edgy. It occurred to me Taale might be at fault here. I made a hurried suggestion. *~ Ask your mother if she and Earlene were getting along with each other. ~*

~ Why? ~ Deloo challenged me silently, as if I were forcing her to do something illicit.

~ I'm just wondering, ~ I answered, feeling flabby. *~ Something is off here. ~*

Deloo frowned. She didn't respond to me or ask my question. I frowned too. Finally I confessed, *~ Okay, so I know she and Earlene fought about something making your mother feel guilty. I think it will help to clear the air if you ask. ~*

Deloo hesitated, but couldn't think of a reason to hold back. "Mom," Deloo asked, her voice a bit whiney, "were you and Earlene getting along? It's odd she didn't chat with you on that last night. The night she gave you my jacket and the check. Were you fighting?"

Taale was jogging upstairs. Caught in mid-step, Taale stopped. Avoiding eye contact, she turned toward Deloo. "A little."

Deloo sensed victory and waited.

Taale retraced her steps to the ground floor, found a folding chair and sat without concern for its stability. "You're right. It wasn't a fight. More like a standoff. It started with your wedding. I asked her to come with me to New Mexico. We'd never been there." A shadow of a grin crossed Taale's lips. "I might have been gloating, too. She and I have never married, but Earlene always bragged about her mystery man. I think she called him BeeZee. She always made it seem as if I was the one who couldn't keep a man and she could. Well, she might have stopped bragging when you got engaged. After all, she wasn't the one getting married. You were. See what I mean? We weren't fighting. At least not out loud."

Deloo nodded, "I see. Now she's missing, and you're feeling all that *hutłanee* stuff."

Taale's shoulders sagged. "Yeah."

"Does Great Aunt Pauline have any magic cures for a guilty conscience?"

Taale shook her head. Deloo treaded on dangerous ground. Circling above them, I told Deloo, *~ Ask her if she ever thought something else was going on. Something Floyd's death might have made her forget. ~*

It was the right direction. Deloo asked and Taale took a deep breath and answered, "Yes. It's the number, 5472. She wrote it in the note she included with the jacket she gave to me the day before Thanksgiving last year. It was like Earlene was trying to bring us back to the old days when we were younger than you are now. We used to have secret codes for messages we put in each other's lockers or passed to each other in a classroom. It felt like that to me, except we haven't done such silly things since her folks died. Also, I don't know what the number means." Taale shrugged and went upstairs.

Deloo decided to take a walk, and went outside to get clean air and a fresh breeze. Her life had taken a sudden left turn she didn't expect. As we walked, she asked me *~ Did anything like this ever happen to you, Baasee'? Cleaning up after someone died? ~*

~ This sort of thing happens all the time to some of us, my hard-working Deloo, especially if you live in a war-torn part of the world. In my case, I knew I was going to die younger than most, and I spent the last two months of my life getting things set up so the rest of my family could escape in time. Earlene did something similar—preparing the future for somebody she loved. ~

Breaking out of commune-mode, Deloo asked, "Did it happen? Did you die young?"

I shuddered and the air around us quivered. *~ Yes. It was near the end of the Ice Age in my part of North America. Some of the glaciers melted all at once. The flooding that happened on the day I died became the Gulf of Maine and the Bay of Fundy. My family escaped, but their* *lives were never the same afterward. Me? I knew I was choosing death over life that day. Some might call it suicide. My grandfather called me a martyr. ~*

"You gave up your life to help your family, Baasee'. That's fabulous. I want to be a martyr. But I'd better stick to helping my family while I'm still alive. I can do that by helping Mom. I'm going to find Earlene."

Deloo returned to Taale's house filled with a new sense of purpose to look for Earlene. In absolute divine spirit-guide fashion, I reminded her she had an eager client in Cambridge, Massachusetts who had already paid her the first installment for a portrait. She wanted Deloo's interpretation of her late husband, Federico. Deloo had never met Federico, so her client, Audra, provided her with a dozen photos and a recording of Federico's favorite music. As soon as she arrived back in Fairbanks, Deloo searched for a large-enough canvas with no success. She could have bought raw canvas. It would have needed stretching and priming, all of which she had learned to do, but not well. So instead she ordered a very large ready-made canvas and it just arrived. Since Woody would be living a short while in Virgil's house, Deloo looked at another possibility in her mother's backyard, meaning a dilapidated shed holding a lot of odds and ends—and dust.

Deloo opened the door and coughed. Peering inside from the top of the door, I communed ~ *It's wide enough. You can use this shelf for your painting supplies. Check to see if this little hut will hold your easel. I think this is a good option for your first layer. ~*

Deloo dragged her easel out of her mother's house, set it up in the shed, and smiled. It fit. ~ *You were right, Baasee'. I should be able to get the base coat and a little of the mood painting done out here. Thanks for the idea. ~*

~ *You are welcome, ~* I said as I changed into a faux-finish smock and donned a lavender and golden beret. Spirit-guide stylishness is very demanding.

Deloo set out her oil paints and brushes beside the blank canvas and put on one of Arthur's huge tee shirts, the one she'd worn when she painted Arthur's portrait. I reminded her to wear an apron as well. The apron swallowed her. Then we both thought about Arthur's portrait. Deloo had painted it months after he died. It was that portrait which inspired Audra to find her Federico the way Deloo found her path to Arthur.

To open Deloo's memories about Federico and Audra, I had her think about a story they had shared. Arthur had had a rough encounter with a horse whose spirit-presence was still in the Goode's house. Audra contributed to the eeriness of the encounter by giving the Goodes a small sculpture of a horse.

"Yeah," Deloo breathed. "I told her that horse sculpture was so powerful, one time I heard it whinny. Audra didn't believe me, but Matty had her own experience with the horse one night. I told Audra her imagination infused the horse sculpture with an essence of Arthur. It reached across to me just when I needed it."

Matty agreed, and told Audra, "It's true. I needed it too."

"It helped to get back to reality with someone like Audra who'd never heard of me," Deloo remembered.

Audra wanted to know what we meant. "Okay, what happened? You're both giving me the willies."

I was at peace in the air above the mortals. We spirits and ghosts often find some pieces of art make good conduits to our mortals. For the occasion Matty was showing everyone a photo album. There was a picture of Arthur on a horse. He was around ten. The horse didn't like him much and bucked before dashing away. Arthur fell off. Later on the horse trotted up and butted him with its head. The horse was Arthur's best friend afterward.

The air around Deloo the painter in Fairbanks was charged by the story. Deloo was mixing a big blotch of white with three other colors, one a mid-tone red, one a bright cobalt blue, and one was a lemony yellow. She aimed a brush rich with yellow at the canvas. Half of Deloo painted while the other half mused about the sculpture. "The horse—Audra's horse—was in Zachary's home office at the time. Matty woke up in the middle of the night. It was 2:20 in the morning when both of us heard a horse trotting out in the hall. They have hardwood flooring everywhere. It sounded like it was right outside my door."

Deloo plugged her ears with cushioned ear phones, set her music player to Federico's style of music, and attacked the canvas, spreading the paint across the white expanse with comfortable passion. In seconds she realized she was irritated with life and everything about it; she hurled the yellow-paint down and picked up a clean brush. This she plunged at the red and white mixture and spread some around, careful to avoid going into the yellows. Then, with calm restored, she nestled red against the edge of yellow, and made sure to bring her brush all the way around to the edge of the canvas on all four sides. If the final painting also followed the curve of the sides, top and bottom, there would be no need for a frame. The painting would frame itself. While it was resting, Deloo thrust a smaller brush into pure red, and made small, irritated designs across the smears of yellow and red. As she moved, the brush became orange. There was no forethought to any of her strokes. It was pure Deloo, expressing a complex of angry and sad emotions. I thought she'd forgotten all about Audra and the horse, when she sank her three pigmented brushes into a jar of brush cleaner. She took several deep breaths and glared at the canvas, whispering to me, hence to herself.

"I thought it was a caribou because it sounded so quick and clattery," she murmured about the sound. "But there was an odd, bluish light in the hallway. I thought of the story about the Boy in the Moon. Mom had told me the story years before, and it seemed like my mother was standing beside me even though I knew she was not. I started talking about how the boy told them he would bring them lots of caribou, but it would all disappear if they killed the leader, the white caribou.

"Later when Mom arrived in Cambridge herself, she told us the story her way, which is spookier. According to Mom the people didn't listen and killed the white caribou first. All the caribou disappeared. I can see where breaking that kind of Athabascan law would get to the person who did it. Even if it was an accident, they'd feel guilty. Making yet another way Historic Trauma gets started. It's *hutłanee*. If your grandfather stopped the caribou from coming year after year, the whole family might starve and remember the reason was your grandfather."

Deloo continued as if talking to someone who was visiting, "Or so we think. Our Athabascan traditions say spirits do things like that. Right after a death, they come by the people who are sensitive in order to send us messages." Deloo grinned, turning her left cheek, the one that dimpled, toward her invisible, unknown visitor. "Or it could be to remind you the stove is still on."

At peace with Deloo's quirky sense of humor, I encouraged her to bring the base coat together with generous smudges of light green and lighter blues. She would let it dry for a day or two after draping a speckled thrift-shop sheet over the canvas. The work had begun as Deloo had learned to do as a toddler. Thoughts and emotions came along with Audra through her horse to blend with Deloo's, Matty's, and Taale's feelings. Underlying all of it was an Athabascan story about hunting wisdom: let the herd leaders go so they can guide the survivors. It was a lesson Grandfather Kwaikit taught me, and I made sure each of the mortals I guided learned something like Deloo's story as well. That's how we spirits try to cure Historic Trauma.

Deloo returned to her mother's house, pulling her late husband's oversized tee shirt off as she walked. She dropped it into her large apron pocket. "This paint will have to dry for a day or two. Lucky for me, this hot, sunny weather will hold for a while."

CHAPTER 7

Day Two, Tuesday morning in Canada

Quite a distance away from Fairbanks, a small family approached the town of Whitehorse, Canada. There were many hours left of daylight. Woody wanted to go to Destruction Bay, about a hundred and sixty miles farther north. He queried his fiancée, Zigwan. Zigwan looked over her shoulder toward their daughter. Nibuna, head tipped toward the middle of the car, slumped. Fortunately they had buckled her into her car seat. Zigwan turned to the guide book. "The Milepost shows a campground at Haines Junction." She glanced at her watch, "but I guess it's too early to stop there." Her back ached and she felt a bout of trapped anxiety welling up.

Woody, sensing her emotional downswing, offered, "Five people have raved about Kluane Lake. I'd like to try there. Two of the people had children with them and were camping. We'll be there by five. Do you need to stop earlier?"

Reading the descriptions, Zigwan sighed and then chuckled. "Of course I need to stop earlier. It would help if I could drive from Haines Junction to the campground along the lake. I won't be as antsy if I drive." When they switched roles at a gas station, Zigwan wondered why Deloo had seemed so determined to drive this boring road.

* * *

Day 2, afternoon in Fairbanks

Taale and Deloo ambled to Great Aunt Pauline's house. At the center of Little Tanana, it was less than a block away from Taale's home. Great Aunt Pauline raised Taale and all of her siblings after Taale's mother and grandmother died in 1977. Taale had vague memories of her mother, Helen, but not many happy ones. Those all belonged to the woman Deloo knew as Great Aunt Pauline, the family and neighborhood matriarch. The house was never locked, so most people walked in without knocking just as Taale and Deloo did.

Pauline inherited the house and most of the land under the houses nearby when her sister Helen and their mother Ruth Dena died. It was then she named her neighborhood Little Tanana after the large village on the Tanana near the larger Yukon River. It was an Athabascan custom to label an ancestral village as home, so while Pauline was born in

Fairbanks, she thought of herself as being from the real village named Tanana.

Taale went into Pauline's kitchen to help cook as she always did. Deloo followed, not quite sure of what to do. As usual, she aimed for the sink and started scrubbing the unending tumble of pots and pans that seemed to live there. She eyed the stove where Great Aunt Pauline and her niece worked on a tasty dish. Most of the time it was moose meat with potatoes, onions and celery. Sometimes they ate caribou. Sometimes it was fish. Great Aunt Pauline never prepared anything else. Nor did she go to commercial stores for anything edible. Her guests brought her the moose and caribou meat, various fish species, and lots of sugary deserts. Pauline grew the veggies. Nonetheless, life is not free. Her wood stove did not survive the 1967 flood and afterward she got an oil stove instead. The oil cost money. She got money to pay for the oil from a variety of sources, including Earlene's Beads.

"When do your guests arrive from Maine?" Aunt Pauline asked.

"They should be here in about two days. By car. They are Deloo's friends, not mine."

"Where are they going to stay?" Great Aunt Pauline persisted.

As if this problem hadn't niggled the back of her mind along with murder and missing persons, Taale pretended she hadn't thought about it. "Oh? Well they can stay with me for a night or two. There's room on the floor."

"Didn't you say they have a child?"

"Yes. Nibuna. She's six," Taale replied.

"She can't stay on the floor. She'd better stay in my place," Great Aunt Pauline stated. Her generation of Alaska Natives, part of the larger Baby Boomers, was known for depriving its men of pride in their Athabascan ways. For instance, if their wives or girlfriends went on welfare, the men often stopped hunting or doing anything useful. Because of loss of pride, Great Aunt Pauline insisted her family would take care of the next generation themselves and not through checks from the white government. They needed everyone to chip in with hard work.

"There's no room here for anyone," Taale frowned. "This is Deloo's problem, not ours."

Pauline eyed her great niece and enveloped her in a hug, "Ah, Deloo. It's hard to believe how much you've gone through in such a short time." Great Aunt Pauline held Deloo back to examine her better. Whenever Taale needed a babysitter, Pauline was the only person then toddler

Deloo would tolerate. Everyone else got an unending concert of scream-ing. Pauline was proud of her status until she realized with only one babysitter, both Pauline and Taale spent most of the time talking in nurs-ery rhymes. Instead of yielding to the pleasure of being Deloo's favorite non-Mom person, Pauline worked on teaching Deloo to be kinder to her mother. Toddler Deloo soon learned to smother her screaming in order to obey her Great Aunt Pauline.

"Tell me about your friend Woody. I hear he and his wife are due in Fairbanks soon."

"Uh. Yeah."

"Where will they stay?"

"Uh." Deloo was poor at conversation with older people and I wasn't helping for a reason. She needed to get better at it. We spirits guide mor-tals to speak in complete sentences. I held back, watching Deloo as she stumbled, but began sounding more intelligent as she explained her plan to house her friends in Uncle Virgil's cabin. They would need wood, but Pauline always kept the electricity on. When she finished, she fixed huge green eyes on the older adults, waiting for them to say no.

On the contrary, Great Aunt Pauline nodded. Pauline's approval was all Deloo needed. Other people, mostly relatives, wandered in and of-fered ideas. A few minutes later they finished wrangling about details. Woody, his fiancée and their daughter would stay in Great Uncle Virgil's cabin for the rest of July. If they stayed longer, Woody would have to pay Great Aunt Pauline a nominal amount of rent. Great Uncle Virgil was blind and living in an elder-care home in Wasilla, near Woody's fu-ture work place.

"Please check in on him every once in a while when you get to Wasilla. He needs visitors."

After Woody and his fiancée left in a few weeks' time, Deloo planned to rent it herself to use as an art studio. I simpered spirit style. Deloo hadn't mentioned this part yet to Great Aunt Pauline, and knew it was better not to bring it up until the guests had departed at the end of July. To keep her from blurting her ideas out in front of Great Aunt Pauline, I urged her to inspect Uncle Virgil's cabin. Pauline handed her the keys. The house was close and we were there in minutes. Deloo opened the door and scurried inside without hesitation. Everything was clean and austere, just as it always was. A ragged wolverine hide had been nailed to the wall. It was obvious the large weasel had died in mor-tal combat with something huge. Two jagged gashes had rendered the precious fur on the shoulders and back useless. Because of the damage, Pauline thought it made a better story than a coat.

* * *

Day Two, Tuesday morning early

At seven the following morning, Taale and Deloo decided to take her car to Earlene's Beads rather than walk, hoping for peaceful together-ness. The first thing Deloo noticed when they arrived was a view of Earlene's car and the unusual design covering it from top to bottom. She'd hired Deloo to paint a chief's necklace on the car to advertise the shop. While simply black and white, the design was recognizable from miles away. Deloo smiled tenderly. It was one of the first things they had done upon arriving in Fairbanks just weeks after their spontaneous wedding. Arthur had helped her by making sure the beads were consis-tent in shape and design on both sides of Earlene's battered car.

An odd odor tingled Deloo's nostrils when they reached the shop. "What is that scent?"

Mr. Cunningham greeted them outside the shop and directed Taale to park to park across the street rather than in the carport in case anyone is watching. "That smell is Death. I used to pick up the parts and pieces of bodies during my second tour in Iraq. It's not a smell. More of a feeling."

~ He's right. Some of what you detect is physical, meaning dead cells from Floyd's body and others, but the rest comes from the spirit world. It's physical for us in the spirit world, if not for you in yours, ~ I con-veyed in a flurried commune. *~ You will not notice it as much later on. ~*

While Deloo had been in the bead shop many times, she and Vindee had played outside most of the time. As such, she couldn't remember much except the exterior was like any other house in that part of town: dilapidated but colorful. The brisk summer tourist traffic encouraged the downtown shops to maintain a look like they were built a hundred years ago. Even though most houses in the neighborhood had been built in the nineteen-fifties, they looked older. Earlene's Beads fit the ideal. It started as a one-bedroom house in the early half of the twentieth cen-tury. By the beginning of the twenty-first century, Earlene added a sec-ond floor with two rooms and a bath. At the same time, she reduced the first-floor kitchen to a dorm-sized refrigerator, a tiny microwave, a sink and two-feet of counter space hidden from customers by calico curtains.

Now three of the walls on the first floor were bare to the studs. The fourth wall, the one farthest away from the flooding water, was intact, but unadorned by furnishings. Mr. Cunningham and the two boys had taken all of the store's merchandize off the wall without regard to what it was. They had piled a lot of it onto the tops of the cabinets near it. Some of the merchandize had been taken upstairs.

Taale fingered a strand of beads on the pile, and stared at the torn-up walls. "Did you say the carpenters would come today?"

"Yes. Tony and Floyd thought all the walls were ruined. They were almost right. I told them to leave this far wall alone because it looked dry to me. Now I see some spots of water damage. The contractor has a tight budget. Maybe he'll tell me we don't need more sheetrock."

"What about the floors? I can see some buckling in places."

"The flooring contractor is due sometime this afternoon. If it has to go, the repairs will take another week." He handed her a packet. "Because it's in a high-crime neighborhood, Earlene left the older locking system in place along with the newer alarm system. This is the alarm code and this is the door code. The alarm code is electronic and will call the police if anyone gets in without entering the code. Those for the door are the kind you punch in. Mechanical. Press these numbers to unlock the doors. The police have both codes."

"Is there a place for me to work?" She looked at Mr. Cunningham, her eyes reddening. "It's odd, now, but it seems wrong to go upstairs."

Mr. Cunningham made encouraging lawyer sounds, making me wonder what kind of law he practiced. He would have been good as a marriage counselor where silence is golden. He prompted her with "Hmmm. I never talked to her in the shop except toward the end. We always met in my office. It's close by."

Taale continued, "In the old days, when Deloo and Vindee were little, Earlene and I, meaning all of us, spent a lot of time in here. That was before she remodeled. After she added the second floor, well…" She gave a tiny shrug to Deloo. "Her brothers were a decade or so older than her. Both died while in high school. Both drowned on the river. Some people think they wanted to die early. Great Aunt Pauline agrees. They didn't know what kind of life they'd have without training. Young native men of my generation didn't get good counseling or job training. Maybe it'll be different for your generation," Taale nodded toward Deloo. She seemed to be lost in thought.

Deloo prompted, "Mom? What about Vindee and Earlene? How long have they lived here?"

"Oh. Sorry." Taale shook her head. "Earlene's folks moved to Fairbanks when it was time for Earlene to go to high school. When she, well, we were seniors, Earlene's mother got sick and died. Then a few months later her father died. My aunt Pauline took Earlene in because of me, although Earlene is not part of the Dena family." Taale looked first at Deloo, then at Mr. Cunningham, eyes focused and very old. "Vindee came along after she moved in with Aunt Pauline."

From my roost above them, I thought of the first time I'd seen anyone with that kind of grief in their eyes. It was fourteen thousand years ago when Grandfather Kwaikit's bleak eyes had fixed on his last wife's, Kesani's, body. Taale must have been in the same place. I was shocked at how much the forty-year-old Taale was coming to resemble the seventy-something matriarch of the huge Koyukon family, her Aunt Pauline.

"Aunt Pauline helped Earlene in all those wise ways she has. She took me and Earlene to an old gravel pit the spring after her folks died. One of boys loaded their mattress onto his truck. She said Earlene had to burn her memories of her folks, clean them out of this house so she could live in it. It was late March or early April when the snow was not quite melted away. We set the mattress in the center of some snow and Earlene lit it with some tinder and a couple of matches. It took a long time to burn. All the time it burned, Aunt Pauline kept up this running patter, knowing it went over our heads. About how Earlene had to feel each flame as a memory of something special. Earlene stood by the mattress with her eyes fixed on the flames like she was memorizing them. After a while Aunt Pauline and I waited in the truck because it was so cold. Earlene didn't notice. In the next few days I helped Earlene wash the walls and get rid of all their clothes and stuff. Earlene stayed with me in my bed at Aunt Pauline's."

" 'You'll pay me back,' Aunt Pauline said when Earlene apologized for staying so long. And she did. It took six years before she made any money at this business." Taale's smile was gentle. "She was proud to buy a new mattress to replace the one she'd used so much. By then I was living in my mother's old house with you, Deloo-Loo. Aunt Pauline hugged Earlene twenty times and kept telling her how proud her parents must be. Then Aunt Pauline said I, Taale, was the one who would get the new mattress. My mother's old mattress was the one we burned next." Taale seemed to lose herself in thought, then said at long last, "I, I would be uncomfortable working in Earlene's bedroom, but Vindee's old room, the one piled high with junk, will be fine."

CHAPTER 8

Day Two, Tuesday morning

They'd chosen one of the inexpensive hotels near the university and turned in early after a long day of flying from Montreal. Due to the time difference, Ming awoke too early, causing herself odd mental figments or visions. The light and shadows played with her mind and its professional training to see architectural proportions in everything. Although she was used to short summer nights in northern Quebéc, she couldn't tell what time it was here in Fairbanks. Exhaustion came to her rescue and she drifted back to sleep and into a familiar nightmare.

A young woman skipped out of the shadows on the other side of the dig site and spotted a man. He was working in a part of the ancient building that was still standing. Gravel spilled around the rest of the old wooden framework. Big trucks were at the street level on the far side of the foundation. Their engines roared, awaiting the signal to begin filling the pit.

"Hi! What do you have there?" When he didn't respond to her call, she tugged at his sleeve.

He whirled at the feathery touch. Even as he turned, he sensed she was female and he drew in a breath to will a sexy grin into every pore on his face. He lifted an object toward her. A spark of bright yellow seemed to rush from the object in his hand into her eyes.

"Ooh!" She smiled and reached toward it.

Still holding it in front of her, he moved forward, stepped to her right, and slid behind her. In a natural reaction to his movement, she turned her head to the right and stepped aside. He slipped the object into his jacket pocket, put his forearm on her left shoulder and used both hands to twist her head hard to the left. She slumped to the ground.

Between the adrenaline coursing through his veins and lifting her light body, shoving her into the gaping hole was easy. Her body replaced the contents he had stolen. Dusting his hands, he put the knapsack on his back before emerging from the gloom. He leapt out of the foundation space and held both fists, thumbs up, to the lead driver. The man nodded and began moving his rig forward.

Ming sat up straight. She was alone in the bed. She felt herself dripping sweat. It ran down her spine, down her neck, everywhere, in rivulets. Chuan entered from the bathroom. He was carrying a wet towel which he draped around his wife's shoulders.

"Another MoLi dream?" He whispered into her ear.

"Yes. The one with that guy. All I ever see is the knapsack. She's trying to tell me something. I could almost figure it out. Not this time."

"What did you dream?"

Ming told him.

"Maybe that's what happened to her. Maybe she was killed on a construction site." Chuan tightened his grip on his wife.

"Maybe. I don't know.…" Ming got out of bed. "Let's go." she told her husband.

"It's four in the morning. Let's rest some more."

Ming opened the drapes. "It's bright as day outside."

"We are in Alaska in July. What do you expect? It's farther north than your mother's village in Quebéc." Chuan laughed.

Ming dropped the drapes and snorted. "I'll take a shower and come back to bed." A few hours later they parked near Earlene's Beads. Are you ready to go into it?" Chuan asked.

Ming's breathtaking eyes were pinched with worry. He could see a little more grey in her hair. "Maybe. I wish I knew what to look for in this place."

"Come. You don't have to say a word."

On the way they drove across the narrow channel known as the Chena River. Ming pointed to a pretty walkway. "We should take a walk over there." Chuan found a nearby parking place and walked around the car to help her get out.

"Come on!" she said, her voice in his left ear. The car door was on the right. He swung around and almost knocked her over. However, she was ready for him and stepped back in time to catch him as he careened beside her.

"Sorry, Honey. It's just that I feel so close to MoLi just now and …. Omigod. Don't turn around." Ming hovered into his chest and peered outward. "It's him."

"Him? Who?" Chuan tried to look around.

Ming tugged his chin toward her and kissed him as she mouthed words between gnawing lips. "He's on the bridge coming toward us. Help me into the car without facing him. I'll drive. You slide in beside me." She reached for the brimmed hat to cover any view of her face. She handed sunglasses to Chuan. He put them on and kept his face down while he looked at the bridge.

"Ah. That's him, all right."

"Told you." She put the car into reverse and made her way into traffic. They were close enough in height that she didn't have to make any other changes to be able to see. "He doesn't know we're here, does he?"

"I didn't talk to him after what happened. He wouldn't like it if we showed up here." He felt around the back seat for the other hat and shoved it down as far as it would go. "He doesn't handle surprises well."

They entered the bead shop at midmorning. It took a moment for Ming's eyes to adjust to the dust, noise of hammers and men's voices. Then she saw rubble mixed with strings of beads and beading tools. When she saw the dark head of a woman bending over something, she asked, "What happened in here?"

Deloo rose up from behind the front counter and stared. "Prize woman!" She ducked out of sight and communed to me, ~ *what shall I do?* ~

~ *First, take a deep breath.* ~ I communed with ultra-wise spirit guide delicacy. I paused until she did as I said. ~ *Now stand up. I'll help you.* ~

Deloo rose and forced a smile to her flushed face. "There was a flood. Someone died."

"Died?" Ming breathed. Her black eyes flared.

"It's you." Chuan sputtered. "I thought we'd seen the last of you in Vermont." He encircled his wife as if my Deloo might leap at her.

"Yes, well, I never expected to see you again either," Deloo retorted.

They eyed each other like short-faced bears about to attack. I barged in and communed to Deloo, ~ *introduce yourself. Then ask them why they are here.* ~

Deloo stuck out a hand and said, "I'm Deloo. After what happened between us, I'm surprised to see you in Fairbanks." Her tanned hands contrasted sharply with the ivory shade of Chuan's fingers. Then she posed Baasee's question with her eyes fastened on Ming. "It's a long way from Vermont or eastern Canada. Why did you follow me here?"

They all shook hands. Ming relaxed. She curved a slim hand around Chuan's and lifted it to her lips. After kissing her husband's hand, she released it and slid out of his grip. "We didn't follow you at all. It's not about you. It's my sister. I've been having bad dreams about her. She won't let me go." Ming, or Prize Woman as we called her, leaned against the counter.

Deloo asked, "Do you mean the little ghost?" They didn't respond. "I mean the ghost of your twin sister?"

"How did you know about her?" Chuan asked.

~ *Tell them what you do know, which isn't much.* ~ I prompted Deloo. Meanwhile, I looked for the little ghost myself and found her peering eagerly at me from the tendril of the giant male spirit who'd taken her from us in Vermont. I communed to the little ghost and her mentoring guide. ~ *How are you?* ~

~ *Greetings Sacred Being Baasee'.* ~ She used my formal, unpronounceable designation as well as a formal version of Eternalese. I beamed at her. ~ *I used all kinds of signs to urge Ming to come here. I'm sure here in Alaska we will find out who killed me. Ming is trying to help. Do you have any ideas?* ~

~ *Hmmm. Too bad neither of us were there when you died. I'll help you find out if it doesn't take me away from Deloo.* ~

Meanwhile, Deloo was telling Ming, "She came to me in New Brunswick and left me in Vermont, I thought, with you. She is a light-hearted person. I enjoyed her sense of humor."

Ming looked encouraged. "Could you see her?"

Deloo shook her head and turned to the workmen, all of whom seemed too busy to listen. "No. I can hear her, or at least I can hear my own guide. Do you see her?"

"I see her in dreams and visions. It's very quick. I wish I could see her otherwise." Ming's shoulders drooped. She leaned into Chuan. "Chuan has been my guide through all of it."

"She seems driven to be here in Alaska. She's angry if we don't do what she wants," Chuan muttered.

"Maybe it's a different ghost. The little ghost with me was happy most of the time." Deloo smiled. "I drew a picture of her. Sort of. Nothing clear enough to recognize her face. Would you like to see it? I left it at home."

"Yes. I would, if you don't mind. Maybe it would help. Maybe it's brought on by the mysterious jackets. I thought her fiancé could help, but he died a couple of years ago. So, we came here because of that beaded jacket of yours. Maybe we can find out in this place."

"Jacket? Do you mean my denim jacket?"

Prize Woman quivered. "It's not your jacket, exactly, but something here. I think it might have something to do with this bead shop. That's why we came here today."

Deloo glanced around the shop. "There aren't any beaded jackets here as far as I can tell, but I've only just started the clean-up process."

MoLi began to moan. Deloo heard it and Ming jumped at the sound. Chuan didn't react, but Deloo cooed as she'd done a few times in Canada. MoLi tried to coo in return.

I was convinced Deloo was maturing in the mystical way faster because she was back home in Fairbanks. ~ *You couldn't see her in Canada,* ~ I reminded Deloo.

Ming smiled at my mortal. "She's at peace again. She must have heard you making that sound. What did you sing?"

Deloo beamed back, "An old-fashioned song she seemed to know. 'Black Velvet.'" Deloo hummed a line of it.

"It was one of those she sang all the time." Ming stared at Deloo with pleading eyes. "Is she telling you anything?"

Confused, Deloo threw beautiful but invisible me, a glance. I had told her many a time I don't live in the ceiling, but she keeps looking, I suppose, just in case. ~ *Tell her she's not talking right now. Ask Prize Woman if she's heard or seen anything to cause her to choose that particular song.* ~

Ming gave Deloo a jumbled account, leaving out most of the recurring murder dream.

Deloo nodded her twenty-one-year-old head as if she understood Ming. "She might be trying to give you a dire warning. My great aunt talks about those all the time."

"Dire warning?" Ming started to frame a question, but her husband cut her off.

"It's not your jacket those guys wanted, anyway. It was another jacket, I guess. I'm sorry I tried so hard to catch you last month. Please forgive me if you can." Chuan hung his head. "We were paid to do it. Now it's over."

"If I see a beaded jacket, I'll call you. What's your telephone number?"

They stared at Deloo, turned as a single unit and left the bead shop.

"Weird." Deloo murmured.

"What's weird?" Taale carried a box downstairs.

"Those people. Those people who chased me around Canada were here."

Taale stared at the door in shock. "Do you mean the one named Edward or was it Gerald? Didn't he get shot right in front of us?"

"Yes. I mean, no. Not him. It was the Chinese couple. I drew pictures of them."

"Should we call the police?"

"I don't think so. She said her name is Ming, and I told her I thought of her as Prize Woman. She smiled. The man apologized for chasing me last month. They looked confused when they saw me. They wouldn't give me their telephone number."

"If they come back, let's call the cops."

"*Hutlanee,* I feel like I'm living in one of Great Aunt Pauline's dire warning dreams. They creeped me out. The man gives me the willies."

"Great Aunt Pauline will love to hear about it."

Moments later Detective Harper walked in unexpectedly. Taale was talking to the carpenters and Mr. Cunningham was talking to the flooring contractor. "Why isn't this door locked? People can just make themselves at home here." He looked after Prize Woman's departing car.

~ He's trying to figure out how to surprise you into revealing more details, ~ I communed to Deloo, *~ Show him your beaded jacket and tell him to contact the police in Canada. ~*

Deloo frowned at the ceiling. Behind her, Taale called from across the room, "Good morning Detective Harper."

"Who are they?" He tilted his head toward the door.

"They chased me through Canada for this," Deloo lifted up the jackets she'd tucked into a corner and told him the story minus details about the startling discovery of gemstones sewn onto it. "You should call the police in Canada for more information. One of them got killed. It's complicated. Lots of ins and outs."

"Oh," Detective Harper said after a long pause, "yes, I'll take the number if you have it."

"I don't have it on me." Deloo said.

~ He has all the numbers he needs. Let his fingers do the walking. ~

Detective Harper's spirit guide must've picked up my sarcasm. "I'll get it myself, thank you." He caught Taale's eye. "I thought you worked for the University."

"There's a lot going on," Taale responded, cheeks suddenly ruddy. "My hours were cut at the University and Mr. Cunningham put me to work here. Is that okay with you?"

Detective Harper shrugged, "I've been wondering why Earlene bought this house."

Taale shook her straight, medium length hair. "She didn't. Her parents left the house to her. They both had serious illnesses and needed to see their doctors often so they moved out of the village to live close to the Chief Andrew Isaac clinic. This house was flooded in 1967 and was not reoccupied until the Shoepacks bought it in the 1980s. It needed a lot of work, but her father thought he could do it. He did a lot before he died."

"What's this thing?" Detective Harper asked, pointing to an area on the wall beside the end of the counter and the craft table. He inspected a sheet of dirty paneling propped beside the largest hole in the wall. "It looks like exterior siding," he exclaimed. "It's seen a lot of water damage over the years. Does it rain often here?"

Deloo, beside him and holding edges of the panel as he twirled it, supplied "we get a lot of snow most winters. It all melts at once in March or April. It rains some, but the damage here is from snow build-up."

Detective Harper touched the upper left corner of the panel. "Look at this odd section. It's not a solid piece of wood with the rest."

Deloo had to stretch to inspect it. "It looks like it could be pressed. I've seen something like this somewhere."

Taale touched the wood and said, "Earlene's parents covered over the old fireplace several years ago with this stuff. It's salvaged wood. It might have been on some other building. See? They put this Monitor oil heater where the fireplace used to be." She felt the air a few inches above the Monitor to make sure it was off. "Mr. Cunningham had the extension opened up last winter after there was a freeze. He thought there might be water damage in there." Taale pointed at the small rectangular heater. "Last summer Earlene papered over the wall. Her father had put the wall up and then died a few months later. She left it untouched until last year."

"I'm sorry to hear about her parents. When did they die?" Detective Harper asked.

"That was in 1993. Both of them, just a couple of months apart. Earlene and I both graduated high school and we were planning to enter UAF. Except her folks died. Everyone was gone in her family. I went to the university alone. Aunt Pauline took over to help Earlene. Earlene stayed with my aunt for a few weeks back then. After a while, Aunt Pauline told us to move out of her place and to my mother's empty house. That was a boon for me, because I got a chance to live like an adult. I had Earlene to thank for keeping me focused, but she was kind of blurry about things. Sometimes I would come home and she would still be in bed. Eventually, Aunt Pauline took her back here. In February or March of 1995, Earlene moved back to her folk's house and started selling beads and furs for her relatives. She didn't go to the University like she said she would."

As if talking to herself, Taale added "Living alone wasn't the best thing for me, either. I met Deloo's father and got pregnant. He left. It was Earlene who knew what to do for me. She started harping about women's rights. She should have been a politician."

Detective Harper wrote some notes and frowned. "So this is just a covering for the addition outside." He nodded and sauntered toward the unlocked front door to inspect the exterior walls.

Taale turned her attention back to the sheetrock carpenters when Mr. Cunningham entered. After consulting with the detective, Mr. Cunningham gave the signal to start mudding the walls. "If the walls are dry enough, they plan to finish this week," Mr. Cunningham said to both Taale and the detective.

Taale smiled and remarked, "Sounds good. I've got work to do." She dashed away. I couldn't help notice her hips swayed a little bit more on the way upstairs and that Detective Harper was very alert to the shape of Taale's disappearing body.

When she was out of sight, Detective Harper smiled at Deloo. "Thanks for the information on that couple." With a meaningful look at Mr. Cunningham, he said, "Remember to lock this door."

Deloo waited a few minutes before calling out to her mother. "He's gone Mom." She ran up the stairs to look around in puzzlement. "You're safe now. I thought I heard voices."

Taale looked around the cluttered den and shuddered. "I hope not. The last thing we need is another ghost."

CHAPTER 9

Day Two, Tuesday morning, Fairbanks

Something felt out of order, but Vindee couldn't identify it. Everything had happened almost as they had planned. With so much to worry about, no one seemed to think of the most obvious ingredient. Would the man around whom they had planned everything so carefully actually show up in dinky Fairbanks when he could go anywhere? She shrugged thin shoulders and caught a glimpse of herself in a window pane. She could tell by the loose way her skirt hung around her butt she'd lost another couple of pounds. She was taller than her mother by several inches, and found it boring to eat enough food.

Shifting back to her current dilemma, she remembered this is where he begins each year, no matter what else he does. He's had the same routine for decades. This time is different. Vindee screwed on the wig that had grown both heavy and sweaty in Fairbanks' hot summer weather. She pondered, wondering if he was there to clean everything out. Vindee whispered to herself, "I'll just stick with details of Plan B. No innovations, especially nothing electronic. Plan B. Now we're doing it. I finally understand. It's not about computers, but about timing. It would be a plus to find out where the money comes from." Vindee examined herself in the mirror-like window. She was getting used to treating the brownish-gray wig as part of her head.

She heard her grandmother's words in her mind. "That's why she's mapped out this much detail on Plan B—so no one will be able to track any of us down." Fay had bent her head while talking and for a brief moment, Vindee couldn't see her grandmother's electric blue eyes. She grimaced at the memory of her grandmother leaning against Vindee's head to show her their family connection. Looking in the mirror, Vindee saw them once again—the eyes had convinced her she was the biological daughter of a murderous monster and the biological granddaughter of a woman who claimed to be his first victim. She already knew she herself was the only child of a woman who was one of his last victims.

"This face and these eyes are why I have paid so much attention to Plan B. He sees his version of these eyes in his own mirror every day. Any change to Plan B and one of us is going to be the next one he kills."

Vindee glanced at her watch and remembered Plan B included buying a donut at the same time every week day at the shop on the way to her job at the bank. The stop allowed her a moment to practice a no nonsense middle-aged pace instead of her habitual youthful slither. She squinted at the pastries. Now that they were actually going through with the plan, she regretted being so thin. As she had done for months, she frowned at her slim waist. She began her daily routine at six AM when she donned the disguise. First, she fished around for the length of fiber-fill that fit into her panties. It gave her a little paunch in front. Then she would slip on the fiber-lined smock. It was great when she first started at the bank in below-zero January. Fairbanks temperatures were now in the seventies and eighties in July. She hated the extra heat. At least it wasn't like the thick fiber-filled belt she wore last winter to add to her middle-aged look. Its fiber replacement filled the loose dress with lighter-weight stuffing. These she had started to wear in June. At least she could take the fake fat off as soon as she got home, and she admitted it all helped to make her look close to fifty years of age when she was barely twenty-two.

Once again examining her image in the window pane, Vindee twisted her hands. "I always imagined he'd know me and love me on sight." She looked at a photo Fay had of her father. In it he wore form-fitted trousers. Her biological father looked the same as he had in the picture when she saw him for the first time a few months ago. Back in November they both worked at the University. Her father never stopped to talk to the new assistant when he breezed through the laboratory at the University of Alaska. Of course, he didn't know her, either. She had been relieved when he brushed past her without a glance. Vindee pulled a silver chain from under her turtleneck sweater and held the key aloft. She released a tiny laugh, "and here's to a gift from my father."

At that time the three women fell silent. Each of them thought about Fay's Bellingham house. It was a bungalow with an attic, Fay's parents had bought it the year they married in late 1939, a year before Fay's birth. They met each other after watching the movie *King Kong,* and didn't think it was funny to name their only child after the star of the movie. Needless to say, Fay learned about peer pressure in school, where she hid her tears and ignored the bullies. She grew up despite her name and fell in love. After they married, Fay's husband was stationed at Fort Wainwright near Fairbanks. She gave birth to her son before his father died. His father was killed in Vietnam in 1970.

Fay stayed in Fairbanks in their first and only house, off Steele Creek Road. It was the house she had called home for eighteen years. Then, while he was still in college, her son bought his mother a ticket to go to Bellingham to help her ailing parents. It wasn't until later she learned he had bought her a one-way ticket. She tried to call him from a pay phone, and found her telephone in Fairbanks had been disconnected.

"It was my own telephone number. A land line in Fairbanks. 'Land lines' were all we had back then." Later she discovered he used the power of attorney she had given him for emergencies to take out a loan for Harvard, of all places. He refused to send her money to return to Alaska. In addition, he told her he had sold or donated all of her belongings excluding the jewelry she had left behind. Because of her parents' various medical needs, she didn't have time to do more than fret rather than ask her son what he was doing and why. Years later when Fay demanded an explanation, he hung up on her.

* * *

Day Two, Tuesday morning

Carmen whispered, "She has his kind of hair, you know. It's not just the eyes. A little straighter than his and of course, much darker." She glanced at Fay. "Suegra, why don't you have any pictures of your son as an adult?"

Now it was Fay's turn to look at her almost-daughter-in-law. "When things go wrong between people, there's never an easy way to fix it." She thought of her son's old dog named Mister, a malamute husky. She told the others, "Mister loved him, followed him everywhere. But something happened one day. I can't get the look on my boy's face out of my mind. His face was smooth, without a single expression. He lifted the tire iron as if it were a spoon and brought it down on Mister's head so hard blood splattered everywhere. His face never changed expression." She shuddered, and said, "He may not have super powers or be a King Kong, but he does have a way to kill without emotion and to stay without emotion after the act. He never said a thing about Mister to me again. My son was ten years old."

"What a horrible thing to do to anyone. He's a terrible human being," Carmen assured her friend.

"It's time for payback, and Earlene has made it possible to make him hurt for what he did to each of us." Fay plucked a tissue from a nearby box and blew her nose. "When we talked about this one night with Earlene, we were trying to believe he thinks like other people. He does not. He is older now, and from what she says, he is just as vicious." As she spoke, her voice got stronger. Some of the confidence she needed flowed into her. "He doesn't reason like we do. When he finds out about what we've done, there's no way to predict what he will do, but we all know how easy it would have been for him to kill each of us at any time. Now we are prepared."

Carmen stood up. "We are prepared. We are always prepared, thanks to Earlene and her detailed Plan B."

* * *

Day Two, Tuesday morning, Earlene's Beads in Fairbanks
Deloo was drenched with sweat. She had been trying to move the stand-alone display case, but it was far too heavy. She leaned on it and gulped in air.

"What's up? You're all red-faced." It was Lizzie, who, like everyone else, entered by the unlocked front door. The heat of the day seemed to make Lizzie's thick hair double in volume.

"Hey," Deloo smiled in surprise. "I thought you were staying in Ester. How'd you get here so early?"

"Mr. Grant dropped me off on his way to work. He was sort of mean about it. Can I get a ride back with you?"

"Sure. Where will we take you?"

"Well," Lizzie shuffled. "It's complicated now Floyd is …"

Deloo put her arm around Lizzie. "It's all right, of course we'll give you a ride."

"I forgot you were related to him on your mother's side," Deloo said.

"Yes," Lizzie said. "I was their favorite babysitter when Floyd was younger because I was an older child. Most of his first cousins are younger than Floyd. He babysat them."

"I babysat Floyd myself, but not very often. Now I know who the competition was. You were the other woman." Deloo sighed. "I babysat Tony more often. I hate to think it could've been him rather than Floyd."

To change the subject, Deloo asked, "How are your folks?" Her voice came out as a chirp. Floyd's mother was Lizzie's maternal aunt. The sisters were both white Americans. Floyd's mother married an Alaska Native. Lizzie's mother, Myrtle, married a white American, Milton Grant. Mr. Grant has a brother who lives in Ester with his wife.

"They went to Texas. I think Mom is taking Floyd's death okay. I talked to her last night. She isn't crying as much as she was when he was k-k-killed." She said the last word as if it had trouble leaving her mouth.

"Where to, Lizzie?" Deloo asked.

Lizzie choked, "As you know from yesterday, I WAS staying with Floyd's mother and father, Mr. and Mrs. Charles. They have a three-bedroom house in Doyon Estates. It's near a bus route close to campus. My uncle and his wife took me in to give the Charles family some space. I don't have enough money for a dorm room." My uncle lives in the Republic of Ester, an old gold mining camp on the west side of Fairbanks. The people of Ester have earned a reputation for being in-dependent from Fairbanks many years earlier.

"Ester is quite a hike to campus and I'm sure it's not on a bus route. Do you have a bike or something?" Deloo queried.

"Not any more. I sold the one I had to pay for my books."

"Ouch!" Deloo whispered. Taale skipped down the stairs in time to hear Lizzie. Deloo caught her mother's eye. Taale nodded. Deloo took it as a signal to say, "Lizzie why don't you stay with us? You can sleep in one of my bunk beds. I use the top bunk, but it doesn't matter to me. When things settle down I'll be moving into Virgil's house, I hope."

Lizzie shook her shaggy brown curls. "I don't want to be a bother."

Taale placed her warm hand over Lizzie's cool one. "You shouldn't be so far away from campus at this time. It's no problem for us. We've been busy working here." She waved her arm, as if to explain everything.

"Oh? I wondered what Great Aunt Pauline meant when she told me to find you here. Last night you said you still worked at UAF."

Taale nodded, "things changed in a big hurry because of what happened."

"Yeah," Deloo said. "It's a mess. Yesterday, Mr. Cunningham need-ed some help, and we are available. It's short-term."

Lizzie looked at Taale. "What about the University?"

"They cut my hours. This job came along just in time." Taale shrugged and added, "Lizzie, it looks like Deloo could use a little help. Besides, there's a murdering prowler tearing through Fairbanks. It would be great to have an extra set of eyes and ears here. I still don't know where things are, like Earlene's computer. Maybe you'll see it."

Deloo butted in, "Also, there are places to do your homework at both Mom's house at home and at the shop—if you don't mind using Earlene's bedroom. Please make yourself at home. We'll leave here in about three hours."

Leroy Cunningham stopped by again an hour later to talk to Taale about her progress.

"I haven't found Earlene's computer yet. It's around here somewhere. Also, what did you decide about flooring?"

"It depends on what the floor looks like in the rest of the store," Mr. Cunningham swooped an arm around the main display area. "Maybe Deloo and someone could move the stand-alone display case in the morning." He smiled, showing his sharp teeth at the carpenter. Old cave-woman-me thought he looked like a dire wolf. The carpenter must have agreed. He found something else to look at. "The main point is we want to clear more space for the flooring people and provide a space for Taale to work upstairs." He looked at Lizzie and asked, "Didn't you babysit my son, Tony, a time or two?"

"Once in a while. I think you had Kathy or Deloo come over more often." It didn't take Mr. Cunningham long to recognize the scent of a poor college kid.

"You can see what a mess we've got here. I need more help than I'd thought. Are you available for a few hours, short term?"

Lizzie brightened and smiled.

"I could use a few hours of work," she answered. They decided on ten hours a week, starting the next day. Lizzie smiled and did some homework while Deloo worked.

Taale came down at five to take everyone home. "Shall we go to Ester to get your things Lizzie?"

Lizzie nodded and looked worried. "I hope the Hills don't mind. They do have the room, but Aunt Hill is not like her sister, my mother, in so many ways," Her smile was lopsided. "It's kind of you to offer your bunk bed, Deloo. Now I have a job. I will be able to pay rent."

Deloo shook her glossy dark hair, smoothing Lizzie's thick brown mop. "What rent? For a bunk? You've got to be kidding. Mom and I don't want your money." She touched the brown hair again, "maybe letting us give you a haircut, but no money." Deloo stopped a chuckle in the midst of a breath. "Hey! We do want your help, though. That's a big need."

After setting the alarm system, Taale ushered them both to the car and aimed it toward the Republic of Ester. She drove in silence. When she reached the Hill's house, she smiled at Lizzie. "Why don't you go inside and get your bag? We'll wait out here."

Lizzie looked long and hard at the Hills' front door and said to the car door in a voice a bat would have had trouble hearing. "They don't like all my Native friends." She cringed and turned to look at Taale,

"Thank you. I need to be with you. They are military like my father is. They… they don't understand me." Lizzie opened the front door and got out. "I'll be just a few minutes."

In the back seat Deloo watched her friend walk to the Hills' front door. She thought toward me, ~ *Baasee', why do bad things happen to such good people, people like Lizzie?* ~

~ *Your friend, Lizzie is better because she has good friends like you and your mother.* ~

~ *Yeah, but Lizzie doesn't have enough money to make it through college even though she's white.* ~

~ *Is not a crime to be white, my dear,* ~ I communed in my most soothing way, wondering if I should put on my alabaster halo or use the old gold one that matches my new polka-dot robe. Each dot was encased in transparent gold light. ~ *It's not a bad thing to be poor either.* ~

Deloo sighed. ~ *I get it. And you do help me understand so many things. It just seems to me you do a lot more for me than other spirit guides do for their people. Although Lizzie's guide does a lot for her. She's alone in Fairbanks, but she's not afraid.* ~

I preened and spun around, trying to see if Zephyr had been eavesdropping. She beamed and aimed a big bouquet of roses at me. Feeling pompous I communed to Deloo, ~ *I'm supposed to follow orders, but no one stops me when I do more. So why not do more? Lizzie's guide got her a job and a new place to stay in a matter of minutes. So does the guide with your mother. There are plenty of us who make a point of helping as much as we can.* ~

Lizzie opened the Hill's front door. We all turned our attention to her. She shook Mrs. Hill's hand and turned toward us with a stiff smile on her face.

"Staying with them last night was hard on them. They are trying to save money on things like fuel oil and gas." She slammed the car door.

Taale said, "We want you with us." She glanced at Deloo through the rearview mirror again. "I'm sorry you will have to stay in Deloo's room. I only have two bedrooms."

Lizzie surprised them with a laugh. "I know. I've been to your house hundreds of times. Thank you very much again for taking me in. Your house is right next to a bus route."

Leaning over the back of the seat, Deloo gave Lizzie a quick hug. "You are welcome to stay as long as you want. You will help me finish all my courses on time."

"I was just going to say the same about you for me," Lizzie turned around in her seat and grinned at Deloo.

Deloo, seated behind her mother, smiled back. As she did so she caught some flickering shape to the right of Lizzie. Or maybe it was just outside the car. She stared, trying to figure out what it was. It was then she realized she was looking at Arthur's face. A huge version of his face. Arthur's big eyes were staring back at her. He was pointing at her chest. She felt the camera, his camera, vibrate. Ever since the day of his death several months ago, she'd carried the camera around her neck wherever she went. It was so tiny, it weighed next to nothing. Her hand went to the camera and so did her eyes. When she looked back at Arthur's face it was gone. *~ Baasee', did you see him? He was huge. Not like he was before. ~*

I'd been busy buffing my fake fingernails when the wraith appeared. By the time I got my ocular pointed in the correct direction, I saw a fragmentary burst of light pointing at Deloo's wedding ring, but no more. Arthur was gone. Instead, I saw her fingers jerking. *~ Deloo, you've been twisting your ring for weeks. Does it hurt? ~*

~ Matty said it was valuable, remember? She said this ring was made by a famous carver in China. ~ We both eyed her wedding ring, but it didn't tell either of us much.

That night Deloo slept on the top bunk while Lizzie slept on the bottom. It gave each of them a little bit of privacy while they slept. It was well after midnight before Deloo dozed off. She awoke to a dream in which she saw Arthur cross-country skiing. Deloo began to shake. I guided her to climb down the short steps from her bunk and toward the bathroom. There she drank some water.

~ Did you see it Baasee'? Could you see Arthur in your dream? ~

~ Yes my dear. I saw him skiing. You are right about his size. He's bigger. ~

I thought about the day her husband, Arthur, died. He'd been struck by a vehicle on Steele Creek Road.

Once again calm, Deloo yawned and snuggled under the covers. *~ I'll check the camera in the morning. Good night Arthur. ~*

CHAPTER 10

Day Two, Tuesday night

Lately, Deloo's absent-minded greetings to her dead husband, Arthur, usually meant that she would dream of him soon. Recording those dreams to review with her later was a key part of a spirit guide's work. This night's dream was typical. As soon as it started, I realized it was Arthur's way of sending her a clue about his unexpected death. He went cross-country skiing that morning. I recalled his final thoughts in their tiny rental home. He wondered when he should explain to beautiful Deloo that he was, in fact, rich. They lived on food a younger Arthur would never put in his cupboards, let alone put in his mouth. He was careful not to confuse her. For instance, the skis he wore cost more than all the food Deloo had permitted them to buy in five months and twenty-three days of marriage.

Those were Arthur's thoughts as I remembered them on that final morning. The visual part of the dream opened with an elegant wolverine crossing his path. The species was noteworthy for its keen hunting ability. The female in front of him was no exception. She stopped, looked to her left, and pounced on a snow berm. The snow buried her. An easy task, since she was barely fifteen inches tall. When she surfaced, her dark nose and ears were speckled with blood. She'd caught a vole. Once out of the snow, she shook her luxurious winter coat, gave Arthur a malevolent glare, and trotted away.

Arthur, always ready with his camera, snapped a photo. His hands were unsteady with the freezing temperatures. He put on his fingerless gloves, as ever amazed. What he used to think of as cold meant little compared to minus twenty Fahrenheit in Fairbanks. I could imagine he wished he had listened to Deloo, who'd held his down mittens out to him. They were great for warmth, but allowed him little control over anything. He pictured my mortal, Deloo, her single dimple flickering at him as he left the cabin that morning.

Suddenly the dream space was filled with sound. Arthur had a rich baritone he enjoyed using. "You're just too good to be true," he'd bellowed. It was their song.

In the dream, Arthur moved his legs forward in clumsy strokes. It was eleven, and time to get ready for another strange dinner at his in-law's houses. Any such Little Tanana dinner started in one person's house for one course, zeroed in on Taale's place for another, and always ended up at Great Aunt Pauline's bigger house for dessert. Today's exception was that he was getting the honor of slicing the turkey. He grinned to imagine his parent's amusement at how Indians in the Far North had co-opted a New England feast.

As Deloo's dream faded, I made a couple of spirit-guide notations to help Deloo remember Arthur. Their entire relationship was so short that by the time I discussed it with her after she'd died herself, Deloo would not remember him clearly. Deloo was destined to live a long time, and few of her later years would remind her of her aborted marriage to Arthur.

It didn't surprise me she forgot to check for his camera again the following morning. She had been avoiding it, I suppose because it was the last of Arthur. I wasn't concerned. I knew about the one photo he had taken before he left the cabin. It was of Deloo, of his sleeping wife. I knew there was no hurry to see herself the way she looked to Arthur on the day he died.

My girl was sound asleep when Lizzie awoke and stood beside the bunk bed. Lizzie peered at Deloo in the light of the Fairbanks night. Deloo's chest moved with each breath she took. Thus reassured, Lizzie lay back on her bunk. Soon, she too was asleep.

While they slept I looked at Deloo's nightstand. That's where she kept her sketchbook as well as Arthur's camera. This time I was looking at the camera rather than the book. I didn't bother to look at the photos inside. That was Deloo's job. Then I noticed a trace of residue on the camera. Using more than my ocular, I studied the residue. Whose was it?

Anyone as old as me can't leave residue. We leave that element behind as part of the maturation process. Young ghosts can. They have a lot of growing up to do. Arthur is a very young ghost so I compared notes with Grandfather Kwaikit and yes. It was Arthur's residue. I didn't touch the residue but memorized it instead. Grandfather Kwaikit would expect no less. He would also expect me to be the spiritual fashion plate I have become. I selected a robe of changeable greens to which I'd affixed an aura of cobalt blue and jade around my slim, but faux waist. I knew I was breath-taking. Okay, if I changed the shape of the air around me, I could sometimes feel my own breath taking temporary residence inside me just like mortal breath. Get it? I'm breath-taking.

* * *

Day Three, Wednesday morning

The next day saw Deloo and Taale at Earlene's Beads with Lizzie. Deloo, as usual, wore overalls. Because she was both short and very slim, the size six overalls hung on her. From behind she looked like a long-haired boy of ten or twelve. July in Fairbanks is often very warm, so Taale wore shorts. When they arrived at Earlene's Beads, Taale, inspected Lizzie with a maternal eye. She took her upstairs. They both could see the shower stall was too clean to have been used recently. Deloo followed them upstairs, but continued on to Earlene's bedroom. Even though she had known Earlene all her life, it was with a child's view of somebody old. She thought of Earlene as 'the turban lady' because she always wore a long scarf. She went back to the hall bathroom where Taale was telling Lizzie, "There's only one bathroom at my place. It's cramped. Why don't you take advantage of a little privacy and shower here."

Lizzie exhaled. "You just read my mind," and she looked around for towels. None of them thought it odd there were only two on otherwise bare shelves. Soon Deloo heard the shower running, and was about to thank her mother when a sheetrock finisher pounded on the front door. He was a distant cousin. She let him in. Since he was a familiar face around Great Aunt Pauline's house, she felt confident about asking him to help her move the display cabinet before they got started.

"I don't do moving," the finisher said, "but Pauline would never forget it if I didn't help out."

Deloo laughed, "I know what you mean." They slid the cabinet closer to the back door. Once it was out of its habitual spot, Deloo saw a thin dark line showing where it had been.

"I'm glad the dog isn't with me today. The blood would drive him crazy."

"Blood? But Floyd was killed back there, on the stairwell." Deloo stared at her cousin for half a beat and yelled, "Mom!"

Taale had started to brush Lizzie's sodden, tangled hair when she heard and felt Deloo's excitement. She and Lizzie looked down the stairs.

"Do you have Detective Harper's number? We found something he should see," my dazzling mortal asked.

Meanwhile I tried my own investigative tools. It didn't help that most of the furniture had been moved and many walls had been taken away. However, I knew the police would discover the one clue worth salvaging from the shop. We would soon know whose blood was on the floor.

Detective Harper and a crime scene investigator examined the stain outlining where the cabinet had been. Tests completed at the shop told them what the carpenter already knew: it was blood. Lab work would tell them more.

Swirling with satisfaction, I communed to Deloo, ~ *These mortal cops are all hampered by physical evidence. Grandfather Kwaikit has taught me, therefore you as well, to use everything we have to disclose the secrets of a crime, or in this case, multiple crimes. I assure you many have died here—Floyd was not the first. Detective Harper will uncover the same truth in due course, but he'd like a little help from his own set of detective spirit guides. He has quite a crew with him. Meanwhile, I want you to be on the alert. Something is going to happen today. Something weird. ~*

In other areas of the Deloo world, things were picking up. Her cell phone lit with a silent call, preventing Deloo from quizzing me further. It was Woody, and they were about to pull onto Airport Way.

Deloo excused herself, and left her mother with the police in order to meet Woody and Zigwan at the huge pawnshop on Airport Way. She saw a little person escaping from her booster seat in the back of a dusty Passat. Nibuna, which means "summer" in Abenaki, was restless and excited to meet Deloo in such a strange place.

I warned Deloo the adults were very tired. ~ *Take the little girl with you to give them some time alone.* ~ It seemed to me Zigwan was no longer as happy or fascinated with Woody as she had been in Cambridge a few weeks ago. Deloo thought Woody's eyebrows had grown bushier in the weeks since she last saw him. His thick glasses slid down his nose, making it easier to see how his brows grew together. To Deloo, he fulfilled her mental image of Sherlock Holmes.

Deloo complied and bounced Nibuna a little. Nibuna squealed. "Would you like to ride with me while your mommy and daddy follow? You'll be able to watch them."

"Yes." Nibuna smiled shyly.

Deloo chuckled, pleased her plan worked so easily. To the parents she called, "Just follow us!"

Deloo stopped first at Great Aunt Pauline's house, knowing the old woman would be insulted and therefore even more bossy if Deloo didn't give her a chance to inspect them before Taale did. After some quick introductions and discussion about the potential blood stain, Great Aunt Pauline handed the young couple the keys to great uncle Virgil's house.

"Deloo will show you the house," Great Aunt Pauline announced. "I'll stay here. You all will come to dinner tonight around six. Be prepared for a crowd. This is a big family, and Taale and her Deloo are my favorites. Deloo has pledged, just as all my favorites do, never to tell the others they are the top favorites forever."

Zigwan laughed with delight and swung Nibuna high above her head. "You are my favorite baby forever!" She turned to Great Aunt Pauline, and asked "What can we bring?"

"Food a six-year-old can eat," declared Great Aunt Pauline. At the beginning of the road trip Nibuna had chosen tiny servings of yoghurt and chocolate covered raisins. They ran out of it that morning. Deloo told them to follow her to a local grocery. With Woody trailing behind, Zigwan perched Nibuna in a cart and followed Deloo down aisle after aisle.

Deloo picked up a few things for her own needs. I noted acerbically her needs consisted of two specialty brands of ice cream and a bag of candy.

~ *Put those empty calories back!* ~ I commune-griped. ~ *It's your time of the month. Eat iron-rich foods. Where are the raisins? Then go to the fresh vegetables to get some green dead stuff.* ~

~ *I need to keep my strength up with the three Cs: calories, calcium and* ~ Deloo looked around for the donuts. ~ *carbs!* ~

Almost as if to support my dietary policies, someone crashed into Deloo's cart and leaned forward to hiss at my mortal. "What did you do with my jacket? Where are my beads?" Deloo looked up at a tall man wearing khaki trousers and a long-sleeved shirt. Woody would later describe the man as wearing the sort of handmade Italian shoes he had envied in Arthur's wardrobe.

I, Baasee' the jaded Wolverine, didn't notice the shoes or the shirt. Instead I swept between my little girl and the stranger. I felt him emit a wave of mixed anticipation and anger. Soon the anger rose to a state of fury of the sort I recognized but didn't allow in myself or my ever-charming mortals. Although I recognized something about him, he was too big to be either of those who had chased Deloo in Canada. Maybe I remembered him from some other time in Fairbanks. While I pondered, I noted with relief the beaded jacket her mother had made for her was safely at home. Nonetheless, I sensed it was time for me to go into spirit warrior mode. I'm always calm about that sort of thing.

~ *Get out of the store!* ~ My commune rose to a silent shriek.

~ *They're after us again.* ~

Deloo murmured, "What? Not this again."

"What'd you say, Deloo?" Zigwan, who was in front of Deloo, asked.

"Mrs. GooGoo said 'Not this again,'" Nibuna responded promptly.

The stranger saw the second cart, pulled his away from Deloo and scuttled out of sight. Deloo stared after him for a moment and then turned to Nibuna.

"Who's Messy GooGoo?" Deloo asked,

Zigwan smiled at her daughter and shook her head, "You are Mrs. Goode, aren't you, Deloo? Honey, Say Mrs. Goode the right way." To Deloo she said, "She is practicing courtesy and prompt recitation in order to be ready for school in the fall." The pair spent the next few minutes in mutual appreciation of Nibuna's language skills. I, Baasee' the Baffled, searched for the man who had just assaulted my mortal. He'd abandoned his cart and was hurrying toward the main door of the store. I was tempted to follow, but thought it best to stay close to Deloo. Besides, she was about to put a bag of potato chips into her cart.

"Weird!" Deloo said as she dropped the bag into her cart.

~ *Stop. You don't need chips. Put the candy back.* ~ Distracted by chaotic reactions to both the stranger and Zigwan, Deloo did as I commanded. In awhile they were finished shopping, paying, and loading the car with groceries.

Once everyone was settled down, she directed them back to Virgil's house. Woody pulled into the dirt track used as a driveway and lifted Nibuna out. He and Zigwan put things into the cabin while Deloo carried two huge sacks of food, and pointed to the wood box. After helping them unload their car, she added, "It's July, and warm right now, but you might want a fire tonight. It will smell good. Besides, it's the only source of heat in this house."

"We're used to cold weather in Maine," Woody assured Deloo. "We'll be fine in this place. It's perfect for our little girl, isn't it?" Nibuna sniffled and reached for her father. He lifted her out of Zigwan's arms. "Tell us about Floyd and the woman who owns the gift shop."

"Gift...?" Deloo was thrown off. I was about to help when Zigwan cut in. Deloo admired her glowing complexion, remembering Zigwan means "springtime" in Abenaki.

"He means bead shop. The woman who left your beaded jacket on Taale's porch last winter. Between her and Clementine, that's all we talked about on the way here."

"Clementine?" Deloo asked.

Zigwan released a big sigh and almost smiled, "Be glad you don't have kids yet. It's a series of children's books for kids her age."

Nibuna yelled, "Clementine!"

"So?" Woody demanded.

I took in Nibuna's energy level and suggested to Deloo, ~ *Let them relax a little. Then tell them about Floyd. There's plenty of time to learn the worst of Alaska.* ~ Following my spirit-guide advice, Deloo found the bag of chocolate covered raisins and poured some into a bowl. After handing the bowl around, she smiled.

"Whoever killed my friend means business. Fairbanks was a lot safer when I was growing up. It all seemed to begin last November when Arthur died." Deloo gave them a quick background on Floyd's murder, and finished with "We found blood on the floor this morning. I think it belongs to Earlene, the lady who owns—or owned the store. They will have to test it to make sure. It might be from a dead moose," she quipped.

"Do you think it's anyone who chased you in Canada?" Woody frowned.

"Yes and no. Yesterday Prize Woman and her husband came to the store. They said a spirit nagged them into coming here." Deloo caught Nibuna's eyes and added, "Or maybe Nibuna." She tickled the girl's chin.

Nibuna thought Deloo was the funniest person she'd ever met and climbed into her lap where I, too, could tickle her with my softest spirit guide tendrils. Nibuna fell fast asleep lying across my mortal's lap. ~ *Don't get me wrong.* ~ I alerted Deloo. ~ *Remember, I don't like kids. Never had them myself. I just helped my best friend raise her fifteen offspring. That's another story altogether. Just let it be known each one of those fifteen children knew with certainty I only loved him or her, never the other fourteen. I swore each one to secrecy.* ~

~*Yes, Baasee'. You don't like kids. Sure.* ~ Deloo eyed the boneless form of Nibuna who sprawled on Deloo's legs.

"Yeah." Zigwan nodded. "What did that man in the grocery store want? I thought he asked for beads." Deloo shrugged and was about to answer when Zigwan continued, "Who do you think killed the teenager?"

"I don't have a clue." Deloo replied.

"At least you and Taale were hired to do cleanup," Woody smiled.

"How convenient."

"It is for the detective in charge. He seemed to think if we were the culprits, it would be easy to put the blame on us. There isn't much in the bead shop any way. Mom is a genius with computers, but we still can't find Earlene's computer. It's frustrating. Now the weird guy in the grocery store wants to know where his beads are. It's the same nightmare I had back East."

"So, in other words, you still don't know who owns those gems," Woody finished.

Chapter 11

Day Three, Wednesday morning

"Not yet. We're still looking in the bead shop. Nothing yet. Even though we know they're probably stolen, figuring out the real ownership is too hard to unearth. We haven't told the detective yet."

Zigwan raised an eyebrow, "Will he be at dinner tonight? I would like to meet him."

"Not tonight. This one is just for you guys. We've invited Earlene's lawyer, Leroy Cunningham, who is an old family friend. He hired us. Maybe you'll be able to find out more about him than we would. "It's unlikely, but he might know something he's not telling us.

Woody looked thoughtful and took Nibuna out of Deloo's lap. "Sounds good. Will we see you around six?"

"Of course," Deloo said. "No one misses a picnic at Great Aunt Pauline's. By the way, expect at least one more picnic with people who don't get enough of you tonight. I'm going back to work at the bead shop. Great Aunt Pauline will tell you where Uncle Virgil keeps stuff, if he's got it. We might put you to work at the store, too."

Back at the bead shop the police had already gone back to their offices, Lizzie had taken a bus to school. Deloo's cousin was applying a coat of compound to the sheetrock tape.

"I'll let this dry and come back tomorrow. Maybe I should bring my dog, just in case."

"Sure. Just bring a leash. Traffic happens on this street. Will we see you tonight? You can meet our friends."

"Wouldn't miss it."

They worked for the rest of the day without further excitement or, in Taale's case, very little success. In late afternoon she came downstairs. "I found a receipt for her computer. It's actually a laptop. I've got one just like it. I've searched for it upstairs and down. She must have a great hiding place in here."

While Taale was talking, Deloo fiddled with the little bookstand that had been on a bookshelf behind the stand-alone display case. It didn't have a smooth base and rocked on its perch at the slightest touch. Holding a handful of books on beading, it rarely got used any other way. Lizzie came back to the shop at that moment. Deloo glanced at the clock, realizing that nearly a full day had passed.

"Did you find more blood?" Lizzie asked.

Deloo waved toward the empty book stand. "I'm trying to fix this to make room on the table for the beads." Deloo had painted some gallon-sized plastic tubs with various colors so that they could sort beads. Each tub sat on its own lid. "I haven't found more blood yet. It'd be great if you can help us sort through all these beads." She pointed to the stylish bins.

Lizzie sprawled her heavy books near her friend. "What's that?" Lizzie asked, pointing at the book stand. "It looks kind of familiar."

Deloo hooted. "I doubt it. Our textbooks would never fit on something this flimsy."

"Let me see," Lizzie bent over the stand that Deloo handed her, her voice unintelligible. "I know what it is! It's about ten times bigger, but look." She rooted around in her pack and surfaced with one of the little pill boxes. "They were giving these away at the exhibit hall the other day." No one heard her. Taale was talking into a phone and Deloo was already at work on a pile of beads.

~ *My illustrious Deloo,* ~ I nudged her, ~ *take a look at what Lizzie has got. Your mother needs it.* ~

"Mmph?" Deloo looked up just as Lizzie pulled a sheet of paper out of a drawer on top of the small book stand. "What's written on the bottom?" she asked.

"Hunh?" Lizzie looked at the other side of the paper. "It says, not for resale." Lizzie tucked the paper back into its slim drawer. "Look," Lizzie touched the edge near the bottom of the back. "It opens just like the pill box does." She pulled another sheet of paper out of a drawer that magically appeared below the first. "It's got writing all over it. Can you read it?"

Deloo snatched the sheet from her friend. Taale was finishing her call when Deloo held up the sheet.

"I can't," Deloo mumbled. "Can you, Mom?"

Taale, still thinking about the last woman she'd called, stretched her hand out and said, "Ugh! She's happy to get her kuspuks back in exchange for the inside scoop on the murder. It's a good thing Detective Grinch told me what to say to people." She looked at the sheet of paper, not expecting it to be anything interesting. "I'm going to have to tell everyone the same story. Whuh?" Something caught her attention. "Where'd you get this?"

"Here, in this book stand," Lizzie answered.

"Hmmm. It's a code sheet. It'll come in handy if I ever find the computer." She looked at Lizzie. "Where was it?"

Lizzie showed them how she found it. "It's like your pill box. Remember? You picked one up, too."

Taale ran a finger along the edge of the little stand. "Hmmm. It wasn't as obvious on that little thing they gave me. Now I see how ingenious it is." She put it on the edge of the counter where she was still standing.

Deloo squeezed in beside her mother. There was scarcely room for one person. The pair of them were pressed together from the sides, and their backs were flush against the wall.

Lizzie pulled her battered smart phone out of her pack and aimed it at them. "This is too good a photo op," she beamed. "Say cheese!"

They both looked at her with same expression: mouths open, quizzical. Deloo's single dimple set her apart from her mother, who had no dimples. Also, Taale was four inches taller than her daughter, and in the places where Deloo looked either skinny or wiry, her mother looked round and firm. Deloo's hair was glossy, dark brown, and past shoulder-length. Taale's black hair was barely shoulder-length. Lizzie caught the unguarded love that shimmered in both Deloo's green eyes as well as Taale's brown ones.

Taale's hand was pinned to the edge of the counter between her belly and the wood.

"Deloo-Loo, would you move out a little. I can't...."

Deloo edged a scant three inches away from Taale, who then was able to move her hand a couple of inches. Because Deloo had more room than her mother in the tiny space, she turned and happened to touch the wooden apron below the lip of the counter near the cash register. At that moment, Taale jostled her daughter's arm and Deloo's fingers made something click.

"What just happened?" mother and daughter said together.

Peering sideways at the click-spot, Taale smiled and said, "Look! I think you struck gold! Let me out of here so I can get a better look," Taale ordered Deloo. Deloo's fingers had found an invisible one-inch by one-inch square of the counter that someone had made with a lot of care. It was so smooth and so small that no one could have seen it by eyesight alone. The square could be pressed. When free of bodies in front, a horizontal rectangle to the left of the square moved outward. The rectangle was cut to a size that fit its contents, more or less eighteen by fifteen with a depth of four inches.

Deloo moved out of the narrow space they'd been in so that Taale could slide the drawer all the way out. "It's Earlene's computer. Trust her to find more ways to hide things." Taale scrunched her face. "I suppose this has as many electronic buffers as we were taught to use in class." She lifted the slender laptop out of its compartment.

Deloo smirked. "That's the way Arthur was about his dissertation and the computer that he had it on. I wasn't allowed to touch it. After his job started at the university, he took it away." She shook her head. "Even though it was all done and in the university system, he was secretive about it."

Lizzie looked perplexed. "I understand Dr. Goode's concern. I'm sure he wanted to get it published. But Earlene? What secrets are in a bead shop?"

"Definitely murder, maybe more," Taale breathed.

They were still puzzling about the secrets Earlene had when Mr. Cunningham entered the shop. After a brief chat with Taale about the morning's bloody discovery, Earlene's computer, and taking another look at the flooring, he decided to replace the vinyl throughout the store. He smiled and said goodbye, leaving them all with a huge amount of work to do. Deloo and Lizzie got busy on sorting the piles of mixed beading into colored bins while Taale called another bead sewer. They kept up the pace for an hour until the younger women had accumulated five bags to take to the dumpster, which was a few yards away from the carport and Earlene's brightly painted car.

Taale decided to examine Earlene's computer upstairs. "I'll take a look at this code sheet."

Thinking of Detective Harper's warning to keep the front locked, Deloo wondered if they needed to do so just to dump out trash. After a brief discussion with Lizzie, they decided it would be safe enough to leave the back door unlocked for a couple of minutes.

Taale finished hollowing out an office nook in the room at the top of the stairs. She used two TV tables for a desk and a box to hold the printer on top. Pleased with her new set up, she took command of the keyboard, taking a quick peak at icons named "Payables" and "Receivables". Receivables included her own beadwork and that of others, beads, clothing, and "Misc." She decided to look at Payables. The first file name was Pauline Dena, known to many as Aunt Pauline, Taale's aunt. She opened it and discovered a signed recurring monthly payment of three hundred eighty dollars. There was no explanation. There were smaller checks made out to her aunt that had pithy explanations, such as "repair window" or "stove". Why did her friend, who was not a relative, pay nearly five grand a year to Taale's aunt?

She got out her cell phone and dialed the familiar number. Pauline answered immediately. They spoke for twelve minutes, most of those minutes with Taale's mouth gaping open.

"I worked for her every week. I did the books, the taxes, and up until last Thanksgiving I balanced the shop's checking account," Pauline's voice, as always, was soothing. "Once a week I let her take four hours off. Most of that time I minded the shop. Sometimes, if one of the kids was available, I'd have the kid mind the store while Earlene took me shopping. She'd pay me the full amount and I would pay the kid out of my own pocket."

"That's still a lot of money. What else did you do? I see these checks go back about twenty years," Taale grumbled.

"I spent a lot of time in the shop when she needed to fix it up during the first year or two. Then, when she remodeled about ten years ago, I lent her the cash and sent the guys from Little Tanana over to do the plumbing, construction, and electrical work. Then the rest of us did the painting."

"Oh, I think I did a little painting, too," Taale mused.

"You did along with half of Little Tanana. It would never have happened without all of us pulling together the way we did. I was very proud that summer."

"So, is part of this paying back what she owed you for the remodel?"

"She still owed me a little up until a couple of summers ago. Then she told me she still owed me for what she called our weekly Sunday afternoon psychiatric sessions. That was when she came over, took me and maybe a couple of others out shopping, and then stayed for dinner."

Taale laughed comfortably. "I was at most of those dinners."

"So you were," agreed Pauline.

"When did you ever have time for a psychiatric session?"

Pauline paused. Taale wondered if she was going to answer, then Pauline said slowly, "those times usually happened late at night. Sometimes she'd call me at three in the morning. I could always tell that she'd been crying before finally calling me. A few times she came straight to my door and stayed for a few hours. She had a lot of pain to work out because of her brothers' deaths by alcoholic drowning; then her parents died when she was so young. She could probably have been able to deal with one or the other kind of death, but not both. Then there's the non-man who got her pregnant. He's a piece of work if there ever was one." Pauline fell silent. Taale knew better than to interrupt. Finally Pauline murmured, "The sessions took less and less time. Sometimes she didn't call except for once or twice a month. I hope she's doing better wherever she's gone to."

Taale felt a shiver grind through her body. "Me too. Thanks for everything, everything you do, Aunt Pauline."

After a few minutes of fighting off worry about Pauline and Earlene, Taale wondered how the work was going downstairs. She got up to chat with Deloo. She was at the doorway when she heard a sound on the stairs.

One spot creaked in the place Floyd's body had landed. It had Floyd's blood stains on it. Both Deloo and Taale avoided the bloody spot on the steps. Taale knew that it couldn't be Deloo, but it might be Lizzie. She waited for a few seconds.

C R E A K.

At first nothing came out of her mouth, then she croaked, "Whoever you are, I've got a gun." Technically, that was true. Taale did have Uncle Virgil's old rabbit-hunting Remington, but it was at home. Taale listened without breathing. Nothing. She counted to ten and ventured a look out the door. She caught a glimpse of a tall man's back as he crept downstairs. She didn't recognize him. His wool cap made him even more unfamiliar.

Invisible to her, Taale's spirit guide, Zephyr, shriek-communed to me, ~ *don't let the girls come in. Someone snuck into the shop.* ~

~ *Stop!* ~ I commune-shouted. Deloo was tossing the last of her black garbage bags into the dumpster. ~ *Both of you! Get behind the dumpster. There's a man in the shop.* ~

In hindsight, that was not the best plan.

CHAPTER 12

Day Three, Wednesday afternoon

Taale rushed after the trespasser who slammed the backdoor just as she reached the stairs. She tripped. Taale managed to catch herself on the stairwell, wobbled down two steps when the backdoor crashed to a close. Taale slid-skittered to the bottom, clutching the smooth handrail as support. She remembered to keep her toes pointed up in order to let the fall do its work. She banged into the door and pushed it open and watched the man gallop toward her daughter. Even in her fright, she saw how his legs moved and could see he wasn't a trained athlete. She'd run the Midnight Sun Run twenty times since she was a kid. The heaviness of his footfalls told her he wasn't lifting his thighs or thrusting his calves forward. He wouldn't make the first mile. Then she saw Lizzie's fuzzy head. Where was Deloo? She screamed and Deloo stood up.

The marauder also spotted Deloo and seemed to aim straight for her. His car was behind the dumpster. She was in the way. When he was even with Deloo, he spun and yanked her toward him.

~ Go with this, my outstanding Deloo, Pretend to faint against his chest. ~

Deloo did as instructed and noticed all he wanted was a temporary shield, not a dead weight.

~ Good. Now knock him off balance a little by slumping forward. ~

Deloo leaned toward the building and away from the man who held her.

~ Now, stand up straight and spread your legs. Notice? He wasn't ready for you. Now hook your left leg around his and pull hard to the right. Feel his nerves jangle? ~

"No," Deloo panted.

~ Take my word for it. They did! This should do it, then. Twist into him, keeping your head up, and take a deep breath. Excellent! Now shout as loud as you can. ~

Deloo shouted the first thing that came to mind, since she had been talking to Lizzie about the attempted murder, "Killer!" Deloo's screech was long and ear-splitting. The man was taken off guard and lifted one hand to protect his ear from the sound. Deloo used the moment to drop to his waist and lean back.

Lizzie, watching all, caught Deloo and helped her scuttle backward, out of sight of the bead shop thief. Together they started running as fast as possible down the alleyway. An old woman watched them dash in front of her porch and stood up.

"Hide! Here! Quick before he sees where you went."

The girls didn't waste time pondering their options, and thundered up the steps toward the stranger, saw she had opened the door, and lunged inside.

The old woman waited until both were inside before closing the door and turning the deadbolt. "I'm Fay. This," she pointed to the dark haired woman beside her, "is Carmen."

Deloo peered over Lizzie's shoulder. Someone gunned an engine and tires squealed.

~ He's gone. It's safe to go back. ~ I, Baasee' the Heedful, remarked to Deloo. *~ Don't stay here. ~*

"He tried to kill you, Deloo!" Lizzie gaped at her friend.

Deloo took a deep breath, wobbled a smile toward the older woman and said, "Thanks for hiding us. He's gone now. Come on Lizzie." The pair nodded at their hostesses and stumbled toward the door. They sprinted to Earlene's Beads. The two women watched from the porch until Fay jerked her head toward the open door as a signal to come back in.

"Mom! Are you all right?" Deloo tried the door, which Taale had locked.

Taale was sitting on the bottom step and reached over to open the door. "I've called the police. Did you see him at all?"

Deloo sat down beside Taale and Lizzie leaned against Taale's knees. Deloo could feel her mother tremble. Deloo whispered, "I caught a quick glance. I might be able to sketch him if I do it now."

~ I'll help. I saw much more of him than you could have done in that flurry. We've seen him before. Remember the tourist shop in Nova Scotia? ~

~ Yes, ~ Deloo thought to me. *~ He's the one who had the tan cube. ~* Her fingers started flying across a sheet of paper Lizzie supplied.

I mused about the man, who not long ago and thousands of miles away, tried to wheedle Deloo into taking one of those cubes. Later we found a bunch more Taale had. Inside those cubes someone had hidden valuable gemstones.

* * *

An hour after Deloo fled the stranger in mid Fairbanks, he arrived at an old gold mining camp now used as a state campground on the Chatanika (pronounced CHAT uh neek' uh) River. It was one of the places his father used to take him when both needed special time together. He didn't notice the vehicle in one of the camping sites.

"Was that who I think it was?" Chuan asked Ming.

"Who?"

Chuan shook his head. "Never mind. I thought it was our noble archaeologist, but he lives on Steele Creek Road, or so he said. There's no reason for him to drive all the way out here. He has a house in some good looking woods."

"What made you think it was him?" Ming strained to catch a glimpse.

Chuan glanced at her. The late evening sunlight flared around her hair. When they left the hotel hours ago it had been damp from a shower. Now it was just like he always remembered—floating around her head and shoulders, moving in its own rhythms. He sighed and said, "I don't know. Maybe it was someone else. It looked sort of like him. But in a town like this any blond man stands out." Chuan bounced his shoulders a little. "I just made a wild guess." He turned toward Ming.

Ming smiled, "You're probably right. It could also be an ordinary thief. Fairbanks has an interesting colonial history. In some ways, it's like northern Quebéc with a lot of poverty showing and a little wealth here and there. Now I know some of the history, and I can see the industrial eras in some of the architecture. At first I wondered why there were so few old houses. Now I know why. That big flood in 1967 wiped out a lot of them and there hasn't been enough money since the old gold miners moved on to do much rebuilding until recently."

Ming leaned over to stroke Chuan's face. "Let's go back to the hotel and maybe tomorrow or the next day we'll see if he's on Steele Creek Road."

Chuan yawned. "Good idea. I have to admit going all the way to Chatanika River to see a burnt out old gold dredge has been fun. But walking around the gravel to see if we could spot a real gold nugget has left your poor, but enchanting, Chinese husband very sleepy."

Ming laughed. "Is that a hint? Shall I drive back to the hotel?" She played with the muscles on his arm. "I wouldn't want my captivating husband to fall asleep too soon."

"What?" Chuan looked at Ming with awakening hope. "Who are

you? The reincarnation of my dazzling wife?" They flirted with each other on the way back to their hotel. Once there they raced to the building as if they were once again the happy graduate students who met at Harvard so long ago.

Ming dropped back a little, pretending to bend over to catch her breath. "Wait! I can't run fast anymore," she begged, looking at her husband with luminous eyes.

He fell for the sparkling black eyes as hard as he had over twenty years ago. He stretched out a hand. She touched it and then slapped it away. He heard her tinkling laughter as she raced ahead of him.

* * *

Taale stood beside Deloo and Lizzie while they studied Deloo's sketches. They had opened the front door for the detectives. After nodding at Taale, Cruikshank went upstairs to make sure the space was clear. Harper turned back to Deloo. "What do you have there?" She showed him the drawings.

The detective looked at the drawings with interest. Detective Harper asked, "Do you know how he got in here?"

Taale nodded, "He was coming upstairs when my daughter and Lizzie were at the dumpster. I was alone. When he realized I was up there, he raced out through the back door. He went straight for my daughter." She pointed to Deloo's first drawing. "These are good, Deloo-Loo. He needs a haircut. There were three or four long wisps of white or blond hair showing around the cap."

Detective Harper looked down at Taale. She had to look up twelve inches in order to see his eyes. She blushed and tried to move away. Lizzie, leaning on her shoulders, kept her in place. Detective Harper cocked an eyebrow and said, "Your daughter is a very good artist." He turned toward Deloo and added, "You should be a police artist. Could I borrow this? We could put it in public places. Someone might have seen him."

Deloo smiled, "Yes, please take it and thanks. What should we do now? There's already a security alarm system, and the front door was locked for once."

Jack Cruikshank came downstairs and shrugged at Detective Harper. "Nothing."

Detective Harper nodded and addressed Deloo's question. "He parked behind the dumpster, as you said. I checked. The backdoor swings shut and locks hard and fast. He either has another way in here, or else waited for someone to go out the back as you two did." He looked around the bead shop and then continued. "Either you neglected to lock the door or else one of you let him in."

"No! Never! We didn't let him in," Deloo bellowed, her voice too loud.

"We left the door open when we took the trash to the dumpster. There were a lot of bags," Lizzie's voice was inaudible.

"There were a number of other people here today," Taale supplied. "We've been calling people to pick up their merchandise."

"This guy is after something," Detective Harper said. "He is dangerous." He looked at Deloo. "By your description of the way he went after you at the dumpster, I know he's had professional training in assassination. If he's the one who murdered Floyd, you need to be more careful. Lock the door each and every time you let someone in or you go out, even for the trash run. Go together to dump the trash," he looked at Lizzie, "Not alone. Oh, and make sure your friends leave their children at home. We're dealing with murder."

"Do you have a gun?" Jack asked.

Taale nodded. "At home. It's under my bed," she said.

"Still?" Deloo squeezed her eyes shut. "Does it have bullets?"

"Oh, great," Detective Harper muttered. Aloud he asked Taale, "Does it? Have bullets?"

Taale shook her head. "I've never needed it. We live in a safe neighborhood."

"That neighborhood is safe. This shop is in the seedy part of town," Jack said.

"Don't worry," Lizzie spoke up, "I'll make sure they get the right ammo and teach them how to shoot." She shook her frizzy hair, a little wild after the morning's event. "I thought you were hunter/gatherers. What happened to that?" She turned to Jack. "I'm a sharpshooter myself. I've won medals in Rifle for all positions."

The two detectives left after a quick technical discussion with Lizzie, or Liz, as both of them began calling her. Disgruntled, Taale locked the front door after them while Deloo made sure the back door was both closed and locked. "Remember what Aunt Pauline always says about the use of firearms in a city: those who use guns for anything but getting food are fools. There are better ways to protect yourself and others than shooting. Look at all the trouble we've got around the world with people shooting each other to prove points invisible to anyone else. That's one of the causes of Historic Trauma. Think about your posters, Lizzie."

Lizzie sighed and said, "you're right, Taale. Shooting without discussion is murder."

"It's not only murder, but an excuse to put your values and righteousness over those of complete strangers. It's time to end such behavior, girls," Taale said.

I listened to the exchange with satisfaction. Taale, and I hoped her daughter as well, would carry on the uneven fight against the ravages of Historic Trauma in the Native American realm. I wasn't so sure about other areas of the world. I also knew it hadn't done much good on Taale's home front.

Once back at the station, Detective Harper watched his colleague fill out his report. When it was done and added to the older detective's stack, Frank said, "don't you want to add something here?" He pointed to a box on the form.

Detective Cruikshank reddened and checked the box. Detective Harper thanked him and continued with a cocked eyebrow, "Wasn't that what some might call a 'moment' back there in the shop? I could have sworn I saw it."

Detective Cruikshank sighed. "Yes. There seemed to be a moment, but …"

"In other words, the young lady is interested. You are interested. What's the hold up?"

"She's twenty-one. I'm almost thirty-two. I'm a cop. She's going to graduate school one of these days," Jack muttered.

"So, have you two talked about it?"

"We both eat at the same diner, usually at the same time. We both prefer the counter seats. We've chatted. Nothing more."

"Who was there first?"

Jack's worked his jaw muscles and he squeezed out the words, "She was" into the air.

"So, you looked around, decided against a table, and joined her."

"Yeah. Is there a problem?"

"How many times?"

"Four. She hasn't been in since Floyd died."

Frank tapped the sheaf and said, "Good report." He added it to his small stack. "I'll scan it before I go home. There's nothing wrong with dating a beautiful woman, you know." He tapped Jack's shoulder.

"Nothing wrong with age difference or having diverse career goals."

* * *

Unaware of the detective's conversation about her, Lizzie examined the book rack again. She looked up, "I understand a little more why Earlene used so many secret devices."

"She lived here in the bead shop," Taale said.

Lizzie looked at both Deloo and Taale, and asked, "She lived here?"

"Yes. For years. She and her daughter lived here."

"Does she have a boyfriend?" my mortal Deloo asked.

Taale looked at the two girls and heaved a sigh. "Yes and no. He was a typical non-man, as my Aunt Pauline says. He had no principles of how to treat a woman. He beat her—badly. Sometimes I'd try to get her to go to the clinic for help, but most of the time she refused. I know she talked to Aunt Pauline about him. Aunt Pauline patched her up. I found the bandages, sometimes. Bloody. I never met him. If I did, I would know who to kill. She would tell me to shut up. Someone should. Say it and do it."

Lizzie punched Deloo in the ribs. Deloo grinned.

Taale continued, "Aunt Pauline supervised everything that went on in the bead shop, had work done. Earlene was tight with my aunt about things I didn't have time for. I'm ashamed to say when Deloo was little, I had time for my daughter and not much else. We talked about the easy stuff, like computers or beading. If I tried to talk about her lifestyle, all I got were those forbidding eyes and a few secretive comments from Pauline. I thought she broke it off with him, but then a while back after she added the upper floor and then a carport, her old boyfriend asked Earlene if he could rent one side, and he would pay for half the costs. Pauline said yes, so there it is. She used to run an extension cord through a crack in the back door to keep the head bolt heater from freezing."

"Yike! I took my folks' outside electrical outlets for granted. Didn't she have anything like it before she made the carport?" Lizzie asked.

"The cabin was built before electricity was possible around here. Pauline is one of the first in Fairbanks to have a carport. Now we all have them in Little Tanana."

"Mom, did you say you've never met Earlene's boyfriend?" Deloo asked.

"No. He was never here at the shop when I was. I think she saw him once in a while in the old days. By the time you were a little girl, I didn't spend much time here. I gather she wouldn't allow more than just talking to him by then."

"Not much of a relationship. Did she have any other friends besides your family?" Lizzie asked.

"No. She was a loner except when we went to classes at the University together. She was better with computers than me, but she didn't want a degree. So when I was taking required courses, she took every computer class she could. I took most of the same classes. She helped me with my homework. It was awesome in the real sense of the word to watch her. She could get into my machine so quick I knew she was a hacker."

Deloo breathed, "A hacker? You're kidding. Did she get into your private accounts?"

Taale snorted. "What private accounts? I'm too poor to have private accounts. I bet she could hack into other accounts, though."

"But if she was so good, why keep ordinary things so hard to find?" Lizzie asked.

Taale heaved her shoulders. "You're the one who has been studying Historic Trauma. In all too many ways Earlene was a living victim of it. Her parents died of tuberculosis. That's one of the typical diseases in areas of high poverty. Both of her brothers drowned while drinking heavily. They were teenagers. As you know, it's typical of Historic Trauma. Then she winds up with a non-man, as Pauline calls them, who never intended to take her seriously as a human being, let alone a significant life partner. It makes her a living victim of intergenerational trauma, exactly as you showed us it happens on those great posters of yours."

Lizzie stared at Taale with her mouth agape.

Taale touched the young woman's chin. "It's okay to be right now and then. The important thing is to learn ways to end it. Aunt Pauline has made it her passion. For now I'll settle for getting something to bring to the party, get home, clean up, and fix up whatever we get in time for tonight." She pointed at a clock. "It's half past four. We'd better go." She picked up Earlene's laptop. "I'm going to keep this with me. I don't want that guy to get at it."

"Great. Let's go. We can get food and ammo. You sure it's a 22?"

At home they started working on a super-sized salad with plenty of locally grown broccoli and carrots. Lizzie said she wanted to teach Deloo to operate her weapon. If it hadn't been for the man in the shop, Deloo would have laughed her off. No more.

* * *

As if he heard her thoughts, the very man who'd been trying to get into the shop stood outside his house. It was several miles north and east of Deloo. He lifted his head, aware of something waiting for him. Although he didn't see her, the wolverine mother whose den was less than a half mile from his house, analyzed him closely. After a while, she relaxed, aware he was not going to hunt for her kits or herself. With a soft grunt, she returned to hunting for the small game her two kits needed.

CHAPTER 13

Day Three, Wednesday, evening

"Where is Uncle Virgil's gun, Mom?"

Taale told her to search under her bed and refused to look at Lizzie. After a half hour, Deloo stumbled once or twice in the routine to load, cock, and unload the gun. Her mouth quirked unevenly as she agreed to do target practice at the university shooting range.

"I didn't know we had any shooting ranges in Fairbanks."

Lizzie muttered something about hunter/gatherers while Deloo skipped ahead of her. "I'm going to be a rock star, Mom. Just call me 'Deloo the Shootist' from now on."

Taale rolled parental eyes at them and told them to wash their hands. "Remember we're all doing this to make sure none of us gets murdered."

Doing likewise with fake eyebrows of intense orange, I followed my charge to the bathroom. She asked me in commune words, ~ *Would you have learned to use a gun, Brassie Baasee'?* ~

~ *That's Baasee' to you, Mortal, and Yes, if they were available, I'd have been a rock star, with a rapid-fire pistol, but guns are noisy. A bola is much more efficient and almost silent for hunting game a few body lengths away.* ~

~ *Bolas! What about big game like moose or caribou?* ~

~ *If the bird or animal is right there, and you don't have time for anything else, yes. Dead falls are better for most large grazing mammals, though.* ~

We, that is, Deloo, took the salad her mother handed her. ~ *I want to learn to throw them the way you used to do. How can I start?* ~

~ *You already did some of the work when you were a child.* ~ Deloo looked confused at my response.

~ *You insist on calling them Eskimo yo-yos. That name doesn't even work among indigenous peoples of the northern coast, or 'Eskimos' as colonialists label them. Call this weapon by a more universal name: bola. Now it's time you begin your training. I trained children on two stones, and added small pebbles as they got better at spinning and then casting the bolas up and out. My rule of thumb is simple: if you can loop the bola around something two or more of your own body lengths away, it's time to increase the number of stones. A five-stone bola is as effective as a six- or seven-stone bola. Why over-do perfection? If the game (hunter talk for target) is around thirty feet away and you catch it, you are doing rock star hunting.* ~ I swished some air around her for emphasis.

~ *Could you teach me some rock star bola tricks?* ~ She found her old bola and wrapped it around her waist. She liked to use it instead of a belt because the students at the Institute of American Indian Arts thought she looked more like an action woman with it.

~ *Your mother would be happier with you if I taught you bola hunting instead of letting you shoot a gun. Remember that raven? It told us you had to learn how to fight. Besides, then you would really earn the name, DelooNa the Ice-Woman, which you fixed on ten years ago as your identity.* ~

"What raven told me to fight?" Deloo asked aloud.

~ *Remember, it said, "Blood, yours or his. It doesn't matter. You must fight."* ~

~ *Yes, I remember. It was at the border just before I reached Vermont,* ~ Deloo cocked her head to one side, pondering. ~ *Does this have anything to do with what you said earlier?* ~

~ *What do you mean?* ~ I blew on a perfectly groomed, ephemeral toenail.

~ *About the guy you said chased Arthur on the day he died. Maybe I'll have to fight for Arthur sometime.* ~ She was making communes extremely well.

~ *Perhaps,* ~ I watched Deloo's vital signs, noting her blood pressure spiked. ~ *But it might be a metaphor, not actual fighting.* ~ I knew I was lying only because my invisible nose started growing.

That evening Taale, Deloo, and Lizzie went together to get Woody and his family. The large group of them walked over to Great Aunt Pauline's house. Great Aunt Pauline's was designed to hold six people for dinner. Pauline had invited Mr. Cunningham and his wife, making eight. I, having observed such dinners over the course of Deloo's life, knew people in the neighborhood would stop by whether or not they were invited. It was expected. She had often invited Mr. and Mrs. Cunningham, since he was an old family friend, and he, too, knew the score. I and most of the spirits present had learned being invited was code for "give us a few minutes of our private time and be sure to bring something to add to the meal."

It was too hot to stay inside. Pauline's backyard was big and she had plenty of folding chairs to accommodate a lot of people. It was an old log house. It had been built in the early part of the twentieth century. Taale, whose house was like her aunt and uncle's, had a very old stove. With an old-fashioned wood stove, they told themselves there was plenty of room for everyone.

After people had eaten and most of them were sitting around chatting, I saw Deloo still had a bola around her waist instead of a belt. I suggested she give some lessons to her friends. She was getting better at her aim, but wasn't strong enough to throw the bola more than fifty feet.

It was then I noticed Zigwan was looking very nervous. I nudged Deloo, ~ *My vigorous mortal, there are too many people here. Zigwan jumps when anyone looks at Nibuna. The little girl is having fun with all of these other kids, but everyone is a stranger to Zigwan. Take them home.* ~ Deloo looked at Nibuna, who was running and shouting with two other small children, and understood.

In one way it was a wonderful contrast to earlier generations of Native American children who were always kept silent if strangers were near. At fourteen thousand plus years, I had seen many a child get stolen by enemies, often by boarding school staff who thought they knew best for "savages." Later they beat the small children with leather straps to eradicate their indigenous souls. Little Tanana children will never know that kind of life. On the other hand, they were the products of too many generations of such bad treatment. Moreover, some of the spirits and ghosts watching had been victims of bad treatment. It's called Historic Trauma. The symptoms were common. For instance, I heard nothing but English spoken. I knew six of the people present had diabetes, a rare disease among some populations. One man kept looking at the clock hoping he could sneak away from sober Little Tanana to get wasted on booze, drugs or both. Many people had no idea how to be like the Alaska Native person they could have been if history had been different. Great Aunt Pauline was one of the few who knew how to take care of many people at once.

Deloo found Woody and made the suggestion they turn in early. "Why don't I take you straight home instead of going for a walk tonight?" Woody took Zigwan by the hand and they collected Nibuna. Having played hard for an hour, Nibuna was having trouble keeping her eyes open.

Deloo put her arm around Zigwan's shoulders. "You've been traveling for a long time. You look like you could use a nap yourself."

Tears coursed down Zigwan's pretty face. "You have been so nice to us. Thanks for walking us all one hundred feet home." She smiled.

"She'll be okay here," Great Aunt Pauline said. "Don't worry about a thing. We're in Little Tanana. We know who's supposed to be here and who's not."

Zigwan gave her daughter a slobbery kiss and held a hand toward Woody. The pair of them followed Taale. Behind them Deloo and Lizzie said their goodbyes.

Great Aunt Pauline wished them goodnight and turned to Deloo to ask, "Does that great spirit of yours give you dire warnings? Has it told you why that man tried to kill you today?"

I wondered if she meant me, Baasee' the Terrifying. I looked at her with an ocular of gold, my best color. I floated upward and a little to the left. Pauline followed my progress and smiled.

~ *Do you, Baasee'?* ~ Deloo commune-asked. ~ *Do you give me dire warnings?* ~

I was grateful to say to my perfect Deloo, ~ *Yes, but you get even more warnings than I give you from other sources. It's up to you to learn which are for your benefit. If you remember, early this morning I warned you I knew something strange might happen today. All I had was a vague warning. As I expected, two things have happened. Why? I don't know, but they've got to be connected. Moreover, each of those events could have ended badly for you.* ~

~ *Thanks, Baasee'.* ~ Deloo used the commune mode. She didn't want her mother to know about me. Since her mother had followed American modes and teased Deloo about her imaginary friend, me, I didn't want her mother to know about me either. Great Aunt Pauline was a much better ally. ~ *Have you been investigating the break-in, too, Baasee'?* ~

~ *I've been using my magical powers to find if anyone is waiting for the door to open.* ~

~ *Yow! Should I tell Mom?* ~

~ *No, she's already had enough put on her plate. There is something about the shop's back door I want you to think about before we go back. Remember how the concrete doorstep fights you when you open it?* ~

~ *Yes. It's irritating. At least is makes it hard for strangers to open.* ~

~ *Exactly!* ~ I knew she would hit on the problem without a second thought. ~ *It's something to tell your mother.* ~

Taale had taken the code book home with her. Deloo went to find her mother, who was resting on her bed. "You know, I've been thinking about the guy who broke in today."

Taale jumped a little. "Oh! Honey! You startled me. I think I've figured out Earlene's computer code. It goes somewhere exotic in cryptography I've never been. I might need some help." She gazed at her daughter, noting this time her baby's eyes were a yellowish amber. Hazel eyes changed a lot. "What did you say?"

Deloo said, "I was thinking about that man or rather, the back door to the shop. You know, the back door is tricky sometimes. Today it swung shut without resistance for those detectives. They are both a lot heavier than me. When I use it, it catches on something before it's far enough open for me to get out. I'm a little woman like you are, so that sort of thing happens to us a lot. The guy who broke in here is a lot bigger than me. That's why he got out so fast." Deloo met her mother's eyes. "I think he's been in there before."

The two women stared at each other for a few seconds, then Taale pulled out a business card. "I'm going to call Detective Harper."

The police station in Fairbanks was a short drive away from Taale's house. He agreed to meet them at the shop. The two men went straight to the back door, over which a double carport gave it shade. They watched Deloo open and close the door several times. Then they did it. Unlike earlier today when they had used more force, it opened after a little work, but not as much as Deloo needed.

"She is right," Detective Cruikshank said. "There's a trick way to open the door."

Detective Harper turned toward Deloo. "Good catch, young lady. There can't be many men who used this door. Whoever he is will be familiar to people in a small town like Fairbanks. Somebody knows him. Somebody has seen him and they'll tell us."

* * *

I dreamed, but didn't know it. My coyotes were with me. I was smug because at fourteen I had formed a truce with a coyote pack. Grandfather Kwaikit told me they didn't work well together because they don't like to follow rules. Grandfather Kwaikit had worked with two dire wolf packs in his past. He got a lot of meat each time, but didn't like being under their control. According to Grandfather Kwaikit, at that time dire wolves made the rules. Humans didn't. You either followed them or you got killed. He figured out what to do: kill them first without regard to yourself and without wasting foolish time in negotiations. Fortunately, he wasn't killed in the bargaining. Coyotes, being renegades, were glad to have me. The leader of the pack expected me to stay. I did. Our deal was simple. I did the intricate work and they did the running and made the kills.

After a while, though, I realized they were getting more out of me than the other way round. My coyotes were bushy and fat. Our hunting partnership was working for them if not for me. Then I planned our biggest hunt ever. Grandfather Kwaikit had given me the idea. A deadfall. I would be building one for the first time.

First, I picked out a cut above a stream in the grassland. The grass grew a little taller than me. I followed Grandfather Kwaikit's advice and I cut a lot of brush. The coyotes disappeared as they usually did. I had to haul the brush back on my sledge without help. Easy enough, but you see what I mean. The coyotes could have helped, but did not stick around when I needed them.

Grandfather Kwaikit told me to cover the brush with hides. I didn't have any extra hides. I tried to explain it to the coyotes. It was hard. They didn't have a mental language to match anything I knew. At last the oldest coyote got the idea and brought me an old dead raccoon. It stank but served the purpose. We found a few more carcasses. Then I needed to cover everything with dirt and cut green grass. By then, the coyotes had understood what I needed and helped a lot. Then we were done except for the big part.

It took forever for them to understand I wanted a herd to run toward me. The smallest of the peccaries would be ideal. We needed meat we could eat and bury for later. I was about to give up when the oldest coyote dashed away, yipping. The others followed him. Praying they had got the idea, I stayed behind to watch. The day was nearly over and I was tired. I lay on the bottom edge of our deadfall, almost asleep, when I felt vibrations in the earth. I recognized the genus if not the species by the feel.

Peccaries. Was it the smaller type? I peeked over the ridge above the deadfall. I couldn't believe my eyes. Yes. It was the right species of peccary. I listened for yipping. Yes again. My coyotes were chasing them toward me. I remembered one of Grandfather Kwaikit's most strict rules: don't kill the leader. Take the second or third, but never the leader.

I followed Grandfather Kwaikit's instructions. I had planned they would fall off to one side of the path chosen by the leader. Following their leader, they would run up to the top of the ridge. A good leader would pause, scan the view, and seeing the cliff in front and stream below, he'd turn to the right. I waited straight ahead of the point where I expected him to make the turn. A deadfall is supposed to prevent the leader from seeing either the stream or the fake slope (deadfall). It would look to him like he was on a hill you could just walk or run down.

If the peccary leader was any good, he would also see the trail heading right and follow it instead. As Grandfather Kwaikit told me to do, I waited for the wise leader to go by and selected a brash and younger peccary. Such a peccary would think it would be smarter to go straight, thus into the trap. When the foolish one took a step into my tidy deadfall, he or she would fall. It worked.

My next job was to make sure we got two peccaries, and no more. In my era peccaries weighed as much as a modern day bull. The coyotes could eat one. Grandfather Kwaikit and I could take the other. So, on the day of the hunt when a second one fell into the trap, I stood up in my hiding place just beyond the deadfall trap and waved a loose branch. According to Grandfather Kwaikit, seeing me in front of them would stop the flow of peccaries toward the deadfall. The rest would follow the peccaries who went right. It all worked as planned. My coyotes all got a half a ton of peccary for themselves. I, well make that Grandfather Kwaikit and I, got the other peccary. He helped me drag it back home.

I slept on a full belly that night.

* * *

"Was that a deadfall, Baasee'?" Deloo's voice slurred with sleep.

Urk! My little one was dreaming with me again. I was about to swirl around her and lull her back to sleep when something occurred to me. I quivered with great intensity. After a pause I said to Deloo, ~ *Yes, my dear Deloo. That was a deadfall trap.* ~

"You're trembling. Baasee', you are making the bed shake! What's happening to you?"

~ *I need Grandfather Kwaikit. There's a hole in this mystery surrounding Earlene. We've got to find the hole.* ~

"Do you mean a hole in something or a flaw in our judgment?" Deloo asked.

I didn't answer. Sometimes even I, the great and noble Baasee', am stumped.

CHAPTER 14

Day Four, Thursday morning
On the next day Taale poked around in Earlene's business records trying to match them with the code sheet. She wasn't getting very far and
Deloo was bored with her piles of beadwork, so I decided it was time
for Baasee' the Magnificent Detective to swing into action by putting a
hook into her metaphysical backside.

"Ow!" Deloo complained.

I used to plug her with such safety devices often when she was
younger, say about two months ago. Now she was ultra-sensitive. I apologized, and explained my mission was to investigate the two women
who had hidden Deloo and Lizzie for a few minutes yesterday. ~ *They
live close by us.* ~

She nodded, ~ *What a good plan, Baasee'. Let me know what they're
doing. Baasee', I feel odd today. I feel like I'm out of tune here. I miss
Arthur more than ever today. Do you think that's normal?* ~

Having been with many widows, widowers, and young orphans, I
assured her she was normal. Since the dream she had last night was
something her awake mind couldn't remember, I didn't bring it up. Even
though it had been my experience with the coyotes, something in it had
a block on it for her.

~ *Some people never recover from a major loss. It's labeled a trauma nowadays. Imagine this kind of trauma repeated from generation to
generation. Without guides like me or some kind of wisdom source to
get you back on track, you'd be lost. This is what's happened to many
Native Americans. We used to have religious traditions to guide the next
generation through those feelings. When the dominating society tries to
force their religious values, there's often not enough meaningful context
to go with it, such as simple love. It takes a lot to recover from trauma.
You've recovered from the shock better than most. Give yourself time to
be a widow before you go through the other stages of recovery.* ~

While Deloo thought about my advice, I swaddled her in a love co-
coon and examined my small arsenal of bugging devices, wondering if I
should contact Grandfather Kwaikit for help. All of a sudden he was beside me, butting his ocular up against my own.

~ *What? Are you bored, Grandfather?* ~ It takes hours, often days to
get some feedback from him. Now, without precedent, he came rather

than called. *~ What's going on with you? ~*

~ I've adjusted my schedule to help you. ~ Grandfather Kwaikit and I are of the Wolf Clan. Some meant more to him than me. For instance, I could swear Grandfather's grin was more like those of the fang-rich dire wolves of yore.

I bathed my grandfather with a dimpled spirit guide smile and communed, *~ That explains what this is about. ~* I showed him the bug I'd found tangled in my lavish tresses shortly after Floyd Charles's Great Walk of Death the other night. I knew Grandfather Kwaikit must have put it there as he did when he hoped his metaphysical technology would impress me. His slightly guilty look convinced me I was right. *~ You're bored stiff. Is that it? ~*

Grandfather Kwaikit flashed his wolfish chops at me and asked, *~ What are you trying to do today? ~*

I explained, and he pointed at a set of bugs he hoped could pick up a mosquito fifteen miles away. *~ May I use this, Grandfather? Something confused me last night when I heard thoughts from two women. I'm not sure who they are. They are counting. ~*

Meanwhile, upstairs in the bead shop, Taale figured out something on her computer. A lot of things about Earlene's code sheet reminded her of some of their mutual computer classes. Then she had it. Excited, she trotted downstairs to find Deloo.

"It's code. She wrote this like computer code. Now that I'm here where we spent so much time doing our homework together, I'm recognizing the style and function of it."

"Should we call the police again?" Deloo looked alarmed.

"No. As far as I can tell, this is all about the bead shop business. There are a couple of entries about my beading, and two about last year's jacket, the one she gave back."

"What about the 'b'? It wouldn't have had anything to do with her bead shop, would it?"

"I think she might have used two or three codes, separate codes for different reasons. Business, fun, and something that's going to take reading more in her diary to figure out. Either that or 'b' refers to something or someone else. Anyway, it's going to take me a while to figure it out." Taale smiled at Deloo and ran back to her tiny nook upstairs.

"Okay," Deloo called after her mother. "I'll just stay down here with all these cleaning supplies and beads. It's endless. You should see this big plastic jug labeled "Mixed Beads." It looks like she tossed every bead that didn't go anywhere else in here." Deloo tucked the jug behind the jumble of stringed beads. "These look like beads she used to hang over there," she pointed to a water-stained wall, but the boys must have taken them all down to make room for new sheetrock. What do you think, Mom?" Deloo didn't wait for her mother to answer. Instead, she got caught up in sorting beads by color and size. The process was soothing and soon she found herself daydreaming about her late husband's handsome face.

Taale didn't try to hear her daughter. Truth is, neither did I, the glamorous Baasee'. Taale's computer was showing us both information that was much more salient. I wasn't the only other worldly entity who thought so. I dropped my inquiries about the counting women and turned to Deloo's mother. As soon as she sat down, I could tell Taale felt it, too. Later I would regret the way I made choices on that day. I should have kept at least one ocular on the counting women.

Taale checked around the room and didn't see anyone. She checked the bathroom. Nothing. She opened the door of a side room. Nothing. It dawned on her that what she called a side room was an oddly shaped closet. She sat down again.

Taale was about to turn Earlene's computer on when she saw a movement on her right side. She looked closer. Nothing was there except the four display cases Tony and Floyd had managed to put in the room before Floyd was killed. Taale turned back to Earlene's computer screen when she saw the movement again. This time, using her peripheral vision, she tried to see it again. There it was. She forced herself to breathe evenly. Closed her eyes and opened them. The vision was still there.

Earlene. Earlene as she'd been when Taale first met her. A girl blossoming into womanhood. Another figure, a female, was beside her. Gesticulating. I knew immediately the second figure was a spirit guide, probably Earlene's.

Meanwhile, Taale saw part of Earlene's face and part of her hands. The other figure was very indistinct. She seemed to be pointing at something. Taale concentrated on breathing. Soon she could see what Earlene was showing her. A book. A notebook. Taale recognized it. She'd seen it and was sure both Earlene and the indistinct spirit guide wanted the notebook. Excited, Taale hopped up. The vision dissipated and then disappeared altogether. Wound up, Taale skimmed over the stairs to find Deloo.

"Hi Mom. What's up?"

"I saw Earlene."

~ *She's had a vision,*~ I supplied, after checking with Zephyr. ~*Smile.*~

"That's great, Mom. Where is she?" Deloo stitched a fake smile onto her face.

"I had a vision, Sweetheart. She's in my head." Taale twirled around. "I should go tell Great Aunt Pauline. Sometimes they are simply caused by loneliness. I'm lonely for my best friend."

~ *Tell her to take a few deep breaths. She'll be okay.* ~

"Mom, breathe. Take a deep breath."

Taale obeyed.

"Great. Now, tell me what you saw."

Taale described her vision in reasonable detail. "It seems to be a notebook. I did find this one, but it doesn't seem to have anything but columns of numbers." She held up the notebook she'd found yesterday.

"That's sort of like the dire warnings Great Aunt Pauline talks about, isn't it?" This last was aimed more toward me than Taale, so I answered.

~ *It's not dire or a warning. It's important for you both to realize the notebook is a major find. Earlene or whatever that was will come back to give your mother more clues. There's no copier here. Why don't you and your mother take a break to make a copy of both the code sheet and the notebook?* ~

Deloo nodded and while her mother jabbered, she began turning off lights. "Let's go, Mom. This is important." Deloo took the notebook and code sheet from her mother's unsteady fingers. "I want to make some backup copies of Earlene's computer today, too." In a few minutes they were on their way to a copy place not far away. Deloo explained as she drove. At the copy shop, they made two full copies of each document.

By the time they finished their work in mortal-based Fairbanks, Grandfather Kwaikit and I finished making a thorough sweep of the bead shop. Grandfather did all the work, but I could watch while I helped Deloo. The first thing he identified were the two women Deloo and Lizzie met yesterday. Grandfather discovered they were not the counters, but were affiliated with the counting ladies in some very precise way. Why? Who knows? We didn't. The second inquiry Grandfather Kwaikit made was about the vision Taale had of her friend, Earlene. Again, he got a little information from the indistinct view of the spirit guide, but not enough to tell us anything.

~ *We'll figure it out, Granddaughter,* ~ Grandfather Kwaikit suggested as he breezed away.

When they finished, Deloo asked, "Should we call Mr. Cunningham?"

"No," said the once again sober Taale, "We're taking a lunch break. Let's find out if Aunt Pauline has anything to say and then go back to work. I've got to figure out a way to translate it."

They reached Great Aunt Pauline's old house. Taale jumped out and raced in the front door. Deloo followed, surprised she had trouble keeping up with her mother.

~ She'll be okay, won't she? ~ Deloo asked me. *~ She's going from tottering to nearly running. Too fast, don't you agree, Baasee'? ~*

~ Of course she is right now. I think this might be her first significant vision. ~

~ Mom's? ~ She entered Great Aunt Pauline's log house. As usual for Fairbanks in July, the outside air felt both dry and hot, but it was cool inside the house. Deloo sat on the edge of the couch while Taale sat in the center of it next to Great Aunt Pauline.

"I'm seeing a stack of books on her lap. Did you?" Pauline asked.

"No. Wait, yes. There were other books on her lap." Taale responded.

"Okay, now she's pointing to the third one down. Do you see what I mean?"

Taale's shoulders sagged. She was crestfallen. "No. I see Earlene and some books."

Deloo intoned, "I'm hearing a lot of buzzing. It's hazy, but I see her pointing to the third book, too."

"Like me. Now my view shows me they are not books. They are more like areas of something very blurry," said Pauline with a gentle smile. "Now I'm seeing the page she's turned to. I can't read it. Can you, Deloo?"

"I see it, but I can't read. Wait. I can pick out the first word. It's got numbers in it: There's a 72."

Pauline said, "I see more than that. I see 5472."

"5472? That's in the note she wrote to me," Taale sang.

"Do you have it here?" Deloo shouted. "Maybe I have selective memory. Maybe I'm remembering instead of seeing it."

"I'm the one who saw the longer number, and I've never seen or heard it before. What does it mean? What kind of note?" Pauline said.

"It's in our house. I put it there," Taale answered. "Do you see more, Auntie?"

"No," Pauline said, "I see the first word has numbers, but I don't think I'm allowed to see more. It's already faded out on me. All I see now is some kind of muskrat. I don't recognize what it is."

Taale gasped. "Me, too. I think it's a wolverine. They are the biggest of the weasel family. With their thick fur, they move well through our snow and ice world."

"Oh my." Deloo sagged downward, wedging herself between Great Aunt Pauline and the edge of the couch. "I don't see anything anymore. I feel tired and confused now."

"*Hutlanee!*" Great Aunt Pauline retorted as she slid an arm around her great niece's shoulders. "You did well today. Sometimes, when the Other Side wants you to do something, they forget you are young. Sometimes it's just between you and a living person who has a strong psychic connection with you. When I was young, I felt revived if I sat with a certain alder tree. Tell your spirit guide to find a safe place for you."

"We'd better find that third book, too." Taale said. "Two of us saw it."

"And when we were still in the bead shop, I heard a voice telling me about many diaries," Deloo ventured.

She'd never told anyone about what I'd said before. I showered her with affection. ~ *This has been a wonderful way to let Great Aunt Pauline know about your growth.* ~

~ *What growth, Baasee'?* ~ Deloo looked at her hands to find the dastardly growth.

~ *What growth? For one thing, I'm talking to you. We couldn't do so last month. You just used every psychic and medium ability you have. Are you dizzy? When I was five, my Grandfather Kwaikit often sat beside me like you did with your great aunt. He could see the future better when I was with him. The problem was I was only five years old. When he left, I would be reeling for days. A tree helped me. I called it the Shrill Tree because everything seemed to shrill at me after being with Grandfather Kwaikit. Sometimes I sat with the Shrill Tree for hours.* ~

~ *What does that mean? Shrill at you?* ~

~ *Do you hear a constant sound? A shrilling? Some people call it buzzing. When I was a girl it helped to sit against the trunk of a certain kind of tree. Let's find your special tree. Alaska is full of trees. Let's see if a spruce tree in your mother's yard will help.* ~

Later, when we were alone, Deloo and I found a tree in her mother's yard that stopped the shrilling. She sat with her back against it to let the world go by. She was fine in less than five minutes.

CHAPTER 15

Day Four, Thursday morning
Detective Harper touched the end button and glowered, "He's going to send me a file. The Chinese couple were suspects in a murder investigation in Nova Scotia, and they were both cleared." He pecked around on his computer and sauntered to a printer. "Here it is." He tossed a sheet of paper at his partner.

"Hmm. I see Deloo's name a few times. Looks like they followed her around three provinces and ended in the States—in Vermont." He looked up. "Weird the Chinese woman is an architect and he's a computer science engineer—none of that has anything to do with beads. Besides, there were no charges. Deloo's word against theirs." He handed the paper back. "Now what?"

If Detective Cruikshank noticed the small print on one of their files, he didn't say anything. Detective Harper shrugged, "Everything else on them checks out on airlines, car rental agencies, and hotels. Their fingerprints weren't found in the shop at the time of the murder. They don't seem to know anyone here except Deloo and this is their first trip to Alaska. They have a right to be here. They don't know our victim. If the Dena woman keeps the place locked up tight, they should be okay." He shrugged. "I think we're looking for a solo male, the one they saw beside the shop today."

"Should I ask the Chinese pair not to leave Fairbanks?" Cruikshank asked.

"Wouldn't hurt." Harper said.

* * *

Back at the bead shop the women locked the back door behind them and went upstairs to the small nook. Taale said, "I'll sit here with the code sheet and you sit in the office chair."

Deloo looked perky. "What's my job?"

"That's the problem," Taale frowned over the diary in her lap. "I don't know what to do. This notebook goes back a long way. And at the same time it seems to be recent. For instance this one entry on me is about six years ago, since it's about moose hide. I stopped using moose hide five years ago. The date in her diary is wrong. If I'm understanding how she's dating things, she claims the moose hide jacket was made two years ago." Taale pointed to a number at the end of the entry. "Look at this numeral she enters after almost everything. It's meaningless to me."

Deloo stared at the number. "I don't get it either." She shook her head. "By the way, did you bring in that note she wrote to you?"

"Yes. She wrote 5472, just like you thought. I don't know what 5472 means." Taale looked frustrated. "Except all of these are four digits long. Hmmm." Taale thumbed through the books on Earlene's shelves, not many, all about beading. "We've been through all of her handwritten ledgers. You have one that looks sort of like a diary." Taale looked at her daughter. "Didn't you and Aunt Pauline see three or more books?"

Deloo shrugged. "These must not be all of them. You've got more in that laptop or on memory sticks or something like them around here. I think the clue is in the numbers." Deloo pointed out a long string of numbers. "See? This one is quite long."

"I know what you mean. They look familiar somehow." Taale looked at her daughter.

Deloo knitted her brow. "What do you mean? They are just numbers to me."

"Omigod. I've got to go home." Taale grabbed her purse and dashed down the steps. "I think this is part of a class assignment we worked on together. Wait here for me, Deloo-Loo. I'll be right back."

Deloo followed her, confused, but sure of one thing. "Let me open the door for you. I'll shut and lock it after you're out."

"Oh. Right." Taale patted her handbag. "I've got my phone here. I'll call you when I get back." She turned left at the bottom of the stairs as if to go out the back. "Almost forgot. I parked next to the front door. It's easier to see who's on the other side of the door that way."

Detective Harper stood on the other side. He held up his cell phone. Taale opened the door and called out to Deloo, "you talk to him." Taale pushed past the tall detective.

Detective Harper stood aside and looked at Deloo with a grim face. "I just stopped by to see if there was any new development."

"I don't know. Mom said she and Earlene did homework together and left."

"Now that sounds very interesting. Homework. I think I will come back later," the detective said and waited for Deloo to reopen the door for him.

He left and Taale returned a few minutes later clutching a notebook to her breast. "I think I've got it." She ran up the stairs. Deloo followed her.

"I think Earlene composed something for me alone. I'll know in a few minutes."

Deloo asked, "What can I do?"

"Just sit beside me," Taale answered, "and have this code sheet ready." Taale's fingers flew across both the keyboard and numerical pad. "We took the beginning computer class together years ago. She caught on right away. I didn't. I needed to sit beside her all the time to get the point of the lectures and the reading materials. If I'm right, this is the first homework assignment we had. That was over ten years ago. You were just beginning middle school."

~ Turn on your recorder, my diligent Deloo, I believe she will soon forget anything other than that the computer screen exists. Record her voice to pick up all the details. ~

~ How do you know, Baasee'? ~

~ I'm listening to Taale's spirit guide. One of the reasons I call her Zephyr is because she's full of light and air sometimes, like now. Your mother may not be as quick on computers as is Earlene. However, Taale is spellbound by computers too. According to Zephyr, she shuts out every distraction in order to work with her computer. You do something similar when you are painting or drawing. ~

"What are the numerals after 'b'?" Taale asked, unaware she interrupted Glorious me, Baasee' the Original.

"Um, yeah, 5-4-7-2." Deloo answered.

"It's what I thought." Taale's fingers flew. Page after page of meaningless numbers and letters appeared and a text file opened. Deloo could see it held a letter addressed to Taale. Just as she was about to read it, her cell phone signaled a call coming in. She fished it out of her purse.

"Hello? ... Oh. ... I'll be right down." She clicked something to end the call and murmured, "That was Detective Harper. He's back."

"I'll open the door," Deloo murmured and ran down the staircase. She let in both Detectives Harper and Cruikshank. "Mom's upstairs." She locked the door after they walked into the store. "This ..."

At that moment Taale shrieked, "No, no, NO," followed by muffled sobs.

Detective Harper lunged upstairs followed by Detective Cruikshank and Deloo. When Deloo reached the top step she could see her mother's shoulders heaving.

Detective Harper hovered over Taale without speaking.

"Mom!" Deloo screeched. "What happened?" She pushed her way

around Detective Harper to sit on the chair on the other side of Taale.

"She's d-d-dead," Taale choked. "Earlene is dead."

Zephyr signaled to me to examine an interior message from Earlene's spirit guide. Using spirit quotation marks, Earlene's spirit said to Zephyr, ~ *Friends like Taale are priceless. I want you to know Earlene's spirit guide warned Earlene as many ways as she could to get rid of that man. He is a murderer who planned well ahead of time to take Earlene's life. Earlene cried herself to sleep after typing that message to Taale Dena.* ~

Detective Harper touched Taale on the back and looked at Detective Cruikshank. The other detective shrugged.

"How do you know, Ms. Dena? I mean, Taale," queried Detective Harper.

Taale jabbed a finger at the screen. "See? It's all here. Read it yourself." She started weeping. Deloo put her arms around her mother while the two detectives tried to read the screen.

"Girlfriend: the man is a murderer. If you're reading this and not hearing it from me, you have proof I was murdered as well. I know he has killed others. Watch yourself. There are a lot of diary entries I haven't got to yet. Look for my text documents. They are all on the main drive somewhere."

~ *Let's go downstairs,* ~ I suggested with spirit guide brilliance. ~ *She needs something hot to drink to bring her out of shock.* ~ There was a microscopic kitchen on the lower floor. I studied its contents and looked for Deloo. Grandfather Kwaikit arrived then and helped Deloo find a cinnamon tea bag. While we foraged, I contemplated some of the background text, the thoughts that went with the entry Taale had found. There was more to the situation than my mortal or her mother were prepared to examine.

Detective Cruikshank followed Deloo down the staircase, unaware of the ancient deadman, my grandfather, who had joined us. Rather, joined me. Mortals. So boring.

~ *This should do it,* ~ Grandfather Kwaikit communed to his granddaughter, meaning me, his cave-baby granddaughter.

Using spirit-guide magic, I handed the packets to Deloo, who started heating some water. I turned to Grandfather Kwaikit. ~ *What are you doing here?* ~

~ *I got an alarm code from someone named Air. The message came from here.* ~

~ That's Zephyr, not Air, ~ I corrected him. *~ My mortal's mother just cracked the code in a murder case. Taale, meaning the mother, has never done clue-finding before. ~*

The water came to a boil. Deloo announced. "I'm going upstairs. Anybody joining me?"

"Who are you talking to?" Detective Cruikshank asked from the stairwell.

Deloo jerked, almost spilling the hot water. Detective Cruikshank took the tray and led the way upstairs. "Frank is talking to your mom."

They found Detective Harper supporting Taale with one arm while she explained "she must have written this on the same night she delivered the jacket to me. Maybe that's why it's addressed to me. She writes here she would have changed what she wrote if she were still alive on the next day." She gulped.

Detective Cruikshank held out a cup. "I've got some tea, Taale. Where should I put it?"

"Here," Deloo said from behind him. "A spot on the display cabinet beside her." He set the tray on top of the glass. She looked at her mother with a nod of satisfaction. "Mom, drink some tea. It's good for you. I put lots of sugar in it."

Detective Harper held the cup toward Taale. She sipped, her fingers too unsteady to hold the cup herself. "She's dead," Taale murmured.

"We found blood downstairs," Deloo agreed.

"She wrote that as a living person," Detective Harper argued. "She might have good reason to suspect her boyfriend of being a murderer, but she was alive when she typed that entry. Before leaping to conclusions, let's go over the facts."

The room, while occupied by a riotous array of beads, boxes of pliers, wires, women's clothing, and display stands, also held several office machines. A cushioned chair faced a small flat screen. Detective Harper pulled the chair closer to the desk. Using a stationary bike for support, he opened his electronic notebook and scrolled through something. "Remember, I'm new to Fairbanks, so I'm going to ask many stupid questions. In other words, I don't know anything about Alaska or Fairbanks. For instance, did you know the owner of this bead shop, Ms. Earlene Shoepack, was reported missing last November?"

Taale gulped and nodded.

Deloo squeezed her eyes shut and asked, "Thanksgiving?"

Detective Harper drew in a deep breath, remembering the other odd fact he had seen. Deloo's late husband, Mr. Arthur Goode, died in a car accident on Thanksgiving Day of the previous winter. "Mr. Leroy Cunningham reported Earlene missing and gave the department some supporting paperwork, including the missing woman's Last Will and Testament. Mr. Cunningham told me he last saw her on the day before Thanksgiving."

Deloo sucked in a lungful of air and stared at him with hollow eyes.

"I'm sorry for your loss, Mrs. Goode. The Lieutenant showed me your late husband's file this morning."

Deloo lowered her eyes and remained silent.

"My wife died five years ago. I still can't listen to flute music. She played the flute."

Deloo met his eyes. "I'm sorry. Real sorry for your loss."

Detective Harper propped his elbows on the bike handles. "I'm here to investigate Mr. Floyd Charles' murder. It looks like the suspect might have done it in this room before throwing the victim downstairs. Will you be able to continue working here, Ms. Dena? I believe you voiced concern earlier."

"Yes." Taale looked at him with a grimace, "This about the River, now. Yes."

Detective Harper waited for a beat and then asked, "What river is that?"

Deloo and her mother looked at each other in amusement. I noted for Deloo's eternal record that they said "Cheechako" at the same time.

Deloo remembered a class she had taken. Most people don't know Native words or history. "Cheechako is a word right from your part of the world. A Cheechako is a trade jargon word from a tribe in Washington, the Chinook. It means newcomer. Another common word is potlatch, which refers to a celebration of any sort. The Chinook tribe in Washington and Oregon takes credit for the jargon."

I swatted Deloo in spirit-guide style and reminded her to be polite. ~ *He's new here.* ~

As if he heard my thought, Detective Harper said, "Even though I am an Alaska Native biologically, I was adopted at birth and raised in the Midwest."

Deloo sat up straight and supplied, "Then I'm sorry for your loss even more. Great Aunt Pauline says that Indian children who have been adopted away from their homelands often suffer from Historic Trauma even more than those who live where they were born. It's weird, but such children often talk, laugh, even move in the same way their biological kinfolk do." Deloo coughed and added, "For most of us in the Interior, the 'River' means the Yukon River. In the old days, that was the main way to get around. Fairbanks is on the banks of both the Tanana and the Chena Rivers, but Earlene's and our families both came from villages along the Yukon River. The Tanana River runs beside Fairbanks. It drains into the Yukon River." Deloo smiled at him, taking comfort in his leadership along the widowhood road. "We should take you to see it."

Detective Harper responded with a stiff, "I would be honored to visit The River, but it will have to wait until this murder investigation is over." He turned his attention to Taale, noting she seemed less tense than a few minutes ago. "Ms. Dena," he began.

"Call me Taale. Everyone does. It's pronounced like tally as in taking a tally."

"Taale, even though we talked about it the other night, for the record, how did you know Floyd?"

"I know his parents. His father is from farther down river than my Aunt Pauline. Floyd sometimes came to my house for supper along with his friend, Tony."

Detective Harper thumbed through his notes again, and remarked, "I have Mrs. Goode down as your only child. I also have her as quite a bit older than Floyd. Why did they eat supper with you?"

Taale looked at Detective Harper as if he had asked why humans have nostrils. I glanced at Zephyr, caught her amused ocular, and turned to Deloo. ~ *You'll have to answer that one, my adroit Deloo. He's a bull in the China shop of Alaska.* ~

"Frank, May I call you that?" my tiny mortal asked.

Various moods rear-ended each other on Detective Harper's face. They registered shock, anger, relief, and delight. Then he remembered his tongue and said, "Uh, yes."

"My late husband, who was an anthropologist, said our neighborhood was a miniature version of Alaska Native, or even Native American cultures. Our friends and relatives have always eaten at our house sometimes and sometimes they eat at Great Aunt Pauline's house or even at their own houses. Great Aunt Pauline made the whole neighborhood safe. We are proud of that honor, because the kids choose to come to us. They never have to go to any of the agencies when they are in trouble, unhappy, or simply wanting company." She appealed to Taale. "Right, Mom?"

"Thank you, Deloo." Taale continued for the detectives, "I'm gratified whenever I see a new face at my table. Sometimes Great Aunt Pauline is too overworked to cook for so many people." Turning to the detective, she added, "My aunt is getting older, you know."

Detective Harper found himself watching Taale's lips move. When it came to him she was waiting for a response, he closed his notebook and said, "Thank you ladies. Now, I'd like to know a little about the missing woman—off the record. Sometimes that's more useful than anything formal. Since I've already shown how ignorant I am of Fairbanks, what can you say about her to teach an outsider like me? I don't want to say so many wrong things I'll get run out of town in my first week."

~ *Smart man,* ~ I remarked to Zephyr. ~ *Does Taale think so?* ~

Zephyr paused before answering. ~ *I think she would like him a lot, but she's fronting the loss of her lifelong friend. She's been thinking she would see Earlene again. Her mind and emotional ways are disjointed at the moment.* ~

~ *Odd, isn't it? Deloo had accepted Frank as a friend because she assumes he is like her in grief. Taale isn't ready to be so open.* ~

~ *You're right, my friend, but this is a changing world.* ~ Zephyr responded.

~ *Yes. Remember when Taale's cousin invited her to that picnic in North Pole. Taale took Deloo, thinking it would be a family picnic. My fears about the event all came true. Two of Deloo's older cousins started drinking and I helped Deloo to hustle away before they got it into their drunken minds to jump her. Instead, they saw her leaving and ran after her. I got her to take a look behind, and then I got busy studying the surrounding landscape. It was no problem to have her dart into the grass on the left side of the trail. Right-handed people think "right" all the time and forget there's a left way to go. She ran about ten feet to the left and I got her to dive down and scramble through the alder bushes to escape. It worked, although she soiled her shirt in the process. When she found Taale a few minutes later, her mother didn't waste a second to get her daughter into the car and back to Little Tanana.* ~

Zephyr glowed. ~ *It took a lot of courage for your Deloo to tell my Taale what happened. Taale was so angry at her cousin, she almost didn't speak to her ever again. I had to use all of my powers to get Taale to confess her cousin's husband, the good looking white guy, put something into Taale's drink. It was supposed to make her pass out, but I figured out what he'd done and planned to do afterward. I made sure*

Taale had a little accident with the glass before it got to her mouth. He didn't notice and started to pick her up to take her inside to rape her. Taale is no dummy. She screamed and got her cousin to see what her husband was doing. They got a divorce while Deloo was in college. The cousin is rid of the rat. ~

CHAPTER 16

Day Four, Thursday morning

Meanwhile Taale and Deloo gave Detective Harper a garbled lecture on Alaska, Alaska Native cultures, and Fairbanks. He leaned against the wall, balancing on three of the five wheels available to the chair. With a frown, he held up a hand.

"Witchen? Who is he? Or she?" He forced himself to leave his notebook alone.

Deloo looked perplexed. She thought about what she and Taale had said and said peaceably, "I think you didn't hear the G in Gwich'in. Someone told me my accent leaves off the hard G sound at the beginning of words. Gwich'in people live upriver—up the Yukon River. They have their own language and history. Some of them live in Canada."

Taale nodded. "Earlene is Gwich'in, or… was." She blinked back tears.

"Let yourself cry," Detective Harper said. "The minister from my wife's church told me to let myself shout all my feelings so I didn't get bottled up. He said the human soul cannot become whole if you try to turn some of it off, whether or not she's dead. That helped me a lot."

Taale accepted a tissue or two or three from her daughter and thanked him. "When Floyd was ten he had trouble remembering Maryland is a state on the Atlantic, and not a dead movie actor named Marilyn Monroe. When he recited state names, I helped him by whispering *"Some Like It Hot"* and then tossing my hair. That made him laugh, and he aced the test. Both of us were born long after she died."

"You've got it," Frank said as he handed her his handkerchief. "Now think of something visual and beautiful about Earlene."

Taale looked at Deloo and they both cried out at once, "her hair."

Detective Harper touched his own short crop and smiled. "I bet it wasn't like this. Tell me something about Earlene's hair I can visualize."

Taale leaned over to Deloo, who rested against her mother's shins, and lifted all of the long, dark hair away from her daughter's neck and shoulders. "Earlene never had a haircut because hers was like Deloo's: heavy, glossy, and did this." Taale let Deloo's hair fall back into place as if on command. "Deloo's hair will do that if I cut it before it gets below her waist. When it's longer, it needs to be brushed. Earlene's hair almost reached the back of her knees because it had a full richness that let it flow. Earlene wore it loose when she was in the shop, here. Otherwise, she had a long scarf she used for binding it on top of her head in cold weather."

"I keep seeing that scarf somewhere in the store," Deloo muttered. "I think of her whenever I see it. Have you seen it, Mom?"

"Do you mean this?" Detective Harper pointed to a length of deep crimson wool. It draped across an oblong box.

"That's it," Taale smiled. "Right in front of us. Earlene would never have left it there, of all places. She was fastidious about her clothing." Her eyes traveled the length of the wool and stopped. "Odd. It looks like there's a footprint on it. Scarves like this are very expensive. Earlene treated it like it had been woven with gold."

Deloo reached for the fabric as if to pick it up when Detective Harper cried, "No! Leave it there. This is evidence." He took photos of it with his cell phone, showing where they found it. Then he pulled a baggie and a pair of latex gloves out of his pouch and draped the cloth along the floor so they could all look at it while he took more photos.

"See?" Taale pointed. "It looks like someone stepped on it."

"Yeah! I see it, Mom. And this dark, straight mark is odd. What's that?"

Taale's head collided with Deloo's as she peeked at the scarf. Every time she reached toward it, Detective Harper coughed. "I see what you mean. Detective Cruikshank and I will have this checked. I think this is from those expensive shoes, like the Ferragamo brand. Do you know anyone who wears five hundred dollar shoes? "

Taking the cue from his colleague, Jack Cruikshank started poking at his cell phone. "There's a photo of a shoe print they took when someone tried to drill a hole in the waterline outside this shop a couple of days ago." Jack tapped a few more icons and announced, "If it is Ferragamo, we're talking an average of seven hundred dollars a pair."

Taale gaped. "Seven hundred! Earlene bought a two-hundred dollar pair of Uggs last year—on sale for sixty percent off. They were the right size and looked good. I can't afford more than twenty dollars myself."

Deloo added, "Me, neither. Besides, this is Fairbanks. No one wastes money on fancy shoes with our harsh weather."

All of them examined the door to the office area for shoes. Detective Harper shook his head and muttered. "Do either of you know when you first saw it here?"

Taale raised her dark eyebrows. "Tony or Floyd might have put it there. Earlene always hung it on her dresser mirror in her bedroom."

Deloo shook her head. "Why didn't she hang it with her coat? There are a couple of parkas and a dress coat down there," my little artist wondered. Have I mentioned she is the smartest and most intuitive detective on the planet?

Taale chuckled. "She did when we were both young. That was during the first few years and before she added this upper floor. She had her bedroom right under this room where the craft table is. Her parents sent both sons to Mt. Edgecumbe boarding school. Earlene wouldn't go. She went to Lathrop, here in Fairbanks, instead." Taale gazed into a time where none of her mortal listeners could go. "She took her parents' bedroom after they moved to Wasilla. The boys shared a room. They put Earlene into a closet downstairs and called it the third bedroom. Ever since she added the upper level, she had more space than she'd ever had. She decided she needed a mirror to keep the scarf straight."

"Hmmm," Detective Harper mused. "Thank you for all of your help. I'll ask Leroy and Tony if they know how this headscarf got here. Did she have more than one? My late wife was a magnet for this sort of decoration. She must have had twenty of them."

"No. Earlene bought a new one every year or so, and tossed or gave away the old one."

"I see," Detective Harper stared at the scarf. "What about boyfriends? Did any of them wear scarves?"

Deloo shrugged. "I never met any of her boyfriends. Did you, Mom?"

Taale shook her head. "Earlene was odd about men. After her folks died she got pregnant by the only guy I ever knew her to date. The relationship didn't last. I don't know of any others. She never mentioned going on dates. Sometimes she mentioned the old boyfriend BeeZee. I never met him although he's one of my customers." Taale sighed.

"Earlene ordered a beaded jacket from me on his behalf every year for the past fifteen or more years. I don't make a lot of jackets, but I have met all of my other customers except for the man who bought the beaded ones. I guess he didn't want to know me. He ordered expensive ones, too."

"Wait," Frank rubbed his temples. He wondered if he needed to take a break away from the women. Taale's lips were swallowing him; moving him into another way of thinking. He wasn't ready for that. Pulling himself together he asked, "Did you say you have never met this ex-boyfriend, Taale?"

"No, I've never seen him or heard him talk," Taale responded.

Frank's eyebrows wrinkled, "Why not? This town is so small, you should all know each other."

"It's easy to go for months or even years without seeing your next door neighbors," Taale grumbled. "There are lots of voting precincts, for instance. I'm in one. Earlene is in another. We couldn't even vote together."

"Well, what if she made him up? What if there is no boyfriend?" Deloo demanded.

"Thanks to Earlene's advice I raised my fee to $2,700 for those jackets. They take a lot of expensive hide and a lot of beading. Maybe Earlene has been paying me year after year just to keep up appearances, but why bother? We've been friends since we were girls. It's not like she's got a lot of money." Taale heaved a sigh. "Or didn't have extra money until a few years ago. She's bought me all these gadgets during recent years. First she gets one of whatever, then she buys me the identical thing the next month. Trying to stop her was like jumping out of the way of a charging bear. Impossible!"

"I didn't know that, Mama. How much money has she spent on you?"

"Thousands."

Detective Harper broke in, "Ms. Dena, I mean Taale, could you give me an example of one of these gifts?"

"This." She put her smart phone on the table. "Every year for the past three years she's bought identical phones for me and her. I used to get those flip phones from Walmart. You know? They're called burner phones. That's what I got for Deloo until she got one herself."

Detective Harper picked up Taale's phone to examine it. "They issue these at the department. I can't afford one on my own."

"Crazy, huh?" Taale picked hers up again. "Earlene paid for the service on mine as well. That's where most of the money for these smart phones goes."

"Hey!" Deloo breathed. "Don't these have an app to tell you where she is? Have you tried it?"

"Of course." Taale shook her head. "Someone, maybe it was Earlene, turned her phone off. I can't find her or her phone."

From our posts above the trio of mortals, Zephyr signaled me with a wave of suspicion. ~ *She tried locating Earlene the minute that jacket appeared on her doorstep. Earlene answers texts or phone calls right away unless she's with a customer. Taale got no reply to any of her calls last winter. I've wondered about it ever since then.* ~

Detective Harper turned his attention to the laptop. "She writes she's got proof, but all I see is this letter," Detective Harper said. "Is the proof in computer code?"

"I don't know. We'll have to wait until Mom finishes her work," Deloo answered before Taale could say anything.

I could tell Detective Harper, whose agenda was to prove he was the right man for his first big case, was impatient. ~ *Taale needs an hour or two more. Have them either go back to the station or sit downstairs where there is more room.* ~

Deloo responded, ~ *Yes I'll tell them to back off. It's too crowded up here. Mom needs some room. Besides, that Harper guy is hugging her.* ~

Grandfather Kwaikit hiccoughed spirit-guide style and butted in, ~ *Don't worry. I think it's helping your mother. Besides, he's not touching her, just giving her less body room than usual. He thinks it's 'comforting' her.* ~ Grandfather Kwaikit didn't commune that Detective Harper also gave off lecherous vibrations.

Deloo convinced the detectives to make room for Taale by suggesting they talk to Mr. Cunningham or Tony about the shoe print. After they left, she assumed her position beside her mother and held the code for Taale to see.

"You can stop anytime you need to take a break, Mom. They are downstairs trying to set up meetings with Mr. Cunningham or Tony and will be up here in a second if you need them."

Meanwhile I communed to Deloo. ~ *We are sure Earlene was more interested in providing proof about her own murder. What's odd is she might be covering for that other pair of women. I see images of little wolverines. They see themselves as wolverines, loners who are violently protective of their young and who prefer to stay hidden. Don't worry my pondering Deloo, Earlene made this set of documents. She knew she was helping us find her killer.* ~ I fluttered my extraordinary, shimmering eyelashes at her as a boost to my comforting style.

~ *Okay, Baasee'. I'll just help her keep calm.* ~

Before long, the two detectives ordered some Chinese food and asked her if she wanted any. Taale didn't hear them, but Deloo did and nodded, "Mom's favorite is the vegetable spring roll—just one. I like Kung Pao chicken." She opened the door for them. "I'll pay you when you get back."

Detective Cruikshank asked Deloo, "Can you eat a whole order of the chicken?" At that moment Lizzie entered the store. They compared notes about how much they could eat and decided one order would do for the three women. Lizzie assured everyone that the restaurant they had in mind imagined all Americans were uninhibited about eating.

"I'll ask for one order of Kung Pao Chicken and some extra spring rolls for the three of you. How's that?"

The two girls grinned at Detective Cruikshank as he left. "He's cute," Lizzie sighed.

"He's almost fifty," Deloo grumbled.

"I meant Jack. He is thirty-one," Lizzie asserted.

A tone in her voice brought Deloo to a halt. She looked at Lizzie and asked "How do you know how old he is?"

"I was at the counter of a diner off Two Street. He happened to take the seat next to mine and we got to talking. That's how I know," Lizzie's face glowed bright pink.

Deloo sucked in some air, looked long and hard at Lizzie, and then brought her up to date on what had happened with Earlene's diary, the scarf, and the shoe print.

"Seven hundred dollars for shoes! Who sells that kind of thing here? Ugh! Earlene was a nice lady—not a snob with power shoes. Sometimes she let me stay in the shop while I waited for the bus." To Deloo's inquiring look Lizzie explained she'd lived in a boarding house last winter. "It was just a room, but cheaper than living in the dorms."

"I didn't know there were boarding houses in Fairbanks," Deloo remarked. "That's brave of you, Lizzie."

"It was cheap." Lizzie smiled.

"Deloo?" Taale called.

"I'll be right up," Deloo said as she flew up the staircase. "Are you finished?"

"No, this will take hours. Earlene and I had a unique way to work out problems because we both found the instructions bad. Earlene figured it out."

"I don't know anything about computers," Deloo commiserated. "I wish I could help."

"This is what Earlene told me that made it all better: Think about beads!" she would say.

"Do you mean the way I keep my beads in order by keeping a bag for each project?" I asked. "Her answer was so sensible to me. 'See, you're already programming Native-style. You use beads instead of keyboards and electronic peripherals.' "

Deloo's mind jumped all over the place, so I applied green lipstick and blew a big puff of calmness into it. ~ *I've asked Zephyr, your Mom's spirit guide, how it works. Easy. You do something like it with paints. Before your mother begins a beading project, she's already decided on what colors, what size bead, how much thread, and so forth. When she's got those all sorted, she puts them into plastic baggies inside the project bag. What Zephyr noticed is that they forget to tell other people about how beads of the same batch will stay together even when they are in a mixed bag. They often roll in the same direction as their mates do. That's the point Earlene was making about programming: look for the natural groups of types of files.* ~

Deloo's thoughts were askew until I sent her images of how she painted. "I get it, Mom," she breathed. "You just imagined how it worked in real life, and then you could program on your own."

Taale grinned. Beyond her Zephyr shrugged dainty shoulders and sprouted a wreath with a complicated pattern of green and dark red-gold. ~ *They just had to tell each other they understood, whether or not it was true. I ended up doing a lot of the work!* ~

I winked a gorgeous ocular at her and beamed at Deloo. ~ *I knew it would make sense to you, my inquisitive Deloo.* ~

Oblivious to the conversation above her, Taale continued explaining. "I just wanted you to know I have found Earlene's real diary." Taale held up the code sheet. "This guides me to a small portion of it. Thanks to another course we took together, I can see the rest with some ease. The files she wanted me to see in the code sheet are all about her boyfriend, somebody named BeeZee. Like I said, I never met him. I don't know if it's a name or code for something else."

CHAPTER 17

Day Four, Thursday afternoon

"BeeZee?" Deloo wrinkled her otherwise unmarred brow. Didn't you two hang out all the time? Seems strange you never met him."

"I know. He was gone so much, it gives new meaning to Great Aunt Pauline's notion of non-men. Earlene and I were inseparable in high school and later when you were little. Then I had to scramble for money. Great Aunt Pauline took the most time with Earlene. She treated Earlene like a daughter and the two of us were raised together after Earlene's folks died. I didn't mind. I would have hung out with her more, but we had odd schedules." Taale chuckled. "I needed every dime I could get. Remember how you helped out one winter? You delivered the Fairbanks Daily News Miner, which meant we both were doing it."

"I'll never forget. We both rolled the papers. Then you drove for a block and waited until I walked through or beside a building or two, then drove me to the next place." Deloo shook her head. "I liked those big apartment complexes. I could warm up in them."

"Those were the years we ate almost every meal with Great Aunt Pauline. If it hadn't been for her, the two of us would have starved."

"True, but you still had time to see Earlene. You did a lot of beading in those years. Thanks to Earlene, you had a place to sell them. This is too small a town for you to never see any of her boyfriends."

Taale glanced first at Deloo with unfocused eyes and then at the wall. "You're right, Deloo-Loo. You're right. I saw men hanging around the bead shop all the time, but was too busy to wonder if Earlene's life was any more romantic than mine. I was so ashamed of being poor; I couldn't stand to look anyone in the eye for a long time."

Deloo hesitated, wondering for the first time if her mother ever went on dates. The topic was too charged because it left her thinking she was the reason her mother might not have got out much. Instead, Deloo smiled at her mother, trying to think of what to say when Taale gave Deloo a gentle shove.

"I smell food downstairs. Could you bring me a spring roll and some tea? I don't want anything else right now."

Deloo grinned. "Okay, that leaves more for me and Lizzie." Deloo brought her mother the spring roll on a cracked plate. Her daughter watched while Taale inhaled the food. Then she wiped her lips and announced, "Baby, I'm going to back the whole set up onto this thumb drive. Then I need to make sure I've got everything off her computer. It will take me about an hour or two to do it right. Then we can go home."

Deloo scoffed. "Is that hacker's code? You just don't want to let me watch how you do it, right?"

Taale grinned. "Oh, no! I was well trained at the University. No one calls it hacking there, either. Earlene did it better than any of the students. That's what Dunbar, the master's student assistant for the program, told me once. He's been told he was the best until Earlene came along."

Taale came down when it was quitting time. Both Lizzie and Deloo looked at her. They all turned toward the front door which someone was trying to open. Taale shouted through the glass, "Hi, Buzz. The store is closed. We're just leaving."

"But Joselin got a call telling her to pick up her stuff," a tall blond man of about forty yelled back. "Let me in. It's hot out here."

"I've got her stuff right here," Deloo signaled her mother. "Let's get rid of it and go."

Taale took the tidy box from Deloo and handed it through the door. "Hey, Buzzy. This is my daughter. Leroy Cunningham hired us to do clean up. Joselin's things are right on top. Could you sign for her?" He signed a form and left. Taale handed the paper to Deloo.

"Who was he? I don't think I've met him."

Taale laughed. "Consider yourself lucky. That's Bruce Ziegler. Back in the day we called him either Buzz or Buzzy."

Deloo gaped. "That's BeeZee?"

"Buzz?" Taale stared at their excited eyes, comprehending her daughter's enthusiasm. "He's too goofy." She twirled a finger in the air above her right ear. "Besides, he's from Manley Hot Springs. Joselin and he have been together since before you were born."

Lizzie piped up, "But he's cute, the right height, and whoever Earlene was seeing had to be from out of town. Otherwise, you would have seen him here."

Taale shook her head, "This is crazy."

Deloo dialed Detective Harper, saying, "Crazy or not, I'm telling Frank."

Just as she waited for Frank to answer, both detectives came in followed by Tony and Leroy Cunningham. Detective Harper took them upstairs to look at the woolen scarf while Detective Cruikshank listened to Deloo's theory about Bruce Ziegler. By the time she finished, the

Cunningham pair returned to the lower level. Neither of them had noticed the red scarf, although the senior Mr. Cunningham remembered seeing Earlene wear it numerous times. The shoe print didn't match either of their shoe sizes.

Leroy protested to the detectives, "Tony can't afford handmade Italian shoes. I was tempted to buy a pair a few years back. They look good, but it tested my sense of good versus bad. A long time ago I chose Fairbanks because of its ruggedness and because of Pauline Dena. She works hard to make it a better place to live. It's not right to live off others and then to claim I'm helping Pauline. When I made that choice, I began to think about what I wanted Tony to learn. I'm proud of the choice I made, just as I'm proud of him."

* * *

Not far from Earlene's Beads, and near enough for Grandfather Kwaikit and me to light our ethereal bugs, Vindee Shoepack stared at her hands through the bathroom mirror. She had just removed the padding she used as a disguise and had pulled on skinny jeans and a tee shirt. A woman watched from behind, stopwatch in hand. A narrow box filled with envelopes rested on the narrow width of the vanity between the basin and the toilet.

"Ready! Set! Go!" The woman clicked the stopwatch.

Using her right hand, Vindee snapped each envelope into the sack that dangled over her left arm. Panting, she looked at the woman's reflection. Their eyes met—one pair a luminous deep shade of brown, the other a captivating blue.

"Twenty-three seconds," she repeated. "Good enough."

"Should we try for twenty?"

"No. Good work, Vindee. You've done it."

"Thank you."

~ *Are they going to rob a bank?* ~ Grandfather Kwaikit asked.

I shrugged with a flare of indigo and pink lights. ~ *She works for a bank, they don't seem like bank robbers to me. No weapons. They aren't talking about what they'll do after it's over, but rather how fast she's doing it. She's worried about one person noticing her.* ~

The older woman, meanwhile, lifted the small key dangling on the chain she looped around her neck like a noose. "Soon we shall find out how much his love was worth." How she came by the key afterward is another story.

Vindee decided to go for a walk after the exercise. Although it was almost seven in the evening, there was plenty of light left for a walk in balmy July. Vindee didn't like to walk at night, but Fairbanks was small and it was so light she didn't think of it as night. As their plans began unfolding, she found she needed a lot more hard physical exercise to keep bouts of fear away. Walking fast, Vindee found herself on the south side of the Chena River. Her mind followed a familiar path: her biological father. Who was he as a person? If he had been a decent man, he would have married her mother instead of using her and then leaving her without a word the way he did. A current of steely anger surged through Vindee, empowering her thoughts of revenge for everything he had done. Vindee turned on her rubberized heel and marched back home.

Grandfather Kwaikit had used one of his long distance, if somewhat weak, bugging devices on Vindee to spy on her for a while. Later, I wished I had kept the device in place for an hour or so more. It would have helped me understand somewhat better.

* * *

Upstairs in the bead shop, Deloo sat beside her mother, watching the smooth tan fingers ride the keyboard while Taale made almost invisible keystrokes. After asking for the first ten or twelve numbers from Earlene's sheet, Taale seemed to find some hidden logic in her own mind, and no longer asked. In a while Deloo got up to stretch. I, wilting with nothing to do, followed. On our way downstairs, I perked up. I added the essence of coffee to my rich chocolate colored aura. Between the caffeine and a resonance of cream color topping off my attire, I could see I was the most glamorous spirit for miles. I added a hint of gold to the remarkable, if fake, teeth I set on top of the creamy aura. Why should teeth be hidden inside a mouth, anyway?

Deloo brought a cup of coffee to Taale, who jerked and planted a thin smile on her lips. "Baby, I'm just getting somewhere here. I need quiet to get at Earlene's diary." She brightened. "By the way, have you called all the beaders and skin sewers who left their stuff on display?"

"Ugh! Sort of. Half of them don't have phones, or else they didn't give them to Earlene. I've sent notes to all those who don't have a telephone number. That's almost half of the inventory. The others are like: Ms. Snow Lin Mountain, Central, Alaska 99730. Central must be so small they don't need numbered boxes."

"It's hard to get to Central. We'll have that one for a while." Taale tipped her head to the side and asked, "Do you mean you've done all you can do downstairs? I thought I saw piles of stuff."

"You did. I should go somewhere to get cardboard boxes for the individual skin sewer's things. We're out of them here. That way their stuff can get mailed out easier."

"Great idea." Taale smiled.

Deloo said, "I need a computer anyway for homework. Lizzie won't be here until late afternoon. Could I borrow your car for an hour or two? It's time to get serious about school."

Taale made sure everything was locked after her daughter left and went back upstairs. I, the perniciously snoopy Baasee', asked Zephyr to keep me posted on what Taale was uncovering.

An hour later, back in Earlene's Beads, Deloo and I, Baasee' the Computer Illiterate, had fun setting up her new computer. Even though my young mortal was a right-brained artist and I, the older, pre-dated the invention of the wheel, each of us had a special way of understanding how it worked. On a tea break, Taale watched Deloo's versatility and called her Amazing Grace.

"What do you mean by Amazing Grace, Mom? The church hymn?"

"Rear Admiral Grace Hopper was one of the first computer whizzes in the United States back during World War II. She's my hero."

"Never heard of her. Just you, Mom. And now Earlene. She's got a big text file I can't open. It's got a separate password from the rest of her stuff. Can you open it?"

"Let me take a quick peak." Taale's fingers jigged on the keyboard for a few minutes. "That's Earlene for you. Hmmm. It's got at least twenty alpha characters and what might be numerals or punctuation marks. Try a few obvious combinations in Gwich'in or Denaakk'e. If that doesn't work, I'll give it a shot."

Feeling stupid, Deloo looked for the Gwich'in Junior Dictionary, which she found tucked under a bag of green beads along with a couple of booklets with Denaakk'e titles in them.

"Whatcha' doin'?" Lizzie asked from the doorway. She'd just bounded off the bus from campus and smelled of books and university-wired mental activity.

"I'm not doing well at picking Earlene's password," Deloo smiled as she showed her friend the new computer. "At least we can start typing lists and labels."

Lizzie looked at the long list of password ideas Deloo had written out and crossed off. "Earlene was Gwich'in and spoke Gwich'in to the old folks from up that way, but she spent a lot more time with you and Great Aunt Pauline. Why not try some Denaakk'e words?"

"Here! You give it a try. I need a break." Deloo went to the kitchenette and asked "Want some tea or coffee?"

Lizzie, already glued to the computer screen, responded, "Sure. Lots of sugar."

While she screeched the same question at her mother and then puttered over tea bags, I flowed around the lower level of Earlene's Beads. It looked better than it had three days ago, but I was puzzled about the gentle gem vibe that emanated from all surfaces.

~ *Maybe it's because she dealt in stolen gems for over twenty years,* ~ my grandfather communed from behind me.

I produced my best imitation of jarring shock waves and snarled at him, ~ *Could you please warn a girl when you're going to be behind her?* ~

Grandfather Kwaikit remarked, ~ *You should be adept at sensing my rugged presence at all times, as you once did thousands of years ago. Once, I might point out, does not make you an expert at detection.* ~

Ignoring his snide remark, I challenged him with ~ *Do you sense it, Grandfather? Am I wrong? I detect the presence of pure sapphire and my favorite, ancient emeralds.* ~

~ *I have since I did that First Walk of Death prayer a few days ago. I don't believe Miss Earlene herself dealt in buying and selling gemstones. However, I do feel the ricocheted impact of excellent and valuable stone cutting in this shop.* ~

I pitched our version of a nod his way and added, ~ *I agree, someone used this place as a significant workshop for disguising stolen gems. The thing is, it seems to be stronger over here where they've still got a lot of work to do.* ~ I referred to the heap of beads Deloo and Lizzie had created on one of the display cases.

Grandfather Kwaikit jabbed at numerous spots on the pile and agreed with me. ~ *That big jar or jug seems to be a key source. Could you ask your tiny mortal to take it out of here so we can check it later?* ~

At that very moment Deloo marched away from the kitchen area with a tray laden with teas and cookies. She removed the smaller plate from the tray and carried it upstairs to her mother.

I, Baasee' had some ideas for things they needed and told Deloo. She agreed and replied, ~ *I'll do that in a few minutes. Thanks for the idea.* ~

While Deloo made herself useful, Grandfather and I made some plans and parted company. We performed the usual bob and curtsies of good-bye our kind used, and he disappeared.

In a few minutes Taale was in another area of Earlene's computer, the one with password protection required many more skills to get into its electronic diary. Earlene's methods of storing the pages followed Earlene's beading rules, meaning they were patterned but not necessarily sequential. Taale put them in an order that would make sense later, making document folders labeled: "Bead Shop Business," "Personal," and "Private." By the time Deloo returned two hours later Taale had created hundreds of files with dated file names, such as 2013 May 01. Then it dawned on her the earliest of the folders she named was 2013, while the shop itself had been open since the late nineties. Earlene kept paper copies of tax files and some backup data for five years in a single file drawer. She'd gone paperless well before that. It was something Earlene had insisted Taale do as well.

Zephyr told me Taale agreed with Earlene, especially when their professors had taught them simple tricks. Taale, prying into secret places on Earlene's hard drive, saw Earlene had pushed the walls out of those lessons and invented many tricks that astounded Taale.

Taale was just about to read one of the files when Deloo asked for something more complicated to do. After five minutes of coaching through the obvious methods of getting into the text file that held what she thought might be ordinary diary entries, Taale saw comprehension dawn on her college-ready daughter's face. The effort was more than Deloo expected, but at least it was better than trying to find phone numbers for elusive beaders. After a few minutes of trying, Deloo succeeded in opening a file and started reading.

June 1, 2001
Dear Taale:
    I wish I had the guts to talk to you in person. I guess Pauline is right: there is something to Historic Trauma. It hurts to be a victim of the White Man, but here I am. God knows, he is a great looking man, white or native. I thought I loved him until today. He's worse than the guy you had—the one who didn't want your cute Deloo. Worse, it hurts to think these very words: I am a victim. His victim. He got what he wanted: seeing my open wounds after he pounded on me until I bled. Pauline says

if I ever get to the stage of saying these words out loud, especially to him, I'll be healing.

The summer when I was seventeen I was feeling sort of grown up, sort of not. After all, my brothers drowned just a couple of years earlier. That hit me hard, but since they were older than me, I didn't know them all that well. Losing Mom and Dad the next year wiped me out.

You and I graduated high school that spring, and we both thought we'd be going to university at UAF in the fall. One day I went to the campus to get a feel for it, and met this handsome guy. One thing led to another and he asked me to dinner. I thought that was all right. We went to one of those expensive places. Afterward we sat outside on a rickety box. BeeZee bent over to kiss me and I tried to dodge him. He ended up falling sideways and some loose boards fell over. That's when I noticed a big hole in the wall of the "addition." It was a false wall hiding the broken down fireplace. Someone had boarded up the spot where it used to connect to the house. I wondered what was in there, but didn't get a chance, because BeeZee put it all back together so fast. Well, he left a few minutes later after kissing me for real. I haven't looked for the hole since that night.

Deloo needed a breath of calming air to think about the kind of hidden violence Earlene faced, stepped outside. In no more than ten strides, her pace had quickened into a mindless march. When she reached a larger street, she stopped. I, Baasee' the ever-so careful, forced her to take a deep breath when I got an incoming spirit guide message: ~ *Deloo should be aware of someone passing.* ~ I forced my speed-demon mortal to look both ways, and we saw her: a brown-haired woman.

"She looks familiar," Deloo muttered, "but around here, who doesn't?" Deloo shrugged impatient shoulders and turned back toward Earlene's Beads. Sitting at her new computer downstairs in the shop, Deloo read the first entry she could find.

CHAPTER 18

Day Four, Thursday afternoon

The next entry turned out to be dated June 4, 2005. Deloo would have been ten and Vindee, eleven. Deloo sighed, wondering if it would help to put them into normal date order.

While ever so tempted to take a short nap in the ether above my mortal, I, Baasee' the Practical, kept my position near Deloo's head and eyes. A lock of her normally straight dark hair fell across my view. What was I to do except pop up to the area above her head and fluff it a little to make a stable perch. Feeling a bit frazzled, I plumped it up with bits of turquoise and cinnamon lights. The lights beckoned me. Okay, I found myself making a glowing bed only the imprudent would leave untested. So I did… fall asleep.

I awoke when Deloo snorted "Black eye? I can't stand that freak! He's a non-man."

Toppling off the turquoise and cinnamon cushions, I squinted at the computer screen to see for myself.

> Dear Taale:
>
> It was good to talk a little bit about BeeZee, even if I froze up about the black eye. Yes. It was BeeZee again. Just like last time, he hit me without warning and charged out of the shop.
>
> He's crazier than me. He's just crazy in a different way.
>
> I think I know what triggered it. He counted out the cash for the jacket. I picked it up and started to sort the bills by turning them all face up and turned to the left. He had them all rumpled and upside down. I looked up to joke with him and saw his fist coming at me. I think he was aiming at my jaw and hit me on the side of the head. The doctor said another centimeter to the right and I would be blind or dead. He wanted me to file charges.
>
> Pauline came in. She's psychic. We all know it. Her usual day to come in to help me with bookkeeping is Monday at 9 AM, but she called to say she'd come the next day. She said she knew she was supposed to come on Tuesday, anyway.
>
> He hit me on Tuesday at 10 AM. She was here at 10:15, just after he left. She must have seen him. She told me she saw someone peel out in a grey car.

I'm ashamed. If she hadn't come in, I wouldn't have done anything. She took me to Chief Andrew Isaac. I couldn't see to walk or talk. Pauline took me home and said something about me not being ready. "Call when you are ready to talk."

Did she send you over? It all happened so quick I didn't have time to put anything away. Pauline must have done it. I found the cash in the register. All the bills faced up and to the left. She taught me to do that.

Someday I'll tell you everything. He'll get that jacket in November, just like the others.

Deloo got up and paced. "Typical! That's almost classic behavior for people who are victims of wife-beating. Even Great Aunt Pauline was acting the stereotypical passive role. They should have got counseling to learn to report and then avoid a brute like BeeZee!"

~ Yes, my little wolverine. Just remember this BeeZee has a simple set of rules to follow. First, someone is always stronger than the next one, and second, be the stronger or else die. So far he hasn't died, and maybe he's got enough intelligence to know when he's dealing with a stronger person than he is. That's the basic formula aggressive carnivores have used for eternity. Having observed your great aunt Pauline for a couple of decades, as you will know someday, she was not acting out a passive role. She's very intolerant of weak behavior, and savvy about stronger types. Instead, she has simply understood that as a small woman, her best chance of survival is to use a variety of techniques. She sizes people up in seconds, and is usually correct. She is a typical wolverine mother. If she had seen him hit Earlene, you can be sure she'd have done far more than report it to the police. Yes, you are angry, but you have to let your mother sleep another hour or so. We'll talk about it later. ~

Deloo flopped back in the rolling office chair and looked again at the next entry and automatically figured she had been eleven and Vindee, twelve, a habit she developed years earlier at birthday parties.

November 26, 2006
Dear Taale:

Do you remember last week when I asked you to bring BeeZee's jacket by the twenty-third? That was a Saturday. You brought it on time and in a box with all the trimmings: the lining was pressed and you put tissue paper around all. BeeZee waltzed in on Monday without calling me ahead of time. He was grinning, walking jaunty, and looking good enough to eat right in front of my beadwork class. Those feelings of sexual desire for a man who tried to beat me to death last June rocked me to my core with shame and yet—almost a sense of wellness. I didn't know I could still feel sexy. Suddenly I knew where I had been in accepting death. That wasn't me anymore. At last. I pulled myself together. I felt myself contorting my mouth into a grin. And power over my fear. Maybe this time it would last. I handed him his box. "Here you are, sir."

He makes as if to open the box but instead reached for my neck and pulled me close. He kissed me right in front of all those beaders!

"If that was a tip for good service, I do not accept it!" I lashed out at him and then pushed him to the door. It was cold that day. Remember? I let him out and turned to close the door on him. He yanked me back outside and said, "I need to talk to you." He closed the door and put his arm around me while I shivered.

"I had problems with the bank today," he tipped his head toward town. "They closed earlier than usual."

"Too bad," I managed to squirm out of his grip. "This is a bead shop, not a bank. I can't help you."

As if I hadn't uttered a sound, he dashed back to his car to pull out a small safe. It was made of solid metal and had a lock on it. "Please, Baby, could you keep track of this for me?" Boy did I get a bad feeling from that box. I shook my head, but before I could say no, he pressed a finger against my lips. "I'll make it worth your while. Say, five hundred a month, including this one? I'll be back in June. That's four thousand bucks for you." He looked into the shop. The single heat source was an oil Monitor.

Pauline had talked to me about how important it was to keep up with the bills. I could use the extra money. "Well," I said.

"Deal!" He pulled out his wallet and peeled out four thousand in one hundred dollar bills.

Without thinking, I put out my hand. He gave them to me and carried the box inside and said "I'll just put it right here." There was a loose panel on the wall enclosing the old fireplace. He moved the panel and shoved in his safe. I'm almost a foot shorter than him, so he bent over to whisper into my ear, "I'll know if you've moved it even one-quarter of an inch." He pretended to kiss my ear and marched out of the store as quick as could be. I had to spend the next two hours listening to every prying question the beaders could think of. One good thing about it is they were my best customers. They were there because they were Gwich'in and knew my family.

Vindee and I will see you and little Deloo on Thanksgiving. If I am brave enough, I will tell you what happened instead of writing it in secret as usual. After all, those beaders of mine all saw him. They saw where he shoved the box. I should show you as well.

P.S. dated November 29, 2006

I just couldn't tell you after all. Sorry, Taale, my friend. I screwed up my courage to tell your aunt Pauline. She told me I will tell you when the time is right. She has more hope for my power over this trauma business than I do.

* * *

Taale found herself once again admiring the beauty of Earlene's code when a ding signaling an incoming call shocked her back to the planet. She accepted the call without looking.

"Holy cow!" she moaned. She'd tried to find a way to write a certain piece of code without her usual clumsiness—and failed. There it was in front of her. Trust Earlene to make it so easy.

Someone chuckled into her ear. "I'd rather be called a holy bull, but I'll settle for reverence in any form. Are you in the shop, Miss Dena?"

"Oh!" Taale's heart, already racing with Earlene's magical computer tricks, pounded too fast for a woman her age. "Yes. Are you outside?"

"Not yet. Jack and I were just about to walk over." Detective Harper lowered his voice. "Or I could come over alone, if you need my, ahem, help." He purred.

Taale pictured slamming an old-fashioned phone into a floor. At the same time, she felt a deep desire to have a sexy dimple like Deloo's. She snapped, "I'd rather see both of you."

Behind him, Jack peered at his associate. "Forgotten your wife already?"

Detective Harper swung around, his face showing a parade of feelings ranging from surprise, anger, and grief. "Never. We were married

almost sixteen years. When she died five years ago I promised her I
would not live in a hole. She was gone four months after being diag-
nosed with cervical cancer. It all came to a head when my patrol partner
had a long talk with me last year. He noticed changes in me I couldn't
see. He said I seemed out of it all the time. Somewhere else. He told me
I should look for a change."

"I'm sorry I brought it up," Jack clucked his tongue.

"Yes," Detective Harper shrugged. "It was time, so then I took a position to investigate international stolen goods. I am good at it, but I like
to arrest perpetrators, especially the violent ones. I asked for more, and
that brought me here to the land of ice and snow."

The two men stared at each other. Finally Jack smiled, "We've got
our share of the cold stuff all right." They walked to Earlene's Beads.

Even as the two detectives approached Earlene's Beads, Deloo was
attacking her new computer. Shortly, she was reading another entry in
Earlene's diary. What she read made her want to check all the doors.
The first entry she read happened shortly after she married Arthur a
year ago, almost a decade after the one she'd founder earlier.

> June 15, 2014.
>
> I started to close the shop on Monday. I watched a taxi pull
> up. It was BeeZee. I had time to run into the bathroom. By the
> time he knocked on the store's front door I recovered from my
> initial terror. I made a quick dusting of flowery-smelling bath
> powder to mask the fear-laden sweat gushing through every
> pore on my body. It was hard to draw in breaths big enough, and
> then to force myself to saunter to the door.
>
> I asked him, "Why in thunder are you here this time?" I let
> him into the shop, and glanced at his bright blue eyes, remem-
> bering the days when I kissed him and could use my hands to
> inspect him, searching for weapons. Over time, we stopped
> touching. He seemed to have a dark, evil secret. In those ear-
> ly days I would play along whenever he acted a certain way
> to give myself a few minutes to calm down. In my Gwich'in
> Athabascan language we'd say he was *ninjigwaazh'ii.* Shitsuu
> said it meant he's sly. Shitsuu isn't here anymore. She would
> have told me what to do. I asked Pauline if she knew a word like
> that in Denaakk'e Athabascan. She said the closest she knew

was *bedzaay ts'otlaage,* meaning he was cruel and dishonest. I liked her word better than mine. It's closer to what I sense about him. That's why I call him BeeZee. It's short for *bedzaay.* He thought it was a love name. Ha!

This time BeeZee said, "All I came over for was my car."

In the early days I would have made him a big meal, and then I would add a powerful sleeping powder to his drink. When I did he slept hard until the next morning. That was then. This time I wanted him to get out of my store and my house, but he wouldn't leave. Even though he said he just wanted to get his car, he didn't go. He lounged at the beaders' classroom table. It was obvious he was waiting for a free meal like I used to make years ago. I didn't move. I was sitting in the chair beside the stove. His eyes drifted toward me. Once upon a time I would have teased BeeZee about the last time he took me out to dinner. When was that? Twenty years ago? I shouted in my head: Can't you get the hint? Go away! Instead, BeeZee stayed.

Then he came out with it. "I looked for you on Sunday. You weren't here. What were you doing?"

Girlfriend, I have read the phrase 'sheer terror' in lots of horror stories. I had no idea what it meant before, but I knew I was feeling it. It was as if an ogre had pitched a bolt of something clear and hard and very cold straight through my chest. I stopped breathing because the thing hurt so hard. Yet, I felt clear about everything, almost as if I had already died. It gave me a new perspective on my life. I saw his fist clenching again and again.

I refused to speak. BeeZee got up and gazed out my window. I think he was looking for witnesses. BeeZee's face was turned away from mine. Otherwise I wouldn't have seen it coming. As it was, I saw his neck muscles bulge. I had time to slide out of my seat and back away from him. I had a cast iron frying pan in my hand when his fist struck the wood. I heard the wood crack. Or maybe it was a bone in his hand. I lifted the frying pan in warning. He blinked first, stared at his balled up hand and let it drop to his side. He said, "You don't have to tell me where you were now. But you will."

I stared at him, my heart pounding. I saw something glinting under his shirt—a key. Desperate for something to focus on, I trained my eyes on the key. I recognized it: a safe deposit key. I had one just like it. It was the one for the bank in town.

He turned and went to the back door for his car. As soon as he left, I checked the laptop. Still no funds on their side, and likewise, only two hundred thousand dollars left in his accounts. I took a deep breath and sent a message to the others. "He's here."

~ Time to look more at Earlene's diary entries. The big thing about her diaries is the thoughts behind her are filled with desperation, but your great aunt gave her a lot of hope. I feel it in every page. ~ Even as I, the ever-hopeful Baasee' communed those sentiments, I couldn't help feeling the desolation that permeated the store. That, combined with how frustratingly random Earlene's diary was, made both Deloo and I read on.

After reading the entry, I commune-urged Deloo to search the building. I floated spirit-style around her. Perhaps it was still here. Twenty minutes later, we knew with certainty the safe was no longer inside the shop, although I felt it had been there as late as last Thanksgiving season.

A few minutes later Deloo went in search of her mother. "Mom, there are lots more of them. I sent some to you just a few seconds ago. It's all about that woman, Fay."

Taale read the entries Deloo had found and gave her daughter a raw look before showing her the one she'd found. They both pulled together all the files they'd decoded so far. Taale said, "I'm confused about the dates. Earlene wrote she originally put them in a text file. We've found a part of them and maybe there are others we haven't seen yet." Taale's palms were sweaty. "She wrote this one just after your wedding. I got back from New Mexico on the third. Earlene asked me to cover the shop for a few days. I needed the money to pay back Aunt Pauline. That's all I was thinking. Now, reading this entry, I know I should have noticed something—but I didn't. He must have been here in this shop the day after I was here." Taale's voice rose to a rasping squeal.

CHAPTER 19

Day Four, Thursday morning

"That man is psychotic." Deloo wanted to shout at her mother while she walked downstairs to let in the detectives. While she let the detectives into the store, Deloo settled for communing to me, *~ Baasee', what would you do with a man like that? ~*

~ In my world, many people hoped the invaders would see how badly they behaved. I didn't. I saw how much damage they could do. I killed as many of them as I could. ~

Deloo straightened her shoulders, muttered, "I would, too."

~ That was fourteen thousand years ago. We humans have learned a lot since then about understanding both friends and enemies. You have to keep reading. Learning how other people think is important work, especially if they ever become your enemies. ~

The next entry was not as violent, and Deloo's breathing settled into a smoother routine, making the guy sound almost normal. Deloo wondered if her late husband might have become violent with her. Having known him a scant seven months, she wondered if she ever knew him at all.

~ That's a good way to think, my girl. Arthur is now a memory, and you are mentally giving him permission to be something other than what you imagined he was. ~

Deloo nodded wisely. Jack and Frank were preoccupied with the files Taale gave them, so Deloo turned back to the screen, not surprised to see the entry was written a decade earlier than the last one, noting the use of the Gwich'in word, shitjaa, meaning my friend.

June 15, 2004
Shitjaa Taale:

BeeZee just left. He paid me for the jacket that you will make soon. I've stuck to the fifteen hundred dollars price for it. He never came back for the strongbox. Also, he didn't bother to flirt or assume he was welcome in my bed. I almost miss the sex, but I don't know what to do about the beatings except to run. Your aunt Pauline is helping.

You know she always shows up on Monday morning and sometimes when I'm depressed at other times. Then she says things like, "You're doing fine. You'll make it." When I hear the "you'll-make-it" part I know she's about to leave Earlene's Beads. I try to give her some proof. All I come up with is a smile. This time I handed her a hundred.

"He just paid me for the jacket in cash. The rest is for Taale," is all I could think of saying.

Pauline eyeballed me funny while she shoved it back toward me. "Keep it for her. She needs the money. She said she's building a trust fund for Deloo."

I snorted. "You mean a 'trust that she will make it on her own' fund!"

"Well, I know it's no more than two hundred dollars so far, but for me that's a fortune." Pauline's lips were white because she pursed them. Her face was brown.

I threw my arms around her and tucked the C note into her purse. "You need a trust fund for yourself."

"Wow!" Deloo glanced at her mother and the detectives. They were all busy with Taale's discoveries, so Deloo continued reading.

June 29, 2004
Dear Taale,

I'm so used to writing to you all my real thoughts, I forget you haven't seen any of this diary yet. You will soon enough. If I had courage, I would just send these pages to you. You know more about computers than I do. You'd figure out all of my codes. That Fay is scaring me. She calls me every Sunday at 9 AM now. She's a year or two older than Pauline. I guess their generation deals in morning visits. She's been harping on my going to BeeZee's/her house. She thinks, but doesn't know, that he goes to Fairbanks in June to order the next jacket from me. I guess that makes sense because he just paid me for the sixth one. She also thinks he goes to the University of Alaska department that lets him use lab space. I suppose he would need to do that. The catalogue says he's an Associate Research professor. I don't know if he ever teaches.

The main thing is, Fay keeps hounding me about spying on BeeZee's house this fall while he's in China. She must think I'd find out how much he's worth or else discover some fabulous wad of money. Hah! She doesn't even know if he still goes to China. I've told her no each week. But I have to admit I'm curious, too.

Taale made room for Jack and Frank at the kitchen counter and left them to read the diary entries she and Deloo had already printed. Deloo settled in her own small area beside the craft table to read the next file. Soon Frank was reading her screen with her.

"November 30, 2004" Deloo read the date of the next entry and did the math. She reported to herself that she was nine. Where was Vindee in all this subterfuge? Vindee would have been ten and an obvious choice to take on this spy work. Maybe.

Dear Taale:

I hope you'll go with me next month. Course, it would help if you knew I wanted you to come with me. I let Fay talk me into going to BeeZee's house. She sent me a copy of her key. Or maybe it's the original one she had. I'll make a copy and then send this one back to her. I'm a fool for saying yes. BeeZee will come after me and kill me if he figures I've been there. Fay has told me the story of how he figured out she had snooped in his bedroom when he was eight and left a stack of pennies on his dresser. He must have been doing it for a while and she didn't notice until then. So, that day she did laundry on Monday instead of Sunday as usual. He was at school. If it had been Sunday she would have left a pile of folded clothes on his bed. Since he was at school, she put them in his dresser instead. She said she didn't search, but come on! I would have searched Vindee's dresser. In this day and age little kids get into all kinds of trouble. Who wouldn't search?

Fay knocked over the pennies while she put the clothes away. She didn't know they were a surveillance trap. That night he saw she had put the pennies back in the wrong order.

He shouted at her "They were in order by year!" After that he locked his door with a padlock. She could have unscrewed it to get in, but didn't. His father died the following month. Sgt. Clerick was in the military. She was used to her husband being gone a lot and had long ago absorbed the fear of his dying in a faraway land. Her son had not. Things were never the same between BeeZee and his mother. She thinks it's because of the pennies. I agree.

I'm glad she never went into his bedroom again. I'm very unhappy she's sending me to do it. I won't let Vindee go with me. It's because of her eyes—just like his. He's unpredictable and I don't want to take a chance with her.

Deloo mouthed a silent prayer for Vindee. "Where are you? Did he find you after all?" She glanced at Frank. He nodded and signaled for her to move the screen to the next entry. Deloo wondered if they got it right. It's odd they took me instead of Vindee.

January 16, 2005

I chose today, a Sunday, for checking on BeeZee's house. For one thing, you and Deloo were available. There's no school for either you or Deloo and without Vindee's small hands and body to squirm into tight places, I needed your daughter, Deloo, to help. Aunt Pauline has agreed to watch Vindee and the shop for a few hours on that day. It's getting close to the big Doyon and Tanana Chiefs' Conference annual meetings and Sundays are usually the day beaders run out and make a quick dash to my shop, so I've been staying open seven days a week.

His car was gone, just as I expected. He'd picked up the jacket, the sixth one according to my records, just before Thanksgiving. I know he leaves right after getting the jacket. I followed him once with Pauline. He doesn't know her car. I was with her at her place with you on Thanksgiving. She followed me out as usual when I was leaving and I spotted him. He was in the backseat of a taxi.

"That's him," I whispered, as if he could hear me.

"Let's go, then," she snarled in my ear. "Hurry. We'll catch up with him at Airport Way."

I didn't argue. We got into her little old Toyota and headed south. Sure enough, we caught up to him at Airport Way. He turned right. Pauline waited for another car to pull in behind him and turned herself.

"There's two possibilities here," Pauline said. "Either he's going shopping at Fred Meyer or he's leaving town. He'll never guess it's you. He doesn't know me."

His cab sped along toward the main airport on the north side of the runway rather than the little airlines on the south. Pauline pulled into the parking lot across from the airport. I'm glad I live in little Fairbanks, where we still have small, outside parking at the airport.

"There he goes," I pointed at him heading into a door at the far right end of the building. "Looks like there's an Alaska Airlines flight heading out pretty soon."

"Where do you suppose he's going?"

"Bellingham," I answered without thinking and regretted it.

"Bellingham? Never heard of it. Where's that?" Pauline asked.

One thing led to another and I ended up telling your aunt Pauline everything I knew about him, Fay and how I got to Bellingham. By the time I finished I was sobbing and my throat was so thick I couldn't talk anymore. She held me in her arms until I was finished crying. Pretty soon I felt so calm I seemed to doze off.

"So when are you going to pull it off?" Pauline asked.

I must have slept a little. I didn't know what she meant or where we were. "Pull it off?" I asked.

She pulled her arm out from behind me. "Wake up!" she commanded. "When are you going to do it?"

I got out of the car. It was Fairbanks in November and forty below zero. I got back in. She chuckled. "When?"

"I don't know. It's too soon. I can't. I don't want to do any of that," I shouted.

She waited until I stopped shaking and started making plans. She figured it out and told me we'd do it in January. I can't believe it. At least you all know everything. I was amazed you agreed with your aunt and that you took Deloo who turned out to be the best part of the plan.

Thanks, Deloo. Vindee would have done it with you. She'll be mad when she finds out about this.

I called Fay right afterward from Pauline's kitchen. I put it on speaker. You all heard it. She knew you were all there, even Deloo.

Just like Fay predicted, the house was almost empty at that

time of year. He couldn't possibly sleep there in such weather. I told them I thought there was another woman. That's when you rolled eyes sideways at your ten-year-old Deloo and smiled. I shut up.

Well, January came and you were there. You know what we got. Some keys and nothing else. You heard Fay tell me to send them to her. She'll see if she knows what it is. I'll send them to her tomorrow. I'd rather not have them any longer than necessary.

I don't like this. Not any of it. Girlfriend, why did you let your aunt talk you into it? Why did I? Of course I would and have done whatever Pauline asks. I always will. Same goes for you, too, Girlfriend. You've kept me going every day. Deloo is like a daughter to me. I changed her diapers as many times as I changed Vindee's. I should be listed as Deloo's official co-mother, even though I've got one of my own.

Deloo re-read the passage to make sure she understood it. Great Aunt Pauline had been in on it all the time. "I thought we were keeping it a secret from her," she said to Frank.

~ *Your Great Aunt Pauline is very savvy, Deloo. That's how she got to own so many houses in a prime downtown area of Fairbanks.* ~

February 15, 2005

Girlfriend: It's been such a long time since I've written in this diary I almost forgot the password. Besides, after we broke into BeeZee's house last month, it's been easier for me to talk to you and Pauline. Pauline points to her chart on Historic Trauma, showing me where I'm at in it. Now that I've taken action about BeeZee, she says I'm doing better in other areas. Thanks to her, my bead shop always makes money, but now I'm making enough to put money away for Vindee's college fund.

I'm almost thirty and got past a lot of things thanks to you and Pauline, it's easier to understand. Most everyone has a lot of trauma, but Pauline keeps harping on Historic Trauma as being different. She tells me I don't know how much pain my mother kept in her muscles and bones. She shows me photos of her. Yeah! I see me in those pictures now. I've got that same timid half-smile. It's in every picture I've got of Mom and every photo Pauline has of me. I'm rich in other ways: family. Pauline isn't a blood relative, but she insists I'm her daughter, just like you are. And you are not a daughter, but a niece. Ha-ha! I get it. Family. They are there to help no matter what.

Like when the front door froze up last November, Pauline sent over the boys, and they had it fixed up good as new in a day. Pauline told me to give them a hundred apiece, and I did. Since then she's been going over my books to see if I might qualify for a loan. She says I should put in an addition and move the beds upstairs. There's no place to put them downstairs. I've tried partitions, but they looked crummy. Ever since BeeZee beat me up a while back, I've got lots of regulars who come it every day for tea, beads and gossip. There's a Tuesday morning group and another on Thursday afternoon. Most of the time I make a treat, but they've asked me to order donuts or other goodies, and they contribute some cash. Now I need more chairs.

With all that, the beds are a problem. That's why Pauline is getting me to arrange for a loan. She'll do all the work to get it done. She's already planning on getting the boys to work on it. We'll be all ready by April 15 to lift the roof. It gets above thirty by then during the day. Kids think thirty in Fairbanks is warm enough for shorts. Not me. There might be a few cold days, but Vindee and I have slept at your place a lot of times when it gets that cold.

Frank looked bored as Deloo breezed through the sentimental parts, and even faster through the sections on house repair, muttering to herself. "Did Vindee stay with her Outside grandmother? I know she likes her grandmother, but I thought she wanted to come back and do a master's degree here in Fairbanks."

~ *That's what she said,* ~ I chimed in, ~ *just remember she's still young and pretty. There's bound to be a young man in her life, just as there are in yours.* ~

Deloo's lively face registered at least ten emotions in the space of five seconds, finally stopping at a big knowing grin. ~ *Yeah! You're right Baasee'. Neither of us dated in high school. I did group dates and Vindee never went anywhere.* ~ "I haven't paid much attention since she took off for college in the city her grandmother lives. Bellingham. A couple of years ago when she came home for Christmas, she had her hair done up because of that guy, I've forgotten his name."

CHAPTER 20

Day Four, Thursday
~ *Jasper Renard. He's a student at UAF here.* ~

"Yeah! That's the one. He couldn't take his eyes off her at Pauline's Christmas party." Deloo sighed. "That was a year before I met Arthur. Arthur would have liked Jasper."

Beside her Frank grunted something 'your loss' and looked at Jack as if to beg him to take his place. Jack ignored him.

~ *Keep reading. This next is from much earlier than Mr. Renard's time.* ~

> June 1, 2005
> Dearest Taale:
>
> You're the angel who was sent here for me. Thank you for helping me close the roof, and arranging with Pauline to have someone stay the night to make sure no one tries to break in. It's a good thing you've got big relatives. Four break-ins since the middle of April. Sheesh!
>
> My Tuesday and Thursday girls have come through, too. Pauline's boys have had plenty of fruit and vegetables every day for six weeks. I'm the one who brings them donuts. It looks fabulous.
>
> Tonight is the first night I will sleep in my own bedroom. I've never had a bedroom all to myself.

"Gee whiz! I've had my own bedroom most of the time until I married Arthur. I never thought about Earlene or Vindee. Maybe that's why she isn't here anymore."

~ *Maybe. Her bedroom was here for a few years before she went to college, though.* ~

Deloo looked at the jumble behind her. Her painting equipment took up the place where Vindee's bed had been. "I remember her in here. She kept it neat all the time."

I recalled the days of Deloo in elementary school. Her room was always a mess.

~ *Vindee was a natural scholar. She got the highest marks in her schools every year. Her daily decisions were different from yours. For her, choosing not to go to college would have been outside of her thought patterns. You are different. You are choosing to go on in college because you now have a career in mind. I don't believe Vindee did that. ~*

Deloo tried to remember if she'd ever talked to Vindee about the future, and agreed. "Vindee was always carrying books around in high school. I usually forgot them. I'd better finish reading this stuff, or I'll never get back to my painting." Deloo thought longingly of her painting area.

June 19, 2005
Girlfriend!

BeeZee came over yesterday to order the next jacket. I've got your money for you. I'll give it to Pauline if I don't see you first.

He was impressed with all the shelving and display cases. He asked if I would consider adding a double carport if he would pay for half the construction. He wanted a place in town to park his car and have it plugged in once in a while over the winter. He offered fifty a month plus utilities and half the construction costs.

I said I'd have to confer with my friends.

This morning Pauline said "no" without even waiting for me to ask. Then a few minutes later she said she'd come up with a cost on the carport, and told me he could rent half. Without his support, there would be no carport this spring.

"Yike! That's a dangerous idea. I'm surprised Great Aunt Pauline ever let Earlene do it," Deloo looked at the ceiling where she imagined I dwelled. "Wasn't that a bad idea, Baasee'?"

Frank looked puzzled. Deloo said, "I mean, Frank."

I wished my spirit-guide powers would stay away from the memories I had. *~ Yes, my dear. He's a dangerous man, and someone has to stop him. In fact, that someone is you. ~*

"Ew!"

~ Keep reading. ~ I admonished Deloo with a breath of spirit-guide worry. You haven't found out what's going on with Earlene.

June 20, 2005

Pauline gave me an estimate of carport costs based on a couple of different features. The most expensive one would

Midnight Trauma

include an automatic three-way head bolt heater outlet. With it, we would both have different turn-on and turn-off times. That one and the next featured a privacy wall between the two vehicles. The least expensive version just had two 120-volt outlets. I could control them both from inside. There was no privacy wall and I liked the simple construction of it. Moreover, it cost two thousand dollars less than the next cheapest. I told her I like that the best, but since he was going to pay for some of it, he had the right to choose.

BeeZee came by that afternoon just when I had a bunch of people in the shop. He disappeared for a while. I know he didn't go upstairs, because the steps are visible from every corner of the lower level. I liked that. From behind me I could hear noises, but it was too busy to stop and check. The shop emptied and BeeZee appeared at my side.

"I like the cheapest carport," he announced. "What about you?"

"Me, too."

We shook, he left and I closed the shop. It had a remote control feature that allowed me to set the pass code as often as I wanted from anywhere within a hundred feet of the front or back doors. Dad would have been thrilled at that.

Remembering the strange noises I'd heard earlier, I checked every corner of both floors. I couldn't find anything.

I love you Taale. Good night, Girlfriend.

Deloo paused, stood and checked on her mother, who was equally busy. "Mom, I'm going to check out the carport. Be right back."

~ *I'll be right above your head.* ~ I smiled with spirit-guide contentment.

Frank joined her. They stepped outside and Deloo examined the wall. "This is what you noticed earlier in the week. He must have put up that easy-to-open wall or door when they were building the upper story and the carport."

They went inside and looked at the odd paneling they'd all seen earlier. "He had something in mind." Beside her Frank touched the wall. "Now we know what he was after. He must have taken the safe."

Deloo looked at the detective and responded, "He must have snuck back here sometime to get the safe, so why does he keep coming back?"

Frank looked at Deloo with unreadable eyes. "I hope we'll find out soon."

~ *Be careful, Deloo. He is a merciless man.* ~

Deloo shivered and nodded. "Merciless."

The next entry didn't improve Deloo's fears.

July 1, 2005

Dear Taale,

It's three in the morning. I woke up about an hour ago. There was a noise. I followed everyone's advice: butcher knife in hand, four other knives in these pants. I've lost a few pounds with all the remodeling, and I'll have to take the pants in. They're the ones with all these knife holders. I didn't find anything, but it feels as if someone is listening. It feels worse upstairs. I've checked every cranny of my bedroom. I've called Pauline. She told me to come over. She'll have the boys check it out in the morning.

You've got the greatest aunt in the world.

July 2, 2005

The boys did a thorough sweep of my bead shop. They found an odd board in the spare room. I looked at it, and told them, "It's upside down. Look at the grain." It was Pete who announced, "I'm the one who put in this wall. I would have mounted this section. I did some of the work myself. Someone else made this cut after I finished. See?"

We all saw it. Pauline came over about then. She studied the hole and said, "How can you be so sure?"

"It was the last one for this carport project. MySon (so called because he was the only boy in a family of five kids) was helping."

Pauline called MySon by phone and commanded him to get over there quick. In twenty minutes MySon confirmed Pete's statement. "It didn't have any extra cuts in it when we nailed it up. I held it while Pete did the nailing."

Pauline leaned hard against it. "Try it Pete." All of them tried it. It felt solid.

Pauline sighed, "I don't want to do it, but we'd better take it down." The boys argued. That would take two hours. They had already wasted enough time. After apologies, they clumped out-side, leaving me with Pauline.

"What do you want to do?" Great Aunt Pauline asked me.

After thinking hard, and suspecting BeeZee had something to do with it, I finally told her, "I'll be fine here." I hugged Pauline. "Thanks for coming today and for letting me stay with you last night."

Pauline left with a reluctant nod. "Call if you hear anything else. We both know who did this."

"That was a mistake," Frank said after they had come back into the shop. He looked sternly at Deloo and added, "Always call the police."

Deloo nodded mutely and turned back to the computer.

August 8, 2005

Okay, Taale! It's time to get serious about school. I haven't taken any courses at the university, ever. I need moral support. You've taken a lot of classes. Today I asked you to take a computer class with me. I showed you which one I needed. It was a general introduction to personal computers.

You compared your transcript to the catalog and said, "It won't do me any good for a degree, but I've never had a computer and don't know the least thing about them. Last course I took was in 1998 when Deloo was three. You haven't got a computer either and we'll need at least one. I can't afford to buy one right now. Can you?"

"Sure," I said. "Pauline says I have to do this for the business. I can buy one for you, too, if you'll help me with the homework. Don't you need as many courses as possible for a degree?"

Taale, you just laughed at me. "Girlfriend Earlene, you'll find out once you start the class. This is the kind that people like you need. It's a basic course to get you ready to work in an office or" she swept a hand around, "run your own business. As for me, I'm still not sure what I want to do when I grow up except I don't want to work in a local business place. I want to do something with computers, though. Programming might be what I want." She looked at the catalogue again.

Taale, standing beside Frank and reading over Deloo's shoulder, said "Yes, I remember. Pauline took me aside one day and explained that with all of her closest relatives dying so close together, Earlene needed time to get over grieving."

After wallowing in self-pity for a while, I pulled away. "She's always talking about Historic Trauma and explaining how I've had all the symptoms. I guess I must have worked my way out of some of it, because she's says I'm ready for this course."

You laughed again. "Or else it's her way of saying your first loan payment to her is coming due soon and you need a job. Come on, girlfriend. We can do this. We're winners now."

We both tried to laugh, but it didn't happen. "Will you need a babysitter for Deloo?"

"She should be good with Pauline. She's eleven. I'll check with Pauline to make sure. Otherwise, I've a cousin who might help out, too. What about Vindee?"

"Same as you. Pauline said she'd help." We both laughed then. Pauline is the greatest person in the world.

We figured out a time to sign up and did it. I paid for both of us since you don't have a computer yet. Hmmm. I'll be looking around for one. I'll find a cheap one for you. My treat, Girlfriend. I owe you!

Deloo chuckled. "I wondered how you got all those computers, Mom. You were too broke to buy rice, let alone a computer."

Remembering how Taale used to search in every corner of the house, including Deloo's room for fallen coins whenever she needed to buy something, I agreed but knew a little bit more, ~ *Your Great Aunt Pauline always knew in her mystical way who would be good at which job. You were good at painting and drawing and your mom was good at figuring things out on a little machine. Your great aunt is clairvoyant. That means she can get pictures of what people do, even if there's no word for it. She didn't have a concept for computer when Taale was born. She always knew about coloring books, though. She knew you would make that way pay off, and you have. ~*

Deloo looked at the canvas waiting for her to start in again. Deloo went back to the diary.

August 12, 2005

Dear Taale:

I'm typing this on your new TRS 80. New to me, five years old in real time. It's got word processing, a spreadsheet program and basic stuff like a PDF file maker. It's cheap enough to throw out at the end of the semester if you find a better one.

Happy computing!

CHAPTER 21

Day Four, afternoon

The detectives took the heap of printed entries, sharing sheets of paper between them. Detective Harper asked of one entry, "What does she mean by 'no funds on their side?' Whose side? What others?"

Taale shook her head and shrugged. "She wrote that BeeZee has blue eyes. Bruce Ziegler's eyes are hazel, meaning changeable, like Deloo's. Sometimes they're blue. Usually they're more brown or grey." She looked at Detective Cruikshank. "Do you remember him, Jack? He's about a decade older than you, but you might have seen him once in a while."

Jack nodded. "He's got a record, Taale."

"A record?" Deloo looked triumphant.

"A record for being in jail last winter. Anchorage. Looks like they might have sent him home on a family emergency. I'm checking into it."

~ Good work, my detective collaborator. You've put together some important clues. The police already reached that place ahead of you, and think they can cross off Bruce Ziegler. What they don't have is your specialized knowledge of the Native crafts Earlene keeps here. ~

With a brief nod, Deloo said aloud to Detective Cruikshank, "I'll look through Earlene's list of artists for other B.Z. combinations."

Taale chuckled. "It's a good thing most of our names are in English. The Z sound is common in Denaakk'e and in Gwich'in."

"Looks like I missed the worst kind of shopping spree," Lizzie said when she entered the shop. She glanced at the merchandise. "All boring stuff." Lizzie shook her head and said in a confidential tone to the two detectives, "If I went with her, we'd get the good stuff, like test tubes and a microscope."

Detective Harper smiled at Taale and said, "Thank you, ladies, for calling us over. We'll take these with us." He stuffed the printed sheets in a thick folder.

After they left, Deloo looked up at her mother with an edgy-expression. "Did you say there was a list of artists here, Mom? Could you send it down to this computer? It will be easier if we could attach them to the boxes. That way we'll see everything at once: artist name, items, and prices. Print them in huge letters so we can read them from ten feet away."

"I agree with making life easier, but there are a lot of files. Maybe fifty or so. I'll send you the whole thing. You can decide."

A few minutes later Deloo told Lizzie about the last entry. She mused, "A geek like Earlene wouldn't want to get behind on technology," Deloo mused. "This whole beading gig seems like a great cover for whatever she does with computers."

"What makes you think she's got a hidden cover," Taale asked. "What else have you found?"

I suggested to my mortal, ~ *It's you, my investigator Deloo, who has seen that bead store is in truth a cover for something else. Not the detectives. It's up to you and me, your invisible side-kick, to see what she hid from us. Maybe the shop itself is hiding something. There are many hidden crannies in here we've begun to see.* ~

~ *Thanks, Baasee'. That man is odd.* ~ To Taale she said, "I haven't found anything. I simply have a feeling."

Meanwhile Taale murmured, "Earlene is a genius," Taale sighed. "I've figured out her system, but haven't done much more. The bulk of her secret files are about the business. I'll forward those to your new computer."

Deloo nodded. I gave her hair a little tug. ~ *There's something about the beads themselves that Grandfather Kwaikit has told me to investigate. It would be useful to have you take a look as well. Something in or near the plastic jar of mixed beads is important.* ~

Later, Deloo and Lizzie looked around the bedroom. Deloo asked, "Mom, has Earlene written anything about this weirdo furniture?"

Taale laughed, glad of a reason to get out of the room where her friend's scarf had been tossed. She moved to Earlene's room and explained, "Not in so many words." Taale shoved her way into the room a little farther, "If you mean this, I've got one myself. You've used ours. It's called a platform lift." Taale removed a heavy cover from it. "She told me once she had been thinking of household hazards, and had put a lift in her bedroom in case of fire. She wanted me to do the same. I didn't have the three to five grand, and turned her down." She pointed to the electrical plate beside it. "Besides, you can't use electricity during a fire." Taale turned away and muttered, "She surprised me with one that operates when the power goes out. She said I'd earned it with all my help on computers."

Lizzie looked around the bedroom with greater interest. "I can see a bus stop from this window. Where's the platform lift?"

Taale showed them. With its beaded cover, it looked like it belonged to someone who treasured the smoky smells of moose hide and the look of hand sewn beading. "This room has two windows. She moved the head of the bed to the south window so she could see the morning sunshine coming through the eastern window. The platform lift is between the windows. See?"

"Wow!" Deloo flapped her arms and crowed like a *dotson* (Denaakk'e word for raven). She'd lifted the beaded cover to the platform lift and clambered into the contraption. "It's like ours, all right. See? It's floating down to the first floor." She waved a hand at the others. Lizzie dashed down the steps at the end of the short hallway. After talking about the merits and problems of the lift, Taale strolled back to Vindee's room, now a computer room. Taale faced the laptop and then turned to say, "I swear Earlene's ghost or something like it was here. It seemed to make sure I saw certain things in the computer. She helped me find entries about his violence, her fear of him, and how she… " Taale shook her head, "she tried to get information from him. Listen to this." She read part of a screen. "I'll print the entry for you. And since you're here, I want to see if there's still some sign of what he did to her downstairs."

While Taale returned to Earlene's computer and clicked a few keys, Zephyr shimmered to me, letting me know we needed to talk.

~ *What's up?* ~ I asked. Zephyr was one of an extinct bipedal primate who no longer had any of her own species to attend. Zephyr studied the mystic environs for a moment before communing. ~ *This,* ~ she pointed at the computer, ~ *is one of those moments Taale and I didn't see, but I was given a vision of it after the fact. I want you to see the vision, too.* ~

Zephyr did something to her metaphysical innards and suddenly a vision appeared to me. In it I saw a replication of Earlene moving quickly, splash whatever she'd been sipping at her assailant, and duck out of reach. It was obvious why Zephyr showed it to me. Earlene's thoughts were so hard they ricocheted across the room dozens of times, explaining why remnants of them shot out at Taale while she worked. This is what Earlene thought but didn't say aloud.

~ *I know you were going to do that someday. I wish I'd been drinking tea, the better to burn your racist hide. I hope you've broken a bone or two. With your ugly thoughts about Indians, those you mouth because I'm just a dumb Indian myself and therefore too dumb to understand you when you correct me about Indian history or culture. Look at you! Hah! You're nothing but a miserable non-man just like Pauline says.* ~

Zephyr and I mused about the echoes that still hung in Earlene's Beads. Then we heard the printer make noises and saw the others shuffle for first place in their hurry to get downstairs. Why had Taale never met BeeZee in all these years?

I caught Zephyr's ocular, and communed, ~ *I'm going to fill Deloo in about his racism later on. Thanks for sharing the vision.* ~

"Any idea how tall the man is?" Lizzie asked, referring to him punching the wall.

"If he's the guy who broke in here the other day, he's about six-foot-two," Deloo said, visualizing the drawing she'd given Detective Harper the other day.

~ *I agree. I've examined my own memories of that hotel in Nova Scotia.* ~

~ *You are awesome, Baasee'. Thank you.* ~ Deloo hopped out of her chair. "So, our guy is about as tall as Detective Harper. How tall was Earlene?" She looked at Taale.

Taale looked from Deloo to Lizzie. "Taller than either of you or me." Taale opened a kitchen cabinet. "There. See? She puts ordinary things, like water tumblers and such on the top shelf. I can't do that because I'm too short. I'm five-foot-four. Lizzie, you are a couple of inches taller. You try that shelf."

Lizzie tried reaching the top shelf. Her fingers touched the first tumbler. "I can reach it, but I'd never put glassware up there because I'd be afraid it would fall. She's either an inch or two taller than me or maybe her arms are longer. My arms are just below average. I hate buying long-sleeved things. They always hang over my fingers."

"Me too, but I'm shorter in every direction," Deloo said. "So, according to her diary, BeeZee hit the wall in this kitchen. He'd have been sitting where Lizzie was. He must have got up, taken a couple of steps toward the stove, and threw a punch, but missed Earlene." She looked at the wall. "His fist would have hit about a foot higher than Mom can reach."

They decided to call the detectives, who came back to the shop a half hour later.

After studying the printout, the pair examined the wall. Detective Harper aimed a fist at the wall. Deloo, who seemed to carry carpenter's tools everywhere, brought out her tape measure and put a small pencil mark where she guessed he might have struck. "See anything?"

"Yes!" Lizzie squealed. "There!" She pointed at a shallow depression in the wall.

~ That's it! She's nailed it. ~ I crowed from my spiritual perch.

"He hit hard enough to do irreparable damage to the wall. He must have held back a little, since he didn't have her in front of him," Detective Cruikshank said as he examined the dent.

Taale said to her daughter and Lizzie, "Ladies, if anyone tries to do something like this to you, don't waste any time. Go to the police. Earlene should have. We wouldn't be here in this room without her if she'd done so."

"Thank you, Ms. Dena," Detective Harper photographed the dent. "We'll call you if there's anything else."

Day Five, Friday

Ever the diligent spirit guide, I, Baasee' the simply beautiful, was busy with Deloo at Earlene's Beads. Grandfather Kwaikit appeared, notifying me he had pinpointed the younger counter's whereabouts. He was going to follow her for a while to the place she worked, a local bank. She left the house by seven in order to have time for a cup of coffee at a tiny shop near the bank a half hour before she was due at work. He watched the young woman make her way along a dusty street, careful to drop her shoulders slightly forward. The shift in balance and weight was enough to give her a slight stoop and the general air of being closer to fifty than twenty. Grandfather had studied the way men and women changed their foot placement on the earth as they aged, and was a good judge of how close they were to death. He was impressed, and told me in detail how Vindee did it.

~ She's no ordinary actress, Granddaughter. She started the walk by tripping along the sidewalk on the balls of her feet. With that gait, she moved faster, held her head higher, and looked the twenty-two year old she actually is. After five or six steps, she adjusted her foot-use by placing the entire foot on the ground at once and shortening her steps a little. I swear I could hear the hairs under her heavy wig turn white. ~

I grinned at Grandfather's wit and listened to his literal recitation of the rest of the subterfuge inside a small coffee shop.

Vindee smiled at the server, who cocked an inquiring head toward the donuts.

"Sure. I'll have a cruller." She was happy that getting the donut now included a cup of black coffee without having to ask. She always left a two dollar tip.

The woman set the hot mug and pastry on the counter in front of

Vindee. "You look nice today," she remarked while pointing to Vindee's silver necklace. "I like that design."

Vindee touched the necklace. "I like it, too. It reminds me of Abuela Consuela." A small smile played on her lips as Vindee caressed the silver chain. An elegant locket dangled from it. Vindee touched the locket's closure and a small key burst from it. Vindee tucked the key inside the locket and smiled at the server.

"Your abuela has good taste," the woman said with a satisfied nod. She measured her conquests in each personal tidbit she worked out of her customers. Needy herself, Vindee recognized the neediness in the server's questions on the first morning she'd walked into the diner. She also saw how she could make use of the server to increase her own knowledge about the comings and goings of her coworkers in the bank. As soon as she tried it, she recognized the knowing look in the other woman's eyes, and more. She recognized a deep mutuality for secrecy and self-protection in developing any form of relationship. She smiled. So did the server. It was an exchange both of them negotiated in tight circles. Neither of them wanted to give the other so much their game would end too soon. Vindee was certain they would work up to exchanging names with each other by summer's end—that is if Vindee hadn't already made other plans for the summer. She slapped a ten dollar bill on the counter and tipped her head toward the server. "See you."

"Yeah," answered the server. She tucked five dollars and five cents into her pocket as she watched the woman cross the parking lot to the bank. The colorful bag that rested along Vindee's back didn't go with the woman's outfit. The server wished she'd had the courage to joke about the mismatch, but figured they'd get to that stage soon enough. By the time she'd tidied away Vindee's mug and plate she had forgotten what it was that struck her so odd about the bag. Later that morning she remembered what it was: the Latina woman was not a handbag type. She liked to walk with both hands free, so she always kept a tiny coin purse in a pocket of her skirt or trousers.

CHAPTER 22

Day Five, Friday

Vindee, using identification and the name of a stranger who'd died long ago, applied at the bank on December twenty-first. It was the coldest day of the year as well as the official beginning of winter. They hired her, now Raelene Clark, as a substitute bank teller because of the paperwork. She claimed Raelene Clark had many years' experience of working in various banks. Raelene had a two-year college degree in accounting and looked respectable.

On the day she started work, she located the employee break room where, on her lunch break, she telephoned someone. No one else had been in the room when she entered, but by the time the other party answered the telephone in English, she sensed someone else was nearby. Switching to Spanish, and careful not to use any names, Raelene broke the connection as soon as possible and turned around to see who was there.

A uniformed woman who looked about fifty smiled back and introduced herself in Spanish as Juliana from Mexico. She was one of the security guards. Raelene Clark stared at the other woman in momentary fascination. Except for a reddish tinge to her black hair, Juliana was her mother's double. Without thinking, Raelene gushed in excitement to be meeting someone so much like her mother—and said so to Juliana. In mid-sentence she remembered the plan. No one at the bank was ever to meet or even see her mother. She forgot that part of the plan when Juliana told her to call her Juli.

Upset because she had broken a pledge, shocked at her unexpected feelings about losing a woman who in fact didn't exist, twin rivulets spurted from Raelene's eyes. "I mean, my de-de-departed mother," she sputtered in English. She allowed the tears to dribble down her cheeks, in awe of the sensation of grief that flooded through her body and sent chills along her arms.

Juli encircled Raelene with a comradely arm and said firmly, "She's still here, Mujer. She'll always be with you." Raelene gazed back at Juli, wondering if she had a newfound talent for acting. During the next several weeks they ate lunch together either in the employee break room or in the security monitor room. Juli told her no one was ever to be in that room unless they were security personnel. Raelene assured Juli she wanted to become a security guard one day, and asked if Juli could show her some of the things she would have to know. It was easy to get permission, since Juli's word was all they needed. Besides, Juli was eager to spend time with someone who knew how to talk real Spanish. Raelene knew the plan was working when Juli kept referring to one of the bank managers as a woman of their age. At first the genuine Vindee inside the Raelene disguise resented the comparison, then forced herself to relax and imitate the way her friend, Carmen, grunted at such remarks.

Thanks to Juli, Raelene had learned everything she needed to know about the security system by the end of March. By then it was time to move to the next phase of the plan. When an opening came up for a vault teller, she applied, and asked Juli for a letter of recommendation and got it. Raelene accepted the relatively short letter of recommendation that Juli handed her as a true certificate of graduation. The bank's branch manager selected her without question. She texted the others to announce it was time. The next phase began when she put her lunch bag into the bottom drawer of her new desk outside the bank's vault.

Each of the steps took time and patience. More than anything else, all of them required training Raelene did not have and couldn't get without Juli's help. Raelene wondered if they would ever succeed when over a week earlier she had caught a glance at her calendar and noted it was already May thirtieth. Her mother had planned everything for the end of June, and Raelene still hadn't finished the training sequence that would take her to the last step of Plan B. Besides studying the security system at the bank, Raelene also had to study the ebb and flow of the bank customers. Raelene was not surprised to learn that other parts of the bank could be busy while the vault remained largely unvisited. She also noted the branch manager prided himself on giving a personal tour to every important banking customer, showing them each part of the public areas of the bank along the way. His tour included the vault. Neither regular safety-deposit customers nor management's special clients ever came to the bank before eleven. Nor did other customers ever visit the vault so early.

Raelene began to put actualities together with Plan B. Thanks to Juli, she knew the security cameras were always concentrated on the bank's common area near the main entrance. Other security cameras covered the doors to the vault area, but were not displayed continuously in the security room. Juli had set up the timers that were programmed to scan the vault and other inactive public areas on an irregular rotation based on industry standards. Juli changed the rotations every Monday afternoon at two PM.

The upshot of all that was Raelene texted the others she would do it on Friday between exactly 10:12 AM and 10:18 AM. If she didn't get caught, she would be in the Plan B lobby before eleven-thirty.

The evening before, Raelene practiced using two padlocks, two nested cardboard boxes to simulate a safe deposit box and hundreds of empty envelopes as pretend money. She was ready.

"You have to do it as if every joint in your body was flowing in hot oil," her partner had admonished her every night for the past six months. "It has to feel as if you've done it all your life. Otherwise, you'll make a mistake and freeze."

"Yes," Raelene acknowledged. "Let's do it again." She flexed her fingers and reached for a jar of ointment. Their research deemed it best for lubricating muscles and stiff joints. At twenty-two, the woman pretending to be fifty-year-old Raelene had no stiff joints but her fingers weren't comfortable enough in making such fine motor movements. They would need to be oiled the next morning. "It's either ointment or get caught on camera and go to jail," Raelene muttered to herself and waited for the signal.

"On your mark, get ready, go."

That was just a few hours ago on Thursday evening. Raelene stared at the clock on the wall. It was time. The day and moment had arrived. Raelene felt a parade of chills along her spine and arms. She stood up at 10:11, touched the closure to the locket and palmed the safe deposit box key. Everything happened just as they had planned it. It took three minutes to open, empty and close the safe deposit box. She put the contents into the voluminous bag she'd brought without looking at it. All she knew was she had money and lots of it. She left a one dollar bill as an insult.

Thinking about the arrangements she'd made the day before to have someone from upstairs take over her position on the pretext she had a dental appointment, Raelene didn't think about the picture she presented with the now full bag dangling from her shoulder. Instead she focused on Plan B, ticking off each step in her mind as she completed them. In the plan, she was to be the only person in the vault once she completed the theft. Mary wasn't due for another few minutes.

She opened her bottom desk drawer, and inserted the heavy bag into the space she had emptied earlier. Loud footsteps clumped toward the vault. The branch manager approached with another man, who stood with his face toward the vaults. She guessed without interest the other person was a valued bank customer. Raelene reached under her desk top for the hidden buzzer.

"Thanks, Raelene," the branch manager murmured when he heard first the buzzer and then the loud click of the vault gate as it swung an inch or two inward. He held the low gate open for his customer, who walked by her desk without looking in Raelene's direction. She kept her eyes lowered which gave her an odd view of the customer. She liked his shoes. He pointed to the appropriate safe deposit box.

Raelene glanced at the man as he signed the log book. He looked a little familiar. As soon as she saw first his name scrawled upside down and then his face she emitted an involuntary gasp. At the sound both men turned to stare at her. Her heavy glasses perched on her nose. They looked huge and grey against her tanned skin and grey hair. She fumbled with a pen and ducked her head down without a word. After a pause, the branch manager led the customer to the vault, smiled unctuously, and lifted the box out of its space and handed it to the customer. "Will this cubicle do or do you need more privacy?"

The customer tipped his head toward the cubicle and replied, "This will be perfect."

Outside in the foyer the branch manager waited until the customer was out of earshot before speaking, "If he needs something, I'll be in my office, Raelene."

The middle-aged woman blushed. "Yes sir, although I may not be here either. I've called Mary to replace me," she continued, "I've got a dental appointment in a few minutes." They both turned toward the sound of high heels clacking on the hard floors. "Here she is now."

The bank customer waited until he was alone before placing the safe deposit box on the small counter in the cubicle. He opened the lid, pulled a plain wooden box from his satchel so he could put the contents inside it and away from prying eyes when he left the bank. Then he opened the lid of his safe deposit box to check for the contents. He stared at the face of George Washington on the single dollar bill that seemed to laugh at him. As if from a great height he saw his hands grab the tiny counter top. The eyes on the presidential face stamped on the bill flared up toward him. He remembered to take a deep breath and to let it out to the count of ten.

He removed the dollar bill and put it on the tiny counter beside the safe deposit box. He closed the lid of his smaller box, the one that would have held all of his five hundred thousand dollars. With his right hand, he slid the still empty inner box bank into his satchel. He knew he wasn't capable of walking without stumbling, so he waited until he regained his sense of balance.

In a couple of seconds he reached into a pocket and withdrew a folding knife with multiple blades. He slid open small scissors. Making sure he controlled his face, he cut the dollar bill into tiny strips. Each strip was precisely the same width as each of its mates. With the same precision he aligned the resulting strips in order, abutting each other on the cubicle's counter. After a long moment of staring at the demolished dollar, he closed the scissors and replaced the knife into his pocket. With exquisite care, he put the slices of the dollar one on top of the next. Then, holding the stack of dollar strips on the countertop with his right hand, he grasped the top of the stack with his left hand and twisted the stack with so much force that each slice of paper seemed to fuse to its fellows. He gripped it in both hands for a moment, fully conscious the force of the torque had heated the tiny bundle a little—enough to bond whatever glues were in the formula of ink in the dollar bill. The man dropped the bundle on the counter. While not as hot as Fahrenheit 451, the supposed flashpoint needed to burn paper, it was hot enough to force the strips to first, stick together and second, for the entire bundle to straighten out and lie flat in front of him.

Meanwhile, unaware he was about to destroy the dollar bill she had left for him, Vindee grabbed the bulky pouch from her desk drawer to make room for Mary, the clerk assigned to take her place. Raelene Clark walked out of the bank and adjusted a lightweight grey scarf loosely over her head looping one end over the other in a single fold. It was hot outside, and Raelene, now fading to Vindee as she strolled on the sidewalk, was glad of the minute shade the scarf offered. The heavy bag dragged on her shoulder but the adrenaline racing through her body didn't allow her to feel it.

Following Plan B, She walked toward the hotel a short distance away, passing through a parking lot full of cars, careful to avoid any vehicles with people inside. Finally reaching the double set of doors at the entrance, she waited with apparent calm as the automatic doors opened. There were cushioned chairs on both sides of the door. She moved right, following Plan B, and chose the grouping of three armless chairs they'd agreed on months earlier. She sat in the one on the right of center. In seconds another hotel guest, a woman wearing a light grey jacket over a skirt or dress that was nearly the same shade as that of Raelene/Vindee's, sat on the chair.

Without looking at the other woman, Vindee slipped the scarf off her head and let its silky fabric slide down her back and onto the chair. If anyone noticed the two women had identical haircuts and hair color, they never mentioned the fact to anyone else. The other woman, her attention focused on the gift shop across the way, removed her jacket and laid it on the chair between herself and Vindee. As it happened, the jacket covered Vindee's bag.

As if she hadn't seen what the other woman had done, Vindee reached over, picked up the jacket, stood up, and pressed her arms into its sleeves. As it had been nearly a year ago, the jacket was a little too big through the shoulders and long for Vindee's arm length. A year ago they agreed that simply bending her elbows a little would make the jacket seem to fit better.

Remembering that lesson, Vindee made her way through the hotel lobby, suddenly busy with tourists, each hustling toward whatever Alaskan delight they had in mind that day. None of them noticed the woman who remained on the chair pick up Vindee's scarf and adjusted it onto her own head. After a moment, she stood up, the handle of the heavy bag caused a slight shift in her gait as she maneuvered her way toward a side door. Each woman exited the hotel without ever glancing at the other.

Once on the sidewalk, Vindee dropped the age-act and walked swiftly toward her apartment a few blocks away. After she'd cleared the exterior entryway and then opened and entered her own apartment, she felt her legs start to shake. Safe at last, Vindee ripped off the brown wig and tossed it into a box. "Plan B is done!"

CHAPTER 23

Day Five, Friday

I suggested Deloo go back to reading more of Earlene's diary entries about the black eye. Although Deloo was stunned by what she saw, there still wasn't enough. "The police wouldn't be able to use this, at least not yet." Deloo saw the next entry was written six months earlier than the last, a week or two after Vindee and her own birthdays. I noticed that Deloo's stomach tightened to remember that birthday party. The two girls had rebelled against the idea of celebrating together, but neither of them wanted to go without cake, ice cream, and presents. Their two mothers had them pegged. I filled my little mortal with loving courage and urged her to read on.

April 12, 2010

Girlfriend! It's midnight. I can't believe what has just happened. His mother was in Fairbanks for the first time in years. I wrote about meeting in 2006. Remember? His mother is Fay Clerick. Must have been a gorgeous woman once with those big eyes and that curly hair. It's white, but I can tell she was a Marilyn-Monroe type with ash blond hair. She's old now. Her eyes are still bright blue. With all those wrinkles, the beauty of the shape has gone south. Seventy if she's a day. Skinny. Jittery way of talking. Everything comes out in spurts. It's hard to listen to her.

So, we've known each other for four years. On the day we met, I suggested going over to the bead shop. It was after hours and I felt weird about having her in my business and home. She wandered around the shop, collected a half dozen items, and I rang them up with the family discount when I noticed she chose stuff from Little Tanana: two pairs of moccasins in ladies sizes, a child's vest, a model dogsled, and a couple of pairs of earrings. Combined with the turquoise necklace she grabbed at the end, it added up to four hundred dollars even with the discount. I boxed everything up and handed her six clumsy bags. Her purse was too small to hold any of it, so I stuffed it all into one large sack. I almost felt sorry for her. It was one of yours, Taale. A cute caribou hide that you sewed, but it didn't go until a year later.

She called to leave me with this zinger. She said they, including my Vindee, saw him in Bellingham. He's got a house in Bellingham. They spotted him in a Bellingham department store last summer. He accidentally tripped. Vindee was walking ahead of him, although at the time she didn't know him. She saw three older boys jump him. They picked his pocket. Vindee was close enough to reach him. About then a security guard came up and the boys ran away. Not Vindee. She helped BeeZee up and spotted his wallet a few steps away. She reached it just ahead of the security guard. It was open and she glanced at it before handing it over to the guard.

"Are you Mr. Clerick?" The security guard asked.

The man on the floor nodded, made his way to a stand and the guard handed the wallet back to him without a word.

Vindee didn't wait for BeeZee to talk. She followed Fay and her mother out of the door and they raced to the car. Fay wondered if her son even noticed Vindee. She's sort of skinny and with her thick glasses on you can't see how big and blue her eyes are—just like his. She guessed he was not suspicious. When he's around me, he usually is. I've never let him see Vindee in the shop here in Fairbanks or anywhere else.

The thing is, Taale, they checked BeeZee's house out when they knew he wasn't around. Once they were all in the car Vindee barked, "It's my father! He's got a house on Harris Avenue." She recited the address. They checked it out.

Sure enough, Fay said he's ten or twelve blocks away from Fay's house. His house is in a rich middle-class neighborhood in Fairhaven, totally unlike Fay's neighborhood. Fay lives in Sehome. That's where Fay grew up. Sehome is an old Salish neighborhood, but not very many Native Americans seem to live there.

You can't see her parents' house from where he lives, but he could spot her old family car whenever he's out and about. She laughed about the bird's egg blue of her car's hood. The rest of her car is tan. The hood was all she could afford to fix. She said BeeZee's house is in a higher priced neighborhood—worth at least a hundred grand more than hers is.

I wonder where he got all that money.

I asked, "Wait, Fay, why didn't he recognize his daughter?

She's got his eyes. My eyes." She reminded me about Vindee's glasses with thick lenses. Besides, we're sure he doesn't know about Vindee since he left Fairbanks before she was born.

Fay's visit has got me all riled up. I'm not sure about all this. I'm going to bed to think. Wish I could be with Pauline. She'd know what to do.

April 13, 2006

Dear Taale: Today Fay Clerick called. Her voice grates when she talks on the phone. High-pitched and wheezy. Maybe she used to smoke. She told me she'll gladly take Vindee for one month every summer. I know most of her willingness stems from the five hundred I gave her to cover my daughter's room and board for four weeks. Fay asked me when I expected to see BeeZee again. I said he paid me to keep a portable safe in my shop and told me he would see me in June to collect it. I'm guessing and hoping he will also pay me in advance for another jacket. Taale, I know, you've always depended on that extra money to make payments during the summer. I have just enough to pay you for the jacket and give the five hundred to Fay for taking on Vindee. Fay's clothes are all very old. My guess is once her folks died and their pensions ran out, she's been feeling a terrible pinch for money. My other guess is BeeZee doesn't help at all.

Fay then suggested we talk again in a week. I was real unhappy and said so. I don't have the energy for that voice for very long, but I didn't say a word about what she sounded like. She claimed to understand, although I didn't say why I didn't want to talk so soon. She is after all, just a person I met at a café and felt sorry for. Now I wonder if she's trying to take advantage of me.

Fay is so wimpy compared to Pauline. Pauline and she may have been toddlers at the same time, but everything about Pauline is like a Marine sergeant compared to Fay. Sheesh! Okay, I don't know any Marines, sergeants or not. Doesn't matter. Pauline is used to being the boss. Fay is not.

Fay offered to call me at any time I suggested. I agreed on May first at noon. I changed it to May third, as that would make it a Sunday. The bead shop is closed on Sundays.

If you were in my shoes right now, Girlfriend, what would you do?

* * *

Far to the north a solitary adult wolverine, enjoying the bleak half-light of a long Alaskan summer night, moved silently between some un-ripe blueberry bushes on his way toward one of the many rabbit trails nearby. While he followed his mother's wordless instructions about life in the boreal forest, he didn't bother to think about her. It was enough to cast about for her usual mental signal. They kept in touch that way, just as he did with his older and heavier father. It was common for wolverine adults, male and female, to hunt with their offspring in adjoining territories. Finding one, thus, suggested you'd be found soon enough by all of them.

* * *

A quick glance at the file named "text" showed Deloo a lot of documents had a variety of styles of labeling and file types, probably a result of changes in technology or Earlene's maturing knowledge of how to make sense of it. She gritted her teeth and plowed on. Deloo saw the next entry was written earlier than the one before. She had been nine when it was written and Vindee was ten. Deloo wondered why two girls so close in age with parents who were obviously best friends had never played much together outside of family gatherings.

I butted in at that point, since Deloo was new to this kind of guessing game, and with my thousands of years of spirit guiding, I had developed a few good techniques. ~ *Little One, the main reason is that you went to different schools in this small town, and since you were always in different grades, you each had your own sets of friends. Yours were mostly from your neighborhood of Little Tanana, while Vindee was in a school many blocks away. Also, she's always liked to read while you've always liked more active things to do. That's why you rarely got together outside of big family events.* ~

Deloo looked up, her eyebrows twisting. "I guess you're right, Baasee'."

~ *I know the topic of her entries depress you and keeps you from reading. Remember this is the life Earlene and her daughter lived, and she lived it because of a lot of dark events that went on in her parents' and grandparents' lives. You have as well. You have to find out if what happened to both Arthur last year and Floyd this year are linked to what suppressed the choices available to Earlene. Someone or something feels they are entitled to things that belong to others. That simple fact is at the root of Historic Trauma.* ~

"You're right, Baasee'. My Arthur must have had something to do with all of this. Everything seems to touch on his life as much as it did on Floyd's," Deloo murmured aloud. Her face relaxed into grim calmness, and she continued reading.

June 15, 2003

Girlfriend, I talk to you almost every day either on the phone or over at Pauline's house, but never with the openness I've heard you use with your aunt, the dream maker of Little Tanana. I don't know why I wrote "I talk," since I don't. I know I don't talk out loud much. In my head I'm quick and funny. In the real world I'm silent and shy. Not like you or Pauline. She's got more courage in one finger than I do anywhere. You do too.

Well, I smile and don't say anything to anyone, I haven't been writing to you like I should. Or think I should.

It's been two months of changes for me. I may not be saying much, but I'm making big changes in my life. For one thing, I've been telephoning Fay every Sunday since May third. I've got used to her whispery way of talking. I suppose that's as bad as my silence. She's sent a dozen photos of herself and Carmen. She sends them by text, not mail. It feels like I'm part of a family the way TV Americans make families: you know, white sheets and fluffy towels everywhere. It's weird, but that's what she is, a white American. I've learned way too much about BeeZee. First, he doesn't know about my daughter, Vindee. He dumped me before I knew I was pregnant. Vindee was born one year to the day before Deloo was: April 30, 1994. Deloo was born in 1995 on the same date in the same city, Fairbanks, Alaska. I sent Fay a copy of the birth certificate. A beautiful baby named Vindee Shoepack was born then.

The thing is, Fay was right to warn me BeeZee was on his way to my store. He showed up yesterday. I told you about that. Now I've got another black eye. I shouted at him and started to dial 9-1-1. He begged me not to and apologized. He ordered another jacket and laid the one grand in hundreds on my counter. I didn't take them even though I need the money real bad. I said the price just went up to fifteen hundred. He made as though to walk out the door and I asked him what he was going to do with the safe in the fireplace area.

He stopped where he was and turned around slow. "Okay, you've got me there. I'll pay you for another six month's rent on the box and twelve hundred for the jacket."

We dickered and he agreed to everything, and gave me fifty-five hundred dollar bills before he walked out of the store, calling over his shoulder, "see you in November." November is his usual month for picking up the jackets.

That's when I remembered he hadn't even looked at the safe. He beat me up for nothing that he knew about. I don't think that's better than dead. I went to the clinic on my own and got four stitches. The doctor asked me if I was going to tell the police. I asked him to put it in writing, asked him to take a picture of it on my new flip cell phone. I didn't say I'd go to the cops, but I wanted to be ready if I did. What I didn't tell him was that Pauline and I spent a lot of time figuring out how the safe worked. We knew what was in it.

Deloo read about the second beating with her gut twisting in knots. The oddness of Pauline working on that safe along with Earlene was intriguing. The next entry didn't help. Unlike my usual loquacious spirit guide self, I could find no joy in these diary entries.

~ *At least we are looking at notes that are a decade old, Deloo, It's all in the past.* ~

June 18, 2003

Dear Taale, I just finished a weird phone call with Fay. She asked me if there was a way to find out how come he has so much cash on him. I have no idea. She said when she left Fairbanks in 1990, she left him with all the cash she could spare: four hundred twenty dollars. She took twenty on the plane. They had one bank account. She closed it to give him the money. The house was paid for by her late husband's life insurance. So was the rickety car. He was twenty, and would turn twenty-one in the fall. She said he would have to get a job. He'd never worked before.

Things got a little clearer when she explained that when her father, that would be BeeZee's grandfather, died in 1997, he left nothing to her or her mother. The bank account had twenty-six dollars in it. The social security survivor benefits were small and mother never worked for wages. At least the house was paid off. All they needed was money for utilities, taxes and groceries. Fay decided to sell off the old man's bedroom furniture. Then she found the stash of coins in the old man's closet. He had four hundred eighteen dollars and twenty-one cents in an old can. Grocery money! Fay and her mother nursed that coin can for almost two years.

The best news came when Fay turned her father's mattress over. There was even more money in the mattress. The mother and father had slept on that mattress for the first forty years of their married life. Then her mother's arthritis got too bad, so she bought a cheap child's mattress, had him build her a box, and that was Fay's mother's bed from 1985 on. Turned out the reason the big bed was so lumpy was the cash Fay's dad kept sliding into it. The older bills were fives and tens. There were hundreds of those on the underside of the mattress. What made Fay a fan of her father were the fifties and hundreds that were stuffed in the top half of the mattress.

Fay said she decided not to tell her mother how much he had stuffed away. Things had been bad enough before he died and he wasn't there to explain it. She used some of it to buy her mother a motorized wheel chair. Then they got smart and went to a couple of medical supply houses who suggested a ten thousand dollar power chair. Who can afford that? So, then they found an excellent one at a local foundation that loans out all kinds of things from canes to fancy wheel chairs. Fay was so thrilled she gave them a check for a thousand dollars then and there. Her mother was able to drive herself to local stores in Fairhaven and one closer to the house in Sehome Village. When Fay's mother began to get bad eyes Fay begged her mother to stop going out onto the street. There wasn't much left of that money or the wheelchair when her mother died. Thanks to Fay's father, they could pay for utilities, groceries and her mother's medical expenses. Both women found other ways to make a little extra money to use for occasional treats.

No wonder Fay wants to come back to Alaska. She's got the frontier attitude that works up here. She would have to get rid of that mean spirit of hers. You can feel her prying into your mind to find a way to hurt. I'm glad you and your aunt Pauline don't give off such vibes. Maybe that's what she did to BeeZee. Maybe that's why he stole her house.

Shocked, Deloo stopped reading and asked me if I thought it was true. "It sounds like this Fay is living in a city without any friends except that woman from somewhere in South America. What would she have done if she didn't have Carmen?"

I agreed and pushed her back to the diary.

November 9, 2003
Dear Taale:

He came in today and asked to see his safe. I'd not touched it. He asked when the jacket would be ready. Last year you finished it about a week before he wanted it, Thanksgiving Day. This time you finished it on October 21. I'd checked it over. Perfect. You're so good at skin sewing. All by hand, even the lining. It looked store-bought and like something a white person would wear. He looked at it with a big smile. He reached across the counter to kiss me, but I dodged him.

"Whoa! What's the matter?"

"Two black eyes and a lot of stitches between them. That's the matter."

"You earned them both."

I gaped. I couldn't believe anyone would ever say that to me. My brain seemed frozen. I didn't answer. He reached for me again. I picked up the first thing my hand touched: a pair of scissors. I stabbed the counter with them so hard they stayed upright.

"Okay. I get it." He chuckled when he walked out the door.

CHAPTER 24

Day Five, Friday

The woman who now had Vindee's bag and scarf silently counted to ten. By then she'd controlled the tremor in her hands enough so she could lift the grey scarf over the brown wig on her head. Glamour was far from her mind as she knotted the soft silk at her throat, tugged the heavy bag to her shoulder, and forced herself to ignore the weight. Turning abruptly toward the side door, she strode to the parking lot where Carmen waited in their old car. Fay opened the car door, slid in with the bag on her lap and released a lungful of air.

"Did everything work as planned?" Carmen asked.

Fay felt inside the bag, her fingers by-passing the paper to find the shape of a cell phone. She puffed out another bloom of air and nodded. "Exactly as planned," Fay's mouth twisted nervously as if sure someone had seen and understood what had just happened. "Let's go somewhere so we can find out what's in here."

An hour later, they sat in the airport's short term parking lot and counted the money. Tears rolled down Fay's old cheeks while Carmen put the last of the bills back into the sack. "There's nearly a million in there. We'll have to figure out how safe it is to spend this the way it is now. Maybe these bills are marked. Maybe they are all useless."

Fay nodded and whispered, "It's done, just like she planned. Plan B." She turned toward her companion. "But why doesn't she want any of this? Or the others?"

Carmen started the car and rolled out of the parking slot. "Just like she said a year ago, there's no way to know how much he had in the first place except by counting the number of houses he owns. We can't touch those, but she figured out how to get to the money he had in banks— enough to make that big transfer last year."

"He must have figured it was her," Fay muttered. "She would have contacted us if she was still alive."

"Si. If she still lived." Carmen motored away from Fairbanks International Airport. "Suegra, are you ready? Can you still do the other three banks?"

"Ha! Just because I'm way past seventy doesn't mean I've passed my prime." She thumbed through the bag. "We should cash one of these to see if it works, and then head out." Fay deposited the bill in the bank she'd used when she first lived in Alaska, intending to use a debit card for regular purchases. There were no problems, and they had packed their bags into the car that morning. They were sure Dustpan would be glad to have the barely used linens. The little food they'd bought fit easily into the car. "Plan B has us going to Tok," she nodded to Carmen. "That's only a few hours away." As she spoke they heard the soft ding that announced a text message.

Fay gasped and reached into her own handbag for the cell phone Earlene had given them a year ago. Even as she tapped the icon to view the text, she remembered they were to throw away the previous phones at the Canadian border. The new device was set up to receive calls in Canada. "It must be her." She glanced at the screen.

"K?" It was the code asking if they had succeeded. Fay texted back immediately. "Y. Plan B. TJ" which meant "Yes. We are driving to Tok Junction per Plan B."

Miles away Vindee whispered softly to her unhearing device, "I love you Grandma."

* * *

A young male wolverine, pleased with his hunting success, lifted his head to watch a solitary car speeding along the Alaska Highway between Fairbanks and Tok Junction. He lifted the remains of his catch in his mouth and scuttled out of sight. His mother had taught him early to avoid all forms of asphalt.

* * *

Meanwhile, at Vindee's former place of employment, the man re-entered the bank vault's foyer after Vindee was already gone for good. He looked at the unfamiliar attendant with a slight frown.

"Where's the other clerk?" He looked for a nameplate on her desk and didn't see one. He tried to remember if the first woman had worn a name tag, but didn't remember looking for it earlier. The customer peered at her replacement.

"She's gone," she smiled.

He forced a relaxed smile and said with a nonchalant tilt of his head toward the attendant, "I think I know her from somewhere, but the memory is avoiding me. What's her name?" He caught and held her eyes with his own spell-binding blue ones.

"Raelene, Sir," the clerk kept both hands on her lap and inched the right one closer to the alarm switch nearest her knee. "Is that all, sir?"

After a moment of silence, he smiled and walked away.

* * *

"Funny. In all these years I've never looked for him in Alaska, even though I know he grew up here. I suppose I've had too little time, and he's always been back east or in China when I needed him," Chuan muttered under his breath.

Ming stumbled the few steps from the bed toward the bathroom. Hearing her husband, she called out, "What did you say? Did you see him?"

"Nothing, yet. He came from here, you know. Last time I looked, he was still on the research staff of the University of Alaska somewhere. It was a cover story. At least they took our money to allow us to say he was on staff."

Ming came out of the bathroom and leaned against his chair. "I thought you checked on all of us every year."

"I did background checks on anyone they told me to follow. That meant all the students on the site in China, the administrators for that university, some of the faculty, and any bureaucrat who got assigned to us. There were always around a hundred new names every spring, and a lot of people they wanted to keep track of in other parts of China."

Ming gave him a peck on his cheek. "Used to be when things were off anywhere, I could talk to him. He always had a way of calming me down. Now that we've made it through that seventeenth jacket business, I think of him as another one of the family. Don't you?"

"Yes. He showed a different side of himself last month. I thought he was one of us. Now I'm sure he's not." Chuan's hands didn't stop pecking at the keyboard even while he spoke. "Oh. He doesn't own property here." He touched a few more keys and waited. "Someone named Fay Clerick owns the two-bedroom house on Steele Creek Road. Might be a wife or a mother." He twisted his head to look at her. "Would you like to check it out again today?"

"Ooh. I'm feeling strong today, but not strong enough to talk to one of them. How about some sightseeing today? Work tomorrow?"

"Great." Chuan looked at her. "I'm glad to hear it. Let's go while you are feeling so good. Maybe that ghost will leave us alone for the entire day."

* * *

A few hours later Deloo drove Taale and Lizzie to Little Tanana, Lizzie took the Mixed Bead jug, while Deloo held a jar of beads on her lap. Deloo, awash with pride for having discovered Earlene's password was little!TANana with three full-cap letters, was babbling non-stop to the others about her good luck. When they arrived at Taale's house, Deloo tucked the plastic jar into Taale's private beading cupboard. It was a well-constructed work of art that featured a large secret space behind the shelves on the upper half. Once safe, Deloo left the cupboard and went to the kitchen to help the others.

Detectives Harper and Cruikshank, who had been in and out of Earlene's Beads all day, had been coerced by Deloo and Lizzie to come home with them to meet the family. Woody and Zigwan, or Zigzag as someone dared call the Abenaki woman were there as well. Someone trotted out a globe and taught a quick lesson in North American geography to the polite detectives.

The eight of them crowded into Taale's small house for Friday night's dinner. Although she had been working all day, making a meal for a lot of people was a commonplace activity for Taale. Since there were a core group of related families involved, making all or part of a family meal happened at least once a month. She pulled a huge pot out from behind some cotton curtains veiling a shelf under the counter. With Deloo on one side and Lizzie on the other, each slicing or chopping, a big vat of stew was simmering on the stove in less than twenty minutes. Woody, Zigwan and Nibuna joined them at the dining room table while Jack and Frank sprawled in the living room. Taale sent her two assistants upstairs to take showers and she sat on the rocker near the wood stove. She brought Woody and Zigwan up-to-date on the investigation while the two detectives dozed, one on a sofa and the other on an easy chair.

Taale rocked while she talked to Woody. All the while she studied Detective Harper to gauge his reactions. He pretended to sleep while watching Taale through slitted eyes. Then he spoke. "Ms. Dena, I received a copy of Earlene Shoepack's transcripts from UAF today. They sent me a copy of yours as well."

Until that moment the easy feel of her house had filled Taale with a familiar sense of peace. Feeling like a bug skewered under a microscope, Taale forced her lips to form a smile. She couldn't speak.

"You told me Earlene was the better computer scientist of the two of you. You went so far as to claim she knew how to hack into computers." Detective Harper smiled at her.

"Yes, she's great," Taale's return smile was tentative.

"And yet," Detective Harper continued, "she didn't qualify to take the math courses required before enrolling in most of these courses in computer programming." He raised inquisitive eyebrows. "You, on the other hand, took all of the math courses you needed for your B.S. and got A's in each of them."

Taale stared at him apprehensively. "I like math, too."

"You are a straight A student, and could have taken more courses than your degree program required. In fact, one of your professors thought you sat through a couple of courses you didn't need. Turns out those were the two upper level courses in computer programming Earlene apparently took and aced even though she didn't have the requisite math classes." He waited for Taale to react. When she didn't he continued, clearly amused. "The professor eventually agreed to give Earlene those two A grades even though he knew you were the one who did the work. Isn't that unusual?"

Lizzie was the first to come down stairs. Her hair, long and still damp, jumbled around her shoulders. She carried a brush and said, "There's no room for both of us in the bathroom."

Taale smiled at Lizzie. "Just what I wanted: your bushy hair. Come here. I've been itching to tackle that head of yours all week!" Taale pointed to the floor, removed the brush from Lizzie's fingers and began the gentle work of tugging at another person's head. Lizzie sat on the floor in front of Taale's knees. Ignoring Detective Harper with all the determination she could muster, she asked, "So, Lizzie, what do you think of French braids?"

"Well, I'm not the girly type," Lizzie began.

"But your hair is saying 'Yes! Yes!' Hear it?"

"Give it up, Lizzie," Deloo called from somewhere near the top of the stairs. "You're going to get the style she wants no matter what. I've been her victim thousands of times." Deloo danced downstairs, grinning. "Mom and Great Aunt Pauline bought or made me ribbons in every color or shape you can imagine." She handed her mother a plastic bucket full of hair gadgets. "Here, Mom. I thought I'd save time and bring these down before you asked."

"Thanks, Deloo, my baby," Taale began sorting strands of Lizzie's hair to twine it in a single thick plait along the center line of her head. "Could you pop that batch of biscuits into the oven? Louise brought them over. They just need to be reheated."

Deloo peered at the kitchen counter, found the biscuit pan, and sniffed the big pot. "It smells delicious. Are you trying a new recipe?"

"No. Great Aunt Pauline gave me some leftovers to add to the stew." She smiled at Zigwan, "It's a must-go type of meal. We started trading leftovers a few years ago when we realized adding somebody else's cooking to yours makes your food taste better."

Surprising them all, Detective Harper spoke up, "My late wife made me eat leftovers all the time. She would have loved the trading idea," He glanced at his partner. "Please call me Frank. It sounds odd to hear you say Detective Harper all the time."

"What happened to your wife?" Nibuna burst out.

"She had cancer." He told them much the same that he had told his lieutenant, adding "she would have loved it here. Loved to be with you all." He shook his head, "She could cook, but didn't. I loved to cook more than she did."

Taale exhaled suddenly and patted Lizzie on the top of her tamed brown hair. "Go look at yourself. We're all witnesses. I expect to see my hard work tomorrow."

Lizzie grabbed her brush with a chuckle. "Come on, Deloo. I want your honest advice about this hoity-toity French thing." A few minutes later they heard a motor sound in the living room and looked up. Lizzie seemed to float down from the sky while Deloo trailed behind on the staircase. Taale recognized one of their cousin's old blouses, and one of her own skirts adorning Lizzie's figure. Jack made a big show of ogling Liz.

Taale dropped her own gaze when she realized Detective Harper's eyes were fixed on herself with sharp intensity. She couldn't tell if his glance was one of suspicion or something else. She stood up. "Supper's on."

CHAPTER 25

Day Five, Friday

Chuan slid out of bed and went to the window. Ming looked at him with a question on her face.

"I feel like checking on him. Want to come?"

Ming shrugged and asked, "Breakfast on the way?"

Chuan nodded, handed her sweater to her and put on his ball cap. "Let's go."

Behind them, invisible to them, MoLi floated near her spirit mentor. He noted she was still shy of him since they had been together less than a month, ~ *So,* ~ he asked in formal Eternalese, ~ *shall we go with them?* ~ He a held tendril toward her.

MoLi perked up and grabbed his tendril. ~ *Let's go!* ~ In a few minutes the four moved together: two visible mortals, eager for a pleasant ride, and two invisible spirits who were learning how to deal with each other.

In a short time they arrived at the woodsy road Chuan targeted as the lookout point. As Chuan pulled in a spot among the willows, a rusty sedan turned onto Steele Creek Road and moved rapidly toward Fairbanks.

Ming pointed and said, "That's him!"

"Yes," Chuan responded in a clipped voice. "Should I follow?"

Ming shook her head. "Let's wait for a while to see if he comes back."

Impatient and unmindful of her twin, albeit mortal, sister, MoLi lured her spirit mentor to visit the now vacant house. Floating above the mortals, the two spirits stopped on the far side of it and he directed his mind at her. ~ *You were a well-trained shaman's apprentice. It's time to go to the next level. The person who owns this house has a powerful mind. To enter it, we have to learn where he placed his shamanic traps and avoid them. I gave you the first lesson a few days ago. First, feel the edges of my mind and then feel for the edges of your twin sister's.* ~ He felt her exploration and praised her when she finished. ~ *Now, feel the edges of the owner's mind.* ~

MoLi reached into the house in a bold mental movement and withdrew when she felt something repelling her. ~ *What is that?* ~

~ *Well done. You used caution. This person is different from most humans. He leaves mental tricks in the specific places. He's never been trained by a shaman or any other type of mystical person. He had to learn the hard way in a land where animals show no mercy. He's spent a lot of time in these woods both in body and then later in mind. Here he has learned from a wolf, two kinds of bears, and a wolverine. Of those, the wolverine is the most merciless and aggressive, and she became his dominant instructor. You grew up knowing that kind of animal in Canada. Use your knowledge here. ~*

MoLi pushed herself toward the mental trap again, studied it, and then continued her mental prowl. In a few minutes she remarked, ~ *I know this man's mind. I don't know it well, but I remember something terrible about him. ~*

Her mentoring spirit had studied her life in detail, including the people who'd interacted with her then. Ming was one of them. So was the man who killed her. ~ *Good. Think about the last week or so of your mortal life and tell me what you find. ~*

MoLi, born and raised in the Canadian province of Québec, had gone to northern China with her sister on an archaeological dig in the last year she was alive. There she was…

~ *It is he who killed me! ~* She shouted mentally to her teacher. ~ *He killed me! ~*

~ *Yes. He is ruthless. He has used his raw, untrained shamanic mind to protect himself and whatever he considered valuable. He learned it from a non-human mother wolverine who had to make a living for herself and all of her offspring. She knew how to embed his mind with key mental devices when she was a month old. He was much older than her, but a good student. Beware of what you might leave in your discovery of him here. ~*

MoLi stilled herself, waited until she had control over all aspects of her ghostly being, and whimpered, ~ *I understand. Shall we go? ~*

As it happened, Ming and Chuan were close. They had decided to take a chance and check the house. They got close enough to spot a jumble of car parts, dirt, and greenery when Ming tugged at Chuan's shirt, "Look, someone is coming this way."

The oncoming pickup was moving on a different country road. Nonetheless, it was enough to spook Chuan. He threw an arm around Ming's shoulder and guided her back to the car. "Let's just watch from the car." They did so, nursing their coffees and hoped the sedan would not come back. But it did. They continued watching.

Day Five, Friday

There was little space inside Taale's house, so eating turned into a pattern of twos and threes seated either inside or out of the house. Woody and Detective Harper talked to each other for a while, separating when Nibuna became restless and started trying to make herself a growth on her father's legs. She followed by leaping from them with enormous crashing noises. I encouraged my mortal Deloo to capture and lift Nibuna as high as possible. The elevation seemed to make her sleepy.

I listened with spirit-guide ears for a while, and was satisfied to hear the pair of law-connected men communicate in their specialized versions of cop shop talk. Detective Harper used Nibuna's interruption to move closer to Taale on her front porch. Jack and Lizzie sat in a corner, perched on folding chairs. Taale, seated on a wooden bench, was watching them with sleepy bemusement. She looked up at the detective with a lazy smile.

Taking that as an invitation to sit beside her, he did. "You're a great cook, Miss Taale," he ventured. "It's my first Alaskan-made meal. I used to be the cook when my late wife was alive, even before she became ill. After she died, I stopped making meals and went into body-building food and exercise. Good for the body, but it tastes lousy."

"You're welcome to eat and cook here any time. I enjoy your company."

"Thank you." Frank looked at her with more than warm eyes, saw her stare and changed the subject, "So, getting back to your brilliant transcripts, I wasn't surprised to see you are an A student." His smiled broadened as he noticed her squirm. "I know Earlene must have taken school work far less seriously than you did, because she had a lot of trouble keeping her grade point average above the acceptable two-point-oh. So I asked your advisor."

"Oh?" Taale concentrated on his face, hoping that doing so would help her regulate her breathing.

"Your advisor has a great deal of, shall we say, admiration for your skills on the computer. How did he word it?" He pulled a folded sheet of paper from his shirt pocket and smiled, "'Taale Dena is talented. After one course on computers, she began to hack her way around the UAF system.'"

"No," Taale protested. "I'm not that good. He's exaggerating."

"Let me continue," Frank said with a vulpine grin. "He said 'She's so good that last September I warned her we would have to expel her if she didn't sign an agreement with us.' Well, that led me to ask for a copy of the agreement because of this case, you see."

Taale covered her face with both hands. "I didn't do anything wrong. I swear I didn't."

"That's what he told me. There's no law against looking at your own grades. It's just that you used the system people like the Registrar use. And you didn't have authorization to do so. He said that even he could not get into the area you found. According to him, that's the place people with official permission use to make permanent changes to their grades." Frank folded the paper and squinted at her.

"I didn't know it was so protected. I just wanted to see my record. I was hoping to qualify for a scholarship." Taale looked at Detective Harper with frightened, dark brown eyes.

Detective Harper stared at her, shook his head, and chuckled. "I'm a homicide detective. I'm paid to poke around in every place I smell a lie. I smelled one in the way you looked, which by the way is beautiful, when you said 'hacker.' You're the first person I've interviewed who has lied about being so good at something."

"Am I in trouble?"

"Not so far. Unless you bashed Floyd on the head with your laptop or hid Earlene in a computer in some geeky way, you're not under suspicion. Just strange, is all I can figure."

Taale closed her eyes and took a deep breath, allowing his words to penetrate. "Just strange?" She peeped at him.

He grinned, "On that note, I dug further. We got some positive feedback today. Thought you'd like to know since this involves Earlene's computer skills rather than yours." He looked at her before continuing. "On June fourteen, an Erinia Pavlov took the flight she mentioned and stayed at an Ontario hotel. The priest, after a lot of urging from California police sources, confirmed he received the laptop computer. There was no evidence anyone made any use of it." He shrugged, "although a good computer techie can do anything on a computer. I also verified you were present in Fairbanks on that date, and your aunt Pauline showed me her calendar. You were busy cooking each day that month at her place. Cooking, she said, for an average of six people a day. A lot of people came to this neighborhood to celebrate your daughter's graduation and marriage on the day in question."

"I didn't lie about Earlene's abilities, though. She didn't care about grades. I do. She and I worked together on those computer courses. It was fun. It brought us together in a way that made our long-standing friendship unique. When I first got into that computer and saw she was expecting me to read her letter—that she thought only I would be able to read that letter, I…" Taale sniffed. "And ever since, I keep seeing her ghost."

Frank fidgeted.

"Oh, I know, that's beyond your official way of doing things, but you're the one who smells invisible lies." Taale let out a breath. "I geek. I admire her in a way that means something special to both Earlene and me. She could hack as well as I could, but we didn't do it to break laws. It was our way of knocking down all those walls that hold us down."

Detective Harper patted Taale's shoulder, "I know what you mean. Detective work calls for a lot of outside-the-box thinking. Don't stop geeking. We're using it to find the man who murdered your young friend, Floyd, and perhaps Earlene."

* * *

I would have stayed to listen in with my spirit-guide ears, but Deloo was hustling away. I was satisfied Detective Harper wouldn't go out of his way to harm Taale. Much to my regret, I had to obey the rules. My spirit guide job is to be with my Deloo rather than Taale. Deloo walked the three Abenaki folks to the Passat. It took a few minutes for Woody and my mortal to shove the canvas into the Passat's backseat.

"Do you want to take this artwork over to the bead shop tonight?" Woody asked, wiping Nibuna-mucky glasses.

Deloo harrumphed, thinking the sound gave her the look of a competent, independent thinker. Since she needed Woody's help, her left cheek with its playful dimple helped her. "It was going to be before supper, but Mom wanted to braid Lizzie's hair, and now Lizzie and Jack seem to be trying to figure out what birds and bees are made of, so I don't know what I should do."

Woody chuckled, "Have they been seeing each other very long?"

"Not really," Deloo snorted. In the evening light, her eyes looked black instead of green.

"I gather they've gotten to know each other in one of those casual relationships where they happened to meet quite a while ago at some coffee shop here in town," Zigwan supplied. "I think the murder of the young man has brought them together in a new way."

"And here I thought they were dancing around some strange Alaskan dating custom which prevents them from touching," Woody massaged his fiancée's shoulder.

Zigwan smiled. "You're an anthropologist. You're prevented from seeing certain kinds of reality by professional training."

"Since we have the canvas in the car, would you mind dropping me off over there at the bead shop? Lizzie could use the time with Jack, and I want to paint as much as I can."

Nibuna attempted to settle the matter by pitching one of her toy balls as hard as possible against an outside wall. Zigwan took the ball away and removed her to the Passat where she snapped the car-seat connections into place around her daughter. "She needs a car ride. It was good driving all this way, because I didn't know how much she was calmed by a moving car. I could take you over myself. Hop in," Zigwan offered.

"No," Deloo assured Zigwan urgently, "Jack and Frank have told us not to let Nibuna or any young person go into the shop until they catch the person who killed Floyd. Leave her here with Great Aunt Pauline for a while. She'll be fine. Then you'll be able to see the shop yourself."

As it happened, Lizzie saw what they were doing and asked to go along. Jack was quick about herding her into the departmental vehicle instead of Woody's car.

"Please leave your child here if you really want to see the bead shop at night. I'll follow you," Jack confirmed, "We're ready to go, ourselves. It was all good eating." He touched his tight midriff, "maybe too good." Zigwan complied when they all assured her they'd get Nibuna within a half hour.

Detective Harper looked at them and said, "I think Jack and I both have the honor of escorting Miss Lizzie back to Earlene's Beads tonight. Isn't that correct?"

"Besides, I don't want to use the shed now because it looks like rain," Deloo added.

Taale spoke up. "That all works for me, too. I'll stay home. You two go. I have to work tomorrow at the University, so I want to sleep in." She squeezed her daughter's hand. "In fact, I'd rather not work at Earlene's until Sunday or Monday."

Deloo smiled and said, "Woody has already offered to give me and Lizzie a ride in the Passat. We have already got the canvas and my supplies in the car. It would be great if you could check out the place for us, though," she smiled at Jack.

"You could let me walk, Jack. My apartment is a couple of blocks that way." Frank pointed south. "It's a short walk to work in the morning."

Without Detective Harper, Lizzie could sit in the passenger seat of the departmental vehicle while Jack drove. Once back at Earlene's Beads, getting in was a little more complicated than they thought. Deloo and Detective Harper went in the front door so that Deloo could disarm the alarm and unlock the back door while Frank checked out the shop. Jack followed Woody to the back door and helped take the bulky canvas inside. The canvas was slightly over three feet by four feet, and four inches deep. It barely fit through the doorway.

Zigwan volunteered to take the paint, brushes, and medium upstairs while Deloo and Lizzie at first tried to put the now-dry canvas on the platform lift. It was too big. Woody joined Detective Harper in the shop's interior to check out the scene of the crime and look at Earlene's remaining beading products. The big canvas was hard to move in the small shop and they found it was easier for all of them to stay on one side of it while they prepared to take it upstairs. Thus, for about thirty seconds, they were all inside the bead shop standing on one side of the canvas, leaving the back door exposed. The thirty seconds in which all of them were focused on the canvas's unyielding configuration was more than enough to allow entry by a surreptitious man wearing dark clothes. He went to the mini-closet inside Earlene's receiving area. No one saw him while they struggled to carry it upstairs.

CHAPTER 26

Day Five, Friday
Fifteen minutes later both vehicles had gone, along with Frank and Jack. Woody and Zigwan went to get their daughter. Deloo and Lizzie arranged Earlene's bed to their mutual approval and flopped on it.

"You're in love with him, aren't you, Lizzie?"

Lizzie gasped, remained silent for three seconds, and finally rolled onto her side to face Deloo. "Yes," she said. "It's like all those stupid love songs I've heard. They always made me laugh. Now I hear them and know what they mean. I've never been in love before. What was it like for you with Arthur?"

Deloo sighed and then chuckled. "Same for me. There was an old song from way before my mother was born that I kept humming on our way to Fairbanks." She sat up and I helped her croon the words.

"You're just too good to be true // can't keep my eyes off of you."

"Yeah! That's it," Lizzie murmured. "It must hurt like mad that you can't …" She broke off, then said, "I'm sorry."

"It's nothing you can do anything about. He'll never be back. I've got to move on. I hope you never have to go through this phase of things," Deloo assured her friend.

Listening with heavy-handed spirit guide knowledge, I sensed that Deloo was about to weep but didn't allow herself that privilege. Instead, she slipped off the bed to start her bedtime ritual.

"I'll just be a minute, if it's okay with you."

Lizzie sighed. "No problem." She slid off the bed. "Hey, I've got to study for my chemistry mid-term this weekend, and I'm too restless to sleep. These short summer sessions are hard. I'll read a little in the other room for a while. You can sleep."

Deloo snuffled. I'm not sure it was for Lizzie or herself. "I'm not sleepy yet. Mind if I join you while I paint for a while? It will help me settle down enough to sleep. My canvas is in there."

"It sure is. It takes up a lot of room," Lizzie called.

They spoke in low tones that the man in the small closet couldn't hear. He assumed silence meant absence. He crept out of his hiding place. It was gloomy but not dark.

I, the worried Baasee', knew he was there and I'd been wondering if I should alert Deloo, but Grandfather Kwaikit told me to do nothing while he was still. Well, now he was doing something and Grandfather Kwaikit was nowhere to be found. I started by causing the stranger to have a brain fart, hoping he would forget to use the staircase. The urge to go up was strong, though, so he went despite my enormous power.

As the prowler moved forward he kept his balance by running his fingers along the wall on his left side. When he ran out of wall, he became disoriented, and despite the fact that he was familiar with the floor plan, he was unnerved to sense the bigger rooms of the bead shop. With my supernatural help, he'd "forgotten" the layout of the stairwell.

My forgetting spell broke when Lizzie went into the bathroom at the top of the stairs and closed it. I tried willing the prowler to want to go away through the back door, so close to him. However, while his head may have turned to the right on the main floor, his thoughts focused on the upper floor. He was imagining the contours of Earlene's bedroom— the one that held my innocuous Deloo and of course Lizzie.

~ *Let him mount the steps,* ~ Grandfather Kwaikit whispered into my right auricle, what we spirits use as hearing.

~ *Where were you?* ~ I groused. ~ *He'll kill them like he did Floyd.* ~

~ *Watch me work this out.* ~ Grandfather Kwaikit sniggered.

Just as Grandfather Kwaikit said he could, I could see a flickering image of the bead shop's owner already mounting the stairwell. It wasn't like seeing the mortal Earlene. She didn't have legs, however, the movement was upward and forward, like legs do.

Grandfather Kwaikit instructed me, ~ *I've got a plan. I'm going to the top of the stairs and will wait for him. You knew her, so you can recreate her face. Then you will cause him to see her face as big as you can make it. Have her face zoom in and out at him. Meanwhile, I will speak for her. I'll amplify her voice to make it warble. That should scare him enough to lose his balance, which I know you will be able to help me do.* ~

~ *Then what? We're not capable of bonking him on the head, tying him up or hand-cuffing him.* ~ I felt a bit touchy because he dumped the complicated plan unexpectedly on me, the Powerful Baasee'. I shaped a gargantuan frown to show him how annoyed I was.

Meanwhile, the prowler was looking around the little space near the back door.

"Hah!" he breathed, and picked up a short length of water pipe Deloo had left there for her next trash run. He began mounting the steps. His mind was a jumble of furious thoughts about the new siding that covered the old fireplace, and even more lethal was an inexpressible anger over the loss of money from his safe deposit box and something else about blue ice. He stepped on a loose board.

Scr-a-a-a-wk!

Lizzie was leaving the bathroom. She'd already taken a couple of quick steps forward when she heard the squeak. Remembering the gun in her backpack, she turned to run back to Earlene's bedroom.

Too late. Having raced up the rest of the stairs, the man took a giant step toward her, and struck Lizzie's head and shoulder with two quick blows of the narrow pipe. Her glasses flew away from her face and hit the wall. The impact was enough to knock her down and slice a wound on her head. The blood bloomed out and high, covering him as well as part of the walls and carpet. He'd hit her in the exact spot and with the right timing to knock her unconscious. Fortunately, the thick braid Taale constructed prevented anything worse from happening. Then he saw Deloo.

Great, I thought in frustrated spirit-guide style. If Lizzie had been the only one there, I could have floated her unconscious body out of his reach and committed a breach of spirit guide rules with no one the wiser. With Deloo as a witness and Lizzie in peril, there was too much to do to keep him away from Deloo as well as help Lizzie. I zoomed past him to get to Deloo. She was already up and on the far side of the bed.

~ *I'll take care of the invader and Lizzie's guide can take care of Lizzie while I cause a ruckus. Ready? Go help your mortal!* ~ Grandfather Kwaikit shouted in our silent way.

Without seeming to move very fast, the prowler loomed over my shocked Deloo, and lifted her with no effort. He held onto her for a moment and then flung her to one side. Her head hit the edge of Earlene's platform lift and she passed out. I watched him then aim Deloo's body to the left rather than the right, as an untrained right-handed person might do. By aiming to the left, the right-handed prowler's orientation was reversed, putting him at a disadvantage. He used exactly enough force to crack her skull if her head connected with anything hard. Instead, her shoulder hit the platform's railing, not her head. Deloo landed on top and slid under the moose hide. The thick hide muffled the man's throwing pitch and Deloo regained consciousness. However, she was very dizzy. I urged her to stay there while Grandfather Kwaikit finished with the man. Then I went to take my position to scare the prowler with Earlene's face.

Suddenly Grandfather Kwaikit, pretending to be the voice of the ghost of Earlene, amplified her fake voice a hundred ways, ~ *You're a lousy coward!* ~

BeeZee, recognizing her voice, stopped moving. He stepped back to stare at Earlene's angry face.

Using all my magical power, I zoomed in and out with Earlene's image, and then multiplied it so he thought she was all around him. As I worked with Earlene's image, which I took from a photo she'd left in her bedroom, I added a glimpse of Floyd on the man's right. Using an image of Ming, I created an impression of the dead MoLi. No matter what he did at that moment he was forced to look at three of the people he thought he had killed.

"Earlene," the man cautioned, his voice both calm and inquiring.

His voice seemed to enrage Earlene's ghost. She, or rather Grandfather Kwaikit, increased the volume on her one line, ~ *You coward!* ~

Grandfather Kwaikit kept repeating 'you lousy coward' and 'you coward' as many ways as he could. Meanwhile, I would have been more impressed had I been less worried about Lizzie, who was very still, much more so than Deloo.

Grandfather Kwaikit took over my face work to shout into BeeZee's mind. The man was both unnerved and off balance. He stumbled backward. He was so close to the staircase, it was a simple matter for me to shove him downward. His hand reached for and grabbed the bannister, but I made it slippery with all the available water I could find.

He gasped, "Stop, Earlene. Stop. You don't know what you're doing."

Grandfather Kwaikit made sure the blood and sweat on the man's hand caused it to slide on the roundness of the stair rail. BeeZee's fingers inadvertently opened. He released his grip on the wood and he tripped over his feet. I spirit-jostled him again to make sure he fell hard against the wall.

~ *You lousy coward!* ~ Grandfather repeated the same line in his ear.

Meanwhile I communed to Deloo, ~ *Do it now! He's not unconscious, but close to it. Use Earlene's platform lift to go down. Call 9-1-1 and those two policemen.* ~ I didn't wait to see if she understood. A piece of me stayed with her while she tapped 9-1-1 onto her phone and clicked the bedroom lift switch to operate the "down" gear. The bigger part of me was already back with Grandfather Kwaikit. I flashed an image of Earlene between the killer and Lizzie.

Detective Harper's cell phone was the last call Deloo made. She called it and he answered by the time she was halfway down. "Frank!

Come back to the bead shop. He's here. Floyd's murderer. This time I think he's killed Lizzie."

Between me pushing the perpetrator with spirit-guide enthusiasm as well as his own fear of Earlene, he fell the rest of the way down. He didn't waste any time opening the backdoor. I noticed his panic seemed to subside as he remembered how to move the door so that it didn't jam on the concrete. Instead, it seemed to glide with him as he leaned some of his weight on it, speeding up his momentum. In seconds he was out the door and running. Before long an engine roared to life and then gravel slapped the under carriage of the escaping car as well as the sides of a wooden structure.

We heard sirens wailing. Detective Harper was still on line with my girl. Frank said, "Let them in. You should cover Lizzie to keep her from getting cold."

"We're too late," Deloo wailed. "He's gone already." She followed this with a more coherent explanation.

After she disconnected the call to Frank, I turned Deloo around to get to the alarm box. She needed to unlock the front door for the emergency vehicles. Then Deloo raced up the steps two at a time. Lizzie lay crumpled on the floor, her long French braid, blood soaked, lay askew beside her head. I, using my talented ocular, could see she was still alive, but concussed. Deloo would know it soon enough.

~ There are big towels in the hall bath. She'll be okay if we keep her warm. ~

Deloo did as I suggested and then pressed a clean hand towel to Lizzie's wound. She could see a crescent of blood spattered on the wall and ceiling. The blood was starting to coagulate, and Deloo was wondering if she should get another towel or simply nestle beside her friend until help arrived. In moments a lot of people made loud sounds downstairs.

Deloo felt a big sweep of energy flow out of her, and stayed where she was. Soon men and women in uniforms swarmed upstairs and filled the short hallway. Someone lifted her up and out of the way. Others began getting Lizzie ready for a stretcher. Someone was asking her a question, and another, Detective Harper, intervened. Frank was about to escort Deloo downstairs when she revived enough to offer another idea.

"Let's use her platform lift." She walked into Earlene's bedroom, unaware of moving her feet. "We'll have to go one at a time. It's not big enough for more." She pressed the wall switch to bring it back up.

"We'll meet you downstairs," Frank said. It turned out Jack stayed with Lizzie while Detective Harper walked down.

No longer interested in them, Grandfather Kwaikit moaned at me, *~ He's not even bleeding. The blood on him is the girl's. ~*

~ That's good news, Grandfather! Her blood in his car will be used as evidence they can trace to this break-in! ~ I gloated. I turned my ocular back to the house on the street behind Earlene's Beads. I wondered where they were.

A half-hour later we witnessed Lizzie being carried down the steps on a stretcher. Bandages and a neck brace almost covered her face. Her eyes were closed. I was glad to see the fingers of her left hand wound around Jack Cruikshank's right hand. He held her glasses in his left hand.

"We might be able to get a faster response from the state lab," Frank muttered as he put a blood-soaked swab into a plastic bag, "now that we have eye-witnesses and this fresh blood." He looked at Lizzie, or rather the thick braid of hair that emerged from the heavy gauze that covered her head, and said to Jack, "I know she's going to hurt when she wakes up, but we've got evidence that's in his car as we speak."

"The best thing to do is wait until she's able to talk. I'll wait with her at the hospital. It will help to see a familiar face." Jack tried to ride in the ambulance with Lizzie, but he settled for driving behind in the departmental vehicle, leaving Frank without transportation. Frank waved the younger man away and looked at Deloo.

"Where did all this come from?" Frank asked, pointing at the ceiling. "I don't remember seeing this hole before you used it tonight."

"It's a secret escape hatch," Deloo shivered. "Mom said Earlene told her to put one here in our house. I've played on our platform lift a bunch of times without wondering why it was there. It just was. Mom had to fix the motor on ours a couple of times because of me." She dimpled at him. "Now I know why it's there: to save people from her evil ex-boyfriend."

Above and around them, I argued with Grandfather Kwaikit about the best way to get Deloo to a safer place. I wanted her to go back to Taale's house, but he thought it would be safe enough in Earlene's Beads.

Meanwhile Detective Harper also realized my very small Deloo was about to collapse with the cold edge of shock. He distracted her. "Is yours just as slow?"

"Mom said there are faster motors, but those were too expensive— for either her or Earlene. Even so, this one is very quiet." Deloo moved closer to the detective in order to point out how the platform lift worked. "Look, I just noticed how she stained the wood on the bottom. It's invisible unless you know it's there. Upstairs in her room, she made a cover for the contraption out of pieces of hide that she sewed together and then beaded." She shrugged without much interest. "I think she used it to escape from her ex-boyfriend because it's so quiet. Mom said I have an over-active imagination."

Frank said, "Earlene wrote her old boyfriend drank a lot."

"Mom said Earlene got or made copies of his keys once." Fishing out her smart phone, Deloo tapped a couple of icons. "I think I'd better call Mom. I don't want to stay alone tonight."

"Good thinking." He tested the platform lift. It held his weight, so he went on up, got a blanket, and rode back down. "Is she coming?" he asked, wrapping Deloo with the blanket.

"Yes. She'll be here in a few minutes."

"Tell me more about the keys Earlene found," Frank said. There was a chair beside the craft table. He walked Deloo over to it.

With my help in keeping her blood pressure elevated, I urged Deloo to remember about the keys. "I think Earlene asked Mom to hide them for her because Earlene was sure her ex-boyfriend would find out about her having them and kill her. Course, I was only ten at the time." Deloo had just sat on the chair when she heard brakes squeal. She saw her mother's head rocking back and forth as her car jerked to a stop outside Earlene's Beads. She swayed as she stood and managed a wave. "There's Mom. That was a quick drive over here."

Indeed, Taale broke a few traffic laws to get to her daughter.

CHAPTER 27

Day Five, Friday

"No. My apartment house is a short walk from here. Besides, Miss Deloo, here," he smiled at my mortal, "was just beginning to tell me something that might be important about Earlene's boyfriend having a house in Fairbanks."

"Before we get into all of that, what happened here?" Taale almost screamed.

Detective Harper told her the official version while Deloo supplied a lot of the drama, with my experienced story-telling help, of course.

Taale repeated, "The suspect allegedly struck the victim twice on the head, and then he staggered around up there yelling 'Earlene' at the top of his lungs. He's a freaking non-man, just like Great Aunt Pauline said."

Frank reported, "The suspect then ran out through the back door."

Deloo picked up her cue and added, "He swung on the door, just like I remembered."

Taale asked, "Where is Lizzie now?"

Frank said. "Jack said she's still unconscious. Someone will call me when they have finished examining her."

"Well, at least we are all right." She tightened her grip on Deloo.

Deloo interrupted before Detective Harper could respond. "He is de-termined to get something from this place. He's killed at least one total stranger for it. Earlene was right about him." Her head sagged against Taale.

Frank leaned forward to see her face and his forehead collided with Taale's who was bending over Deloo as well.

"Sorry," Detective Harper muttered, rubbing a bump on his head. He looked at Deloo. "Is she still conscious?"

"Deloo?" There was a rising shriek in Taale's voice. "Deloo, don't fall asleep!" Using the miniscule kitchen, Taale made everyone some hot, very sweet tea.

Once Deloo was alert enough, Detective Harper took out a tape re-corder and asked permission to record their conversation. So much for family fun. I noticed with wry spirit-guide amusement that Detective Harper, who'd been so reserved earlier in the week, didn't even ask if he could turn on the space heater for Deloo. Deloo was glad to sit while the older pair bustled around her.

"I am speaking with Mrs. Deloo Goode, who is about to describe some keys Earlene Shoepack took from her boyfriend, currently known as BeeZee. Mrs. Goode?"

Taale nodded at Deloo, "I'll have to notify the Charles family about Lizzie. They just lost Floyd, and now Lizzie's in the hospital. Maybe I'll start with Great Aunt Pauline. She's good at these things."

Deloo was feeling cozy with the steady heat of the stove and had a hot cup in her hands. She replied, "That's good, Mom. By the way, do you remember when Earlene used that key I found? I was in fifth or sixth grade and we all went out to some place off the Steese. What did we do there?"

Taale took a deep breath and spoke toward the tape recorder, "Let's see. Deloo is twenty-one, so that was eleven years ago. December. Deloo was not quite ten at the time, a year younger than Earlene's daughter, Vindee. I'll show you." She hopped out of her chair without explanation and dangled a key at Frank. "I should give this to Mr. Cunningham, but I think it's just as safe to give it to you. It's Earlene's key."

"What does it open?" Detective Harper asked, fingering the key.

"The key to Earlene's former boyfriend's house. This is the copy she made of the one I think his mother gave to her and I have another set at my house. I'll give that key to you as well when I get a chance. I don't want it back."

That prompted Detective Harper to point to his recorder. "Please, if you don't mind, have a seat Ms. Dena. Shall we get started on the story behind the keys?"

After official beginnings about time, date and address, Taale started in, "So one day she and Pauline called me over to the bead shop. They were excited because someone had mailed this key to Earlene." She touched the one that looked like a typical house key.

"Who?"

"They wouldn't tell me. I think it came from the guy's mother, Vindee's grandmother. They wouldn't confirm my suspicions, but I remember she used to live in the house, and now the ex-boyfriend lives there. Earlene sent me out to make a copy of it. When I got back they told me a lot of whoopla, but I agreed. The former boyfriend lived out toward Fox, northeast of town. Earlene had the address. She said he never took her there. She wanted to go in my car. She said he wouldn't recognize it. We had to wait for a Sunday, since otherwise I'd have to leave Deloo with Aunt Pauline. Pauline was willing, but Earlene wanted Pauline to be in the shop with her own daughter, Vindee. She said she didn't want her daughter to meet her biological father because he was such an evil man. So, my aunt Pauline ended up babysitting."

"So we all went: Earlene, Deloo, and me. She made me park across the road from his house so he wouldn't see tire tracks the day we went there. As it was, she was peculiar about our footprints. She told me and Deloo to follow in her footsteps. That meant stepping where her feet stepped. Not only that, she brought brooms for each of us. If Deloo or I landed outside of her prints, we had to brush it just so in order for the brush marks to look natural. 'I don't want him to go after you, too.' She kept droning over and over."

I thought back to the moment as well, using spirit-guide oomph. I recalled noticing the trap BeeZee had put on his bedroom door. In my mortality I'd used something like it myself by stringing blades of grass together. Where I used small piles of rocks to hold my grass in place at an entry way, BeeZee had taped a length of thread to the door jamb. He positioned it about four inches from the floor. Taale and the others kept their winter boots on due to the frigid weather, and didn't feel it. It was Earlene who broke the trap. She didn't notice the string on the dingy carpet any more than the others did. I was the one who pointed out the trap to my little mortal Deloo, who was then a ten-year-old. She showed it to her mother and Earlene. They saw what it was and put it back together when they finished.

Meanwhile, I left a bit of myself to capture any thoughts he might leave afterward. Since he'd be gone for weeks, I doubted my makeshift 'bug' would last that long. Grandfather Kwaikit said they were only useful for ten or twelve days.

Taale continued, "It was cold that winter. Minus fifteen was a high temperature for us that year. Deloo went into the house with us. It was a few degrees cooler out there on Steele Creek Road than here in Fairbanks, so I worried about my daughter. There was no heat or electricity at his place. It was so cold icicles formed in the electrical outlets."

As her spirit guide, I wanted to wrap Deloo in one of the blankets from his couch, but Earlene instructed Taale not to do that. He'd know, somehow that my tiny one had been prevented from freezing.

Taale continued as if my spirit-guide input meant nothing to her. "Earlene posted the two of us at his front door to tell her if the former boyfriend was coming. He didn't."

Deloo brightened. "Arthur and I used to live on Steele Creek Road."

Taale eyed her grown-up daughter fondly. "Things have changed a lot since you were ten. It was a two-bedroom house, newer than either Earlene's Beads or this one. I'm just guessing about that because it had flat siding on the outside. Earlene and I have log walls. But it still looked kind of old. We spent a solid two hours there. It was hard to keep you busy. There were no electrical lights. No candles." She smiled at the old memory, "We were on best behavior in her ex-boyfriend's freezing-cold room. I made you stay bundled up in your parka."

"I remember freezing. I had to keep my jacket on and scarf over my nose," Deloo supplied.

Taale continued, "I brought some books. You were studying the planets, so we wrote your science report, a book report on something else, and then you read your favorite book, *The Witch of Blackbird Pond*. You've read that book at least a dozen times over the years. Anyway, it started to get a little dim, and Earlene wouldn't let me light his kerosene lamp. She kept saying he would see it or smell it. All that did not keep your interest for a whole hour so I sent you back to help Earlene, hoping she would remember you had a child-sized bladder and would need to go soon. The two of you came out of the big bedroom an hour later. Earlene had the notebook that she kept pressed to her chest. I suspect whatever she wrote is stored on her laptop, too. She didn't tell me what she found then, but I got the details from Deloo afterward."

"That house was strange, considering he was a man. It was as neat as a pin, but barren. No pictures on the walls or furniture. It felt hollow. Earlene said he was a fanatic about neatness. She was terrified of his rages. Anything that seemed different always gave him a reason to go into a rage. So we didn't touch anything except what we brought. Finally we were out of there like ravens diving for a free lunch."

~ It is true, my mortal. I knew from the thoughts he left inside there that he had killed both humans and animals if he thought they had violated his things. Knowing that, I made sure you didn't touch anything. Even when you, Earlene and, of course, invisible me, were messing with his things in the bedroom, she was careful. She didn't let you move anything, and did not touch the paperwork she found. She was looking for three things, bank names and addresses, types of account, and how

much he had in those accounts. I knew it would matter to you one day and that day has finally arrived. She took photos of what she wanted. Your mother will find them in Earlene's computer somewhere. ~

"So, two hours, one in which Mrs. Deloo Goode was working with Earlene Shoepack, and the other on school work." Detective Harper said into his recorder, "Mrs. Goode, what did you do at the residence?"

Deloo took a moment to answer the question. The heat and comfort had done their work of getting rid of the symptoms of shock. I used spirit guide magic to nudge Deloo's memories and she answered, "We used flashlights to look for hiding places in the floor and walls. She must have already looked in drawers before I came in. She found lots of loose flooring. One of the places had a bunch of money in different colors, like pink or silver, with pictures of men or buildings. She left those alone. Then she told me to look at the walls and floors. She told me to look for anything that looked like a push or squeeze could trigger something. The kind Earlene used to hide her computer. We found a cabinet in his bedroom wall that had stuff in it. She took lots of photos of the hiding place." Deloo pressed her eyes in an effort to remember.

"She told me to crawl under his bed with my face up to look at the bedframe. I didn't see or feel anything except for glimpses of his mattress between the slats. His mattress was thinner than the ones on my bunk bed. Maybe half as thick. Earlene told me to feel the mattress for any place that bulged. I found a big lump and she decided to lift up the mattress to check."

"'Another safe deposit key,' is all she said. I think she might have slit the mattress open, because I saw her take something out of her pants pocket and then put something back in. Then she remade the bed and we left."

"Yeah," Taale smiled at her daughter and added. "That was harder than you'd think. She told me and Deloo to walk backwards in her original footprints. I decided it would be easier to have Deloo stand on my feet while I walked backward. That worked. Earlene followed. We swept our way back to Steele Creek Road. Then it turned out he was gone for the rest of the winter. By the time he came back, which was sometime in June, the winter snow had been melted for a month or two. I'm sure he couldn't tell anything had been in his house by then."

After Taale spoke, Detective Harper asked Deloo a few more questions. Then he asked Taale, "Do you remember anything else?"

"Yes. Earlene was paranoid about him getting into the bead shop. That's why she has such a complicated lock on it. She asked me to keep a copy of her old boyfriend's house key, and I did. I kept it upstairs in my dresser. Earlene asked for it a couple of years ago. She seemed to have forgotten it until then."

"A couple of years ago? Do you remember the date?"

Taale said in a matter of fact voice, "It was sometime in late December, maybe even January. I don't remember the dates. Deloo was ten or eleven when I got it from Earlene. I did think it was odd she didn't ask me to go with her again, if that was why she asked for the key. She must have been confident he wasn't in Fairbanks at the time."

Frank scribbled a few notes, made sure the recorder was still on, and asked, "Do you know what she was after?"

"I don't know for sure," Taale twiddled with the lacey edge of a doily. "We avoided talking about the reason and just dealt with what she wanted. Just the same, all Earlene seemed to get excited about was banking information and her eyes got a certain look when Deloo found that safe deposit key."

"Why do you say that?"

"Isn't it obvious? She told Deloo she found 'another' safe deposit key, and she's got more money nowadays. It's in her diaries, in the new things she's bought for her store. It's obvious in her daughter, Vindee. She sent Vindee to an expensive out-of-state university. I could only afford a two-year-degree in a school for Indians for Deloo. You must have noticed other differences. Also, there was something odd about a woman she keeps mentioning in her diaries. Fay. That's the past boyfriend's mother." She dropped the doily and looked at Deloo. "The house you rented with Arthur was on the other side of the road from Fay's house. It's odd, in view of what's going on now. Do you think Arthur knew he was there?"

"We had a lot of strange neighbors out there," Deloo said. "The woman who gave us rides to the university was nice. Remember your friend, Agatha? She liked to tell me all the goings on in that neighborhood." With a shrug, Deloo added, "but she never talked about Fay or her son."

"Thank you Ms. Dena and Mrs. Goode. That was useful information, ladies," Detective Harper said. "All of it." After making sure the recorder was off, he glanced at Deloo.

"Would you show us your old rental sometime, Mrs. Goode? I know it will be painful, but I'd like to check it out."

Deloo paled. "I guess so, I'd like to find out if Lizzie is okay first, and I was hoping to get a day of painting in tomorrow. I've got a commission for a portrait, so I've got to get something done even though all that's going on has got me way out of the painting mood. That doesn't matter. My client is very impatient for the painting. Could we find out about Lizzie now?"

CHAPTER 28

Day Five, Friday

Detective Harper called Detective Cruikshank's cell. Jack answered. They spoke in coded phrases and then ended the call without a goodbye.

"Lizzie is still unconscious."

Taale's face, which had been pasty at best, now creased with renewed worry. She looked at Deloo. "Maybe I should stay with her tonight. She's a member of the Charles' family, and with Floyd's murder, she'll probably want to stay with us. She's not close to that aunt of hers."

Deloo nodded. "I'll stay with her, Mom. You need to get some sleep."

Detective Harper intervened, "Don't worry, Ms. Dena, Jack said he would stay there at the hospital with Lizzie." He didn't bother to suppress a wry grin. "In fact, I'm sure he would be very annoyed if anyone tried to chase him away right now."

After Detective Harper walked away from the shop, the two women decided it was best to watch the store rather than go home that night. They tucked themselves into Earlene's bed. Deloo started to cry. "That crazy man might have killed Lizzie, Mama."

"We'll get him, Honey. Shhhh."

As they soothed themselves to sleep, I, the tediously vigilant Baasee', circled Earlene's room, leaving a residue of myself in the fissures between Earlene's ghostly thoughts and those of her attacker.

Grandfather Kwaikit appeared just then. His spontaneous visits were becoming a welcome habit. ~ *Granddaughter,* ~ he admonished, ~ *you are very nervous tonight. You haven't left a residue track like this in centuries. Maybe more.* ~

After Grandfather left I looked at my residue and grimaced. He was right. Everything about Earlene's place reflected its chaotic past. I needed to resolve Deloo's part in it soon for both of us. I dwelt on my issues for all of two more seconds and resumed reviewing the thoughts of Earlene. It was obvious she understood the killer in a way his own mother never attempted.

He, Earlene's attacker, reminded me of the coyote male who befriended me in my youth. A good hunting partner, but unaware that I was a human rather than a coyote as he was. He did things his own way and didn't like other coyotes or me to be around when it was his time to do things his way. I followed him once. He found an immature coyote of about four months old and ripped it apart. The coyote pup screamed for about five minutes and whimpered for another hour. There was nothing I could do to save the pup. I sensed its death and walked away. That was the last time I worked with coyotes. My Deloo was right, we were close to the perpetrator, yet all too far from seeing the truly complex monster he has become.

* * *

A few minutes later Taale gave in to a full week of one trauma after another and fell into a deep sleep. Deloo dozed for a while. I remained watchful over my girl for an hour, then I did something I was sure would get me a long lecture by some spectral busybody or another about spirit-guide morals. I peeked into Earlene's computer. Sure enough, I found a simple text file that seemed to explain all of Earlene's thinking. It was easy to follow, and I found myself enjoying both the words she wrote, apparently to her best friend, Taale, but which she was sure Taale would never see. In other words, Earlene didn't hold back a single thought when she typed. I didn't notice Deloo when she wandered into Vindee's old bedroom, alias the junk room.

By then I'd flipped open the laptop the way Taale did and used the screen to help me meander through Earlene's complex thinking. Hours passed. Suddenly my spirit guide privacy was blasted to smithereens when my tiny mortal, Deloo, sat on the computer chair and started reading as well.

Suddenly we were stunned into yet another reality. "What are you doing, Mrs. Goode?" Leroy Cunningham asked.

Deloo jumped and swung at him, stopping herself just in time from slamming a book in the attorney's face. "Oh! It's you. I thought you might be that man again." Deloo sat back on her wheeled chair and whispered. She pointed at Earlene's room and made a shushing sound. "Mom's asleep in there. I thought I could look at Earlene's computer for a while." After a flurry of questions and distracted answers, Deloo pointed to the screen I, her annoyed spirit guide extraordinaire, was nursing. "So, we decided to stay tonight. Detective Harper knows about it. Would you like to see what I've got?"

"Yes, please," Leroy's voice sounded apologetic.

She nodded at Leroy, still not sure why the computer was open to the file she realized was named, Shaa Gwaandak, meaning "my story" in the Athabascan language, Gwich'in. Deloo guessed the same title on this computer meant it was Earlene's diary. She smirked secretly to me.

~ *Did you find Earlene's actual diary, Baasee'?* ~

~ *Yes, I did, my little genius. Now find out why he's here.* ~

Deloo stabbed a finger at the computer and looked at Mr. Cunningham. "Mom found all these files on the computer this week. She's been printing them out and giving them to the police. I was just looking them over." Deloo smiled. "Would you like copies, too? You might find something the police might not see."

Mr. Cunningham looked interested, then thought about his already daunting workload, and shook his head sadly. "Thanks. I'll let the professionals do their work. I don't need another job. I'm sorry you and your friend were targeted by that murderer."

Meanwhile, unobserved by either mortal, Zephyr joined me in reading the diary. I had been taking the easy route when Deloo came up behind me, by looking at Earlene's diary on the screen. It was a little more difficult, but not much, to read the diary in the computer's background areas. I adjusted it to make room for Zephyr. She sucked in the essence of the entry I, the erudite Baasee', was reading. She remembered the day and clamored at me to come. ~ *This is it, Baasee'!* ~ Zephyr communed. ~ *She robbed that rotten skunk. Read this.* ~

Confused, I took the passage inward, ran it through three of my analyzers and remarked, ~ *We're going to need Grandfather Kwaikit for this. I'm calling him now.* ~

~ *But why?* ~ Zephyr wailed. ~ *All we need is common sense and a bunch of lies to make it work. You can do that, easy.* ~

~ *Lies? Me? I do cosmetic corrections, not lies,* ~ I retorted, trying to suppress my humor. ~ *Grandfather always sees the big picture. This affects way too many lives, my Deloo for one, to handle with a 'bunch of lies.' Although I do recall having used that tactic from time to time, we can do a better job here.* ~

Zephyr gnawed invisible fingernails to the bone and complained, ~ *If you say so. I knew you'd call in the ... uh-oh.* ~

Grandfather Kwaikit bumped into me, shifting the mortal airways a little. Leroy shivered and tugged at his coat collar. While he complained about the chill of the morning, Zephyr, Grandfather Kwaikit and I read the entire diary entry. Grandfather told me flatly, ~ *Get rid of the cop.* ~

~ *He's not a cop, Grandfather. He's an attorney,* ~ I observed with fake spirit guide civility.

~ Same thing. Get rid of him and don't let her make any more print-outs. ~

Shrugging elegant, if invisible to the mortals, spirit guide shoulders, I puffed some air around Leroy Cunningham's neck. He shivered again.

"Brrr. It's chilly in here. Odd for July in Fairbanks. Are you cold?" the attorney asked.

Deloo had piled a thick terry cloth robe around her shoulders. "Huh? Oh, no. It's fine for me. Why don't you tell me why you're here?"

"Me? My son saw the lights. The bead shop is supposed to be closed, you know."

Deloo smiled. "So much has happened lately, I don't know what is supposed to happen and when. It's good of you to worry about Earlene without much information from her. How long have you known her?"

"I've known your Great Aunt Pauline for years. You know Pauline. She made me draft the first formal papers for this shop about sixteen years ago. My father had already drafted some paperwork for her. When your great grandmother Ruth died, for instance, he did the legal work of transferring Ruth's house into her name and your grandmother, Helen's house into Taale's name. I took over shortly afterward."

"You must be the one who drafted the legal document all of her tenants have signed about not having alcohol in the houses they rent from her."

"That's what I started. There's a lot more involved than the first warning we gave tenants. If they got caught with drugs or alcohol, I worked on all the paperwork that got the inebriate into jail and eventually prosecuted. There's a lot of time and cost involved. She's borne the brunt of it," Leroy said.

"She's changed a lot of lives by insisting on sobriety," Deloo said.

Grandfather Kwaikit said, *~ Baasee', you can say the same thing about your mortals. ~* While we waited patiently for the attorney to skedaddle away from my cool airflow, Grandfather shimmered at Zephyr and said, *~ How are you, Air? ~*

~ She's Zephyr, Grandfather Kwaikit. Call her Zephyr. ~

Grandfather Kwaikit chuckled our way and asked for details. *~ So Earlene was trying to make changes herself. Let me soak that entry in. ~*

~ Just wait a minute, will you? ~ I turned my attention to Deloo. *~ My brilliant mortal collaborator, it's time to get rid of the lawyer. This passage explains a lot neither he nor the police should see. Smile and say goodbye. When he's gone, I'll show you what we've found. ~*

Looking confused but polite, Deloo smiled and thanked Mr. Cunningham for stopping by. His smile was bleak as he saluted Deloo and told her to make sure the door was locked after he left. As soon as he was gone, I used spirit-guide flare to display the screen with Earlene's diary entry about a day in June a year ago.

* * *

I wore a lilac-colored skirt-suit I had tailored to fit. I wondered if the fabric would hold up after a night in an airline seat. I had to wear it to make a one-day turn-around flight. I should have spent the extra ten dollars a yard on the better fabric. At least it matched the lavender sandals. They're comfy, if cheap. Not like those expensive shoes BeeZee wears all the time. Handmade Italian loafers, indeed! I packed the prettier pumps in my bag for afterward. I could have called Taale, but I'd have had to explain everything to her, so I drove myself to the airport. I bought the tickets weeks ago. Matched it to my spreadsheet of BeeZee's financial and travel records. No one was available to fill in for me. Taale was not available and I didn't want her to know about this, anyway. It's too dangerous.

Once beyond the security gates, I arranged for C to meet me. After the aircraft landed in Seattle around midnight, I had to trot to the parking garage. We decided it was simpler and would attract less attention than if we met in Bellingham. I knew it was her. She has dark hair. Like me. Greying. Mine was grey as well, but I wasn't sure if I should dye it like she did. Then I muscled up. We eyed each other like fighting dogs. I broke the ice with a "Hi."

She looked tentative. "I brought it." She handed me a manila envelope. "He said it's reliable."

I told her "Thanks," took it then sucked in a breath. "Here's something I'd like you to take to the police if anything happens to me. I've booked a flight for Sunday morning. Can you get us all together?" I named a restaurant at a SeaTac airport hotel and a time to fit my flight schedule.

Then we just stared at each other. Fascinated, just as we had been from the first moment we met, by the similarities in our faces.

"He didn't pick us because we looked like his mother," I said to her.

The other woman snorted, "Ay, que si. Who can guess what that man thinks?"

* * *

As far as Deloo and I could tell, this entry was made in June, around the time she and Arthur got married, and about when all of Deloo's generation were graduating: Vindee Shoepack with a B.S. in Biology from Western Washington University, Deloo with an A.A. in Art from the Institute of American Indian Arts, and her new husband, Arthur with a PhD in Anthropology from the University of New Mexico. Ironically, not one of those degrees was as valuable as what Earlene, who had no college degree, had written. More of Earlene's writing appeared, and all of us, spirits and mortal alike read it with fascination.

Being with her made me feel more in control of the situation, I went back through airport security to board my flight to Los Angeles. I slipped my own Alaskan drivers license into one of the hidden pockets and put the manila envelope at the bottom of my big bag. My fake name for the trip was Erinia Pavlov.

A few hours later I, Erinia Pavlov, with grey, permed hair, and feet sweating in the tight lavender pumps that matched my fitted lavender suit, checked into a hotel in Ontario, California. My feet must have swelled up with fear. The pumps were hard to wear, but I kept on going. After a cup of coffee in the hotel's restaurant, I took a cab to a nearby computer store. There I bought a laptop with a wheeled case and walked back to the hotel. I, or rather, Erinia ate lunch before making a series of bank transfers. Sitting in the overstuffed hotel lounge chairs, I hacked into the hotel's system and used the wireless hotel internet service.

When I finished, I went upstairs to Erinia's room and changed from the killer pumps to my lavender sandals. I reformatted the hard drive and installed a standard office suite of software, also just purchased from the computer store. After a thorough look at myself as Erinia, I felt ready, so I descended to the main floor with the computer rolling behind me. I, Erinia, located a Catholic church two blocks from the hotel and assured a surprised priest the computer was brand new, had good software, no viruses, and I was making a personal donation.

"Mother was adopted, you see," I, Erinia offered, trying to make sure my face smiled with angelic assurance and my words explained everything. "The church was very helpful in finding a family and then bringing solace to my mother later in life." I, Erinia coughed then. It sounded so uncontrived, delicate, and Russian. I continued as if my throat had so filled with tears that words could not squeeze through it. "It's been many years and my mother has passed on. I'm not at liberty to tell you her name or any more details." I entreated the priest. I placed the computer case's handle in his open palm. "Please take it and pray for me and my mother."

Elated and unquestioning, the priest accepted the gift, and Erinia Pavlov.

Back at the hotel, I bought a sleeveless black silk dress dotted with tiny lavender flowers. Its fitted bolero-style jacket showed off the flare of its skirt as well as my, or rather, Erinia's slim legs. Best of all, it matched my easy-fitting sandals.

At five the following morning, I as Erinia Pavlov, checked out of the hotel and rode its shuttle service to the airport, once again wearing my handmade lavender suit. Before going through security, I tucked the false ID away and put my Alaskan driver's license back into my wallet. Four hours later the real me, Earlene Shoepack, arrived in Seattle and took a cab to a nearby hotel.

CHAPTER 29

Day Six, Saturday

After Leroy left, Deloo and Taale made themselves comfortable on Earlene's bed. Taale fell into a sound sleep. At five AM I, Baasee' the Opportunistic, rattled Deloo awake. ~ *Come, Deloo, let's work on the computer for a few minutes.* ~

"Why, Baasee'? That's Earlene's computer and that's Mom's job. I don't want to mess her up."

~ *Your mom hasn't slept well for weeks and she has to work tonight. She's figured out where Earlene buried her secret notes. Come on! It won't take long.* ~

In fact, Deloo merely touched five keys and an entry dated a little over a year previously flooded the screen.

* * *

The restaurant looked like one I'd just left in L.A. I saw the others already seated at a table, cups and plates in front of them. Upon reaching the table, I bent to pat BeeZee's mother on the shoulder and to shake Carmen's hand. Vindee was beside her grandmother. As always, I felt the urge to stare at the face that was so like my daughter's. So like Vindee's. Equally, I submitted to their fascination. We couldn't help ourselves. We had known each other for years. Now it was different. Now we had drawn the bow, so to speak, and released the first arrow.

I sat across the table from Carmen and said, "Thanks to Mr. Hauser, I mean, your father, everything worked just as we planned."

"You did it?" Fay asked.

"It's done."

Three faces looked at me with expressions varying from outright distrust to awe.

"When can we use it?"

"Now. I've checked. All three point six million is in our bank's possession, if not our actual hands. I deposited nine hundred thousand into each of your accounts. You can access your shares whenever you wish."

They looked at me with various shades of distrust. Fay said, "You could have taken it all. Carmen and I would never know."

"You said it would be only one million, two hundred fifty thousand for each of us. Why is it more?" It was Carmen again.

It was a nearly empty dining room. The other diners were seated at distant tables. Nonetheless, their eyes darted around, looking for eavesdroppers. After a moment I calmed myself and nodded my head. I resumed, "It was three point eight, less than it was last year, and less than the previous year. Plus, I used some for this trip. As far as I can tell, he usually gets around three and half million for himself. I didn't want to disappoint you if this was another bad year. I left him point two in case he forgets to check the balance himself before he uses it." I shrugged, "I doubt if that will happen, but I didn't want to risk a surprise from the bank. It would tip him off too soon."

Fay's eyebrows knotted over the bridge of her large nose. "How can that be enough for all the traveling he does? He must spend a fortune just in airfare, not to mention his other expenses."

"Twenty years ago he received and spent a quarter of a million per year for the first two or three years. Last year he spent the better part of four million—like I said, there must be a cycle, but I couldn't figure out what it is."

"He's bound to find out the money's missing."

"That's the plan."

"He'll kill you."

"That's not the plan, but in case he does, I brought these." Earlene placed two identical packets on the table in front of Fay and Vindee. "These are copies of every transaction I've traced. Carmen already has her set. So far, we will proceed with Plan A. If anything happens to me or to any of you, we'll follow Plan B. Any problems?"

The others looked at each other as well as me. I expected that. Then, as if controlled by a puppeteer, all of them dropped their eyes to the table.

"If we go to Plan B, that probably means you are dead," my daughter said.

"Yes," I nodded with regret toward my daughter. "As we agreed last year, when any of us is down, possibly, probably dead, we shift to Plan B. He's finished a cycle, and is due back in Fairbanks in a few days. He'll be there for three or four weeks. Never longer. Then he's gone for four months at a time. If anything has gone wrong, this is the time he'll be checking up on me. You as well, any of us, wherever we are."

My daughter's brown hair was bound tightly into a single braid. Her glasses slid off her nose, allowing one and all to see her glorious blue eyes. Carmen's black eyes searched mine with multiple shades of panic while she clutched Fay's hand. "What will we do if he comes after us?"

Fay intervened, "That's what both plans are all about, ladies. Carmen's father gave us these disposable phones. We will text only using the codes chosen for Plan B. We agree if any one of us fails to respond, then she is dead or unable to act. Plan B calls for constant moving and no direct contact except within the two teams. Me and Carmen, you and Vindee." She eyed her granddaughter with glittering blue eyes. At one time Fay had used mascara to blacken her lashes. It always heightened their impact. Now well past seventy, she no longer felt the need to stand out. "Carmen and I will take a house or an apartment in Fairbanks for a while. He'll never look for us there."

They separated without finishing breakfast or saying good-bye. I met Fay's burning, bright eyes across the table. We seemed to have like minds. As if she heard my thoughts, she lifted her chin when I did, a signal of silent agreement. Then she turned away. When I saw I'd been left with the bill, I tossed five twenties onto the table before leaving the restaurant. It was twenty more than the total bill. Too much for a tip? Would any-one remember? I shrugged. No time to worry about that small detail and I went to the front desk to ask for a shuttle. The others were already out of sight by the time I made my way to the van and then to the airport to go back to Fairbanks. My daughter used a separate itinerary.

* * *

Deloo stared at the computer for a minute or so before she realized the entry pulled a lot of the layers of mystery away from her mother's friend. She thought to me, ~ *I don't know who those other women are, Baasee', but I suspect all they wanted was Earlene's talent and courage.*

Mom will understand what to do. ~

We both stared at the laptop for a long moment, trying to take in what we had just read. I couldn't help use my spirit-guide powers to try to locate Earlene's two friends or Vindee. Something flickered when I asked if they knew anything about what had happened to Earlene. Flickering is not a specific answer. I didn't think to ask if I had ever met Fay or Carmen. I knew Vindee. If I had known them all, I would have got a bright, steady light, meaning yes, Yes, YES. However, I didn't think to pose such a query.

What's a gorgeous, invigorating spirit like me to do?

* * *

"Deloo? Why are you awake so early?" Deloo looked up when she heard someone knock on the front door. She saw a short ponytail poking straight up and guessed whose hair it was.

"Morning, Woody. Is that Nibuna with you? What are you doing here at the bead shop with her? It's too dangerous here."

~ Take them to breakfast somewhere. And take all those print-outs for his reaction. ~ I communed silently and a bit enviously. I would have loved to play with Nibuna, myself.

Without a pause, Deloo smiled and invited Woody. "Let's get some coffee. I'll get a much-needed dose of Nibuna, and you can read these." Deloo tapped the paper, "Let me check on Mom and lock up." She showed him the sheaf of paper. "You might finish before I come back down."

Woody said, once Deloo was in the Passat, "I'm letting Zigwan get a little sleep for once, so Nibuna and I took a little turn around town in the car and saw the lights on here. Why are you up before most swallows start singing?"

They reached a small coffee shop. Deloo filled him in on what happened in the few hours since they'd parted company the previous evening. "This has turned into a horrible nightmare, Woody. Worse than when you rescued me in Vermont."

Woody leaned forward so his elbows dug into his knees and the mug rested between chilly palms, he bathed his face and glasses in the rising steam of the coffee cup. "I'm sorry, Deloo. I'm so new to Alaska, I don't know what to tell you. I'm sure the secret is right here, though. That's what you thought when you were back East. Whoever Earlene is, she's got money. Maybe that's the thing to look for. For instance, do you remember how long the upper floor has been there? It looked old last night, but nothing here is as old as Uncle Virgil's house. I thought it might be ten or so years old."

"You are right. Earlene added it on about a decade ago when her daughter got big enough to want some space of her own. Vindee got her own room and Earlene wanted to take computer classes. She urged Mom to go with her. Ten years later Mom graduated—broke but with a college degree. Earlene never declared a major, but things started looking up for her. That was the year something changed in a few ways for me and Mom, too."

"Oh!" Woody was suddenly alert.

I remembered his police background and flashed Deloo an image of a badge and a Sherlock Holmes-type hat. Deloo choked on a giggle.

~ *Remember, my mortal collaborator, when there's money lying around, you have to be careful. Everyone wants a cut—even a friend like Woody. Until we, ourselves, learn what's going on here, be watchful,* ~ I warned.

Deloo nodded at me and smiled at Woody. "It's nothing special for my mother and me. It's just with Great Aunt Pauline helping her, Earlene made money at this shop, and she shared it with us." With prompts from Woody, Deloo recited the small changes she had seen over the years. "Ever since I was ten, I was able to do things for money, like helping Mom with beading. My sewing stitches are still bad, but I could work the pliers to put beads on O-rings. Mom was more focused. Earlene helped her with what she called small loans. Once in a while she handed me a fifty so I could put it in the utility bill fund. See what I mean?"

"We weren't just a typical single mother with her kid to Earlene. Even though she was raising her own little girl, Earlene helped Mom with money and little jobs. It all helped Mom get a Computer Science degree. Mom didn't know how much she wanted that degree until Earlene talked her into taking a couple of classes. They needed each other to figure out what the professors were saying. So, after what happened last night, I'm seeing another side of things. Earlene wasn't after a degree. It wasn't a hobby, either. Mom said she got into trouble for geeking. She says Earlene's code is so good, she never gets caught. Now we know a lot more, it's clear Earlene was up to something in a big way."

"What do you mean?" Woody's face lit up eagerly.

"Mom told me Earlene's homework was always hit-and-miss. Some of her assignments were pathetic dabs that did not fit the assignment.

Mom would patch them up so Earlene would pass the course. But Mom thinks there's more to what Earlene learned. For instance, what she's done to hide that diary is incredible. She thought of solutions to specific types of problems that are beyond my mother, and Mom is famous for her computer work. What could that be except hiding from the mysterious boyfriend?"

Woody frowned, "So, why would she bother?"

"At first I thought, since he or somebody killed Floyd, that Earlene knew something about him, like him robbing a bank or something. But Mom says there's something about the code that leads her to think it is even worse. You know Prize Woman and her husband are here? Remember them? Their names are Chuan and Ming. I thought I was done with them. I think Earlene found out what they were up to, and this BeeZee came after her or else his loot."

Woody and Deloo looked at each other before Woody shrugged. "I don't follow."

"It's a combination of things, like the way Earlene always kept the computer hidden from view. Then there's the times she stayed over at Mom's house in my room while I was growing up."

"Were you roommates?" Woody queried.

"It only happened twice when Vindee started college in Washington and I was still in high school. Each time Earlene dragged my bunk bed away from the window and kept the door shut. When I asked her questions, she'd say things like 'Don't ask. It's for your own good.'"

Deloo took a sip of coffee. "I've been looking for diary entries in that year, but no luck. Mom got all of these 5472 files open, but Earlene left a lot of password-protected text files. After what happened to Lizzie, I'm more serious about finding them." Deloo set her cup down and rubbed her palms together.

Once they reached Earlene's Beads again, Woody nodded earnestly, his eyes taking in the shop with a quick sweep. "The way she locked up the shop is not standard for a house or a business as homey as a bead shop." Woody's thick eyebrows knotted. "These locks are set up to keep serious criminals out. Your mother said last night her attorney changed both the alarm code and the door locking system the last time he saw her, which was the day before Thanksgiving."

He looked at Deloo. "Compare that to the casual way she handled the gems. That bothers the cop I used to be. Remember? That happened on the day you said she left a package on your mother's doorstep—the jacket had those beads on it. I'll never forget your mother brought us those beads, which contained three million dollars in gems, in her carry-on bag."

"That's it," Deloo said, "We think BeeZee couldn't get back into the shop by opening the door. Mom thinks he made some other arrangement Earlene didn't know about."

"Yes." Woody said. "This funky piece of plywood must have hidden a secret way into the old fireplace. It's odd, but even stranger is why did he wait so long to try to use it? I think he must have gone somewhere for a few months, because he made that hole in the summer just when your Alaskan sun never sets and everyone can see him."

Deloo looked at Woody with desperate eyes. "And yet that's not the way he came in last night. The carpenter took down the panel he gimmicked up, but he keeps trying to get in. Mom thinks he's still after Earlene. Well, Earlene is gone, and we think he killed her. I think he hid something of his in the bead shop. But what and why? I don't understand what he's after."

"I get you. You haven't found what the killer thinks is in that bead shop. What I think, after hearing what you've said about that little trip eleven years ago to Earlene's mystery boyfriend's house, is that Earlene was just as secretive as he was. She has moved it, maybe sold it, whatever he wants. Or left it on your mother's doorstep?" Woody expanded his pacing by hopping off the porch. "Based on the timing, I'd say Earlene didn't sell it, because he would have retaliated long before this."

"When people don't do as he wants, he goes into a rage. That's what Earlene said over and over again eleven years ago." Deloo said, "That's why a kid like me when I was ten, learned to be so quiet when I was with Earlene. She was scared of him and I was, too."

Woody picked up a very restless Nibuna. "Looks like I'd better be heading back to Zigwan. Can I do anything for you at Uncle Virgil's house?"

"I've got some ideas for my painting, so I'll be busy. Besides all that, Mom is going to work at the university this evening." She lifted her camera off her neck and looked at Woody. "There is one thing you could do for me. Arthur took some photos just before he died. He tried really hard on the day he died to make sure I kept the camera, and later in Cambridge, I had a dream about the camera. Could you take a look at the photos Arthur took on that last day he lived? Something keeps me from looking at them. Maybe you can do it. You were his best friend."

CHAPTER 30

Day Six, Saturday

Woody took the camera, "No problem." He stretched his arms out again. "Could I move your mother's car first? I think it's in an illegal parking space. How about that empty carport space?"

Deloo said, "Mr. Cunningham told us not to. That's the space she rented to BeeZee, the one we think may have killed Earlene. If he's watching the carport, he might use it as an excuse to come in here. There's a place on the street we've been using, just around the corner from the store. I'll get Mom's key. Could you come back to the shop after you've had dinner? I'd like to find out what you think of these diary pages Mom found. She's sleeping in today, and then she leaves for work at the university around five or so. I'm also late on getting that painting done. I want to block in more of the design features."

Woody smiled, "I'll be back."

As soon as he had parked Taale's car, Deloo went upstairs to Vindee's old room to glare at the large canvas. She glanced at her notes from Audra, and squirted three blobs of paint onto a palette. Although, of course, painting on canvas had not been part of my, Baasee' the Adroit, artist training way back when, even I knew the biggest blob should not have been black at this stage. I dropped all pretense I would be able to take a much needed nap while Deloo painted. Instead, I stationed myself next to her head and watched her smear a solid black, jagged line from one edge to the other. Deloo was about to thicken the blackness when I intervened.

~ Deloo, didn't Audra say she wanted to remember Federico as a fun-loving man? Isn't a black gash too angry to represent playful? ~

Deloo stopped and stared blindly at the canvas. Without answering, she dipped her brush into the red paint and aimed the red and black mix at the unsuspecting canvas.

~ Stop! ~ I commune-shouted into Deloo's mind. *~ Think about what you're doing, Deloo. You have an elderly, African-American client who trusts you to represent the passionate love she felt for her late husband. What are you trying to say with those harsh colors? ~*

This time Deloo's shoulders twitched. She dropped the paint brush and looked around the room. She spotted the rolling chair her mother had been using and fumbled her way to its seat. Sensing Deloo wouldn't notice if I set the shop on fire, I used a tendril to pick up the paint-brush with its dribble of black and red oil paint. Spying the unopened can of turpentine in the corner of Deloo's workspace, I peeked at Deloo. Her face was aimed at the wall in front of her rather than the canvas. Taking her inattention as permission to open the turpentine, I did and then tipped the can over a politely waiting jar. When I had tendrilled the brush into the jar, I turned back to my mortal. By then Deloo was no longer staring at the wall, but cupping her face into hands. Tears splattered on the floor.

I enveloped her in a curl of tenderness and waited for her heart to slow before I reminded her wordlessly of my presence. By then I had decoded a dozen half-formed memories of a tall, blue-eyed girl—the girl who usually sat next to Deloo at every family event, the bead shop owner's daughter, Vindee. I remarked silently, ~ *You've been very strong, Deloo, to put your worries in the background this week while your mother has been struggling with fear for her best friend. Vindee is a capable young woman. She's as smart as you are. Trust her to fight for herself.* ~

"Fight?" Deloo murmured. "Is she trapped somewhere?"

Answering her questions was likely to arouse Taale, I mentally nudged Deloo. ~ *Let's take a walk. Your mother needs her sleep.* ~ In a few minutes Deloo found herself a few blocks away on Airport Way. It was one of Fairbanks' main roads and lots of cars rushed noisily by. I worked Deloo toward one of the several parks nearby and urged her to sit on a handy park bench. In a few minutes she began talking about the little girl, now a young woman, with whom she had laughed and fought all her life.

"I haven't seen her since I was fifteen," Deloo sobbed. "That's almost six years ago. I probably wouldn't recognize her if she came up to me today."

It was true Vindee hadn't been visible for years, at least not to Deloo. Since she was a year older and went to a different school than Deloo, they only met at family functions or at Earlene's Beads. Vindee went to Western Washington University because it was in Bellingham, Washington, her grandmother's home town. Fay Clerick lived fairly close to the WWU campus, which made going there logical to everyone. When Deloo married Arthur in New Mexico the year before, Vindee was busy graduating from college. Excited by all the details of starting her own adulthood, Deloo hadn't given a thought to Vindee.

"Where is she, Baasee'? She should be the one who's searching for her mother, not me and Mom. Why isn't she here?"

Since I had been pondering that very question myself, I had been trying to track her down in the spectral way with no results. ~ *All I can tell you is I've been trying to figure out what Earlene was doing when she was last in the shop. Vindee was with her. They were in a state of fear and panic. I was hoping there'd be something that could explain more in Earlene's computer. Why don't we go back and read more of it?* ~

"Vindee was with her mother in the shop? Do you know what date it was? Why didn't she call me?"

I raised lovely, ephemeral eyebrows in frustration. ~ *People who are frightened don't usually have mundane thoughts about the date and time. They rarely think, 'I should call Deloo.' If we are lucky, we'll get some answers in Earlene's computerized diary.* ~

In a few minutes I convinced my mortal to walk back to the bead shop. She had already scanned the diary pages Taale had found and knew there were few comments about Vindee in them. Since Taale was still asleep, she tiptoed around Vindee's old bedroom-cum-messy-office space. After another impatient glimpse of the diary pages, she shrugged and turned to the paint. It never occurred to her to wonder about the open turpentine jar. The walk had cooled her unstable emotions, and she spent the next few hours working out a design she thought would please Audra. When she was finished, she went back to the diary and read with greater calmness. In early afternoon her mother awoke and came to check on her daughter.

"Why haven't we heard from Vindee, Mom?"

Taale put down her coffee and frowned. "That's the question I've been thinking about all week. There was the strange visit Earlene made to L.A. and Seattle that had something about Vindee, but not much. I wish she had written more or else that I could find more of her diary."

"Did you get to see her in Fairbanks after she graduated from WWU?"

Taale's eyebrows knotted briefly. "Here? She didn't come back here. I thought she stayed in Washington with her grandmother. What makes you think she was here? Did you see her?"

Deloo stared at her mother uncomprehendingly while I communed, ~ *I think Vindee was in Fairbanks on the sly. I can find signs of her using my spirit guide tools, but she didn't leave any clothes or toothpaste anywhere. Just tell your mother you thought you saw her a while back and leave it at that.* ~

"I thought I saw her a while ago. Her hair is almost as long as her mother's. Even though it's brown instead of black, from behind, they look alike. She didn't stop when I called, though. I must be wrong about seeing her," Deloo shrugged.

Taale looked at the clock and decided she had time for a quick nap before officially getting up. She fell into a deep slumber without transition, so Deloo continued to assault me with silent questions about Vindee. Finally, I supplied a thought, ~ *I think that Seattle trip happened while you and Arthur were driving toward Fairbanks last summer. Of course you don't remember it.*

Muttering to herself, Deloo said, "None of this explains anything about what happened to Earlene or where she is. What good is calling all of his evil behavior part of Historic Trauma? Is that just an excuse for letting it slide? Was there anything like this when you were alive, Baasee'?"

I examined my mortal with some consternation. By comparison with her world, mine was one of constant life and death struggle. I thought for a bit, and then replied, ~ *Yes, but it would seem more like endless slaughter to you. The invaders often killed without cause. They ... ~*

Suddenly, I couldn't continue. A bad memory flooded my mind and shocked me. The trouble was, it was a fourteen-thousand-year-old incident that happened to someone else, not me. I grappled with the whole issue of intergenerational trauma, realizing my memories and me, her spirit guide were a serious part of Deloo's unstable world because of what I brought to her.

Deloo studied the air. "Baasee'? Are you there, Baasee'? Baasee'?!"

~ *Ooh,* ~ I waited until I regained a sense of balance. ~ *I'm here, Little One. You surprised me. Then I remembered something terrible. I had to wait for my mind to clear.* ~

Impatient because I fell silent a second time, Deloo queried, "Baasee'?"

~ *Yes, sorry. I recall a story so horrible it's made me ill even now. It's about Njootlan.* ~

Deloo wriggled into a childlike tell-me-a-story pose. It called for coiling her legs under her butt while sitting up straight. I detected pain signals emanating from her knees.

~ *Don't sit like that, Deloo! Let your legs dangle as usual. Now, where was I?* ~

~ *Njootlan,* ~ Deloo prompted happily.

Privately I felt disgusted with myself and Deloo because we both enjoyed my stories. In this case I knew what I was about to tell her had put a little boy into a catatonic state of mind for several years. I offered him a mental apology before starting the story.

~ *All right, as you recall, way before I was born there were the tall people called the Tuudzaado or Shadow People. My Grandfather Kwaikit is Tuudzaado. The people we think were first in Zana were the Hutlan. I am mostly Hutlan as far as any of us can tell. Invaders came afterward. We called them Death Runners. The Death Runners killed, maimed, and destroyed many of the Hutlan, who were very short people. They were easy targets for the Death Runners. One of their intended victims lived and suffered every day of his life because of them. His name is Njootlan. He was my Great Uncle Zaandan's hunting partner, a Hutlan man seven or eight years Zaandan's senior.* ~

~ *The Death Runners had a savage custom they thought would boost their strength. Their notion of strength was to be able to attack anything without hesitation—like wolverines. They hunted boys who were about to enter adulthood to get that kind of strength.* ~

"Ew! What did they do to the boys? Put them in cages?"

~ *No. Caging them is bad, but not as bad as what the Death Runners really did. They hunted the boys, slaughtered them, and ate their testicles raw. Actually, they ate all of their victims raw. That's what they planned to do to Njootlan. He was nine years old when he showed the early signs of manhood. His mother tried to hide him and failed.* ~

~ *One day his mother heard the Death Runners chanting. She screamed for Njootlan to run and tried to block them with her own body. Njootlan ran as fast as he could. He glanced over his shoulder to see if his mother was behind.* ~

"Uh oh." Deloo drooped, eyes enormous. "Was she?"

~ *She stopped shouting in mid-scream. As he turned, he saw a spurt of blood where she had been. He thought he was doomed too because they were big men who could run even faster than he. Then he saw a very tall figure come out of the grass just ahead. He'd never seen anything like her: She was a female, all white, some fur, mostly pale skin. She was taller than anyone he'd ever seen. She signaled for him to come to her. Then he heard a bellow from behind. He couldn't think any more. He just ran straight toward the white woman.* ~ My mind froze on the image of Njootlan's mother as he had last seen her. I pulled myself out of it, remembering I was a strong psychic. However, Njootlan's horror was still alive in him and therefore me as well. Little did I know I wasn't the only one receiving images from a man far away from us in both time and space.

"There was another person, wasn't there, Baasee'? Another boy. Who was he, Baasee'?"

I stared at my psychic Deloo, who leaned forward, panting as fast as Njootlan must have done. If I could have done so, I would have gasped for air myself. Being lungless, I couldn't do any such thing. Instead, I nodded, then communed to Deloo, ~ *He was Njootlan's childhood friend, a Hutlan boy who'd come to visit. He witnessed the attack on Njootlan's mother and he pitched himself at the Death Runners, perhaps to save her. They killed them both.* ~

Deloo and I fell into a bond of mutual grief over two people we would never know and a terrified third who'd escaped because of the white stranger.

"Who was the white person? What happened next?" Deloo asked.

~ *Njootlan doesn't remember. I've heard that story a dozen times, hoping he could recapture the moment after the white creature picked him up.* ~

Deloo looked perplexed. "But he was able to tell you the story, so maybe he passed out and then came out of it later. Did he?"

~ *That's just it. Typical of anyone or anything that's been terrorized by brutes, he can't remember anything about what happened after his mother and then his friend died. The creature who saved him, we call her The Naan, conveyed to him that she picked him up and ran for her own life. Fortunately, she had extremely long legs and out distanced the Death Runners in a hurry. Then she ducked into the grass, dove for cover under some shrubs, and waited until they passed before she moved again. Afterward she carried Njootlan for miles, taking him to, and up, a tall cliff. When he saw the cliff in later life he couldn't believe anyone could climb it because the stony face was smooth and sheer. There was no pathway up.* ~

"How did The Naan do it?" Deloo asked.

~ *We, that is Grandfather Kwaikit and I, guess she knew exactly how to ascend rock walls like that. Some animals like mountain sheep seem to fly up cliffs expert human mountain climbers don't dare attempt.* ~

"Hmmm? So, what happened to him? He must have awakened to eat or pee at some time. What did she tell him?"

~ *The odd thing about The Naan is she didn't speak either in mouth words or by mind the way I do with you. Besides, Njootlan said he doesn't remember much until he was about thirteen or fourteen. Even then, he doesn't remember anything except flashes of scenes that disappear as fast as they come. Finally, when he was about sixteen or so, he remembers she took him to an encampment of Hutlan people. Their language was different from his, but he could pick out familiar words here and there. They were mountain people. One person among them was Zaandan. At first Njootlan thought Zaandan was a full grown man. Later, Njootlan learned that Zaandan was only nine years old compared to Njootlan's then sixteen years. He was the tallest person in the camp. Over the next few years, Zaandan grew another two feet. ~*

"Sweet! So they got to be friends. What did The Naan tell Njootlan about the new people?"

~ Nothing. She never spoke to him at all, but later on the two met from time to time. He always knew what she thought, even if it was all wordless. He somehow learned to understand her. Zaandan told me their kind, the Naan's kind, weren't sociable. He often saw her with Njootlan, but whenever he got close enough, she always melted out of sight. ~

"Gee," Deloo said. "I've heard of that kind of amnesia. They say it happens sometimes to people who've had a shock so bad their entire being, body or mind, can't remember it."

~ Exactly. Only in this case, as in the case of many who suffer from Historic Trauma, when the people around you, including spirits like me, have all experienced the same kind of horror, there's a kind of group amnesia that happens. Both mortals and spirits don't, as you put it, come out of it. The horror is too strong. Njootlan is just one of the hundreds I've met in our spirit world who have had gruesome lives they can't recall. Something keeps them from remembering the worst of it. ~

CHAPTER 31

Day Six, Saturday

Deloo decided to go downstairs for a cup of tea before continuing. I encouraged her to add a lot of sugar. At least the next entry was back to when she was ten. She remembered all the late hours her mother had spent with Earlene on their computer homework.

November 3, 2005

Taale, Shitjaa! I'm getting this course. I can't believe I, little Earlene Shoepack, get programming. I am keeping up with it. Sometimes I'm even ahead of you. It only makes sense when I pretend I'm working with beads. Programming and beads have a big thing in common—being more sensible if they work together. You know how a beading project gets when you start fighting with the beads.

5472: that took us from six PM when I closed the shop doors to two AM. We did homework last night. I finished, but I don't get it. I think you got it at seven or maybe as late as seven oh five. You're so patient with me.

This is the first time in my life I've ever wanted to stay up so late to do homework. I wish I'd met computers and programming in '98 when I first had the chance, but Pauline is right. I do not remember 1990 or my brothers. All I know is they drowned because they were drunk. Then my parents moved to Fairbanks. I was old by then: fifteen. I was old enough to remember playing with them or something. I just can't. I don't remember much of the year my folks died. 1993 is just a blur to me. I remember being in the room where Deloo was born. I think I might have started waking up then. She's so pretty with the green eyes. I've offered to chaperone her on her dates. At eleven she just grins.

November 26, 2005

Dear Taale, my best friend.

We both got A's on our midterm. I wouldn't have done it if you hadn't coached. I get so shivery when exam time comes around, even when it's for my teeth. I guess that's why my teeth are in such good shape. Heh-heh.

It's so cold out there. Minus thirty and dropping. Just a month ago in October it was a balmy fifteen or so! Fay called from Bellingham to wish me a happy Thanksgiving. She said it was about 35 degrees and raining. Lucky.

I've been baking bread for tomorrow's dinner. You always feed so many on Thanksgiving Day. I've made four dozen rolls.

It's already ten PM. BeeZee called today to tell me he would stop by on Friday to get the jacket. He reminded me to plug in his car. It's been plugged in since noon today.

What was that noise?

I just did a full inspection of the upstairs and the shop because I heard something. It sounded like a squirrel or something. Pauline is right. I need a security system. Whatever it was gave me the willies. See you tomorrow, Girlfriend. Don't be surprised if it's a little after midnight instead of noon!

Deloo took note of the date of the last entry. It happened almost a year after she and her mother had gone with Earlene to sneak into the scary boyfriend's house. Deloo shrugged. Eleven years ago. Nothing happened then. Why now? The next entry explained a little more.

November 28, 2005
Dear Shitjaa:

What a fattening Thanksgiving dinner. I must have gained a couple of pounds.

Pauline is right about the security system. I called today and they came over to give me some ideas of what to do before they get it all installed. I heard noises again last night. I think it was the dog in the house behind me.

Maybe. Didn't sound much like a dog. Sounded like someone in the shop. I went down there with a knife in my hand and a shorter one stuck in my belt. I didn't find anything, but I think I smelled something. Something like cinnamon. The security team will be here on Monday. I'm going to call you in the morning to see if you'll stay with me or else if I can stay with you.

I'm scared.

Deloo shivered. Whatever had been going on eleven years ago had to be related to why Earlene was missing now. But why?

Deloo searched the computer for more entries, but found none. She decided it was time to work on her painting for Audra. She checked on her mother, and saw her roll over, lift her head and then groan. Deloo turned and tried to tiptoe out of the bedroom. Before she took more than two steps, Taale called her.

"Deloo, is that you? I'd better get up. It's time to go."

"Mom, it is only two-thirty. I was just checking to see if you were okay. There's time for you to sleep some more."

Instead of resting, Taale sat up on Earlene's bed and let her feet feel around for her slippers, which would have been there if they had been at their own house.

"We're at the bead shop, Mom. Your slippers are back home."

"Oh." Taale padded to the bathroom and found what she needed for a shower. "Is there anything to eat downstairs? I'm hungry. " Her stomach rumbled loudly.

"No. I think Mr. Cunningham cleaned out all the perishables." Suddenly Deloo's stomach growled. They both laughed.

Taale was about to step into the shower and called, "Let's go out together. There are a lot of good places close to here. I should know. Earlene and I tried them all."

"That's great, Mom. Let me clean up my painting while you're in the shower. Then we'll go out."

Deloo hurriedly added another design element to the painting to introduce her interpretation of Federico's love of music. I watched as I always had. Taale had seen the preliminary underpainting with horror. I, Baasee' the Courageous, have had that reaction a few times, however, Deloo knew what she was doing as long as I kept her use of black under control. Deloo is good.

On emerging from the shower, Taale asked, her voice low and soft. "How soon do you think it will be ready for Audra?"

"I'm still working on the background areas, trying to set the mood and pace. When this coat dries, I'll be ready to begin the painting itself." Deloo turned away from the canvas and said, "I'm ready for food any time you are."

Taale, still mesmerized by the oil painting, touched the paint brush she found on the table. "It's ugly, but you know that. Right?"

Deloo chortled. "Very ugly. But the red is how she feels about losing her husband, Federico. If she's like me, and she thought she was, right now she's going through passionate denial. That's the way I felt about Arthur until I finished his portrait. I could accept his death once I went through all of the feelings I had. Some of those feelings are ugly. If I'm right about Audra, then the intensity of our love of our dead husbands will come through in this underpainting."

"That makes, sense."

They busied themselves, and negotiated where they'd go for a late lunch. Soon they were headed toward a Mexican restaurant on the south side of Fairbanks.

"Mom, have you read all of Earlene's diary?"

"No, Babe. It's too depressing. I've skimmed most of it. Have you?"

"Yes, before I tackled the painting today. There's a couple of entries I want to show to Woody. Do you mind?"

"Woody?" Taale looked probingly at her daughter. "What's up? Did you see something?"

"There's an entry about her meeting Vindee's grandmother, and a bunch of others reporting how the grandmother sort of badgered her a lot. I just want to get Woody's take on it. Did you ever meet that woman? Her name is Fay?"

"Fay? No. I remember talking to Earlene about it a long time ago, and wondered then if the woman was on the up and up. Did you get something that I should have seen?"

"Just a feeling. That's why I want Woody to see it. And there's Earlene's version of what we did that day out at her boyfriend's house. There are some small differences between what I remember and what she wrote. Plus, there's the weird trip Earlene made to California. Do you remember that? She disguised herself."

Taale toyed with her rice and beans. "I read that section two or three times. Show it to Woody. He might have some idea about it I didn't get." Taale glanced at her watch and said, "Time to go. I'll drop you off and then head on over to the university."

While Deloo waited for Woody to stop by, she sorted the computer entries into date order. She was almost finished when Woody tapped on the front door downstairs. After making sure the front door was locked, she showed Woody upstairs and handed him her sheaf of printouts. Small pieces of colored paper stuck out here and there.

"I've got them sorted, now. You can save some time by skipping to the key entries."

Woody pulled up a folding chair, handed her a digital camera and a plate of cookies. "Here's Arthur's camera. I've looked at all of them. No surprises until the end. In fact, since you are in most of them, you have probably seen what he did."

Deloo's dimple flicked on and off. "Thanks, Woody. You said there was a surprise or two. What was it?" Her fingers had not moved to touch Arthur's camera.

Woody could see her fingers shook, so he took the camera away and said to her, "I took the liberty of copying them onto this." He showed her a gadget that looked like a cross between a camera and a jump drive. "This makes it easy to get prints. So," Woody produced a sheaf of papers, "I did." He picked up her hand and gave her a piece of paper with the blank side up. "This is the last photo he took of you. If you're not ready for it, just leave it and look at the others."

Deloo looked at the back of the print and finally turned it over to see a photo of herself sleeping. She turned pale, gulped, and said, "Thanks, Woody."

"By the way, Zigwan baked enough cookies to feed everyone in the neighborhood. I brought these for you."

Deloo's smile was a little soggy, but she picked up a raisin cookie. "Thanks, Woody. What's on the others?"

"There are two. I don't know what kind of animal this is. Do you?" He produced an image of the black and red nose of an animal nearly fully covered with snow.

Deloo's eyebrows knotted. I, the mighty hunter, Baasee', knew she didn't recognize it and communed silently to her, ~ *It's a wolverine, Deloo. It looks like it dove into a snow bank to get a mouse or something. There's blood on its snout.* ~

"Oh!" Deloo almost chuckled. "It's a wolverine. I had just told him to keep his eyes and ears open in case he saw one. They are vicious hunters."

Woody nodded and turned the last one over. "This one really bothers me. Do you know who this man is?"

Deloo studied the last image.

"He's got sun glasses on, probably to avoid snow blindness. I like to paint eyes, not jaws or hands, so no. Not exactly. I think I've seen someone like him, but I don't know him. He must be the guy who lived across the street. His garage is in front of it. See?"

"Do you know what he's carrying?"

"No, why? What is it?" Deloo asked.

"It's a Chinese jadeite figurine. Whoever carved it is really good. Look at how delicate the projections are. In fact," he pointed to Deloo's wedding band. "This is made out of jadeite, too. Maybe yours was carved by the same person. Those parts that stick out are extremely well shaped, just like those of this figurine."

Deloo and I studied her ring. I communed to Deloo, ~ *He's right, Little Wolverine. Remember what your father-in-law said of the value? Your ring is worth fifteen thousand dollars.* ~

Deloo grimaced. "Zachary said this ring was worth fifteen grand when he bought it for Matty. How much is that statue worth?"

"It's probably about eight inches high while your ring is an inch or two at most. The man is holding it in his hands. See? At a really bad guess, I'd say the carving is worth a million dollars. Someone will have to get it appraised."

Deloo stared at the image, transfixed. "Who is that man? Do you know him, Woody?"

"I hoped you knew him. He's smiling at Arthur. I'm guessing they were friends. You recognized the house. Doesn't that tell you anything?"

"Omigod," Deloo turned desperate eyes toward the ceiling. ~ *Is this Earlene's boyfriend? Is this the man who killed my Arthur?* ~

~ *Deloo, breathe slowly. Yes, he is the man who lived across the street for a long time and is the owner of the house you and Earlene broke into ten or so years ago. His name is Brent. Do you recognize him? You should. You've drawn his face without sunglasses.* ~

Turning to Woody, Deloo said, "I wonder if this is the mystery man we've been looking for. If so, he's the guy who was following me in Canada. He tried to break into here a couple of times. I think his name is BeeZee. Look at this!" She shuffled through the papers she had assembled. "The important one is marked with red ink. I told you about the day Mom and I went out to Earlene's boyfriend's house to break into it." She waved at the paper. "Read it!"

Woody read, looked up from time to time, and then carefully put the papers aside. "So-o, what do you think, Deloo? You were right there."

"Even though I was just a kid, not much older than Nibuna, I thought it was weird. Her diary is not very much different from what I remember. What do you think?"

Woody answered thoughtfully, "First, those two women were terrified of him. The mother especially. She had a key and the legal right to enter, but didn't have the nerve. Why not? Then there's Earlene. She's a cold blooded planner. Does your mother think of her that way?"

Deloo looked at him in surprise. "Cold blooded? Earlene? I never did. That's worth asking Mom, for sure. There's a lot more here you should read. Look at the big section on what she did last summer. It was about a year before you and I met in Vermont. If that's the case, her old boyfriend was near us, I think." She pulled out the set marked with yellow highlighter. "Here it is."

Woody read, first a little too fast, and then starting over, he read each word slowly. When he looked up, "What were you doing at this time?"

"I was still in New Mexico. This was when I met Arthur and then you. Mom used up all her money to fly down to be with me just about when this happened. Mom and I both thought Earlene was with her daughter, Vindee, who graduated from a university in northern Washington. She doesn't even mention it here. There's something about Vindee, too."

"Odd. What do you think Earlene was doing in Los Angeles besides making some sort of transfer and then giving a computer to a church?"

Deloo shook her head. "If we weren't talking about Earlene, a woman I've known pretty much all my life, I would guess she was robbing somebody. But look at this place, Woody." Deloo waved a hand around the room filled with junk. "It's so tiny this whole building could fit into the Goode's big living room—if we included their dining room as well."

Woody stood up and looked at the junk more carefully and then walked downstairs. Deloo followed. Finally Woody said carefully, "Yes, it's tiny, Deloo. But some of this furniture is brand new. Then there's that platform lift," he pointed at the bottom of it above them, "which your mother has in her house. Taale said the other night the lift is worth several thousands, and Earlene bought two of them." He walked slowly around the lower level, "and there are a few things in here that must have cost a lot of money."

Woody studied the store area and then turned slowly back to Deloo. "Could I see the records of sales and purchases she's made recently?"

Deloo nodded and produced the record books she'd worked on earlier in the week. "Most of the stuff has already gone back to the beaders and skin sewers."

Woody scanned the pages carefully and muttered, "Just a Nickle and Dime business. She sells some things for a lot of money, though."

Woody's fingers drummed on the back of one of books. "There's just enough for a small profit. It would pay for that lift and a little more." He smiled at Deloo. "It was probably a real stretch for her to send her daughter to an Outside university."

"Stretch or no, she did it," Deloo said defensively. "Sending me to IAIA was hard for Mom, but we both worked at it. I had to work part time and still didn't have anything left over for more than a single cup of coffee."

"That's what I mean. So here's Earlene making mysterious bank transfers and then giving away a computer she's only used once. Where'd the money come from?"

"What does it mean, Woody?"

"It means you and I need to do a little investigation. Did you say you used to live out there where this guy had a house?"

"Yes. And last night Frank told us he wants to go visit it."

Woody glanced at his watch. "It's too late now. I told Zigwan I'd be back at eight." He looked at Deloo. "How far away is it?"

"About ten miles. The road is crooked."

"Tell you what," he smiled at Deloo. "Let's make a field trip with your mom and Detective Frank tomorrow morning. Call her to let her know. While you're at it, we should call Frank."

"Mom," Deloo forced a smile to her lips and repeated Woody's request for Frank to come.

"Really? Isn't having the police come a little too much?" Taale asked. Woody could hear her, as Deloo had turned on the speaker.

"Mom, Woody is right here. Let him explain what he's thinking."

"Taale, Woody here. With Lizzie in the hospital and all the stuff that happened to you and Deloo last month, I think the most important thing to do is get the cops in on this as soon as possible. I feel it in my bones."

It was time for me, the cave-girl gumshoe to butt in. ~ *He's right, Deloo. The people who chased you through eastern Canada last month were using deadly force. Moreover, I'm getting strong warnings that you'd better do something as early as possible tomorrow or lose the perpetrator.* ~

Deloo studied the ceiling where she keeps assuming I hide and heaved a sigh. ~ *You're right, Baasee'. I'll tell Mom.* ~

After a flurry of argumentation, Woody could hear Taale suck in a gulp of air. "Okay, Baby. I'll call you in a few." The line went dead. Woody and Deloo went back upstairs where they ate more cookies and waited. A tinny version of "Moonlight Sonata" wafted into the bead shop. Deloo had chosen it as Taale's ringtone because of her name, Naagheltaale, which refers to the Big Dipper. "We'll be there at six thirty tomorrow morning."

"Six-Thirty?" Deloo looked questioningly at Woody, who nodded wordlessly. "Okay. We'll be there." After she clicked off, Deloo turned to Woody. "Frank must think it's as important to be there as you do."

Woody looked around the shop. "I know you think you're safe here, but I don't. I'll take you home tonight and then pick you up at six, Deloo. I'm going that way," Woody offered.

Deloo nodded vigorously at me in secret as well as Woody, who stood in front of her. "I'll take you up on the offer to go home, Woody. I'm kind of scared."

The two carefully took the record books, Earlene's computer and Zigwan's cookies before locking up the store. When they got to Taale's house a few minutes later, Woody said, "I'll be in the Passat tomorrow morning at six."

"Thank you Woody, and thank Zigwan for me."

While Deloo munched on a bowl of cereal for dinner, I went through my list of her fighting skills. First, she had a gun, but didn't know much about shooting. Scratch the gun. Second, she knew how to throw a two-rock bola, which she usually called an Eskimo yo-yo. She did not know how to use it as a weapon—yet. Third, she could climb just about anything vertical as long as I made sure she had a strong enough grip on something. Hmmm... I thought about the house we would be investigating in the morning. It was one-story tall and the only trees near it were very scrawny willow or spruce. On the other hand, she is bony, so maybe that would work. Okay, make climbing number one, and it was time to practice a little harder on that bola. And then there was her secret advantage: Spirit Guide Baasee'.

I slung my ephemeral six shooter into its equally gauzy holster, and nailed a spider web with one spirit shot. We were ready!

Deloo managed to keep one eye open during an hour of watching television. I doubt if she understood she was looking at a game show in which one team of ordinary people played a dreary game with a troop of wannabe actors. By the time I organized her in the bathroom to brush her teeth, I was certain she didn't remember seeing her mother's old-fashioned television set—it was the cathode ray tube sort that often didn't work. She was asleep by nine PM.

CHAPTER 32

Day Seven, Sunday

A wolverine mother followed by her two kits traveled along a powerline trail. She decided to rest beside a birch tree about a mile from her den, but still well within her territory. She settled the kits into a shelter about one hundred feet from BeeZee's house. An hour or so later her keen nostrils were prickled by tiny tendrils of smoke. She awoke instantly, completely sobered by fear of yet another wildfire. Then she picked out the smell of the human resident of the house. She'd been curious about him and his frenetic behavior. She let her kits drowse a little longer while she examined the man.

He was busy scurrying between his house and the smaller garage. Her alert ears heard a ripping sound and then she heard a whump as something as soft as bird feathers exploded. Then more smoke drifted from one of the windows on the far side of the house. A man backed out of the door. The wolverine heard another muffled explosion and this time saw a few flames follow the man out of the house. He turned and ran down the short flight of steps on the front side of the building. She nudged the kits awake and they began to meander toward their primary den. Her path moved them behind his house, giving the wolverine one last chance to figure out what he was doing. Or maybe not. Thin flames were already reaching for the clouds high above the roof. Just as the wolverine mother rushed her twins to the east rather than straight for the den, she saw a vehicle obstructing her path a short distance away. Then she remembered seeing it before. In fact, she'd seen it several times during the past two weeks. She snorted to urge her kits into a faster scuttle past the car. It was then she observed it contained two living humans, a woman and a man, as well as an ethereal being who seemed to guard the woman.

As the wolverine moved beyond the reach of the two people in the car, her sharp ears picked up the sound of another vehicle arriving on the scene. On another day, she might have dashed her kits away from the encroachers, but something held her back. The second car pulled up near the burning house.

Frank, unaware that some of his hair displayed a fetching bedhead look, jumped out of the car as soon as he muttered to empty air, "Stay in the car."

Taale's door closed on his words and she ran toward the house and up the steps. She screamed "Earlene!"

Not as alert as he had been on other occasions, Frank followed her and shouted again, "Stay in the car!"

Taale later told the doctor she'd rushed to the house because she had seen a person dash into the flames. She thought she saw Earlene's face and without hesitation, flew out of Frank's police car and ran toward her friend.

Frank scuffled with Taale, trying to keep her from entering the fiery living room. "Get out of there, Taale. Go back!"

As Great Aunt Pauline would have observed, Taale had never learned the command "stay" and rushed deeper into the house. A hungry flame reached toward her eagerly.

The man, presumably the owner of the house, who'd been in the garage, reached Taale before Frank did. He was taller than any of the others, and used that fact to race toward her, acting on defensive impulse and fury. He threw her, kicking and shouting, into the flames. Then he jumped out of the way. Instead of watching her burn, he ran off the porch to get away from both the flames and the people who invaded his private home. Since he had a lifelong habit of jumping off the porch to stroll to the backyard, that's where his feet took him one last time.

Frank Harper, who should have slowed himself to take stock of the situation as his police training dictated, stopped acting like a cop. Instead he ran past the tall man and jumped into the house after Taale. Even as Frank struggled to save Taale, several things happened at once. Another car screeched to a halt beside Frank's. Woody jumped out of the driver's side and Deloo raced out of the other.

She shrieked, "Mom! Stop! Get out of that fire." Once out of the Passat, she ran toward her mother.

I, bursting with spirit-guide energy, managed to get her to remove her bola from her waist as she dashed forward. Knowing that Deloo didn't have to worry about her mother as much as she needed to get the man who had done so much damage throughout his life, I aimed her legs to the far corner of the burning building.

BeeZee, the man who'd been lining his garage with beautifully carved jade, thought he had escaped the strangers. He reached halfway along the far side of the house, not knowing the wolverine family was cloistered just beyond him. Too late, he saw the wolverine female. Her kits were beside her. BeeZee was moving too fast to control his direction and tripped over one of her kits. She assumed, as indeed, who wouldn't, he had attacked her son. The wolverine, six or seven times smaller than her enemy, flung herself into action.

Although the wolverine had attacked him, he was big enough to beat her off his chest. She landed on the ground and twisted herself around and back by using her youth and taut muscles in a coiled leap. By then, Deloo on the ground and me in the ether around her, put into action her new expertise in snapping a bola. Her aim was good, but her throwing strength was still poor. Never mind! I hadn't guided hundreds of young hunters into correct use of their bolas for nothing. I made a minute adjustment to her aim and used magic on the thrust. The two rocks spun around BeeZee's blond head perfectly.

The man fell while his arms thrashed wildly. His scream filled the shadowy areas of the spruce forest. The wolverine made short work of him by slicing through his carotid artery. After a moment of anger, she turned her motherly attention to her wounded kit, whose brother was washing his face. She hustled them away from the burning house, and then she cleaned them both with her long tongue.

Inside, the fire was extremely hot, very hungry for anything in its path, and began to lick at Taale's clothes. She screamed in panic until she accidentally inhaled a flame. The shock of what was happening combined with having worked all night overpowered her. She fainted. Frank threw her over a big shoulder and leaped out of the burning building.

Ming, when she heard all the yelling, rushed toward the melee, Chuan inches behind her and MoLi soaring, ghostlike, above them both. They reached the edge of the glade where they might have seen the tip of the wolverine's tail as she urged her kits into the underbrush ahead of her.

Meanwhile, Frank carried unconscious Taale out of the house. Both of them were burned, Taale far worse than Frank. Local people, alerted to the smell and noise, arrived. Frank appealed to Woody to take them to an emergency room. A neighbor donated a set of wet, clean sheets to drape carefully around Taale and Detective Harper. In negotiating quickly with Deloo, Woody agreed to drive the departmental car for emergency medical help in Fairbanks. Thus, Deloo could drive Woody's Passat back to Little Tanana.

Deloo turned toward the garage on her way to the Passat. I noticed the man and woman who'd chased us with so much persistence, and helped Deloo to stop. She was shocked to see both Ming and Chuan taking things out of the garage. In hyperventilated statements, they explained they were investigating Brent on behalf of the Chinese government. They'd been doing so for almost a decade.

"These two," Ming pointed to small jade carvings, "we got permission to use as decoys to see if we were right in the first place. We were absolutely correct. Brent took them."

Chuan grimaced, "Yes. He took these two. It's obvious he didn't know jade from colored glass or he would have seen these were worth nothing."

"They're beautiful," Deloo said, running a finger along the edge of the figurine. "What's fake about it?"

Ming lifted it up to the sun. "See how the light looks through this one? Now look at the light through this older one."

"Ooh!" Deloo whispered on seeing the light of the older. "What makes the difference?"

"The older one, the one you're admiring, was made in the seventh century by someone who worked each of the features by hand," Ming said and pointed to Deloo's wedding ring. "It's like the one on your finger. That's a great ring, but since I know the artist personally, it's not very old."

By that time Chuan closed the lid on the trunk. "It's time for us to get away from this blaze." He ushered his wife into the car and called to Deloo, "I'm sorry we didn't get to understand each other very well. Maybe next time."

Ming looked at the wood on the side of Brent's house. "Is Brent still alive?"

Deloo shook her head. "Last I saw was a big fountain of blood." Using spirit guide anxiousness, I propelled her to the Passat as she shouted, "I think he's dead!"

~ *Don't worry, Deloo. Now it's time to take care of your mother. She's got a bad burn on her head. I'm afraid she'll be sporting a hairstyle as short as Frank's for a while.* ~ While I talked, I checked for my own reflection in the Passat rearview mirror. As usual, nothing of beautiful me showed up. ~ *Now that we've finished this ugly business, it's time for my freelance artist to get back to work. You have a painting commission due back in Cambridge, Massachusetts.* ~

"Thanks, Baasee', for teaching me to use a bola. It felt right to get revenge on that terrible man for what he did to Floyd a few days ago. He killed a lot of people for no reason. Do you know what attacked him? It looked like a small wolf or a wolverine."

~ A wolverine. He tripped over one of her kits. They are one of your three great Athabascan spirit animals. ~

"Fitting," Deloo grimaced.

Day Eight, Monday

Great Aunt Pauline and Deloo sat on stiff chairs beside Taale's hospital bed. Taale's body was covered from neck to toe by a thin blanket. The two visitors were silent until Taale's hand crept from under the blanket to her face and crabbed at one of the gauze bandages.

"Stop!" Great Aunt Pauline snapped. "They'll be here soon to swab your face. Don't touch it yourself."

Taale's chest expanded, held a long breath, and released it. "Mmmph!!!" She may have been trying to swear, but the bandages prevented all facial movement.

A woman tiptoed into the room. Deloo gasped, but the figure put a finger to her lips. Great Aunt Pauline grasped her grandniece's hand and Deloo relaxed.

"Shitjaa? Taale, it's me, Earlene. Can you hear me?"

Taale's mouth opened. Great Aunt Pauline intervened, "No talking, Taale. Yes, it's Earlene. Let her speak. You can talk tomorrow."

"Taale, they wouldn't let me bring flowers or your old Porky Pig doll, so I bought you a brand new one. They said I can leave it with your aunt."

Taale's lips moved from a smile into a broad grin. When they opened, Great Aunt Pauline remarked again, "No talking!"

Above them Zephyr and I did a spirit-guide jig. Then another person walked in and we subsided.

"Miss Shoepack?" It was Detective Harper.

Earlene whipped around, eyes wide. On seeing him, she smiled. "Oh! Hi."

"Hi Frank! Do you know him, Earlene? He's a cop. He's new in Fairbanks. Frank, this is the woman you've been trying to find, Earlene." Deloo stopped with a nervous smile. "Frank, the doctors aren't allowing Mom to talk until they take off her bandages. That might take a while."

They could hear a muffled argument in the hall. Great Aunt Pauline stepped out to see what the problem was, and ushered the latest arrivals in. "Could you let us have some folding chairs? The girls will bring them in." The nurse capitulated. Great Aunt Pauline orchestrated who sat where, and resumed her seat. Deloo sat between Pauline and her mother's bed while Vindee, one of the new arrivals, sat on one of the folding chairs next to Pauline. Earlene sat on the opposite side of Taale's bed. Detective Harper shuffled his feet until he obeyed Great Aunt Pauline's pointing finger and sat next to Leroy Cunningham at the foot of the bed.

"I see you've got bandages, too, Detective," Pauline said with a tight smile when he was seated.

Frank nodded, "It's nothing as bad as what happened to Ms. Dena, here. My doctor told me I would be able to report back to work in a week to ten days. I just came here today because it's my first case in Fairbanks, and I wanted to see it through."

Pauline nodded peacefully. "I admire your work ethic. My niece's doctor has allowed us all to be here for thirty minutes so that you can take Earlene's statement in public. I understand the murder investigation of Floyd Charles is closed, as well as the disappearance of Earlene Shoepack, and the assault on Virginia Grant. You are here to put all the final statements in order. Correct?"

Frank glanced at Pauline, managed a sidelong glance at Leroy, who nodded, and chuckled. "Yes. We just need a brief final statement to put in a file. Ms. Shoepack, could you explain what happened to you?

Before Earlene could speak, Vindee stood up. "I can tell you more than Mom can, because she was knocked out. Would you mind?" Her big blue eyes implored Frank. He nodded.

"I was in my room when my biological father, Brent Clerick, barged in the back door and demanded his jacket. Mom made him take his safe first, then he could come in for his jacket. She'd already signaled me to stay upstairs, so when he came back in, I didn't see him punch my mother, but I heard the glass break and then the door slam shut. I came down, and took her to the emergency room. They said there was no concussion and she'd recover in a few weeks. When they asked how it happened, I told them the lie Mom basically dictated. Then I took Mom to my place to recover."

Despite the cumbersome bandages on his hands, Detective Harper was able to print his report. It was short. He held it out for both Earlene and Vindee to sign, and smiled at Taale's bandaged face. "I'm sorry for your burns, Taale. They told me to go back to bed once I finished this report. Leroy offered me a ride today."

Pauline looked at her protégé, Earlene. "What about you, my girl?

What does the neurologist say about your walking problems?"

Earlene spoke up. "We'll know more in a few months. I collapse without warning just when I'm not expecting it. I'm not sure if I'll be ready to work or live at my bead shop for a while because I'm not safe on the stairs. I'm glad I installed the platform lift, though."

"And how about you, Deloo?" Pauline patted Deloo's hand. "You've been a widow such a short time, do you feel better about Arthur, yet?"

~ Just tell her you are taking it one day at a time. She'll feel better, and it's the truth, ~ I communed to my gentle Deloo. I am after all, a top-notch spirit guide.

"So much has happened, especially to Mom and Earlene. I'm glad that man is dead and the Chinese people are getting some of their stuff back," Deloo said. "Did they ever say anything to you, Frank?"

"They checked in with me before leaving. They showed me their paperwork on the few items they took, and there was no reason not to shake hands and wish them well." Frank shrugged. "The Chinese government doesn't have any information about what else might have been taken, so if he or his comrades sold it, it's gone. Nothing we can do about it now."

Pauline summed it up. "In other words, we're all better off without him or the hassles he made for all of us. Now he's dead. We're alive, and we all wish Floyd was here with us."

"Or as my late wife would have said, there may be something else to find, but no point in wasting our taxpayers' dollars on it." He and Leroy stood and nodded goodbye to the others before they walked out.

CHAPTER 33

Day Fifteen, third Monday

Deloo guided her mother into the house. She was still bandaged, but not much. If Taale's burns healed well, or as they hoped, proved themselves to be first degree burns rather than worse, she would be fine in a week or so. All of them understood that "fine" meant alive rather than dead. Deloo had already talked to her former in-laws about seeing a cosmetic surgeon near their home in Cambridge, Massachusetts. Taale objected, but was careful not to protest too much. Everyone agreed it was healthier to be at home than in the hospital. Taale was eager to be released, eager to eat junk food without being criticized, and happy to seek the refuge of her own easy chair.

The door opened without a warning and Earlene and Vindee walked in. After the usual song and dance of greetings, the group sorted itself into two zones. In the kitchen Deloo and Vindee compared photos on their phones, while the older women made themselves comfortable on the couch. Pauline sat at one end beside Earlene. Taale sprawled across Earlene's lap with her head on her aunt's knees. Using surgical tweezers, Pauline and Earlene carefully removed Taale's dressing. Both of them had patched up enough people and cleaned moose or caribou hides to know what they were doing. The process was so comfortable that Taale dozed. After studying her friend's face, Earlene remarked, "It's healing properly. Don't you agree, Pauline?"

Pauline sucked in a breath and finally murmured, "Hmmm. Except for this area," she pointed to her niece's forehead near the scalp, "I think she'll be fine. I guess we'd better wait another week or so." Together, the two women redressed Taale's head. Then Pauline pushed her niece upright and looked at Earlene.

"Your turn. Let's look at that scar." Earlene traded places with Taale. After her two friends poked around at the scarred tissue, Pauline called Vindee over.

"This looks decent, kid. What did you use for a salve? Most of what we have in Fairbanks leaves this kind of wound a little dry, but Earlene's skin looks almost as good as new."

Vindee took a small jar from her purse. "Mom has a friend in Anchorage who makes this salve from devil's club and some other stuff. Used wrong, it's a poison, but if it's made by a trained healer, it's the best thing to put on a cut or bruise. Have you used devil's club before? It doesn't grow this far north."

"No," Pauline observed. "I'd like a jar of my own. Maybe your friend could sell this through the bead shop."

Deloo heard a tapping on the door and let in Jack and Lizzie. Detective Francis Harper stepped in behind them.

They all gathered around Pauline's living room, staring at Jack and Frank. Pauline tapped Jack's arm. "Now that we're away from the hospital, we want to know what's really happening."

Jack grinned and leaned back in his chair. "We all know it started last winter with the death of Deloo Goode's husband, whose death was satisfactorily documented as an accident. Questions about Dr. Goode's last few hours have surfaced because of a photograph Dr. Goode took. We conjecture that Dr. Goode recognized the items he saw and then photographed in Dr. Clerick's garage. Further evidence has come to us that some of those items belonged to the Chinese government, and should not have been in Dr. Clerick's possession. We believe Dr. Goode's professional interest was likely aroused because he was an archaeologist as well as an astute scholar of international business. With his family background as well, he might have known that these items were contemporary goods, rather than the sort of thing an archaeologist like either Dr. Clerick or Dr. Goode would have studied."

Jack stopped when he saw the stricken look on Deloo's face. "Sorry Deloo. I'm sorry I didn't get a chance to know your late husband. His associates from China have known Dr. Clerick for years, and they have proof the items in Dr. Goode's photo were stolen. We believe Dr. Goode, your husband, recognized them as such and said so to Dr. Clerick. The driver of the car that later struck Dr. Goode testified that he saw someone running toward Dr. Goode immediately prior to the accident. The other witness never came forward, and now we think it might have been Dr. Clerick."

Pauline signaled Deloo to sit beside her, "I didn't know him well, either, Deloo. Your husband was very astute about money, but he didn't brag about it. Most rich people are only too happy to show off how great they are, but not Arthur. Do you remember when Cindy came rushing in to the party we gave to welcome Arthur into the family?"

"Yeah," Deloo frowned thoughtfully. "Wasn't she trying to round up enough money to get to Anchorage? I think her husband was rushed there when he broke a leg while out hunting."

"Yes. She and her husband are back now, and he managed to keep his job. Well, I was going back to my bedroom to get some money for Cindy. I figured a couple of hundred would do it. I didn't have more, anyway. When I got up, so did Arthur. He bumped into me. We laughed. He held me until I regained my balance, just like I think a gentleman should. Then I learned what a gentleman he really was." Pauline patted her jeans. "I usually like to walk with my hand in this pocket. Have you noticed?"

Taale spoke up suddenly, "Is it because of that arm? You started doing that a year ago when you broke that arm." Taale touched her aunt.

Pauline looked chagrined. "Yes. It still bothers me." She pushed Taale's hand away in irritation. "So, back to Cindy's problem. I was going to give her two hundred. I put my hand in my pocket after Arthur assaulted me, and what do I find? Two five hundred dollar bills. I was so surprised, I just handed them to her."

Deloo's jaw dropped. "What? Where was I?"

"You were outside, talking to people. I don't think anyone noticed. Arthur had ducked out the door to join you by then. He's the only one who could have put that money there." She hugged her great niece. "Did he ever say anything about it to you?"

Deloo shook her head, stunned. "We lived like paupers because I thought he was as poor as me. I knew he had been lying to me when I got to his parents' house. He was dead by then."

Pauline laughed gently. "He must have loved you more than you will ever know. Honor his discretion, and honor him for seeing past what must have been outright poverty in order to be with you as much as possible."

In response to a prod of inquiry from my confused mortal, I cuddled Deloo with a warm and fuzzy memory of her late husband. ~ *It was one of those things, my child. Arthur tormented himself daily. Once he realized that you thought he was poor, at first he thought he could use your methods of pinching pennies to prove to his parents that you had not married him for his money. By then, it was too late to say anything that wouldn't hurt your feelings.* ~

Deloo nodded slowly. "I took that place on Steele Creek Road because it was all I could afford. I assumed that Arthur wouldn't get a paycheck until he started his job at the university. That meant my little paycheck from the library would have to do for three months." She shrugged unhappily. "It never occurred to me to ask if he had any money. He never brought it up."

Lizzie patted Deloo's shoulder and said, "One of those times I waited for my professor, Arthur saw that I was fiddling with a single glove. He looked around and asked me where the other side was." Lizzie smiled at Jack with embarrassment. "I told him that I'd lost it a week earlier and that I couldn't afford another. Deloo, he didn't know we were friends, ever! He turned toward his parka and took his gloves out. He apologized that they were probably too big. He wouldn't take them back."

When Deloo's tears wouldn't stop flowing, Lizzie hugged her friend. "You were lucky to have him even for those few months, Deloo."

"After all this time of being without him, Lizzie, the only thing I wish I had known was that he gave you his gloves. It would have helped me get past the pain a little easier to know how generous he was."

Jack slid a hand into the crook of Lizzie's left arm and smiled at Deloo. "Now I know what I have to live up to. Lizzie and I have something to tell all of you." He held up Lizzie's left hand to show off the new ring she wore. He smirked, "Now I'm going to wonder if she is interested in me just because she's seen that I own two pairs of gloves."

Lizzie giggled and pretended to slap his hand. Then she turned to Deloo and said, "We wanted you to be the first to know." She looked quizzically at Frank. "Frank was outside when we walked in. He was actually here first."

Pauline took that as a cue to take Lizzie's other arm and announced, "As surrogate grandmother of the bride, it's my duty to offer and your obligation to accept my hosting your wedding party."

After a few minutes of congratulations, Deloo inadvertently turned the group attention toward Detective Harper by taking a spot on the floor next to her mother. All of them looked expectantly at Frank. Earlene bounced to her feet. She shook Frank's hand.

"Thank you!"

"Are you ready to explain everything, Ms. Shoepack?"

"Please, Inspector, you do it."

"Inspector?" Taale frowned. "What does that mean?"

"It means that until a few days ago I was an investigator for an international insurance adjuster. My record is on file at the Fairbanks Police Department." He shrugged, and continued. "It was an interesting position, often putting me between multiple law-enforcement agencies. I learned that what's a crime in one area of the world is often not noticed in another." He grinned at Jack.

"What he means is that a few days ago he accepted the position that he took as a cover for his previous employer." Jack chuckled.

Frank nodded, "I was after Clerick for his part in a major insurance fraud case that I've been investigating as part of my employment with the insurance adjuster. When I saw him toss Ms. Dena into his burning house, literally as if it didn't matter that she would die, I realized that my now previous employer, the insurance adjuster, might fire me for rescuing her. In their world, my job was about stolen goods, not about living human beings. Their policies put the insured objects first, and human lives second. Since I had taken the position as police detective as a cover for the insurance adjuster, I did some serious thinking about my purpose in life. In short, I turned in my resignation with the insurance adjuster and took the one with the police force here."

After an awkward silence, Pauline Dena started clapping, followed by the others.

Bowing in her direction, Frank straightened, "This was a complicated case and a lot of people took time to help me, including Ms. Earlene Shoepack many years ago. Actually, it was due to her courageous appeal to go to the police with evidence, meaning her black eye in 2005." He nodded to Jack.

"I was new to the department then," Jack supplied. "Like any newbie, I was doing everything by the books. I looked Clerick up. He had an interesting record: no arrests, but there were three ongoing investigations of him and his collaborators. A couple of names came up that led me to some people in China." Jack looked at Deloo. "You know them. They were busy investigating you last month, and weren't surprised that you are in the thick of it here."

"Do you mean Prize Woman?" Deloo asked, her eyebrows making dives at her hair.

Pleased that it was all coming out at last, I gripped my mortal in a tight, ethereal grip, I communed ~ *Let them talk. Pretend you aren't surprised.* ~

Deloo took a breath, smiled and fell silent.

"Yes, someone in Vermont forwarded testimony in which you allege Prize Woman's accomplice attacked you," Frank smiled. "I've got a very thick file on you. Your friends in Canada and on the East Coast have assured me that you are honest. Crazy, perhaps, but honest."

Jack nodded, "In the end, we had all the information we needed regarding Dr. Clerick and his mother, Fay Clerick. Of more interest is Mrs. Clerick's companion. She uses the name Carmen Hauser as well as many other aliases. It wasn't until 2014 that we had enough on them, thanks to both Earlene and Vindee Shoepack. We were able to follow their trail through Canada because of the bills Frank's agency supplied through you, Ms. Shoepack." He smiled at Vindee cheerfully.

"Where are they now?" Vindee asked, frowning.

"They are no longer together," Frank supplied. "When Mrs. Fay Clerick insisted on a separate room at Destruction Bay in the Yukon Territory of Canada, Ms. Hauser took that opportunity to steal their car and drive away. The RCMP caught up with Ms. Hauser at Muncho Lake.

"Mrs. Fay Clerick was voluble when interviewed, clearing up a lot of confusion about her son's actions back here in Alaska. It appears that she texted him using one of the cell phones the insurance adjusters supplied Miss Vindee Shoepack as part of the sting. We intercepted the text message to Brent Clerick in which she instructed her son to 'Run'. He might have succeeded if he hadn't assumed that the Fairbanks Police was, as he reported to his friend Chuan Liu, 'a backwoods farce.'

"As some of you know, both Earlene and Vindee Shoepack have been working closely with my former employer the insurance adjuster regarding Ms. Hauser and Mrs. Clerick. My former employer paid Vindee to stay with her grandmother in Bellingham and during this past year to take positions of a particular nature back here in Alaska. The agency, in fact, paid for Vindee Shoepack's apartment in Fairbanks, Miss Earlene Shoepack's medical expenses after Dr. Clerick assaulted her, and issued funds to give the suspects the impression there was more money to come.

"It was deemed essential that Mrs. Clerick and Ms. Hauser remain convinced that Earlene Shoepack was dead and that Miss Vindee Shoepack was in hiding. Ms. Hauser in particular has been a person of interest in a number of international jewelry thefts, and thanks to both Shoepacks' exceptional cooperation, has been placed under arrest. Mrs. Clerick's situation is being evaluated, but I'm no longer involved in the investigation. Therefore, I'm no longer in the loop regarding updates on that case."

Jack, face ruddy, said stiffly, "About Frank, we had a position open. I was surprised when they gave it to a complete outsider who wasn't even from Alaska. No one filled me in on why they did that until Friday night when Lizzie was in a coma. My boss came to the hospital to tell me off, I suppose. I was so mad by then that I told him off instead. I was shocked when he listened, and then he explained who Frank was and who he was really working with besides the Fairbanks Police Department. I wasn't that surprised when he told me Ms. Pauline Dena was involved as a police advisor as she has been many times over the years."

Pauline smiled at everyone. "I think your boss really meant to include all of us in this room. I know that Taale was horrified at what she read in Earlene's diary, as was Deloo. Everything that Earlene described is called a number of things. While part of the larger pattern of Historic Trauma, we see all too much of Battered Women's Syndrome as well as learned helplessness in Alaska. No matter what label you give it, for us in Little Tanana, it happens and it's time to do something about it."

Taking her cue from both the words and Great Aunt Pauline's nod in her direction, Deloo poked around in Taale's beading cabinet. Moments later, she produced the plastic jar of mixed beads and poured out its contents onto the large bath towel that her mother had spread over the kitchen table. Surrounded by the others, Pauline quickly sorted the contents into two piles: ordinary beads and gemstones, and waited for the comments to end before turning to Detective Francis Harper.

"Deloo located these beads while cleaning Earlene's store. She placed them in this jar. I understand that there is a similar collection in Cambridge that is possibly from the same source as these," Frank smiled.

~ I thought so! ~ I crowed silently. *~ Now we're getting somewhere. Who owns them? ~*

Deloo asked Frank, "What Mom and I have been wondering for weeks is who owns these stones?"

Frank cocked an eyebrow at her, "It depends on who you ask. If you ask me, the insurance adjuster, I'd probably side with my former employer, and say they have a legal *interest* in them. In truth, they do not have a legal *right* to them any more than does the Chinese government. Ms. Earlene Shoepack and Ms. Taale Dena could wrangle over them, as well. Now that I'm officially with the Fairbanks Police Department, I checked. The gemstones are officially *not* stolen items in Fairbanks."

Earlene and Deloo looked at each other and laughed. "They've caused me quite a lot of trouble, thanks. I'll bow out of the discussion," Earlene shook her head.

"So, Ms. Pauline Dena asked me for my policeman's opinion of an idea that she has. Ms. Dena?" When Frank smiled at Pauline, all heads turned toward her.

"As I said earlier, we are doing all we can in Fairbanks to combat Historic Trauma and one of its usual outcomes, the Battered Women's

Syndrome. I've connected with a network in Fairbanks that is more or less like an underground railroad. It helps women escape, get medical attention, get jobs, and take back their lives. It's not an agency, but a group of caring women who make things happen—which official agencies that are bound by red tape and nine-to-five jobs can't do. Their methods are obscure. For instance, the police have an unidentified Eskimo yo-yo, which is also known as a hunting bola. The bola seems to have been used as a defense weapon. There's no way to tell, but they think that an expert Native marksman ultimately saved Earlene's life the other day. If Dr. Clerick had lived, he would have found his way to Earlene's shop and probably have killed her without warning. Nonetheless, someone who knew how to use it as a weapon happened to be there and got the job done, although it was actually a wolverine that finished the man off. That's what I call obscure methods." Pauline looked at the ceiling and smiled.

~ *You are a hero, Deloo,* ~ I, the ruthless bola instructor preened toward Earlene's senior guide, who smiled in return. Zephyr encircled Deloo's head with a crown-shaped tendril.

Deloo's mouth wobbled toward a smile, uncertain of whether to confess what she had done in front of Jack and Frank.

Pauline coughed, "What I have proposed to Earlene and Taale, the women most involved with these gems, is that we collaborate with the underground network to make something happen in our obscure ways. For instance, other such networks have found it's best to avoid having a specific building or a single place to house the victims. On the other hand, having a system of providing transportation, food, medicine, and protection costs money, and now we've got some gems. Can we use it that way without building a red-tape trap?"

Taale put her arm around Earlene and looked at her friend. "I hope we can, as long as we use some of it to get you some cosmetic surgery. Those wounds are going to stay ugly unless we get it done ourselves."

"Thanks, Shitjaa," Earlene rested her head against Taale's. "What about you? They said you should get something done in a few months. Indian Health Service can't afford to do it here in Fairbanks, but we could go somewhere else."

Taale looked askance at her friend. "Okay, I'll do it if you do it with me." They smiled at each other. "How much do we have for foolishness?" Taale looked at her aunt.

~ *Let your gemologist tell you, Deloo. Your Aunt Pauline made good money with local jewelers, but she did more good for others with Little Tanana. Then when they figured out what Brent was up to, Earlene and your great aunt figured out how to replace a few of his stones each year with those of lesser quality from Alaska. Brent Clerick never caught on. Later on Pauline would trade them to the local gem dealers. Earlene and Pauline made a lot of money over the years and used it for women and children who needed help.* ~

Pauline touched the gemstone pile and said, "Speaking as a gemologist, I think we've got all we need here or else in Cambridge."

Jack looked concerned. "Who's going to run it?"

Pauline gave him a serene look. "It will have to be people who know how to run their lives on a tight budget, limited time, operate computers, and above all else, who know how to keep secrets. While the mysterious gemstones we've got are worth a lot for one person, we've got many lives to save at any given time."

Frank scanned the room, eyed Jack and smiled. Jack hugged his fiancée tighter, and nodded. "I believe those people are all right here."

ABOUT THE AUTHOR

PHYLLIS ANN FAST, winner of the North American Indian Prose Award, is an artist (painter) and a woman of mixed descent (Tleeyegg'e hʉt'aane, which is also known as Koyukon Athabascan and white American). She was born in Anchorage, Alaska in 1946 to Elsie and Oscar Fast, graduated from East Anchorage High School in the year of the 1964 Alaskan earthquake. She earned a BA in English from the University of Alaska then centered in Fairbanks, later an interdisciplinary Master of Arts from the University of Alaska Anchorage, and concluded her education with a PhD in Anthropology from Harvard University in 1998. After teaching at the University of Alaska Fairbanks and the University of Alaska Anchorage, she retired Professor Emerita in 2014, when she turned to writing fiction. She now lives in the Washington state.

Please visit her website: PhyllisFast.com

PRAISE FOR
HALF-BEAD OF FUNDY

Half-Bead of Fundy — Native American Paranormal
5 stars
"A 5-star blend of cultural interfaces driven around in a used Passat by a young Native American woman who hears a 'voice'. The 'voice' belongs to Deloo's metaphysical spirit guide Baasee'. Then there is the Chinese connection, the Cuban spirit healing, the Canadians, the Boston Brahmins and the Harvard alums. All told with a Native American curved story line involving murder, cross country chases and scaling tall buildings while dodging bullets. It would take a Native American anthropologist with a Harvard PhD to make it work. So it does.

"For readers interested in Alaskan Native American culture there are words, references and philosophy that all add to the telling. The most intriguing part, for me, was the relationship and machinations between Spirit Guide and guided mortal. Is this the author's vivid imagination or does she have a special connection? Is a chance meeting a coincidence or a connection? We may find out if there are sequels.

"While the author avoids any form of clichéd cliff hanger there are hints of further adventures of Deloo and Baasee, perhaps on the metaphysical side. I've read several other 'paranormal mysteries' but this is the first that provided me with more than just a glimpse of how paranormal may work. I look forward to future, hopefully far reaching, adventures of Deloo and Bassee." –DL, 2016

Half-Bead of Fundy
5 stars
"A must read Mystery. Entertaining and elegantly written. The story races along with passion between the mystical spirit world of Baasee and the Koyukon Athabascan, Deloo, to unravel the twists and turns of this thriller!" – JH, 2016

Half-Bead of Fundy
5 stars
"Fast has created an engaging mixture of mystery and humor. The narrative, told from the viewpoint of Deloo's spirit guide, swings through maritime Canada to Boston as the young Athabaskan solves the mysterious death of an innkeeper." – JKR, 2016

OTHER BOOKS BY THE AUTHOR

These three are also available as ebooks.

Fiction / Native American & Aboriginal

Half-Bead of Fundy

First in the Native American Mystery series.

Deloo had always welcomed the pull of a myriad of oddball spirits. ~Pull a 180!~ Baasee' shouted into her head. Deloo wasn't used to spirit guides like Baasee', but the crazy people following her didn't know or care. They wanted her beaded jacket at any cost. It was up to Alaska Native, Deloo Goode, to figure out what was so important about her mother's beading— or else be killed like the innkeeper at the Secret Spirit Inn.

270 pages

ISBN 978-0-9974977-2-4 (trade paperback)

Midnight Trauma

Second in the Native American Mystery series,
sequel to *Half-Bead of Fundy*.

Someone has killed a teenager at a bead shop in remote Fairbanks, Alaska. Moreover, the owner, Earlene, is missing and the shop keeps getting broken into. Deloo Goode and her mother try to unravel the mysteries surrounding the bead shop. Luckily, Deloo has an invisible weapon: her playful spirit guide Baasee', who can see things others can't—sometimes. Will they force the murderer into the open? Can they untangle the clues and surprises before anyone else gets hurt?

252 pages

ISBN: 978-0-9974977-3-1 (trade paperback)

The Dire Wolf Alliance

A Native American Saga
Prequel to the Native American Mystery series.

The prehistoric story told by her spirit guide Baasee' and her Grandfather Kwaiikit, helps Deloo, the protagonist of *Half-Bead of Fundy* and *Midnight Trauma*, come to grips with her own recent widowhood.

"Go where?" Ping asked Chebucto. "You've been banished twice. You have nowhere to go." Growing up, no matter the era or place, can be terrifying. Chebucto understood what the medicine man told him to do, but couldn't do it by himself on the ancient northeastern coast of North America. Meanwhile, adults in a local group called the Dire Wolf Alliance, tried to rescue and find homes for widows and orphans traumatized by the violent Death Runners bludgeoning their way through Zana.

260 pages

ISBN: 978-0-9974977-6-2 (trade paperback)

JUVENILE FICTION / Animals / Deer, Moose & Caribou

Tepi, the Girl Who Helped the Deer

Story and illustrations by Phyllis Ann Fast

Tepi finds herself in communication with a deer spirit who wants her to go into the forest and help an injured deer in need. This is the story of how Tepi found her calling.

66 pages, full color

Trade paperback

ISBN: 978-0-9974977-1-7

JUVENILE FICTION / Animals / Elephants

Brella and Her Umbrella, A Baby Elephant Story

Story and illustrations by Phyllis Ann Fast

Brella, the baby elephant, is so curious that she dreamily follows a pretty bird. She wanders away from her family and is suddenly LOST! Her spirit guide, Umbrella, attempts to keep Brella safe from danger.

68 pages, full color

Trade paperback

ISBN: 978-0-9974977-5-5

Available at Amazon.com and other retail outlets.

Northern Athabascan Survival
Women, Community, and the Future
(North American Indian Prose Award)

by Phyllis Ann Fast

The Northern Athabascan peoples of the Alaskan interior and the Yukon have survived centuries of contact and attempted domination by outsiders. Their lives today are rich in meaning and tradition yet are also complicated by numerous challenges such as poverty, alcoholism, domestic violence, suicide, and troubled leadership.

Combining scholarly analysis, first-person accounts, and her own experiences and insights as a Koyukon Athabascan artist and anthropologist, Phyllis Ann Fast illuminates the modern Athabascan world. Her conversations with Athabascan women offer revealing glimpses of their personal lives and a probing assessment of their professional opportunities and limitations. Also showcased is the crucial but ambiguous role of Athabascan leaders, who are needed to champion reform and social healing but are often undermined by conflicting notions of decision making, personhood, and leadership in Athabascan society.

A troubling observation of this study is the vast extent to which addiction—manifested as both substance abuse and economic dependency—pervades Northern Athabascan society and threatens to curtail its cohesion and aspirations. But Northern Athabascans are far from victims. As Fast discovers, Northern Athabascan men and women are well aware of these widespread social problems, and many have undertaken initiatives to deal with and heal them. Rigorous and compassionate, *Northern Athabascan Survival* provides an uncompromising view of a remarkable and troubled world.

When Spirits Visit
A Collection of Stories by Indigenous Authors
Compiled and Edited by MariJo Moore

WHEN SPIRITS VISIT contains stories centered on spiritual visitation – animal, bird, and people. Some are fiction, some non-fiction, and some faction. Discernment is left to each reader.

Writers included are: Susan Deer Cloud, **Phyllis A. Fast,** Gabriel Horn, Amy Krout-Horn, Evan Pritchard, Jim Stevens, MariJo Moore, Sean Milanovich, Clifford Trafzer, Dawn Karima Pettigrew, Lois Red Elk, Willliam Yellow Robe, Jr, Dean Hutchins and Denise Low—all respected published authors in the Native American realm of literature.

This book is unique in its presentation of the fact that "...many of us do believe in the mysteries of the universe, even if they cannot be 'proved' mathematically or scientifically. There are spirit beings who help us, who guide us, and there are spirit beings who can confuse us as well. Spirit beings are all around us at any given moment. These spirits have their work to do in helping us, so they need us as much as we need them."

www.ingramcontent.com/pod-product-compliance
Lightning Source LLC
Chambersburg PA
CBHW031315170626
46807CB00001B/432